USA Today *bestselling author Julia London creates a world of daring passions and dangerous loyalties in her wonderful novels . . .*

THEY WERE THE LOCKHARTS.

A FAMILY WITH A NOBLE HISTORY.

A SECRET TREASURE.

AND A ROMANTIC CURSE.

"London's characters come alive on every page and will steal your heart."

—*Atlanta Journal-Constitution*

"Finely crafted characters and polished writing rich with the author's deliciously tart humor are just a few of the delights awaiting readers in the superb love story."

—*Booklist*

"Sprightly and fresh . . . quick with humor. . . ."

—*Publishers Weekly*

"A perfect blend of passion, poignancy, and humor. . . . The likeable characters, intense emotions, and depth of sensuality only add to a story that tugs at your heart."

—*Romantic Times*

Also by Julia London

The Hazards of Hunting a Duke
Highlander in Love
Highlander Unbound

JULIA LONDON

POCKET STAR BOOKS
New York London Toronto Sydney

A Pocket Star Book published by
POCKET BOOKS, a division of Simon & Schuster, Inc.
1230 Avenue of the Americas, New York, NY 10020

ISBN-13: 978-1-4165-2388-8
ISBN: 1-4165-2388-X

This Pocket Star Books paperback edition September 2006

10 9 8 7 6 5 4 3 2 1

Cover art by Franco Accornero

Manufactured in the United States of America

One

Talla Dileas, near Loch Chon, The Trossachs of the Scottish Highlands
1817

They needed money. Banknotes or coin, it mattered not, just so long as there was plenty of it. All seven Lockharts agreed that they had no choice but to return to England and attempt to find the ancient family treasure, a solid gold beastie with ruby eyes, to stave off certain ruin. They would *not*, however, dispatch Liam to fetch it.

That had been their first blunder—Liam had returned from London with a woman and a bonny young lass. But not the beastie.

No, this time, Liam's younger—and dandier—brother, Grif, would go.

Yet Aila, the lady of Lockhart, had reservations about a second attempt at retrieving the beastie. "'Tis certain disaster," she said as the family reviewed their latest scheme at the supper table. "We tempt fate, as we've no' the slightest notion where the beastie may be. We know nothing other than Lady Battenkirk took the blasted thing!"

"And gave it to Amelia," Ellie, Liam's bride, pleasantly reminded the lot of them.

Everyone paused to look at Ellie as she blithely continued her meal.

That was because Ellie had stolen the beastie from beneath Liam's nose, then sold the priceless ornamental statue for a paltry amount to a Londoner she'd encountered in a small shop of knickknacks and household wares in Cambridge. Now, the only thing they knew for certain was that the Londoner's name was Lady Battenkirk, and that Lady Battenkirk had said at the time of purchase that she intended to give the beastie to her friend Amelia. That was it—the sum total of what they knew about the precious statue. Everything else was wildly imaginative conjecture.

But Grif was confident in his ability to bring the beastie home, and affectionately squeezed his mother's hand. "Liam went as a soldier, no' a gentleman, like me. He was ill-suited to acquaint himself with society, whereas I am perfect for it."

"Society!" Liam muttered. "Ye can have the bloody lot of them!"

Liam, a captain in the Highland Regiments, was, kindly speaking, a little rough around the edges. And while Grif could be just as rough if push came to shove (he was, after all, born and bred a Highlander), he fancied the life of a high-society gentleman, a desire that had been firmly entrenched after two years of university in Edinburgh.

That had been, by his measure, an eternity ago, when the family had means, before they began to buy out the tenants who could no longer support Talla Dileas, the remote family estate in the Highlands near Loch Chon. When Grif returned home five years ago, it was to a different place, where crofter's cottages stood empty and the old mansion had begun to fall into a state of disrepair. The situation had only worsened—not a fortnight past, the roof over the original kitchen had collapsed, and they could do nothing but board it up.

Grif missed his former life on Charlotte Square, where he and his lifelong best friend, Hugh MacAlister—who was seated across from him now, trying gamely to swallow the stuff in his bowl—had been the most popular of the young gentlemen vying for the attentions of the debutantes. The prospect of London—*London!*—was perfect for a young man such as himself.

"Aye, Aila, what choice do we have, then?" Carson, the laird of Lockhart, asked wearily. "We've no tenants to pay rents, the cattle are so few in number as to be laughable, and we lose money each day. All around us are sheep that graze the Highlands much easier than the blessed cattle. If we donna do something rather soon, the sheep will put us in debtors' prison, they will."

He spoke true. For all their misgivings, one fact remained indisputable—the beastie, that ancient piece of valuable art, the one thing that the English and Scottish Lockharts had continued to feud over the last several hundred years (in spite of the family chronicles showing quite clearly that it rightfully belonged to the *Scottish* Lockharts, thank you), was the key to their survival. Only it had been stolen back and forth for centuries, and their damnable English cousins had last pilfered it around the time of the Battle of Culloden in 1746. Since then, it had languished in a fine London salon, a trophy for the English Lockharts.

But the English Lockharts were quite wealthy. They didn't *need* it. The Scottish Lockharts, on the other hand, needed it desperately.

"Ye have me word," Grif said to his mother, "that I'll no' skip merrily to London and hie meself home again with a wife and bairn—"

"I beg your pardon!" Ellie interjected, as she was the wife Liam had hied himself home with, along with her daughter, Natalie.

"Forgive me, Ellie," Grif said, turning from his mother and instantly grabbing Ellie's hand and bringing her knuckles to his lips. "Ye know I adore ye, but ye're no' exactly what we had hoped for, are ye now?"

"Oh no—Liam has made it perfectly clear that I'm not," she admitted cheerfully.

"But Grandfather says we are much better than that old beastie," Natalie sniffed, earning a tweak of her cheek from Carson.

"Of course ye are, Nattie," Grif quickly reassured her. "And we'd no' have it any other way . . . but if only ye'd come to us *without* selling the beastie—"

"Hone$tly, Grif!" This interruption from Mared, the Lockharts' only daughter. "Ellie's atoned for it, has she no'? She single-handedly turned ye into a gentleman—"

"I beg yer pardon—I was a gentleman long before our Ellie walked through this door, if ye please!"

"Aye, but ye canna deny she's taught ye to dance and to walk and to talk like a proper English gentleman, as well as taught ye all their customs!"

"Aye, she has, indeed," Grif grudgingly admitted.

"And the letters of introduction she's penned for ye—why, they're brilliant, they are!"

"Thank you," Ellie said, clearly pleased.

"Ye think it is easy, then, to introduce Griffin MacAulay, laird of Ardencaple?" Mared demanded.

"That name . . ." Hugh said thoughtfully. "I donna understand why ye willna go as yerself, Grif. What harm can come of it? It all seems a wee bit complicated."

"*Ach,* now," Liam said gruffly. "Is it no' as plain as the nose on yer face, then, MacAlister? Look here, *I* traveled to London and let it be known that I was a disgruntled outcast from the Scottish Lockharts, and thereby managed to ingratiate meself to our cousin Nigel. But then the beastie was stolen, and before I could set it all to rights, *I* was forced to depart abruptly"—that remark prompted everyone to look at Ellie again, who colored slightly—"so we canna be entirely certain if the English Lockharts know the beastie is even *missing,* can we now? And if they *do* know she's missing, have they connected her disappearance to me? Or worse, perhaps they might be prodded into *making* a connection if they discover me very own brother in London. 'Tis all quite simple, lad!"

But Hugh shook his head in confusion. "Aye . . . but have ye no' forgotten one thing, Liam? Grif *looks* like ye! How can he hide it?"

"He's right," Aila agreed, looking at her son Grif. "If Nigel Lockhart lays eyes on ye, he might very well recognize Liam in ye."

Liam snorted at that. "*No,* Mother, Cousin Nigel is a bloody *sot.* He'd no' recognize his own toe without help, I'd wager. And there is difference enough between us—if Grif has a different name, Cousin Nigel will no' put it all together. Of that I'm bloody certain."

"I'd no' be so certain," Aila said warily. "Ye know what they say of the beastie—she'll 'slip through the fingers of a Scot, for she's English at heart.'"

"Hogwash," Carson said. "I put no more stock in that than I do Mared's curse," he said, waving his hand dismissively at his daughter.

Mared colored instantly and stole a sheepish glance at Hugh, embarrassed by the medieval curse, which stemmed from the tragedy of the condemned first lady of Lockhart. The daughter of that unfortunate woman was cursed with her mother's shame and her father's hatred, and took her own life in 1454. Since then, and for reasons that were no longer clear, it was said that no daughter of a Lockhart would ever marry until she looked into the belly of the beast—or faced the devil, as it were. And it was true that no daughter had ever married—some were never offered for, and those who did receive offers died or watched their lovers die before a betrothal could take place. Wiser heads argued that the deaths were merely a coincidence, the result of human carelessness. But most in and around these lochs believed the deaths were the work of the *diabhal*, the devil himself, and that Mared, the first daughter born to a Lockhart in almost one hundred years, was cursed.

"This plan is really much better than the last, Mother," Mared said now, before Carson could say more about the curse. "And we've thought it all through, have we no'?"

They had indeed carefully thought it through. They knew that Grif could only succeed in finding the beastie if he had money, had entry into society, and a place to reside that would convince the *haute ton* that he *was* legitimate, even if he had assumed a false and rather lofty identify.

"And all the obstacles have been resolved, have they no'?" Mared continued.

No one could dispute it—Mared and Griffin had pored over old books and family trees until they finally landed on the fictitious Lord Griffin MacAulay, laird of Ardencaple, a title that was passed to the duke of Argyll one hundred years prior and was later abolished by the duke as redundant. There was nothing left of Ardencaple now save a few crofters. *"Ardencaple. Who could possibly know that old name?"* Grif had laughed.

Once his identity was established, Liam and Ellie took over, schooling Grif daily on the habits and haunts of London society and many social protocols. They enlisted Dudley, the Lockharts' longtime butler-cum-manservant-cum-groom-cum-gardener to accompany Grif and lend credibility to his being a lord.

But it was the wee lass Natalie who had handed them a bit of a quandary one day when she remarked, from amid her collection of Mared's old dolls, "I think he must have a valet if he is to be a lord."

They'd all stopped talking at once and stared in horror at the lass. "Dear God, I had forgotten," Ellie muttered.

Carson came up with a brilliant solution, and enlisted Hugh, the son of his oldest and dearest friend, Ian MacAlister, to play the role of Grif's valet in exchange for a small percentage of what the beastie might bring. Not only was Hugh willing to pose as Grif's valet, he also knew of a place they might take up residence. Hugh's maternal grandmother, Lady Dalkeith, had married an Englishman after her husband died, and he knew his grandmother's house on Cavendish Street sat vacant and unattended while she accompanied her husband to France every summer.

The Lockharts celebrated with several tots of Highland whiskey, for not only had they access to a vacant house in London for several months, but proper letters of introduction, expertly fabricated by Ellie.

That left them with one last hurdle—money. As the Lockharts had scraped together all they had to send Liam to London, their pockets were now decidedly empty. But Grif had an idea. "I think we've no other option, then, but to ask Payton for a small loan," he suggested. "He's the only one with money in these parts."

"Traitor," Mared hissed.

"Payton Douglas?" Hugh asked.

"Bloody Douglas, that's who," Carson said, as he was wont to do anytime the name Douglas came up, and then instantly softened. "Aye, he'd be a Douglas, but a decent sort, if there's such a thing."

"He's been right clever," Grif said carefully, knowing how the subject rankled his father. "The sheep have served him well, and I hear he plans a distillery. He's no' an idiot, that one," he said, and added, for Hugh's benefit, "He's suggested an arrangement of lands between us, he has—one that would benefit both Lockhart and Douglas."

"*Ach,* ye're a fool, Grif!" Mared said instantly with a dismissive wave of her hand. "He's a Douglas! Lockhart and Douglas have never seen eye to eye!"

"Aye," Liam said on a weary sigh, "but Grif is right. Douglas is our only hope."

"Then Mared must ask him," Aila said. "He esteems her greatly and always has."

"Mother!" Mared cried. "I'd rather be drawn and—"

"Quartered!" Aila exclaimed with her. "I know, I *know, mo ghraidh*. But it doesna alter the fact that he's sweet for ye—although God knows why, the way ye treat the poor soul. Yet he might be favorably inclined to make a small loan to yer father . . . if ye were to ask him nicely."

With a moan, Mared covered her face with her hands.

"There now," Liam said kindly. "It's no' as if ye must *kiss* him," he said, and he and Grif laughed roundly at her muffled cry.

Two

Payton heard them coming before he actually saw them—the screech of rusted iron from the Lockharts' old landau echoed across the little valley, drifting in through the open window and startling his poor cousin Sarah so badly that she put down her teacup with a clatter.

"What in heaven is that horrid noise?" she asked, daintily covering her ears with her hands.

"A carriage. Ye've carriages in Edinburra, no?"

"Payton!" Sarah chided him. "I'm no' accustomed to the country, and well ye know it."

"Aye," Payton said, already walking to the windows that overlooked the drive.

Below him, the old Lockhart landau had come to a stop. Captain Liam Lockhart was standing with his brother, Grif Lockhart. The two of them, leaning forward, were peering into the interior of the carriage. Liam's voice was raised; Grif was calm and smooth, as always. And then he heard the familiar voice of their sister, Mared. Except in that particular moment, it sounded more like a screech.

At that moment, Payton's butler, Beckwith, entered the room. "Beg yer pardon, milord, but the Lockharts are calling."

"That I see." Payton nodded thoughtfully. "The question is, *why?*"

"I couldna rightly say, milord."

Neither could Payton. The last time a Lockhart had entered this house was . . . actually, Payton couldn't remember a time.

"Who are the Lockharts?" Sarah asked.

"Neighbors."

"*Oh!*" Sarah exclaimed excitedly. "Invite them in—"

"No' that sort of neighbor," he quickly added. "I'll be but a moment," he said, and strode out of the room before Beckwith.

Walking down the corridor, he could hear the voices of the Lockharts over that of the footman who was showing them to the small receiving salon just off the main entry. As Payton entered the room, Grif was standing at the hearth, wearing a dark brown suit that Payton admired, one leg crossed casually over the other, his hands in his pockets. Of the brothers, Grif was decidedly the handsome one, always dressed to perfection. And there was Liam, wearing a kilt, naturally, a proud Highlander who refused to succumb to modernity.

Then there was Mared.

She was standing at the back of the room next to the heavy velvet drapes, wearing a plain gown with a sash tied just beneath her breasts, a rich emerald color that caught the color of her eyes and made her confoundingly pretty—ink black hair, beautiful rosy skin, eyes as green as moss . . . Ah, but that was the problem with Mared—she was as pretty as she was insufferable.

"Payton Douglas!" Liam boomed cheerfully, walking forward, his hand extended. "Ye'll forgive us for interrupting, will ye no'? We'd no' come at all if we could help it, truly."

Payton could certainly believe that was true. "Captain," he said cautiously, shaking his hand, then looked at Grif. "Grif, ye look well."

"Thank ye, sir. Of course, ye noted our sister, aye?" Grif asked with a charming smile and a nod toward the back of the room.

Noted her? The woman haunted his bloody dreams. "Miss Lockhart," he said simply, and recalled, with not a wee bit of perturbation, the last time he had seen Mared Lockhart. It was on the occasion he had gone to complain to her father that she and her bloody dogs had penned his sheep again. As he had departed that astoundingly unsuccessful meeting, Mared had opened a narrow slip of a window high above him at Talla Dileas, leaned so far out that he feared she would fall, and called a jaunty "Good day!" to him, her lilting laughter taunting him. His eyes narrowed at the memory.

"Laird Douglas!" she said stiffly, and instantly received a bit of a frown from Grif for it.

"To what, then, do I owe—"

"*Ach,* Douglas," Liam said, sighing. "Ye canna begin to understand our troubles. We've come to speak about a wee but urgent problem—"

"Urgent?"

"Oh, *aye,* very urgent indeed," Liam said, nodding gravely.

He was instantly suspicious. "What is it, then? Has one of yer coos escaped her fence?"

Liam laughed; Grif smiled and said, "'Tis much more urgent than *that* . . . is it no', Mared?"

"Aye," she said, and added a very reluctant sigh. "Much more."

Now, Payton couldn't help noticing, Liam was frowning at her.

Mared frowned right back, but took one long step away from the drapes and fixed her gaze on Payton. "It seems that ye are the only one who can help us, Payton Douglas."

All right, then, now he was *extremely* suspicious. Mared was the last person on earth who would ask for his help. "If this is some sort of trick—"

"Trick?" Liam scoffed, and clasped two huge hands over his heart. "Ye *wound* me, Douglas!"

"Aye, and I shall wound ye with me bare hands if this is trickery. A Lockhart would no' seek the help of a Douglas unless there was some tomfoolery—"

"Have I ever done ye harm?" Liam demanded. "Or me brother?"

"I canna say that ye have," he said honestly, but looked pointedly at their demon sister, who at least had the decency to blush. "All right, then—what is this trouble?" he asked impatiently.

Mared sighed again. Lowered her gaze for a moment, then raised it to the ceiling. "Laird Douglas, how gracious ye are to receive us."

"*Gracious?*" he echoed in disbelief.

"Oh, aye, ye are indeed," she said, walking forward. "'Tis true what they say—ye are a gentleman."

And it was true that she was the spawn of the *diabhal*. Payton folded his arms across his chest, narrowed his gaze on Mared as she glided so prettily toward him. It was so unlike her that he was quite tempted to laugh.

"The fact is," she said in a husky voice as she came to stand before him, "we find ourselves in a wee bit of a quandary. There is something in London that rightfully belongs to us, and if we donna fetch it soon, we could very well lose our land. Ye know quite well that would kill me lord father," she said, looking up at him through dark lashes with her dark green eyes.

For a brief moment, Payton was lost in those eyes . . . until her words began to sink into his consciousness. He was hardly surprised to hear they were on the verge of losing their land. Carson Lockhart was a good man, but his way of thinking was firmly rooted in the last century. Payton had made overtures countless times to the old codger, but each time he did, Carson had rebuffed him and vowed to raise cattle until there wasn't a breath left in his body.

Payton eyed her suspiciously. "What of yours is in London?" he asked. "A pirate's treasure?"

Grif and Liam exchanged a look, but Mared's smile brightened. "In a manner of speaking, aye, ye might say so," she agreed. "But we canna say more than that."

So they had latched onto a scheme of some sort—just like the Lockharts, barmy lot that they were. "And what has this to do with me?" he asked, his gaze sliding to the décolletage of her gown.

"Our Grif must go to London, then. He'd be gone now, he would, except that . . ." Mared paused. "Except that we are a *wee* bit short on funds," she said, holding her thumb and forefinger a hairbreadth apart to show just *how* wee short. "A-And, we'd no' ask, indeed we wouldna, but this is right important. Our only hope is, ah, that . . . that . . . *yewillhelpus*."

"I beg yer pardon?" Payton asked, not hearing her.

"Diah!" she suddenly exclaimed, exasperated that

she had to repeat it. "I *said*, our only hope is that ye will help us, Douglas!"

"Help ye *what?*" he asked, and smiled as a fire lit in her eyes.

"What she is trying to say," Grif said, quickly stepping up, "is that we've no funds of our own, and we've come to ask if ye might see yer way to lending us a wee bit of yers."

Money? They wanted his *money?* The proud, stubborn, we'll-all-go-down-together Lockharts, who'd not take the shirt off Payton's back if they were naked and freezing in the dead of winter, wanted to borrow *his* money?

Judging by the way Grif began to prattle, they obviously mistook his silence for denial instead of the shock that it was. "We need enough to go to London and fetch our . . . *belonging*, but when I return, we shall have enough to repay the loan," he said quickly. "With interest, of course."

"Soldier's honor," Liam chimed in. "Ye have me word it will be returned to ye, every last pence."

"We'd no' ask if it wasna so *important*," Mared pleaded. "*Please*, Payton."

Please, Payton . . . He could count on one hand the times he had heard Mared use his Christian name, and looked at the three of them standing there—especially Mared, who'd once said she'd not want a prayer from him even on her deathbed. Her cheeks were flushed a dark red—she was remarkably shamed by this request and Payton had never seen Mared shamed, not once in the many years he had known her. Oh no—this woman had the grit of the gods.

"How much would ye look to borrow?"

"Three thousand pounds," Grif said quickly.

"Three *thousand* pounds?" Payton half spoke, half choked. "Have ye lost yer bloody minds?"

Mared's face was flaming. And as much as he would have liked to enjoy her discomfort, for some reason Payton saw this outrageous request as his one viable chance to integrate the Lockhart and Douglas lands and make them the premier Highlands sheep producer. He'd no longer have to worry about encroaching on their lands or their bloody cattle encroaching on his. They'd all prosper.

He strolled to the sideboard that held several crystal decanters filled with Scots whiskey and French wines, his mind rattling through all the possibilities as he helped himself to a tot of whiskey and tossed it down his throat.

"And if ye are no' successful fetching this . . . thing?" he asked casually, pouring whiskeys for Liam and Grif. "How will ye repay the money?"

Grif smoothed the sleeve of his coat. "We'd repay ye with a piece of our land."

Payton almost choked, but managed to keep his expression stoic as he handed a whiskey to Liam. He handed the other to Grif and looked at Mared. "How it must pain ye to come here and ask this," he said.

Mared rolled her eyes and looked away. She was the most exasperating of all the Lockharts by a furlong or more, the one who made his blood boil every time she opened her accursed mouth. Aye, but since she was a wee lass, she could light a raging fire in the pit of him, one that never ceased to glow when she was nearby.

"I'll agree to lend ye the money if ye can manage to repay me in twelve months' time."

"Done," Liam said.

"And I'll ask six percent for me trouble."

Grif and Liam glanced at one another. "Fair enough," Grif said.

"And if ye *canna* repay me?"

Grif was already nodding. "We'll give ye a portion of the Lockhart lands equal in worth to the original loan, and the six percent—"

"No," Payton said, shaking his head amicably. "If ye canna repay me . . . ye'll give me Mared."

For a moment, no one spoke a word, and the silence, Payton was pleased to note, was deafening. But then Mared gasped her outrage. "Why, ye *bloody*—"

Grif instantly and desperately jumped behind her, clapped a hand over her mouth as he yanked her into him, and held her captive while he exchanged a worried look with Liam over her head.

"Ah . . . Douglas, are ye *certain* ye know what ye ask?" Liam asked.

"Aye," Payton answered calmly.

With a well-placed heel to Grif's instep, Mared wrenched free and stumbled toward Payton to stand directly before him, arms akimbo, her green eyes flashing angrily. "Who do ye think ye are, a bloody feudal king? Ye'll no' make claim to *me*, ye scoundrel! Do ye think I am property to be bartered like an old hairy *coo*—"

Liam grabbed her, clamped *his* hand over her mouth, and smiled sheepishly at Payton. "She's a wee bit of a temper. Are ye *certain* . . ."

"Aye," Payton said, enjoying the look of horror in her eyes. "*Quite* certain."

"But . . . but there's a rather wretched *curse*—" Grif tried.

"Ye'll no' frighten me off with yer bloody curses," he said resolutely. "If ye want the money, gentlemen, ye have me terms. I'll give ye the evening to think on it."

And with that, he turned and walked to the door and opened it, continued on down the corridor, smiling broadly at the sound of Mared's shouting against Liam's hand.

As luck would have it, Sarah had wandered into the corridor just as the three Lockharts came storming out of the salon behind him. Payton chuckled at the look of alarm in Liam and Grif's eyes as they noticed his genteel guest, and almost laughed aloud at the haste with which they tried to retreat.

But Mared looked at them all with disdain as she went striding out the front entry, muttering furiously under her breath with each step.

Aye, she had the grit of the gods, that one.

Three

Mayfair, London
Several weeks later

Caught in a snare of carriages, wagons, beasts, and people at Piccadilly Circus, Viscount Whittington's brougham came to a complete halt, which gave his youngest daughter, Miss Lucy Addison, yet another reason to complain.

Seated on the bench next to her mother, and directly across from her older sister Anna and their father, Lucy sighed very loudly, squeezed her eyes shut as if she were suffering from some spectacular pain, and rested her chestnut-colored head against the plush velvet squabs.

"There now, Lucy, you'll not make it any more tolerable with your impatience," Mother softly chided her.

"Oh, what's the use of attending at all?" Lucy huffed, opening her eyes and leveling an icy, amber-eyed glare at Anna. "It scarcely matters if we are late or not, for regardless of which gentleman may catch my eye, *I* will not be allowed to entertain *any* offers!"

Anna rolled her eyes at Lucy's attack of vapors—which were becoming entirely too commonplace, really.

"Lucy, darling, that is not very kind," Father said. "Anna is not purposefully trying to cause you grief."

"I don't know how you can be so certain, Father," Lucy sniffed. "She makes no effort at all to gain an offer. I think she rather enjoys hurting me."

"How very silly of you, Lucy!" Mother said sharply. "It is not our Anna's fault that she hasn't entertained any offers recently," she added, looking hopefully at Anna. "She'll find her way soon enough, and you'll still be young and beautiful and marriageable."

"No I won't!" Lucy cried with all the charm of a petulant five-year-old. "I'll be old and sitting on the shelf next to Anna!"

"I beg your pardon, but have any of you noticed that I am actually *in* the carriage with you, and therefore can hear what you say?" Anna asked them all.

She received a fatherly pat on her knee in response. "Don't be cross, dear," Father said soothingly. "Lucy is quite understandably concerned—after all, she had such a smashing debut last Season that she should expect to make a good match, and *would*, I daresay, perhaps in as much as an instant, were it not for . . . well, *you* know."

"Yes, I *know*," Anna said impatiently. "My sister reminds me at least daily that no gentleman of any import has offered for me in the three long years since my debut."

Honestly, her family's growing fear that dear little Lucy was missing hundreds of viable offers was beginning to wear very thin. Lucy might be the prettiest of the three Addison sisters, but did that make her the most important of them? And really, Anna could scarcely care less if they married Lucy off before her—she gave that ridiculous custom no thought and had said so, many times. Unfortunately, the rest of her family did.

"Dear Anna, won't you at least *try* this evening?" Lucy asked sweetly, looking, all of a sudden, all innocent and damnably pretty. "The Darlington ball is one of the most important events of the Season. . . . If you'd just try a *bit*, you might attract at least one gentleman."

There were times, such as this, when Anna wished they were still children and she could tie Lucy up and leave her in the wardrobe when she was such a horrid little bother. "And what would you have me do, darling Lucy?" Anna asked just as sweetly. "Smile and bat my lashes like you?"

"There now!" Mother warned. "I'll not abide your quarreling. Conduct yourselves as ladies, if you please!"

Lucy fell back against the squabs again in a pout. Anna ignored her.

Perhaps if she were in Lucy's perfect little slippers she'd be just as insufferable, but it wasn't as if Anna was keeping her from receiving offers on purpose. And it wasn't as if she hadn't had at least an offer here and there—of course she had! Three, to be exact—all deemed unacceptable by her parents. Not that it had bothered Anna, really—she scarcely knew the men who offered, and she did not feel an all-consuming desire to marry.

No, Anna had realized the Season she'd made her debut and had attracted only the attention of a man who had a bug collection and a declining fortune that she did not fit the desired mold of what the more exciting bachelors of the *ton* sought in a potential wife. The realization had been rather hurtful, and she had retreated to the training of hunting dogs—a hobby that had made her one of the most renowned trainers in Devonshire. But Anna had begun to accept the fact she might end up a spinster.

She did not want to end up a spinster. Quite the contrary—she had long ago dreamed of falling in love, of being swept off her feet by some dashing man, of marrying for love and bearing children, and laughing and living . . . and she dreamed of Drake Lockhart.

Drake Lockhart . . . She stifled a sigh. Lord *God*, how she admired that man! Had admired him desperately since her introduction into society. Was there anyone more dashing? More handsome? More accomplished or gentle or charming? Sadly, no . . . and while Anna wasn't certain that he held any particular esteem for her, she had her hopes. He flirted shamelessly with her, and since he had come home from his Grand Tour of the Continent at Christmas, he seemed even more flirtatious than he'd been the year he'd left.

She could scarcely wait to see him tonight; she had worn her best ball gown, a shimmering pale green, embroidered at the hem with a garland of flowers that matched the embroidery of the high bodice. Mother proclaimed it lovely, but Lucy, adorned in gossamer white and looking very angelic, said it looked rather matronly.

Anna had ignored her—she harbored no false illusions about her appearance. With auburn hair so dark that it was almost brown and brown eyes, she was what her father called a handsome woman. Not so handsome as to be considered uncommonly pretty, and not so *un*handsome as to be considered plain. Just somewhere in between pretty and plain. Along with a thousand other unmarried women.

Nonetheless, Anna had high hopes for tonight's ball, and smiled when the carriage suddenly lurched forward.

There was a crush of carriages in and around fashionable Berkeley Square, all vying for a position in front of the Darlington mansion. The crème de la crème of London's *haute ton* was expected to attend. Only being on one's deathbed was sufficient reason to miss the event.

Peter and Augusta Addison, Viscount and Viscountess Whittington—Anna's parents—were no different. They were among the privileged ranks of the *ton*'s very elite. Lord Whittington had been a distinguished member of the House of Lords for several years, and Lady Whittington was known as the consummate hostess.

Furthermore, their three adult daughters were renowned for their good looks and manners. Bette, the oldest, had married a parliamentary protégé the year after her debut and was now the happy Lady Featherstone, mother of two children, and following closely in her mother's footsteps. Miss Lucy Addison, the youngest, was known as the prettiest of the three, and, in fact, many said she was uncommonly pretty, and the one with the sweetest countenance.

That left Anna Addison, the middle girl. While there were those among the *ton* who would quietly say that Miss Addison was a true Original, there were many more who thought her a bit artless for the Quality. Anna had heard enough parlor gossip to know that she had what some said was a "difficult personality."

Frankly, she did not understand why. Well, all

right, to be fair, her argument with Lord Mathers over Catholic emancipation at a very large supper party had not exactly been her shining moment, but his lordship was so *unbearably* stodgy on the subject!

Nevertheless, she was reasonably accomplished by the *ton*'s standards. She knew all the things a young woman was supposed to know—the harp, a little geography, a little embroidery. She might not be the most demure woman circulating amongst the Quality, but she had never picked her teeth with her fork or stepped on anyone's toes in the course of a dance, or been caught in a compromising position . . . as much as she might have liked to have been involved in something so excitingly scandalous.

Unfortunately, the only thing that could be said about her was that she found the endless, circuitous life of the *ton* rather boring . . . and even that was not something she was foolish enough to voice aloud. Well . . . not very often, at any rate.

Her less-than-enthusiastic acceptance into society was something of a mystery to her, but not one that she dwelled upon now—she had far more important things to think about, such as her dogs and the course of training them for the hunt. And at the moment, as the carriage inched forward, moment by interminable moment, she was thinking about Lockhart, the only bright spot to her otherwise exceedingly dull existence.

At long last the carriage rolled to a stop outside the main gates of the Darlington mansion, and the four of them spilled out.

Lucy and Anna fell in behind their parents and stood patiently as they waited to be announced. Lucy took the opportunity to give Anna's gown a bit of critical study and opined, "You should have worn the pearl necklace. It would go well with your gown."

Anna shot a look at her. "Do you mean the pearl necklace *you're* wearing? *My* necklace? The one you said you simply had to have or you'd not attend tonight's ball?"

"Did I really say so?" Lucy asked with a pert toss of her head. "Well I—*Oh!* Who is that?" she asked, going up on her toes to peer over her father's shoulder.

Anna looked to where Lucy indicated and caught a glimpse of a tall, broad-shouldered man's back as he turned the corner and walked into the gentlemen's gaming room just as the Darlington butler intoned, "Lord and Lady Whittington . . . Miss Anna Addison . . . Miss Lucy Addison."

Their father offered his arm to their mother, and the four of them glided into the ballroom.

Several young dandies instantly flocked to Lucy, who was, to her great delight, already rumored to be this Season's most desirable debutante. Anna stood patiently by with a smile pasted on her face, just as she had done all her life next to one sister or the other, alternating between feeling quite self-conscious and rather insignificant as Lucy received the young men's warm salutations.

She was thinking she'd just as soon find a quiet corner than stand there when she felt two gloved fingers on her elbow.

She glanced over her shoulder, felt her body's heat surge into her neck and face, for the hand on her elbow belonged to none other than *him*—tall with golden brown hair, a charming smile, and mysterious brown eyes. "Why, Mr. Lockhart," she exclaimed with a sly smile. "Fancy meeting you here, at a tedious ball."

"Tedious?" he asked, cocking a brow. "I cannot imagine what you mean, Miss Addison, for nothing could keep me from the pleasure of viewing the loveliest ladies London has to offer." His gaze flicked the length of her. "And might I add that seeing such a radiant image of femininity and good health is most sublime."

The warmth in her neck was rapidly spreading down her body, and Anna laughed low, flicked open her fan and looked covertly about the room over the top of it. "Have you come alone, Mr. Lockhart? Or will we have the pleasure of meeting your brother and Miss Lockhart, too?"

"Naturally, my sister has come in the company of my parents," he said, smiling as if he knew what heat he caused in her. "Unfortunately, my brother, Nigel, is in Bath this Season, taking the waters there."

Sobering up was more like it, and everyone knew it. It was no secret among the Mayfair drawing rooms that Mr. Nigel Lockhart was fonder of drink than food or women or sleep. Anna had heard from Bette (who knew everything about everyone) that when Drake had arrived home from the Continent, he had instantly sent his younger brother to Bath in the company of an elderly uncle until he could free himself of the demon drink.

"What of you, *ma petite* Anna Addison?" Drake asked, stepping closer, so close that he was almost touching her. "Have you come in the company of your parents? Is there perhaps a chance that a gentleman might have the pleasure of your company for a walkabout in the gardens when the moon is full? Or would the gentleman be forced to endure the presence of her venerable papa, too?"

Anna laughed. "I assure you, sir, if a gentleman

were to escort me on a moonlit walk about the gardens, my father would be the last to hear of it, directly after the vicar."

Lockhart grinned. "Oh my, Miss Addison, how terribly wicked of you. I shall certainly have to seek you out and request the favor, shan't I?"

It was all Anna could do to keep from nodding eagerly, but she slanted him another look over the top of her fan. "Perhaps," she said with a slight, noncommittal shrug.

"Until the moon, then, Miss Addison," Lockhart said, and with a sly wink he stepped around her and walked to where Lucy was standing, still in the midst of several young gentlemen.

Anna watched him surreptitiously, hoping feverishly that he would greet Lucy and walk on. But when he spoke to her, Lucy's face erupted into a lovely wreath of smiles, her amber eyes sparkling, and Lockhart was caught in her perfect little web. Lucy had an enviable way with men, an innate quality that Anna could not explain.

Nevertheless, she told herself that Lockhart did not care for Lucy's attention, but was simply being polite, and then she tried hard to believe it. Yet watching it—the charming tilt of his head, the broad smile—was so painful that she felt the urge to march into their midst and break up the happy little reunion.

It was her sister, Lady Featherstone, who stopped her by suddenly appearing at her side.

"At whom are you staring so intently?" Bette asked after kissing her on the cheek.

"What?" Anna asked, feigning surprise. "Why should you think I am staring? There's hardly anything or anyone who captures my attention."

"There's someone who might," Bette said, and slipped her hand into the crook of Anna's arm, forcing her to walk along the edge of the dance floor. She leaned in, whispered conspiratorially, "You shall *never* guess who is in attendance tonight."

"Who?"

"No, no . . . *guess*," Bette said, poking her in the side.

"Bette!" Anna exclaimed. "I can't possibly guess! *Who*, then?"

"Oh, all right," Bette said, frowning at Anna's incompetence at playing her game. "The *Scot*."

Anna instantly perked up at the mention of the Scot. She had been intrigued from the first mention a month or so ago, when reports of a Scottish earl with business in London began to make the rounds of drawing rooms. He was making quite a splash, all told—it was said he was quite entertaining, quite wealthy, quite handsome, and quite in need of a wife—the latter being pure speculation, of course, but the fact that he was a Scot added an air of intrigue to the usual game.

As it happened, Anna had met a Scot once before—last Season, when Captain Lockhart had come into the *ton*'s midst for all too brief a time.

On that occasion, she had been at the Lockhart ball, and as Drake had not yet returned from the Continent, she had been quite bored. Until Barbara Lockhart, insufferable Philistine that she was, had introduced Anna to her Scottish cousin, and instantly Anna had been captivated by his accent, the air of impatience, and the scar across his cheek. That evening she had made a game of following him about, and when she'd found him, alone, poking about the Lockharts' small study, she had been highly titillated.

Her reward had been a very passionate kiss that had left her breathless and weak-kneed and *dying* to know more. Unfortunately, that ruggedly handsome Scot had disappeared without a trace just a few days after that . . . *at the same time the reclusive Ellen Farnsworth had disappeared.*

That extraordinary coincidence, coupled with that extraordinary kiss, had fascinated Anna.

Some speculated that Miss Farnsworth went willingly with the captain—after all, she had something of a reputation in that regard. Others said the captain had kidnapped her, and that old Farnsworth was too much the penny-pincher to pay the ransom. And even wiser heads argued that there was no connection between the two disappearances whatsoever, very tiresomely insisting that the Scot had simply returned to Scotland and Miss Farnsworth had returned to Cornwall.

Whatever the truth, Anna had built it up to a great romantic adventure in her mind, and the story had so deeply ingrained itself in her imagination that she had, over the last year, devoured all things Scottish, from historical accounts, to travel volumes, to old maps. Scotland sounded magical, a land where time did not march so ploddingly along as it did here, in the Mayfair district of London.

Therefore, the mention of a *new* Scot excited Anna, and she very much wanted an introduction.

"There he is," Bette said, tapping her arm with her fan as they strolled along the southern wall of the ballroom.

Anna looked to where her sister indicated and saw a group of men conversing. She recognized one strong back as belonging to the same gentleman she and

Lucy had glimpsed as they waited to be announced. That surprised her; she had assumed the earl was an older man. The Scot was tall, like the captain, but not as thick. His hair, almost black, was slicked back and was longer than most, but nonetheless coiffed in the current fashion. His shoulders were perfectly square, his waist trim, and not fish-bellied like so many gentlemen of the *ton* seemed to be.

"Introduce me?" Anna whispered. "Come on, say you will!"

Bette laughed. "He *is* pleasing, is he not? But I haven't been properly introduced, either." At Anna's imploring look, she laughed. "All right, then, I'll see what I can do." With a wink and a tap of her fan against Anna's shoulder, she went sailing off to find someone to introduce them, leaving Anna standing alone against the thick brocade drapes.

Anna flicked open her fan, held it up so that she could scan the room. The Scot and the other gentlemen remained deeply entrenched in conversation, and much to her dismay, Drake was still in the company of Lucy. From where she stood, she could see Lucy coyly laughing.

Unable to watch the flirtation between her sister and the man she so admired, Anna turned away—at which point she happened to see Miss Crabtree, alone, perched on the edge of her seat, her hands folded tightly in her lap. The poor dear—she had the dual misfortune of being quite plain and rather soft-spoken. The combination of the two always kept her apart from the rest of the crowd, and even on those rare occasions a kind soul would take pity and attempt to draw her in, no one could hear a word the girl said.

Anna could hardly abide it—the *ton* could be so cruel at times—and began walking purposefully in Miss Crabtree's direction, intent on speaking with her. But as she moved toward Miss Crabtree, she noticed that the Scottish earl and Mr. Fynster-Allen were likewise walking toward Miss Crabtree, and it became plainly evident that they meant to speak with her.

Poor Miss Crabtree had noticed them, too, and white as a sheet, she tried to sit a little straighter.

Mr. Fynster-Allen was the first to reach her, and bent over to speak. Miss Crabtree was instantly nodding, allowing Mr. Fynster-Allen to help her to her feet, and glancing uneasily at the Scottish earl, who at that moment stepped from behind Mr. Fynster-Allen and bowed deeply.

A breath caught in Anna's throat as he stopped fully in her view. Dear heaven, but he was *extraordinarily* handsome, with a square jaw, an angular nose, and deep-set, gorgeously green eyes. And when he smiled—a frighteningly *charming* smile—it was so bright and warm that she could feel her belly flutter as Miss Crabtree dipped a terribly awkward curtsey, from which the earl rescued her by reaching for her hand and lifting her up.

Miss Crabtree (all right, and Anna, too) almost swooned; she looked up at the earl, tipping her head all the way back to see him, her mouth agape.

Much to Anna's considerable amazement, the earl extended his arm, onto which Miss Crabtree laid a trembling hand, and he led her onto the dance floor.

The parting of the Red Sea could not possibly have been more dramatic, for not one person in the ballroom missed his exceptional act of kindness.

He moved Miss Crabtree effortlessly and gracefully about the dance floor, and tiny talons of envy pricked at Anna's insides. The couple swirled past the small orchestra, beneath the six circles of beeswax candles hanging from the ceiling, and past the floor-to-ceiling French doors that led out into the gardens—but then something else caught her eye, and Anna nearly dropped her fan.

Just behind the beaming Miss Crabtree, Drake and her sister stepped out into the night.

Her heart sank; she instantly started in that direction, moving against the crowd, navigating her way through the chairs and people and the ridiculous number of decorative plants until she found her way out onto the veranda—but Lockhart and Lucy were nowhere to be seen.

Oblivious to the couples standing around her, Anna stood there for several minutes, debating whether she should walk into the gardens and confront them or simply hope it was not as it seemed and return to the ballroom. But as she believed her heart could not bear the sight of them locked in some moonlit embrace, she finally lowered her head, turned, and walked back through the French doors—and almost collided with Miss Crabtree, who, with a sheen of perspiration on her brow, was grinning wildly. "Miss Addison!" she cried buoyantly and very plainly. "I didn't know you had come this evening!"

Anna gathered her wits. "I shouldn't miss it," she said, lifting a smile to Miss Crabtree. And *oh!*—the Scottish earl was standing behind her. Her gaze traveled up to his dark brows, one cocked in amusement above his green eyes.

"Have you had the pleasure of making Lord Ardencaple's acquaintance?" Miss Crabtree asked, and Anna could only shake her head as her gaze fell to his lips.

"If I may present my good friend, Miss Addison."

Somehow Anna managed to lift her hand and dip a curtsey. He smiled pleasantly, took her hand in his big one, and bent over it, his lips grazing her gloved knuckles. "A pleasure to make yer acquaintance, Miss Addison," he said in a lovely, lilting accent.

Her gaze steady on his smile, those lips, those lovely yet masculine lips, Anna muttered, "The pleasure is certainly all mine, my lord."

He cocked a curious brow, but Anna couldn't speak, could hardly even move. Lord Ardencaple shifted his smile to Amelia Crabtree. "Shall we take a wee bit of air, Miss Crabtree?"

"I'd be *delighted,*" she said, beaming up at him.

"Will ye excuse us then, Miss Addison?" he asked.

Too dumbfounded to find her tongue, Anna nodded helplessly and stepped aside. As they passed, the earl smiled, but Anna couldn't tear her gaze away from his mouth.

Those were extraordinary lips for a man, full and ripe and *quite* enticing, which Anna should know—she wouldn't forget those lips in her lifetime, and had thought of them practically daily since she had kissed an almost identical pair one year ago at the Lockhart ball.

Four

Having met his sixth Amelia since his arrival in London a month or so ago, Grif was coming round to the conclusion that being one of their number likely meant that the poor female was rather young and plain or old and fat. This one, bless her, was even plainer than the first young Amelia, who at least had a rather jovial spirit that made up for her large beak of a nose and tiny mouth.

None of the Amelias he'd met thus far were acquainted with Lady Battenkirk. But Grif had high hopes for *this* Amelia.

She was practically floating beside him as they toured the gardens. It would seem that Miss Crabtree's opportunities for such walkabouts were rare indeed, and judging by the way her little hand clutched his arm, Grif thought it might be a bit of a struggle to extract himself from her company. Better to get it over and done with, then.

"Quite a lovely moon, aye?" he asked, looking up to the watery image of a half moon, obscured by the sooty haze from thousands of chimneys.

"*Oh*, my *lord,* I think it perhaps the *loveliest* moon I have ever *seen!*" she exclaimed with great enthusiasm.

If that was the loveliest moon she had ever seen, he pitied her, for she, along with all the bloody Englishmen, had no idea what inspiration one could divine from the big, milky white moon that hung ripe over Talla Dileas. The lass would think she'd passed through the pearly gates to heaven.

"'Tis quite amazing how the moon can look so very different from place to place. Have ye been abroad, Miss Crabtree?"

She blinked two small blue eyes. "Abroad? Ah . . . my family has a country home, in Yorkshire. We are back and forth between here and there."

"That's the travel ye've done, then?"

"Yes?" she asked, biting her lower lip as if she feared he might be cross with her for not having ventured farther into the world.

Grif couldn't possibly have cared less if she'd traveled as far as the ladies' retiring room or not. "There's quite a lot to see in the world, there is. Ye must rely on the tales of yer friends who go abroad."

"I suppose . . . Well, of course!"

"I'd wager they bring ye trifles now and again."

"Trifles?"

"Wee gifts."

She bit deeper into her lip. "Well . . . I *suppose* they might. If they traveled very far, that is. But what with the Season upon us all, my friends are rather firmly rooted in London," she said with an uncertain smile.

"All of them, really?"

She nodded.

Grif smiled. "Are you acquainted with Lady Battenkirk, then?"

Miss Crabtree's wee eyes went wide with surprise.

"Lady Battenkirk!" she exclaimed. "Certainly I know of her, but . . . but I could not fairly count her among my acquaintances."

Bloody hell, then. Grif shrugged. "Ah. I had heard she's had the good fortune to travel quite extensively," he explained, "and I should like to inquire if she's ventured as far as Scotland."

"Oh! I suppose you'll have to wait for a time before you may ask her *that,*" Miss Crabtree said, obviously pleased to know something after all.

"And why is that?"

"I am given to understand that she has gone off to Wales to study cathedral ruins."

"I beg yer pardon—to study *what?*"

"Cathedral ruins. Cathedrals are rather large churches—"

"Miss Crabtree, I'm no' such a heathen that I donna know what a cathedral is," he said with a wink. "But a study of them?"

"The architecture, that sort of thing."

Ach, for the love of Christ! Did the English have nothing better to do with their time than study architecture? In *Wales* of all places?

"I beg your pardon . . . did I say something wrong?" Miss Crabtree asked meekly.

Grif forced a polite laugh. "No' in the least, lass," he said. "'Tis that I'm a wee bit surprised to learn that the study of architecture is in vogue among the ladies. Perhaps ye've spoken to Lady Battenkirk of her travels?"

"No, my lord, for I scarcely know her at all." She smiled uncertainly again; Grif returned her smile and turned her sharply about and started the march back to the house, where he intended to deposit Miss Crabtree at a table with a cup of punch.

As they strode down the length of the Darlington gardens, and Miss Crabtree spoke of the weather this Season, he nodded politely and glanced around at the other couples availing themselves of the garden shadows. As they neared the house, and the golden lights of dozens upon dozens of beeswax candles spilled out from the ballroom windows and illuminated the lawn, he caught a glimpse of a woman with hair the color of chestnut and turned to look.

She was very near to being locked in a man's embrace, but Grif could just see her angelic face—alabaster skin perfectly smooth, her eyes luminous, and her lips dark and full. She was smiling up at the man who held her in such rapture, coyly batting her long lashes at him, laughing a little at whatever he said to her. As the man slipped his arm around her waist, Grif noted she was delightfully feminine in the curve of her body.

Beside him, Miss Crabtree made a clucking sound. "Oh dear, I rather think Lord Whittington would be quite displeased," she said when Grif looked curiously at her.

"Beg yer pardon?"

Miss Crabtree didn't answer, but frowned disapprovingly in the direction of the angel. "It's rather unseemly for a debutante to be cavorting about," she whispered. "Especially with a man of such reputation, and *especially* Miss Lucy Addison, as she is rumored to be the Favorite of the Season."

The favorite what? Grif wondered, and thought that while it might appear unseemly to a lamb like Miss Crabtree, it was actually an awful lot of jolly good fun to go sneaking about lush gardens. Perhaps that was what was wrong with the English in general, he mused. They really had far too many rules that barred any merriment.

Grif smiled down at the mousy woman on his arm and wondered if she'd ever know the pleasure of cavorting about moonlit gardens. "What a pity, that," he said low, "for I know one lass I should very much like to cavort with in the gardens."

Miss Crabtree gasped and blinked. Then smiled beneath a furious blush.

Grif winked, but said nothing more.

He managed to extract himself from Miss Crabtree easily enough, although he didn't care for the pitiful look she gave him—it made him feel a wee bit like he was leaving a puppy on the wrong side of a door.

She was quickly swallowed up by a number of couples and ladies who were ready for their supper.

He made his way back to the ballroom, smiling at any lady whose eye he could catch . . . which seemed to be all of them. He might have stopped to flirt with as many as he could, for that was a sport he excelled at, but he was rather determined to make Miss Lucy Addison's acquaintance. Aye, if there was one thing on God's earth that Griffin appreciated, it was a bonny woman, and Miss Lucy Addison was definitely bonny.

He found his friend, Mr. Fynster-Allen, in the place he had left him—standing a little behind one of the ridiculously overgrown potted palms, apparently enjoying the sight of the ladies as they waltzed by on the dance floor.

It had been Grif's good fortune to make Fynster's acquaintance at a gentlemen's club shortly after his arrival in London. What had begun as a friendly game of cards had turned into a friendship. Fynster was a rotund, practically bald man who stood a full head shorter than Grif. He was likewise a bachelor, and possessed the most pleasant countenance Grif had ever encountered in another man. Unfortunately, Fynster was painfully shy when it came to women, and did not avail himself of their company nearly as often as Grif did, if ever.

Fortunately, however, Fynster seemed to know everyone among the *ton,* had even heard of Lady Battenkirk, and even knew a batch of Amelias.

Furthermore, it appeared that everyone among the *ton* knew Fynster; he was invited to all the important events, and it was indeed his influence that had garnered Grif's invitation to this ball. Grif liked Fynster well enough to feel abominably guilty for the number of lies he had told him, beginning with the reason for his search for an Amelia.

Fynster was watching a woman in a blue gown when Grif clapped him on the shoulder, startling him. "*Ho* there, Ardencaple!" he exclaimed, jumping a little. "By God, you startled me!"

"Dreadfully sorry, lad," Grif said, grinning.

Fynster glanced around Grif, saw he was alone. "She was not your Amelia, I take it?"

"She was no'," Grif said, affecting a sorrowful look.

"There now," Fynster said with a sympathetic smile. "There are more Amelias. Squads of them, I'd reckon. You'll find her, I'm quite certain."

Grif smiled sadly and looked out over the dance floor, wishing he wasn't forced to tell a decent chap like Fynster such a god-awful lie about Amelia. He had made up the outrageous tale one night over cards and with the considerable help of whiskey. His story went something like this—that his Uncle Angus had sired Amelia in an illicit but passionate love affair (the details of which had Fynster's eyes bulging quite out of their sockets). But, alas, Uncle had been forced by family tragedy to return to Scotland, and Amelia's mother had married an Englishman. It had been his uncle's dying wish that Grif find Amelia and give her something that had belonged to her true father.

It had worked—Fynster had been so touched by the tale that he had immediately and earnestly set out to help Grif find as many Amelias as he could shake from a tree. He had high hopes for this ball, which he said was one of the more important events of the Season, but sadly, only one of the Amelias known to him was in attendance tonight . . . and she was the wrong Amelia. Which, to Grif's way of thinking, left him a clear opening to ask after Miss Lucy Addison.

"By the bye," Grif said as they both watched the woman in blue sail by again. "The young woman just there," he said, nodding in the direction where Lucy Addison was now holding court with three gentlemen. "Do you suppose her Christian name is Amelia?"

Fynster looked to where he indicated and laughed. "Ah, so you'd join the ranks of gentlemen smitten with Miss Lucy Addison?"

Grif shrugged. "She's a bonny one, she is."

"She certainly is. I'd wager there isn't a man in this room who hasn't dreamed of her, myself among them. Very well, then . . . come along and I'll see if I can't give you a leg up."

Grif grinned. "Ye'll have me adoring ye yet, Fynster," he said jovially.

"That's quite unnecessary," Fynster said, turning a little red of face as they started off.

Miss Lucy was entertaining the gentlemen around

her with some girlish tale as they walked into her charmed circle. Something about having twisted her ankle, which had the men gathered about *aahing* at her misfortune. She looked up at Fynster and Grif, and smiled prettily at Grif. "Good evening, Mr. Fynster-Allen. How very good to see you," she said charmingly, her gaze still on Grif as Fynster bowed over her hand.

"My pleasure, Miss Lucy, to be sure," he said. "Might I beg your pardon? I should very much like to make a proper introduction of my good friend, his lordship Ardencaple."

Her smile deepened; she was an old hand at this game, Grif could see, as she snapped open her fan and fanned herself. "I should think you may, sir."

A bit too theatrically, Fynster intoned, "My lord, may I present Miss Lucy Addison."

Miss Lucy daintily held out her gloved hand; Grif instantly took it and bowed deeply over it. "Ye canna know what a pleasure it is to make yer acquaintance," he said, and thought he heard one of her fawners snort.

"My lord, I daresay the pleasure is *mine*," she said, her smile perfect as Grif raised himself up. Her hand slipped from his. "Have you been in London long?"

"Scarcely more than a month."

"Ah," she said as her eyes quickly flicked the length of him. "And how do you find the weather here?"

"Quite pleasant, aye."

"Isn't it? I'm rather pleased, for I am *quite* cross when it is dreary."

"Really, Miss Lucy! You've not a cross bone in your body!" one of the other men said with a laugh.

"I swear that I *do*, sir, and it is most likely to present

itself when the weather is dreary," she said, and smiled at the laughter of the men.

"Miss Lucy, I believe if you will check your dance card, you will find my name written against the quadrille," another one said, edging forward.

"Oh! That *is* a quadrille they are playing, is it not?" She looked at the dance card dangling by a ribbon from her wrist. A very full dance card, Grif could see, for there was not a blank spot on it. "You are quite right, Lord Preston. I promised the quadrille to you."

The lucky man stepped forward, his arm extended.

Miss Lucy snapped her fan shut, smiled adoringly at the others. "I do beg your pardon," she said sweetly, and glanced at Grif from the corner of her eye. "A pleasure to make your acquaintance, Lord Ardencaple." Before she could say more, Preston had clamped his hand down on hers, was pulling her along, ready to be gone from the throng of admirers.

Fynster sighed as she glided alongside Preston and the other men drifted away. "There you have it, then, Ardencaple. The most desired debutante in all of London. It's the subject of much speculation as to who will win her hand."

Aye, but it wasn't exactly her hand that interested Grif.

He accompanied Fynster to the game room for a time, and when he'd lost a few more pounds than he cared to lose, he decided it was time he joined Hugh at the town house they had overrun, and left Fynster to carry on.

He took his sweet time making his way through the crowd, going against the tide so to speak, smiling and nodding at dozens of women who passed him by, but his head was filled with the lovely images of Miss

Lucy Addison and her chestnut-colored hair—so filled, in fact, that he almost collided with a woman who stepped in his path near the main entry.

He recognized her instantly—Miss Crabtree had introduced them—yet he could not for the life of him recall her name.

She smiled pertly at him, her coppery brown eyes sparkling beneath dark brows dipped in a vee. She looked, he thought, delightfully devilish.

"Why, Lord Ardencaple, we meet again," she said happily, clasping her hands before her.

"Aye, that we do," he said, racking his brain for her name.

"You *do* recall our introduction, do you not?"

"Naturally, I do, and it was indeed a pleasure," he lied.

"If it was indeed a pleasure, then I should think you might recall my name," she said as the corners of her lips curled into a daring little smile.

That, more than anything, caught Grif's attention. He'd been in London a month now and had learned that the many lovely ladies of the *ton* were, by virtue of their many societal rules, prisoners of decorum and propriety. Of all the women he'd met—and there had been quite a lot of them, pretty and young and terribly enticing to the man in him—he had yet to meet one who was quite so . . . *saucy.*

Grif paused to have a closer look, and couldn't help but like what he saw—her hair was an earthy maple color with strands of dark auburn. It was swept up in bunches of ringlets as was the current fashion. Her nose was straight and delicate, her lips full and pleasing, and her neck long and slender. Her copper eyes were flecked with bits of deep gold. She was a very attractive woman, certainly, and he noticed, as he clasped his hands behind his back and smiled down at her, that her eyes were her most remarkable feature, for the sparkle in them clearly betrayed the vixen in her.

The vixen lifted her head, smiling playfully. "Oh dear, my lord, have you perhaps *forgotten* our introduction?" she teased.

"How could I possibly forget ye, lass?" he asked, his gaze drifting to her lips.

"Then say it—I *dare* you," she said, her smile broadening.

"Why should I? Just to please ye?"

"Yes. Just to please me."

Saucy and impudent. Grif grinned, blatantly letting his gaze wander the length of her. "How dare a gentleman deny such a request? All right, here ye have it, just to please ye . . . Miss *Dragh,*" he said, using the Gaelic word for trouble, and winked.

That took her aback; the lass blinked up at him with those coppery eyes. "I beg your pardon?"

"Do ye no' recognize yer name in *Gàidhlig*, then?"

The saucy smile instantly returned, and she lifted her chin. "There, you see? You don't recall my name! For I am certain that Miss *Addison* is Miss *Addison* in whatever language you choose."

Miss Addison? The same Addison as the lovely Miss *Lucy* Addison? It surprised him, but Grif was skilled at the art of flirtation and did not flinch. He just smiled deep into her eyes. "Miss Addison it is, then," he said. "I shall no' forget it. And now, I must bid ye good night." He allowed his gaze to sweep over her once more before stepping around her and walking on.

"Before you take your leave, Lord Ardencaple?"

she called, stopping him. "I was wondering if you might know an acquaintance of mine from Scotland?"

God's blood, why was it everyone in London supposed he knew every other Scot in the blessed world? "And who might that be, then?"

"His name is Captain Lockhart."

She could not have stunned him more if she had kicked him in the shin. Grif stood almost paralyzed for a moment, his smile frozen, peering closely at her, assessing her. But she smiled innocently. "I canna say that I do," he said.

"No?"

"No. Good night, then, Miss Addison," he said, and bobbing his head in something of a bow, he continued on.

"Good night, my lord!" she sang after him.

Grif could feel her eyes on his back all the way out the door. Once outside, he drew a breath of relief, but his mind raced wildly. How could she *possibly* have known Liam? His brother hadn't mentioned any women, had not even hinted at a woman besides Ellie. All right, then, the only plausible explanation was that Miss Addison must have met him at a social function, something like this ball. Aye, it was nothing more than that. A strange coincidence.

But for the entire drive to Cavendish Street, where he and Hugh lived like kings in Hugh's grandmother's house, he could not shake the rather unpleasant notion that Miss Addison knew something about him.

Five

The next morning started with a row between Grif and Hugh, as Hugh had been out all night again, gambling with the money the Lockharts had borrowed and smelling of cheap perfume. Grif angrily reminded Hugh he was to be a valet, not a scoundrel. Hugh shoved the toast points he'd made at Grif and complained of feeling trapped. Before their argument was said and done, Grif had extracted Hugh's promise there'd be no more gambling or trawling about the city at night, and no more women of questionable character to darken their door.

Hugh had gone off to bed in foul temper, muttering his unflattering opinion of the new Earl of Ardencaple. Grif determined he needed some air. He left Dudley to keep an eye on his old friend and set out with the intention of calling on the lovely young lass he'd dreamed about last night.

He had to inquire of Fynster-Allen how to find Lucy Addison, but Fynster-Allen was amused by Grif's ardor for her, and with a chuckle sent him to Whittington House on Audley Street.

On Audley Street, Grif was slightly taken aback by the grandeur of Whittington House—not that he hadn't seen grand houses, but when he thought of

Miss Lucy, her circumstance was not exactly the first thing that came to mind.

When he lifted the heavy brass knocker and let it fall, a footman instantly opened the door. Behind him stood a butler. "Sir," the butler said stoically, bowing slightly before extending a silver tray.

Grif retrieved a calling card from his breast pocket and placed it on the tray. "Good day to ye. Lord Ardencaple calling for Miss Lucy Addison."

"Of *course*, sir," the butler said, as if Grif were somehow expected. "If you will follow me." He pivoted sharply about, strode into the ornate foyer.

Grif stepped inside, quickly tossed his hat and his gloves to a footman, and hurried to catch up with the impatient butler before he lost him.

The butler turned from the foyer into a large corridor and strode to a pair of highly polished oak doors. "If you will kindly wait here, I shall inform Miss Lucy that you've called," he said, and pushed open one door; Grif barely had an opportunity to step inside before the efficient butler closed the door behind him.

"Thank ye," he said to the closed door, and turned around to have a look about the room. Yet it seemed as if he'd scarcely begun before the butler was once again at the door. "If you will follow me, sir."

Grif hurried after him again.

They walked to the end of the very long carpeted corridor, past portraits and large porcelain vases full of hothouse flowers and brass wall sconces. At the end of the corridor, the butler paused in front of another set of doors, pushed them open with a flourish, bowed deeply, and announced, "Lord Ardencaple calling."

Grif stepped across the threshold and saw the

angel, Miss Lucy. She was perched like a pretty bird on the edge of an embroidered chair, her back straight, her hands folded in her lap. When she stood, it reminded him of the way the morning mist rose on the loch. "Lord Ardencaple, what a delight."

"Ah, but the delight is mine, lass," he said with a bow, and it wasn't until he was striding forward to take her hand with a ridiculously broad grin on his face that he noticed he wasn't the only caller in the room.

There was a man seated on a divan, who was eyeing Grif disdainfully. Directly across from him was an elderly woman with a matronly cap. The chaperone, he presumed, as her attention was on a piece of needlework in which her needle flew in and out. And there was one more person—a man standing at the window, his hands clasped behind his back. Grif recognized him as the man with whom Miss Lucy had been in the gardens at the Darlington ball last night.

Nevertheless, Grif bent over Miss Lucy's hand and smiled into her amber eyes.

"May I introduce you to Mr. Effington," she said, nodding politely in the direction of the man on the divan.

Grif and Effington exchanged a curt nod.

"And Mr. Lockhart," she said, nodding to the man at the window.

Lockhart! His English cousin. Grif stared at the man—he was so shocked that, for a fraction of a moment, he wasn't certain what to do.

"Ardencaple, is it?" Lockhart said, strolling across the room, his eyes narrowed slightly.

"Aye. Pleasure to make yer acquaintance, Mr. Lockhart," Grif said, quickly recovering, and extended his hand. Lockhart took his hand, peering at Grif so intently that he might have, in another circumstance, taken offense, but he wisely stepped away from him and turned a bright smile to Miss Lucy, who had resumed her perch on the edge of the chair.

"Please, my lord, be seated," she invited him, gesturing to the chair next to her. Grif flipped the tails of his coat and sat.

"Did you enjoy the Darlington ball?"

"I did indeed," he said with a broad smile.

"I so enjoy dancing," she said, and as Grif wasn't certain what to say to that, he merely nodded. "Do you enjoy dancing?" she asked.

"I do," he said honestly. "I hope to demonstrate how very much at first opportunity, if ye'll allow it."

Miss Lucy smiled at that, but Grif's cousin sneered and strolled back to the window.

"I beg your pardon, Miss Lucy, but I must take my leave," Mr. Effington said, coming across the room to bow over her hand. "Thank you for allowing me to call."

"Oh, but thank *you* for calling, Mr. Effington. Good day."

He smiled, glanced up at the others. "Good day to you all," he said, and strode toward the door, which a footman quickly opened, then just as quickly shut behind him.

"Lord Ardencaple," Miss Lucy said, drawing his attention back to her as she smoothed the lap of her gown. "How do you find the weather today?"

What was the English fascination with the weather? She'd asked after his impression of the weather last night as well. Did the lass aspire to some sort of meteorological occupation? "Rather pleasant," he said. "The sun is shining." As if that weren't obvious from the way it was streaming into the room, and if he had any doubts as to how ridiculous he sounded, he caught Lockhart in a slight roll of his eyes.

"Yes," Lucy said, clasping her hands again. "It *is* shining, and quite brightly on such an early spring day. I had a walkabout earlier, and it felt quite warm."

"Did it?" Lockhart asked. "But you asked for my cape, as if you were chilled."

"Yes, and you were quite generous with it, Mr. Lockhart," Miss Lucy said, glancing at him from the corner of her eye. "But then you will also recall that I returned it to you after a time, as I said I was warm."

Lockhart smiled and nodded his recall; Grif wished to high heaven the man would hurry along and take his leave so that he might have a moment with Miss Lucy.

"Does it become very warm in Scotland, my lord? It seems so frightfully . . . *north.*"

"Aye, there are days of warmth," he said. "But I'd wager not as many days as ye enjoy in London."

"Ah, time has escaped me," Lockhart said, pulling a timepiece from his pocket. "I'm afraid I must be going. You will have to carry on your delightfully riveting conversation about the weather without me."

Diah, but Grif would have liked to put a fist in the middle of that contemptible smile. It was true what he'd always heard—the English Lockharts were a sorry, despicable lot.

Grif did not bother to return Lockhart's cold smile as Lockhart strode across the room to Miss Lucy, who stood (which she had not done for poor Effington) and extended her hand to Lockhart. He took it, bowed deep, kissing her knuckles and lingering there for a moment before finally lifting his head. "I shall wish you a lovely day."

"Thank you, sir."

Lockhart dropped her hand and looked at Grif, who had come to his feet. Grif was slightly taller than his cousin, his shoulders broader, and, he thought a little smugly, decidedly younger. Lockhart bobbed his head, muttered, "Ardencaple," and moved for the door without waiting for a reply.

Miss Lucy waited until the footman had closed the door behind him before she very carefully resumed her seat and once again smoothed the lap of her gown.

Grif sat, too. "I see that ye are quite the favorite lass, what with all yer gentlemen callers," he remarked pleasantly. "'Tis enough to make a man a wee bit jealous."

"Are you jealous, my lord?"

"Aye," he said, leaning forward. "I'm jealous that I wasna there when ye needed a cloak. I'm jealous that another gentleman was allowed the favor of yer company. I should very much like to have a walkabout with ye, Miss Lucy."

"Would you indeed?" she asked, smiling coyly. "Perhaps one day I might be so inclined."

"Ah, now ye've given me a ray of hope, ye have," he said, and sat forward a little farther as he stole a glimpse at the chaperone, and with his hand, brushed Lucy's knee. "When might I have that walkabout, do ye suppose?"

She smiled at his hand still on her knee. "Why, Lord Ardencaple," she murmured, lifting her amber gaze to his. "I couldn't rightly say—so much depends on the weather after all." And with a seductive smile, she brushed her fingers across his.

"Miss Lucy, I beg your pardon, but it is time for your music lesson," the chaperone suddenly said.

Lucy moved her hand from Grif's and rose gracefully. "I thank you for calling, my lord."

"But . . . I've only just arrived!" Grif protested, gaining his feet.

"Would you make me tardy for my music lesson?" she asked, and gave him a sunny smile. "Good day, my lord!" She dipped a small curtsey and walked past him, out the door.

While Grif was trying to make sense of Miss Lucy Addison, Miss Anna Addison was trying to make sense of Drake Lockhart.

She had intercepted him as he had emerged from the sitting room, having wrenched the names of Lucy's callers from the family's butler: Lockhart, Effington, and Ardencaple.

At the mention of Drake, Anna hid herself in the salon just before the foyer, the door cracked so she could watch who came and went from the sitting room where Lucy held court.

She had waited for what seemed an eternity before she saw Effington come out, followed by Drake several minutes later. As he strode down the corridor, she slipped out of the salon, stood with her back to the silk-covered wall just before the corridor opened into the cavernous round foyer.

Surprise washed over Drake's face when he saw her there, but then a smile spread his lips. "Miss Addison, what a pleasure," he said instantly, reaching for her hand.

Anna quickly gave it to him. "Mr. Lockhart, I was not aware you had called on us."

One brow arched high across the other and his thumb caressed the bare knuckles of her hand. "Indeed? Your butler did not inform you I had come to pay my respects to the prettiest pair of sisters in all of London?"

"Why, *no,*" she said, twisting her hand in his so that their palms were touching. "He did not say you had called on anyone but Lucy."

Lockhart smiled, glanced surreptitiously into the foyer, then stepped closer to Anna, so that she had to tip her head back to see his face. "I shall have a cross word with him then, for depriving me of your company," he said, his fingers skating up her wrist, and inclined his head toward her, so that his lips were on her temple. "How lovely you smell, Anna."

His compliment sent a delicious shiver through her, and she boldly lifted her face so that her lips were only inches from his. *"Indeed?"*

"Indeed," he said softly, and she knew, she could *feel,* that he was just a fraction of a moment away from kissing her . . . but with an enigmatic smile, Lockhart stepped away from her.

"Regretfully, I've a previous engagement and must take my leave," he said, and with a polite nod, walked on, into the foyer.

Her heart pounding, Anna heard him walk across the marble entry and darted across the corridor. Now she could hear him speak to the footman, and with her body pressed against the wall, she leaned to her left to have a peek around the corner.

"Is he gone, then?"

The sound of the Scot's whispered voice caused her to shriek softly and clamp a hand over her heart as she whirled about. "Lord Ardencaple!" she cried. "You frightened me!"

Ardencaple laughed, his teeth snowy white. "I certainly did no' mean to frighten ye so, Miss Addison. I rather thought ye heard me . . . but I suppose yer attention was elsewhere, eh?" he asked with a sly wink.

Anna's face flamed—had he *seen* her with Drake? This was exactly the sort of thing that sent her mother into fits. She self-consciously smoothed her damp palms against her sides before folding her arms defensively beneath her bosom and glaring at the Scot . . . *handsome* Scot, actually, what with his dark wavy hair and lovely green eyes. And his *lips* . . . dear God, those lips had her heart pounding all over again.

Her hand drifted up to her throat. "I see that you have found your way around London's sitting rooms well enough."

Ardencaple lifted an amused brow. "I suppose I have."

She was unable to take her gaze from his lips. "I should think, in fact, that likely you've found your way to the sitting rooms of *all* the debutantes."

His eyes filled with something akin to mirth. "No' as many as ye might think, Miss Addison. I've left one or two of the lassies for the good English gentlemen."

"How very kind of you. I'm certain they shall all be indebted to your largesse."

He chuckled as his gaze lazily drifted the length of her, leaving a peculiar trail of warmth in her. Unnerved by it, Anna blurted, "How ever shall you choose, my lord? There are so *many* debutantes to swoon over you."

His smiled deepened. "All but one, apparently."

There was something very intent about his green eyes, and Anna abruptly pushed away from the wall, saying indifferently, "Oh, my lord, you should not concern yourself with *me* . . ." She strolled into the middle of the foyer, and over her shoulder added, "I assure you I am quite content to let the young ladies brawl for your attentions."

Ardencaple laughed at that and followed her into the foyer. "How very considerate of ye, Miss Addison. Yet I confess I'd no' mind another fair lass in the thick of the brawl. The more the merrier, as they say, and I should think it would be quite . . . *entertaining* to see ye brawl."

She gave him a pert toss of her head, looked up at a painting of her grandfather, sighing as if she heard that sort of thing all the time. "I am hardly affected by your attempts to charm me, my lord—there's enough gentlemanly charm in Mayfair to suffocate us all. I confine my interests to academics."

"Do ye now?" he asked, startling her with his nearness. He was standing at her back, so close that she could feel his body behind her. "And under which course of study would ye classify Mr. Lockhart?"

Of all the nerve! Anna shot him a frown over her shoulder. "Mr. Lockhart is a gentleman," she said coolly.

"Of course he is," Ardencaple amicably agreed. "And what is it ye study besides the *gentleman* Mr. Lockhart?"

"As a matter of fact," she said, turning round to face him. "You might be surprised to know that I am a student of Scotland."

"Are ye indeed?" he asked, his brows lifted in surprise.

"I am. It seems a rather charming place."

"Oh aye, she is that."

"And where would the seat of your earldom be, Lord Ardencaple?"

Ardencaple said nothing at first, but his wolfish smile slowly faded. "Near the foot of the Highlands."

"The foot . . . would that put it somewhere near Stirling?" she asked curiously.

With a slight frown, he looked at her closely. "Are ye familiar with the geography of Scotland, Miss Addison?"

"Yes . . . a bit," she said, even more curious about his sudden change in demeanor.

"Then ye know the Highlands are quite large with many small glens and rivers and lochs."

"So I've surmised."

"Then ye would have likewise surmised it's near to impossible to describe where everything lies, aye?"

Anna blinked, confused. "Do you mean to say that you can't describe where your seat is?"

His reaction to that question was to suddenly and inexplicably reach for her hand and bring it to his lips. "No' at all. I would describe it just as I did—near the foot of the Highlands. To explain any further would require a map of sorts, and ye are far too pretty to worry with it," he said, and kissed her knuckles, his lips warm and soft on her skin. "Now, then, if ye will kindly give me leave, I should best be on me way," he said, and dropping her hand, he turned and walked to the opposite end of the foyer and the entry.

Confused and a little perturbed, Anna watched him go, wondering if he had just insulted her intelligence. Did he think her incapable of grasping the simplest tenets of geography? That she couldn't think in the abstract?

As the footman opened the door, Ardencaple turned, gave her a strangely cool smile, and stepped outside.

Anna instantly whirled about and marched to the curving staircase leading to the floors above.

Frankly, she didn't need some dandy Scottish earl to tell her where the seat of Ardencaple might be—she had her books and her atlas and she had managed quite well without him until now, thank you. The next time she saw Lord Ardencaple, perhaps she'd explain to *him* where his seat was.

In her room, Anna pulled out the heavy atlas of Britain from her vanity, flipped the thick pages until she found Scotland, and began to scour the pages for Ardencaple. She found nothing like Ardencaple at all, which really didn't surprise her. Lots of peer names had changed over the centuries.

A trip to her father's library, and Anna returned to her rooms with the voluminous *Debrett's Correct Peerage* and began a painstaking search for Ardencaple.

After an hour or more, she found it. Her eyes widened, and she squinted at the page, read it again, using her finger to trace every word to make sure that she did not miss anything. And when she had finished, she slowly sat back and stared blindly at the wall in front of her.

There was no earldom of Ardencaple! At least, there hadn't been since the Ardencaple title and lands had been assumed by the duke of Argyll decades ago. Which meant that Lord Ardencaple was . . . some sort of *fraud?*

Now *that* was an intriguing notion, Anna thought as a smile crossed her lips.

Six

First the remark about Liam, and now the questions about Ardencaple—Miss Addison was beginning to vex Grif.

As he strode away from Whittington House, he had the distinctly disquieting feeling that the lass knew too much. Or something, at least. Or perhaps she simply had the ability to unnerve him with too many questions.

He'd have to be more astute in avoiding her, wouldn't he?

Grif walked on, tipping his hat and nodding at the passersby as he strolled through Mayfair and north across Oxford.

As he turned onto Cavendish Street, he noticed, much to his chagrin, that Lady Worthall was striding toward him with that insufferable little ankle-biting dog jumping alongside her. Lady Worthall was their intrusive neighbor, who had, apparently, appointed herself Grand Inquisitor. She'd been the first to arrive at their door to review the letters of introduction and was constantly walking up and down the street, peering up at their windows, and God forbid she catch one of them in the street.

"Lord Ardencaple!" she trilled loudly from half a block away.

"Good evening, Lady Worthall," Grif said, clicking his heels and bowing curtly as she sailed, not unlike a royal barge, to a halt in front of him.

"Been abroad, have you?" she asked, peering up at him as she yanked the leash of her dog, Sirius, who yelped with each yank. "How fortuitous to encounter you here! I've just been delivered a letter from Lady Dalkeith."

Grif's heart stopped beating for a moment—Lady Dalkeith was Hugh's grandmother, from whom they had filched the house. "Did ye indeed? I trust she is well, then?"

"Oh, *quite* well," Lady Worthall exclaimed. "French air agrees with her, I think. But she's determined to come home to England, and avowed in her letter to me that she'd come straightaway this autumn. That's *months* away!"

"So late in the year, is it no'?" Grif suggested.

"Indeed it is," the woman said, peering at Grif suspiciously. "I thought it rather odd that Lady Dalkeith did not mention her houseguests in her letter. One would think she would encourage her old friend to welcome her guests in her stead and until her return, wouldn't one?"

Ah, but he knew what the old battle-ax was about and smiled charmingly. "One would think it, aye. But then again, Lady Dalkeith would no' yet know that we've arrived a wee bit early, would she, then?" he asked. "And therefore, any such encouragement would come in her next letter, would it no'?"

Lady Worthall's pudgy face scrunched up in confusion.

"Good evening, Lady Worthall," he said, and, tipping his hat, he walked on before she could question him further. He did not look back, walked directly to the house, jogged up the steps, and quickly stepped inside. Only then did he release his breath and have a look out the small portal window to see if she'd followed him.

Dudley joined him there, trying to peer over his shoulder. "Worthall," Grif said gruffly. "God blind me, but that old woman is a meddlesome bother!"

"There's bound to be some talk, sir," a stoic Dudley said as he calmly held out his hands for Grif's gloves and hat. "We canna avoid it."

Dudley was right, of course, Grif thought, stepping away from the window. They would eventually be discovered, if not by Lady Worthall, then by someone else. Not one of them believed they could perpetuate this lie forever. The question was, how long could they? A month? A year? A day?

"I've been to the kirkwarden to review the parish registers, sir," Dudley said as he put Grif's things away.

"Aye? And?"

"*Mi Diah!* Ye've no' seen such confusion! There's register after register, and no' a legible Amelia found in any of them save the ones ye've already found!" He picked up a silver tray upon which were two folded pieces of vellum. "I think ye'll have better luck finding our Amelia among the likes of these," he said.

Grif grinned; the vellums were addressed to The Honorable Griffin MacAulay, Lord Ardencaple. Quite honestly, he loved the sound of that.

He broke the seal on the first one. It was an invitation to another ball, this one hosted by Lord and Lady Valtrain. He had been introduced briefly to Lady Valtrain at the Swindon Ladies Society tea. Apparently, he'd complimented her well enough to be remembered.

The second vellum was likewise an invitation, to a supper party, extended by Lady Seaton. In her handwritten note, Lady Seaton claimed to be both delighted and thrilled to have made his esteemed acquaintance, and that she very much hoped he could attend, as this would be an "intimate affair." Grif had been in London long enough to know that *intimate* meant no fewer than two dozen persons, perhaps even more.

He turned a broad grin to Dudley and held up the invitations. "We'll find our Amelia yet, by God. I'll send ye out with the replies posthaste."

"Aye, sir," Dudley said. "Ye'll find parchment in the sitting room."

Grif happily started in that direction, but was brought to an abrupt halt by the unmistakable sound of a woman's voice. For a moment, he stood frozen, then slowly turned and looked at Dudley. "MacAlister?"

Dudley looked to the corridor that led to the kitchen stairs and sighed wearily. "It would seem we've gained a *cook*, sir."

"A cook my arse," Grif growled, and slapped the invitations in Dudley's hand. "Put them in the sitting room, would ye, while I have a word with me valet."

He strode down the corridor to the narrow hallway and the stairs leading to the kitchen below. But as he started his descent, the scent of something wonderfully delicious reached his nose. As he and Hugh and Dudley had failed miserably in the task of cooking, smelling something *that* delicious slowed him a step or two.

He saw Hugh first, leaning against a long wooden table, his arms folded across his chest, watching intently as a woman chopped carrots with the efficiency of an executioner.

"Ah!" Hugh called cheerfully as he caught sight of Grif. "Ye smelled a heavenly aroma, did ye no'?"

Grif didn't answer, just slowly walked into the room, his eyes on the young red-haired woman. She did not spare him a glance, just kept chopping.

"I'd like to introduce ye to our new cook, Miss Brody," Hugh said, obviously pleased with himself. "Miss Brody, curtsey if ye would to the right honorable Griffin MacAulay, earl of Ardencaple."

Miss Brody curtsied without missing a stroke. Hugh beamed proudly.

But Grif was frowning—Miss Brody was no cook. Miss Brody was a bonny lass, and he'd wager it was her plump bosom that had Hugh drooling. All right, then, it *was* a lovely bosom, but nevertheless, they'd had an agreement! No gambling, no trawling about, and no women! Grif looked at Hugh, who still wore that silly grin on his face, and said in Gaelic, "I thought we agreed—no women."

"Ah—" Hugh interrupted him, holding up a finger. "We agreed no women of questionable character. We said nothing of a cook."

"A *cook?*" Grif laughed sardonically. "I'm no fool, MacAlister!"

"I agree," Hugh answered amicably. "Quite the contrary, lad. Ye are far too clever to turn yer back on a woman who can cook."

Grif looked at Miss Brody. He could not deny that whatever she was about, it smelled bloody fabulous. Still . . . "And how do we pay her?"

Hugh chuckled. "Now *that* I've given some thought," he said, and there was a wicked glint in his eye. "Leave it to me."

While Grif was loath to leave anything to Hugh, his nose and his belly overruled his good sense. "All right," he said gruffly in English. "More importantly, when might we sample her efforts?"

Hugh laughed, clapped him on the shoulder. "Soon, *mo caraid*. Soon."

Seven

By the time the Valtrain ball rolled around, Grif's trousers were a wee bit tight.

It turned out that Miss Keara Brody was indeed an excellent cook. She was not, however, a woman who was easily seduced by the likes of Hugh MacAlister. Miss Brody was Irish, had come from Dublin with her older brother in search of work. "Our parents are dead and gone," she'd told Grif one morning over a plate of eggs. "Our sister looks after our younger siblings."

There were six younger siblings at home, dependent upon what Miss Brody and her brother were able to send back. She seemed rather single-minded in her purpose and had no patience for Hugh's interest.

But Grif and Dudley were too fond of her cooking to let Hugh's lack of sexual triumph chase her away, and were, in fact, quite content to let his whining fall on their deaf but fully sated ears.

Unfortunately, Hugh had grown quite smitten with Miss Brody, and he was incorrigible. Miss Brody had, in fact, banned him from the kitchen entirely, which was why he was seated on a chaise longue in the master suite of rooms the night of the Valtrain ball, smoking a cheroot and eyeing Grif critically as he buttoned a white waistcoat.

"*Diah,* ye look like a bloody Sassenach, ye do," Hugh said irritably as Grif donned the black-tailed coat.

Grif glanced at Hugh over his shoulder—his shirttails were out, his neckcloth dangled haphazardly down his chest. "And ye look like a man who's hired his very own cook only to discover she willna touch his sausage and eggs."

Hugh snorted, picked up a whiskey glass from which he had been sipping, and tossed back the contents. "She'll come round," he said, pointing the cheroot at Grif, and in the very next breath moaned, "*Ach,* I give the lass a bloody occupation, and this is the thanks I get? She's such a bonny thing, Grif! Did ye see her? Hair the very color of a Scottish sunset? Eyes as green as moss?"

"I hadna noticed," Grif said cheerfully, and straightening his snowy white neckcloth, he stood back, admiring himself in the full-length mirror.

"'Tis hardly fair," Hugh continued morosely. "Night after night, ye have quite a time of it, while I'm forced to sit behind these walls as if I were a wretched servant!"

"But ye *are* a wretched servant, lad," Grif reminded him. "Perhaps the most wretched valet in all of England's history."

Hugh cursed him in their native tongue for that, but Grif just laughed, adjusted his neckcloth once more, and strode out of the master suite, whistling a cheerful tune.

Fynster was waiting at the Fordham Gentlemen's Club of Leisure on Regent Street, as they had previously agreed, and from there they took Fynster's carriage to the Valtrain residence.

There was the usual mad crush of carriages and horses and people dressed in the latest finery, and that sent Grif's spirits soaring. Unlike his brother, Liam, Grif loved balls. He loved women whose pastel-colored gowns swirled about their legs on the dance floor, loved their bright glowing faces and the shiny baubles they wore, the way they felt in his arms when he danced, so small and delicate, moving at the command of his body.

And he loved to be surrounded by fine things. In the weeks he'd been in London, Grif had seen splendor that went beyond anything he'd ever known or imagined. And Grif had imagined—he and Hugh both. They used to talk of owning their own bank or lending company, or perhaps shipping goods from Scotland across the Atlantic to Caribbean ports. As young men, they believed they'd be wealthier than their wildest dreams, that they would live a life of luxury. A turn of the economy in Scotland had grounded their dreams, but Grif still imagined himself in a position of importance one day, a man who would be invited to all the right events, attached to all the right women. He had imagined something like his life in London thus far. . . .

But *this* ball—held in honor of young girls who had just been presented at court—surpassed anything he'd seen to date.

Crystal flutes of champagne and wine seemed to float on silver trays, carried high above the crowd by skilled footmen. Pristine white floral arrangements, made up of roses, orchids, daisies, and irises, littered the corridors and ballroom in enormous porcelain vases. Beeswax candles burned brightly in silver chandeliers. The strains of a six-piece orchestra floated throughout the mansion, and a dining room had been set up with three rows of long, cloth-covered tables upon which dozens of china settings had been placed.

In the ballroom, Grif's smile of pleasure deepened. There she was, Miss Lucy, a vision of beauty, waiting for the dancing to begin. Not surprisingly, she was surrounded by men. Foppish, overly elegant men. Men who wouldn't last a day in the Highlands, who could not, by the look of them, even wield as much as a fencing sword without spraining a wrist.

It was into that *petit-maître* milieu that Grif confidently strode, smoothly stepping around the many debutantes being honored tonight with nothing more than a smile for their hopeful looks.

As he neared Miss Lucy, she smilingly tried to extract herself from the attentions of one of the bothersome gnats that surrounded her.

Grif ignored them all, walked straight to her, boldly extending his hand for hers. "Miss Lucy," he said, bowing over the hand she graciously gave him and kissing her gloved knuckles. "How bonny ye are this night."

"I'm charmed, Lord Ardencaple," she said silkily, withdrawing her hand.

"I had hoped to find ye here," he said meaningfully, smiling down at her. "There is, I hope ye will recall, the matter of a dance."

"Of course I *do* recall." She glanced demurely at her dance card. "As it happens, I am without a partner for the fourth dance," she said, lifting her gaze to him. "It's next. A waltz."

"I'd be quite honored if ye'd allow me to put me name just there."

Miss Lucy smiled, held out her arm, and as Grif wrote his name with the little pencil that dangled from her wrist, she looked past his shoulder and lit up like a bloody lighthouse. "Mr. *Lockhart,*" she said happily, turning from Grif. "Might I assume, sir, that you deigned to come and take a peek at my dance card after all?"

"Is it necessary?" Lockhart asked. "I thought we had an agreement, you and I. A waltz, was it not?"

"Oh yes, that's right," she said clasping her hands together. "Unfortunately, I've just given away the last one," she added with a deceptively sweet smile.

A look passed over Lockhart's face that was not the least bit pleasant. Miss Lucy, however, seemed to enjoy his displeasure. "Ah, there it is now, they are playing the fourth dance," she said, looking wistfully at the dance floor before turning her smile to Grif and extending her hand. "Lord Ardencaple?"

Grif took her hand, laid it on his arm, put his hand protectively over hers, and flashed a smirk at Lockhart for good measure before leading her to the center of the dance floor. The music began; she curtsied, placed her hand very lightly on his shoulder. Grif slipped his arm around her back and pulled her close to him as he swept her into the rhythm of the music.

She smiled politely and looked away.

Grif took the opportunity to smile at her cleavage. "Now that I've succeeded in standing up with ye, I must gain yer promise for a walkabout."

Miss Lucy kept her gaze on the dancers around them. "Perhaps you will call one afternoon when we might enjoy the sunshine."

"But I had in mind the moon. On the veranda this

very evening, I'd hoped we might gaze together at the moon. Perhaps we might stroll the grounds, aye?"

"I suspect you're rather indecorous beneath that charming exterior, my lord," she said coyly.

"Would ye like me to be?" he asked low, squeezing her hand a little. "I'd be happy to oblige ye."

She tilted her head and glanced at him from the corner of her eye. "You're quite bold! I shan't take as much as one step onto the veranda without your solemn promise to be a perfect gentleman."

"Ye ask too much, lass. I can only promise I'll be perfect," he said with a grin, and winked.

"My lord!" she exclaimed, feigning shock. "I insist you speak of something else altogether!"

Grif laughed at her false modesty. "All right, then. Perhaps ye might help me. My friend Mr. Fynster-Allen is quite smitten with a lass, and it would be me pleasure to put his name on her dance card."

"Then why don't you?" Miss Lucy asked, her gaze drifting to the other dancers again.

"Because I donna know who she is. He's only mentioned her by her given name."

That instantly gained Miss Lucy's attention. "Her *given* name?" she repeated suspiciously. "How very odd! Pray tell, what is the given name?"

"Amelia."

Her brow wrinkled as she thought of it. "Amelia," she repeated. "I don't believe I know any Amelia. Perhaps one of the debutantes? But why should Mr. Fynster-Allen be interested in a debutante? He's practically . . . *old*."

Fynster was a year or two older than Grif. "Ah well, perhaps he'll manage fair enough on his own, then," he said, and twirled her about.

Grif attempted to make small talk, but Lucy was too intent on the others on the dance floor to converse much. When the music at last came to a halt, Grif brought them to a full stop. "Ye willna forget me, lass, on the veranda, aye?" he asked as he let go her hand.

"How could I *ever* forget you?" she demurred, dipping into a curtsey.

How indeed. Grif led her back to the edge of the dance floor, and just before they reached her contingent of admirers, he nodded toward the doors on the opposite end of the ballroom, whispering, "I'll meet ye just there," before he bowed and walked away.

He found Fynster, who was, as usual, staring wistfully at a woman on the dance floor. Grif felt a little sorry for the man, and passed a bit of time remarking on the lovely gowns as the ladies passed, exchanging smiles with more than one of them. But when he began speculating about the color and shape of their drawers, the gentleman in Fynster would not engage in Grif's play and excused himself, wandering around the edge of the room until he came to where Miss Crabtree was sitting. How odd, Grif thought, that Fynster flipped his tails and took the seat next to the little mouse.

Never mind that—Grif was ready for his moonlit stroll, and looked across to where Lucy was standing, catching her eye. He nodded almost imperceptibly at the doors leading to the veranda. The lass nodded slyly and opened her fan, which Grif took as a positive sign. He walked the length of the ballroom floor before slipping outside.

It was a wee bit chilly out, and there were only a few hardy souls about on the veranda. Grif withdrew a cheroot from his pocket and lit it, then made his way to the corner to have a look at the gardens below.

Before too long, he'd smoked half the cheroot, and wondered idly what could be keeping Lucy. The orchestra had begun a minuet, and a few more people strolled out onto the veranda for a breath of the cool night air.

When the minuet ended, it was painfully clear to Grif that Lucy was not going to join him as she had said. He tossed what was left of his cheroot into a planter in the corner, tugged on his waistcoat, and was about to return to the ballroom and find the wench when he heard the sound of a woman's footfall behind him. *Lucy.* With a smile, he turned about—but his smile instantly faded.

"Lord *Ardencaple*, how do you do?" she drawled.

It was not Lucy at all, but her older and permanently vexing sister, dressed in a pale pink gown of shimmering satin with a very modest décolletage. Her hair was simply done up at the crown, and from her ears single pearl drops hung.

Grif bit back the frown of disappointment, trying not to scowl impolitely as she dipped into a curtsey.

Miss Addison rose and clasped her hands behind her back before stepping to the railing to stand directly beside him. From there she looked out over the garden. "How surprising to find you wiling away the time here—after all, you seem to enjoy dancing so."

Grif gave her a sidelong look. "Yer powers of observation are quite keen, are they? Why is it ye're no' enjoying the dance instead of standing off in the corner?"

He meant to startle her, but she just laughed and gave him a bright smile. "I'm not as enamored of stiflingly crowded ballrooms as my sister. She enjoys them enormously, you know—why, I believe this is her third waltz, and her second dance with Mr. Lockhart," she said, and snapped her fan open, waved it lazily at her face, smiling a little at the frown Lockhart's name brought to Grif's face. "Dear Lucy, she must be exhausted—she's not missed a dance, I think, and there are so many more to come."

Envious, was she? Well, she should be—Lucy was light and angelic to her darkly exotic look, Lucy's eyes bright where this one's dark copper eyes glistened with a devilish gleam. There was something about her that seemed almost forbidden—an exotic woman dressed in such an angelic color.

"How fortunate for yer sister that ye enjoy keeping count of her dances."

Miss Addison just smiled and looked away, but her fan went perceptibly faster. "I pay her dancing no mind, my lord."

"Aha. Just Lockhart, then."

Did he detect a wee bit of spine stiffening?

"Apparently, so do you."

"No' in the least," he said with a wry smile. "My attentions are only for the ladies."

"Or their décolletages," she muttered.

That cheeky comment startled him so that he laughed. "Ye're no' one to mince words, are ye, lass?"

She glanced at him over the top of her fan. "Why do you act surprised, my lord? If I were a man, you'd agree with my observation."

"Aye, but ye're no' a man."

"Honestly, women wear low décolletage so men will notice them. All rational adults are quite aware of it. Why not let's just admit it?"

"To admit it would take the sport from the game," he said, feeling mildly disappointed she was not playing the game with her modest neckline.

Her brows knit in confusion and her fan stopped waving. "*What* game?"

"A game ye'd understand were ye a man. Now, Miss Addison, if ye'll excuse me, I'll leave ye to the counting of yer sister's dances."

"What?" she asked, lowering her fan. "You're going so soon? I thought you'd at least make an effort to put a mark on my dance card."

Diah, the woman was astonishingly brash—so brash, in fact, that she reminded him a wee bit of his sister, Mared. As if sensing his reluctance, Miss Addison jiggled her wrist before him, making her card dance.

He laughed. "*Mo chreach,* woman, ye're an impudent one! I donna believe a lady has ever been so forward as to ask me to stand up with her!"

"Another bothersome custom," she said with an insouciant shrug. "Why shouldn't a woman ask a man to dance if she pleases? And besides, I should think you of *all* people would appreciate my impudence, sir, considering the impudence you've brought to London."

Whatever could she mean by that? The remark astounded him. "*Me?*" he choked. "Ye think me impudent?"

"Perhaps not outwardly," she demurred with a smile, "but you do have your secrets, do you not?" And she laughed.

He narrowed his gaze, openly studying her. If she knew something, she gave not even the slightest hint of it, and, in fact, smiled brightly, jiggled her dance card before him again. Women like her, he knew from experience, had to be put in their proper place before they ran amuck.

"And here I believed ye to be no' so enamored of the dance, Miss Addison," he said gruffly.

"I should have clarified that it depends on the circumstance. In this circumstance, I am willing to give it a go." She jiggled her wrist again. "Do you truly find it so objectionable? I'm really quite a good dancer," she added cheerfully.

He would have liked nothing more than to walk off, leave her standing in all her glorious cheek.

"I'll leave you quite well alone afterward," she said.

He hoped to heaven that was a promise, and muttering a slight Gaelic curse under his breath, he reached for her dance card . . . which was near to empty. He glanced up at her. "What's this, then? Have ye no' thought to threaten yer fellow countrymen with a dance?"

Her rosy cheeks turned rosier; she tried to pull her hand and the card away from him.

"How is it that I have become the object or yer badgering instead of any number of the fine Sassenach dandies in there?" he demanded, gesturing toward the ballroom.

She shrugged, tried to move her arm again, but it was too late for that—she had started this silly game, and Grif was not the least deterred. He suddenly took hold of her wrist, his fingers closing around the fragile bones, and pulled her arm toward him to have another look at the card. "I swear I donna understand why ye think to vex me so, lass, but ye've succeeded," he said hotly. "If a dance is all that is required to free me of ye, then—"

She gasped and tried to jerk her hand from his grasp, but he held tight. "What are you doing?" she cried. "You think all of London won't see you hold me in your grip? Unhand me, sir! I was merely amusing myself—you needn't stand up with me if you are so revolted by the notion!"

"*Ach,* What foolishness!" he said shaking his head. "Ye canna deceive me. I donna give a damn what London might see, but ye wanted yer dance well enough to ignore every wee bit of decorum, and now, by God, ye shall have it!" He gave her a determined grin as he lifted his free hand and yanked the small pencil tied with ribbon to her wrist. He hastily wrote his name on the card, then tossed the pencil onto the floor behind them. "Ye'll no' be needing it by the look of things. There we are—ye've an entry for the next waltz, which, ye may have heard, is just starting. Shall we?" he asked, and extended his arm with a cold smile.

An expression darkened her copper eyes, and for a moment Grif thought she might actually resort to punching him. She lifted her chin defiantly, slapped her hand down on his arm with a little too much force. "Why, I'd be *delighted,* my lord."

"As would *I,* Miss Addison," he said, and placed his hand on hers, and gripping it tightly, marched her inside, right into the middle of the dance floor.

When the orchestra struck the first chords of the waltz, he bowed, and Miss Addison curtsied perfectly. He instantly snaked an arm around her waist, his hand to the small of her back—a perfectly trim back, he couldn't help notice—and jerked her hard into his chest at the same mom[illegible] he simultaneously led her into the stream of dancers.

Her eyes glittered with indignation.

Grif laughed and let his gaze drift to her mouth. "What is it, then? Do ye no' care for a Scotsman's dancing?"

"It is a little *close,*" she remarked through gritted teeth.

"*Ah,* so *now* ye'll fret about propriety, is that it?" He laughed sardonically and pulled her closer.

Miss Addison pressed her lips tightly together.

Grif looked at those lovely lips, at her pure complexion. She was an exasperating woman to be sure, but a man had to like the feel of her in his arms—she was lean, surprisingly firm, yet supple. He wondered how she managed it, since his impression thus far of society ladies was that they did quite a lot of sitting about all day. Miss Addison, however, had not gathered any dust, and her body gave him a deliciously hot feeling of pleasure.

He smiled again—he liked seeing the furious glint in her eyes. "What is it now? I should think ye'd enjoy this waltz, as I will no' be so commanded again."

"You flatter yourself, my lord," she said coolly. "I did not *command* it. I merely suggested. Perhaps you think that forward at Ardencaple—or wherever you claim to hail from—but in London it's naught more than a *suggestion.*"

Grif wisely ignored the remark about Ardencaple and went straight to her bald-faced lie. "Ye didna *suggest* it, lass—ye practically planted a boot in me arse and kicked me out here."

Miss Addison gasped self-righteously. Grif responded by twirling her about and pulling her closer into his body, so that his lips were grazing the ringlets above her ears, and he could smell the sweet scent of rosewater in her hair. "And I really donna believe ye care in the least if ye are forward or no'."

"Don't be ridiculous," she said, pushing back against his shoulder. "I hardly care what you make of it, but instead of all your prattling, I'd rather you occupy your thoughts with directing us to the east end of the dance floor."

Grif laughed incredulously. "I beg yer pardon, but would ye now command the *dance?*" he exclaimed. "What a shameless lass ye are!"

"And what, pray tell, would you have against the east end of the dance floor?" she demanded as she struggled to see over his shoulder. "I should think one end as good as the other, particularly when one is so very determined to be off of it and away from such a *'shameless lass'!*"

That prompted another laugh of disbelief from Grif, and he abruptly twirled her about again, to see for himself what she was trying so hard to see. He knew instantly, of course, for there was Lockhart, at the very edge of the dance floor. "*Ach,* how could I be so blind?" he asked with a chuckle, and instantly and effortlessly waltzed her in the opposite direction of Lockhart. "Ye donna mean to torture me at all!" he laughed. "Ye mean to *use* me to torture another man, God have mercy on him."

"I have no idea what you are talking about," she declared, and tried to turn him. Grif held fast. "Do you *mind?*" she snapped.

"Aye, I do," he retorted cheerfully. "I donna know what ye may be accustomed to, Miss Addison, but in Scotland a man will lead the dance unless he's been gelded."

"Oh dear God!" she cried. "What possible difference could it make?"

"All the difference in the bloody world. I willna allow ye to curry the favor of another man whilst ye dance with me. I've me honor to protect."

"Your *honor?* You barely deigned to dance with me at all, and now you would pretend to be insulted? I should hardly be surprised—God only knows what else you pretend, Lord Ardencaple!"

"Any number of things, particularly in yer company."

"So I've surmised!"

"Ye have a rather unpleasant habit of surmising quite a lot," he said with a frown. "But ye should at least have the decency to remember that ye trapped me into this dance to make Lockhart jealous and therefore at least give me the attention I'm due!"

She gasped. Her face turned red. "I beg your pardon, I did *not* trap you in this dance!"

"I canna for the life of me see how ye might argue it!"

"Do you mean to say that if a lady makes a *suggestion* as to the dancing that she has *trapped* a gentleman?"

"Aye, that I do mean to say, absolutely. And now we may both be at peace, for the dance has come to its inevitable end," he said, and dropped her hand, stepped back, and bowed.

"Thank God," she muttered, and dipped a barely discernible curtsey while making a show of smoothing the hair at her nape.

"I beg yer pardon?" he asked, slowly straightening.

"I said, 'Thank *God,*'" she repeated, only louder.

That infuriated Grif. He'd done what she wanted, and now she'd pretend it was distasteful to her?

Criosd, he'd never, not once, suffered a more aggravating woman. And instead of turning and walking away as he ought to have done, instead of leaving her to stand alone in the middle of the dance floor as she so richly deserved, he suddenly grabbed her hand again, and forcibly put it on his arm.

"What are you doing?" she demanded, stealing one last look at Lockhart over her shoulder.

"Ye want to incite a man's jealousy?" he asked, not really desiring an answer, and marched toward the doors that opened onto the veranda. "Then ye must give him something over which to be jealous!"

"My lord!" she haughtily exclaimed as if he was loathsome, and tried to jerk her hand free.

"Uist!" he spat in Gaelic, surprising her into silence.

For a moment.

"What do you mean to do?" she exclaimed hotly as they marched through the doors onto the veranda, out into the cool night air where the only light was that spilling out from the windows. Grif glanced over his shoulder at the many backs facing the dance floor in anticipation of a quadrille, and shoved Miss Addison up against the railing. He stepped in front of her, put a hand on her shoulder.

The wench opened her mouth to complain, but Grif was too fast for her—with his other hand, he grasped her jaw and abruptly planted his lips on hers.

She tried to gasp for breath, and he opened his mouth, let her breathe him, intending to startle her senseless before letting go and giving her something to stew about.

But somehow his body got ahead of his mind, and he realized that her lips were soft and lush beneath his, her breath sweet. Before Grif knew what was happening, his tongue had slipped into her mouth, earning him a scintillating little gasp. His hand, of its own accord, apparently, was suddenly at her waist, anchoring her to him, the other cupping her face, tilting her head just slightly so that he might kiss her deeper.

In the cover of darkness, on a public veranda, her body was pressed against his, her breasts against his chest.

And then Miss Addison made a sound, something like a moan of pure pleasure, and slipped her tongue into *his* mouth. The moan and her darting tongue brought him instantly and harshly to his senses, and he recognized he'd just suffered an astounding slip of control. It rattled him; Grif suddenly reared back, breaking the kiss, and gaped down at the woman.

Her eyes were closed; black lashes formed dark, velvet crescents against cheeks stained the color of fire, the same intense heat that was coursing through him. Her lips, full and wet, were still pursed, but tilted up at the corners in a devilish smile.

Grif dropped his hands from her as if he had been burned. Miss Addison slowly, dreamily opened her eyes. His gaze slipped to her mouth again.

She smiled.

He growled. "Now ye have something with which to make him jealous," he said, and abruptly walked away from her.

Eight

It was several minutes before Anna could catch her breath, several minutes more before she could stop shaking.

Just beyond the door, dancers whirled by, and Anna slowly lifted her hand, touched her lips where Ardencaple's powerful kiss still lingered. Her head felt as if it were covered with a shroud; she couldn't think, couldn't seem to do anything but clumsily feel his kiss on her lips.

After a moment or two, she realized how ridiculous she must appear, standing on the veranda alone, in the dark, and even though it felt as if that kiss were branded across her face, she woodenly moved inside, cautiously glancing about as she entered, wondering if anyone had seen such an untoward, unladylike, indecorous, absolutely *brilliant* kiss.

Dear God, had she dreamed it? Had it really happened? Just like that, so suddenly, so unexpectedly, as it had almost a year ago with another Scot? *That* kiss had been tantalizing, certainly—but this one, Mother of God, *this* one felt entirely different. This one had been *blistering*.

In truth, it had almost brought her to her knees, had begun a flood of coarse feelings and desires in the pit of her belly, flashing out to all her limbs, warming her to the point that she desired to rip her gown open so that she might feel cool air on her flaming skin. That naked desire was still racing through her, making her blind to the people around her, deaf to the music.

She paused in her aimless promenade around the ballroom to desperately fan herself, staring absently at the line of dancers moving through the quadrille. Did *every* woman feel such brilliance when they had been so thoroughly kissed?

She was so caught up in the wake of that kiss that she didn't see Drake until he was upon her. "Miss Addison?"

The sound of his voice startled her, and she sucked in her breath—was her skin red from the heat inside her? She fanned herself, turning slowly and madly wondering if Drake's kiss could be as provocative as Ardencaple's.

He must have seen the flame in her skin because he was looking at her curiously, one dark brow rising above the other.

"I, ah . . . good evening, Mr. Lockhart," she said, smiling unsteadily, and dipped into a curtsey.

"Are you quite all right? You look rather flushed."

That was all she required—her panic was instant and furious. "Flushed?" she demurred, and averted her gaze, lest she look as guilty as she felt. "It's rather warm, that's all."

"Are you well enough to stand up with me? I had hoped for a space on your dance card," he said, moving a little so that he was in her line of sight.

"Did you?" she asked coyly, slanting a glance at him, and almost laughed out loud with hysteria.

Having wished so for this moment, all she could seem to think of was Ardencaple—who, incidentally, had danced as if on a cloud, what with all the effortless twirling. Unthinkingly, Anna glanced across the crowded dance floor where the quadrille was ending, and she saw him in the company of Miss Netherton.

"I beg your pardon, but shall I take that as a yes or a no?" Drake drawled.

Anna jerked her gaze to him again and forced a smile. "You know very well that I would be honored, sir."

He smiled confidently, took her hand, and led her onto the dance floor as a minuet began. He took her through the steps, smiling down at her, his gaze boldly wandering the length of her, lingering on her bosom.

Anna didn't shy away from it; she stood straighter. A soft giggle escaped her, and she wondered what sort of unmarried woman went about kissing men here and there on darkened verandas. A happy one, certainly.

"If I may be so bold," Drake said during one pass as he pointed his right foot at her, "I would ask if you might do me the pleasure of walking about the Valtrain gardens."

Anna responded to his toe point with one of her own, bowing perfectly. "Goodness, Mr. Lockhart! You ask after that pleasure so often that I think you merely delight in the asking."

He laughed as they stepped sidelong in perfect unison. "I must beg your forgiveness, as I was unavoidably detained at the Darlington ball."

Anna twirled about and faced him again with a toe point. "Come now, sir! You must think me a foolish girl."

"Not foolish. Patient," he corrected her.

"Patient!" She laughed. "And why should I wait patiently for a silly walkabout?" she asked as she bowed and stepped and twirled again.

"You know very well why, Miss Addison. You desire the pleasure of my company so I might regale you with tales of your beauty and wit and charm."

She couldn't help herself; she laughed at his banter and glanced gaily about, saw the Scot smiling charmingly at Miss Netherton, and quickly turned her gaze to Lockhart again. "Perhaps you confuse me with my sister," she said daringly.

"Surely I do not," he said pleasantly. "Your sister is lovely, but she pales in comparison to you."

"Mr. Lockhart, your flattery is obvious!"

"Flattery? How could I possibly flatter you? You are far too clever for it."

Really, she was, but she nevertheless enjoyed the playful talk, and laughingly shrugged, twirled about, stepped to her right, and glanced about. Her gaze inadvertently landed on Ardencaple again. This time he was looking directly at her, wearing a very knowing smile on his face. *Damn* him!

Anna pretended not to notice at all as she faced Drake again. "Very well, you have succeeded, Mr. Lockhart. I should very much like to stroll about the gardens with you," she said, and went about the rest of the minuet without looking once at Ardencaple.

When the dance ended, Drake escorted her into the gardens, where several of the guests had come out for air, including, she noticed with mild interest, Mr. Fynster-Allen and Miss Amelia Crabtree, who walked along slowly, obviously caught up in deep conversation.

Who could blame them? It was a fabulous night for strolling along—a rare cloudless night in London. A cool breeze kept the air clean of soot, and the torch-lit gardens looked magnificent. Anna and Drake walked down the center path, remarking on the many rose-bushes in full bloom.

They paused at a wrought-iron bench beside a hedgerow that had been cut to resemble giant chess pieces. Beneath the bishop they sat, side by side, admiring another stand of roses, until Drake looked up at the moon and said, "Moonlight is very becoming to you." He lowered his gaze and smiled warmly at her.

Anna's heart fluttered. "Thank you."

"You are indeed a handsome woman," he added with a smile.

Handsome? Her heart stopped fluttering—why did that remark always make her feel like someone's spinster aunt? Why couldn't she be beautiful, or, at the very least, pretty?

Drake put his hand lightly on her knee, and Anna stared down at the hand in surprise, willing it higher.

"Ah . . . the moon *is* lovely, isn't it?" he asked absently.

"Yes," she said, and watched, fascinated, as he squeezed her knee, then caressed it with his palm. She was distantly aware of more people walking about, another couple on the other side of the hedgerow—and she could hear the girlish laugh of a woman. But her attention was riveted on Drake's lips now, hoping fervently that he would kiss her.

"This night reminds me a bit of a poem," he said absently as his fingers casually stroked her knee. "Would you like to hear it?"

"Yes, please," Anna urged him, and shifted a little closer as she tried to block out the light chatter of the couple on the other side of the hedgerow.

Drake glanced at the moon again and said, "*In the moonlight was her heart thus taken; a chaste kiss, another vow forsaken. And when the sun rose again on her lovely face, there she did lie in love's sweet embrace.*"

Anna sucked in a slow breath and lifted her face, nearer to his. "It's lovely . . . who is the poet?"

He laughed low; his gaze fell to her lips. "Would it surprise you if I said it was me?"

Now her heart was beating wildly. He would kiss her. He would *kiss* her! "I did not know you were a poet," she murmured, lifting her face higher.

"I merely dabble at it," he said, and as Anna closed her eyes, she heard Lucy's laughter somewhere close by. Drake pressed his lips to her cheek at the same time he removed his hand from her knee.

Anna opened her eyes; Drake was not looking at her, but down the path. "Would you like a refreshment?" he asked absently. "A cider to warm you, perhaps?"

"No, I—"

"It's really rather chilly," he said, standing. "I'll fetch a cider for you. Rest here and I will return forthwith." And with that he went striding off into the dark, leaving her to sit alone on the wrought-iron bench.

Blast it! Anna folded her arms beneath her bosom and fell back against the bench, pondering what might possibly have gone wrong—after all, she was on a garden bench in the moonlight, practically sitting on his *lap*, for goodness' sake. . . .

She heard the woman's girlish giggle again, and

realized another couple was still on the other side of the hedgerow.

"Aye, of course we've a name for it," she heard the man say.

Ardencaple! Anna sat up with a start—Lockhart momentarily forgotten, she quickly inched to the left side of the bench, leaning as far back as she could, straining to hear without actually shoving her head into the hedge shaped like a bishop.

"What do you call it in gallish?"

"*Ach,* lass, 'tis *Gàidhlig,* then," he said pleasantly. "And the word is *gealach.*"

"Oh, I don't think I can say that!" the woman said, laughing.

I don't think I can say that, Anna silently mimicked her.

"All right, then, let's try another, aye?" he said. "What is your given name?"

"Catherine," the woman said, and Anna instantly deduced it was Catherine Peterhouse, whom she had seen earlier this evening openly ogling Ardencaple.

"Catherine, lovely," he said. "Can you say 'Caitriona'?"

"Kay-tree-una," Miss Peterhouse said very carefully and ar-tic-u-late-ly.

"Aye, ye said it perfectly, ye did!"

"*Did* I?" she squealed, and Anna rolled her eyes, twisted on the bench, and leaned toward the bishop-shaped shrub, pushing aside some of the branches in the hopes of seeing him.

"Let's have another, shall we? Perhaps ye know someone named . . . Amelia?"

"Amelia?" Miss Peterhouse repeated, sounding

perplexed. "Umm . . . yes, of course, there is Amelia Crabtree."

"That's the only Amelia ye know, then?" he asked, sounding, strangely, as if he was slightly disappointed with Miss Peterhouse's answer. Confused, Anna quietly pushed farther into the giant bishop, but her foot kicked the torchère next to the bench and made it wobble. She instantly grabbed it, righting it before it fell over. When she turned to the hedge again, she froze—she could see his leg just inches from her face.

"Yes, she's the only one," Miss Peterhouse said uncertainly. "What is the name Amelia in your language?"

"Alas, it doesna translate," Ardencaple said with a sigh. "Ah, here's one, then. Lady Battenkirk! Would ye happen to know her?"

"Lady Battenkirk," Miss Peterhouse said carefully. "I'm afraid I'm not acquainted with her."

"Pity, that," he said, and sighed again. "I would think she'd have a splendid Christian name to translate."

Now he was talking nonsense! Anna's frown deepened. He moved again, and then when he spoke, Anna realized he was even closer, and dared not move.

"I'll teach ye another bit of *Gàidhlig* if ye'd like. Ah, let's see . . . what would ye call a very silly person?"

"A fool?" Miss Peterhouse eagerly answered.

"Aye, a fool. Here we are, then. If ye were to encounter a *complete* fool in Scotland, ye would say of him, *fior òinseach.*"

"Feer awn-shok," Miss Peterhouse dutifully repeated.

"Very good indeed, Miss Peterhouse! And what would ye say to the *òinseach* if ye were to meet her?" A moment of silence followed. "Why, ye'd say, *Moi nàir'ort!*" he exclaimed so loudly that Anna jumped.

Miss Peterhouse laughed. "Oh my! What does that mean, my lord?"

"It means 'Shame on ye!'" It sounded as if he was standing just above her, so frighteningly close that Anna reared back, and the shrub rustled in her wake.

"What was that?" Miss Peterhouse asked.

"Naugh' but *fior òinseach,*" he said with a laugh. "Well, then, Miss Peterhouse, it is unfair of me to keep ye from the other men who desire to dance—"

"Oh no, it's really quite all right!" she exclaimed.

"No, no . . . I willna be accused of monopolizing yer charming attentions. Shall we?"

"Oh . . . yes, well. I suppose we must," she said slowly, and there was a bit of rustling.

Anna didn't move until she heard the sound of their footfalls far down the path. Then she twisted around, folded her arms petulantly across her middle. The man was an insolent, overbearing goat who thought himself entirely too clever! And she was still smarting at having been discovered when she saw Drake coming down the path, a cup of cider in one hand and Lucy in the other.

Oh, *splendid!*

Nine

After exhausting all four of the Amelias in attendance, as well as some suspected Amelias, Grif did not linger at the ball. He left Fynster in the hands of Miss Crabtree, although both had looked a little perplexed as he had strolled from their midst.

He found a hack, returned to Dalkeith House on Cavendish Street in something of a huff. Not only was he no closer to finding the correct Amelia, but he could not shake the uncomfortable notion that Miss Addison knew *something* about him. *Damn* her devil eyes!

A morose Hugh was in the drawing room before the hearth, his bare feet propped on a footstool directly in front of the flames, a near empty bottle of whiskey beside him. He glanced up as Grif strode into the room. "Ah, our dashing young dandy doth return," he said in his best English-accented acerbic voice.

As Grif was accustomed to Hugh's pouting, he ignored it, looked around the room. "Where's Dudley?"

"Abed, lad. His gout is flaring again, and by the bye, have ye no' seen the clock?" Hugh asked, gesturing lamely at the clock on the mantel.

Two o'clock in the morning—Dudley would have been abed hours ago. Grif took a chair across from Hugh. "And how was yer evening?" he asked Hugh.

Hugh laughed. "Full of dreams of a bonny Irish lass, with hair as red as blood and eyes as—"

"No, *no,*" Grif groaned. "I canna bear to hear another ode of lament to Keara Brody."

Hugh made a sound of displeasure and reached for a cheroot that was languishing in a tray nearby. "What do ye expect, then? What else am I to do, locked away as I am? I'm no' allowed to gamble, or to soothe me ruffled feathers with a bonny lass. At the very least, ye could regale me with tales of dancing ladies and fine wine and good gaming."

If only he could, but unfortunately, Grif brought only two things away from the Valtrain ball: One, that he had reached another dead end on the Amelia trail—and the trail was looking bleaker all the time. And two, that he had never met a more exasperating person than Miss Addison. "I'll regale ye, I will," he snorted disgustedly, "with the tale of a bloody wench who knows what we're about!"

Hugh took a long draw of his cheroot and casually released the smoke into small circles. "What do ye mean, then?"

"I mean, Miss Addison—"

"Yer favorite—"

"No, no' me favorite! Her sister! Her endlessly vexing and bloody impudent older sister, the most aggravating female on the face of God's earth!" Grif exclaimed. "First she asked after Liam—*'Would ye know me friend, Captain Lockhart?'* " he mimicked in falsetto voice. "And then, at Whittington House, she asked where she might find Ardencaple—*'Where would ye describe it as being?'* And again, this very evening, after the wench connives to get me into standing up with her, she has the bloody nerve to imply that I might be less than honest and hiding something!"

"Oh aye, I can see why that would upset ye so, as ye bloody well *are* hiding something," Hugh casually observed.

"Mark me, Hugh, she *knows* something. I'd swear it on me life! The hell of it is, I canna determine *what* she might know."

Hugh took another draw of his cheroot as he considered it. "Impossible," he said at last. "She knows nothing, for how could she? Unless she's been to Scotland. Has she been to Scotland?"

"How in God's name should I know if she's been to Scotland?"

"Ye stood up with her," Hugh patiently reminded him as he poured more whiskey into a tot. "Did ye no' converse with her as a gentleman would?"

"No," Grif said petulantly.

"No?" Hugh echoed incredulously, a small smile playing at the corners of his mouth.

"*No.*" Grif repeated emphatically. "I'd rather gouge at me very eyes than make polite conversation with that devil's handmaiden," he muttered. "She likes to see a man squirm, that one."

"There's only one thing to be done for it," Hugh said gravely.

Grif looked at him.

"Do yer squirming *on* her, lad!"

Grif glared at him, but Hugh laughed. "All right, then," he said, still smiling, "why donna ye write yer brother and *ask* him about the lass? Perhaps he can shed some light, aye?"

"Aye," Grif said, nodding. "Aye, that's what I'll do, then."

Hugh chuckled, picked up an empty tot, and poured Grif a shot of whiskey. "There now, Lockhart!" he said congenially. "Have yerself a spot of good Scottish whiskey before ye collapse into sobs like a wee bairn. How could she know what ye're about? If she suspected, she'd have all of London on yer head."

That much was true. But he'd write to Liam all the same. With a snort, Grif ignored the tot Hugh offered him and reached for the bottle instead. Bottle in hand, he propped his feet up next to Hugh and joined him in staring morosely at the fire . . . while the memory of that searing kiss continued to frolic at the corner of his mind.

In Mayfair the next afternoon, Whittington House was once again besieged by admiring young men come to call on Miss Lucy, and Miss Lucy greeted them all with a thinly veiled yawn and the serious study of her manicure.

As she explained to Anna later that afternoon (who had been commanded by her mother to accompany them on a walkabout of Hyde Park), she found all her callers rather boring all in all, and really, there were only one or two who had sparked any interest.

"Who?" Anna asked as the three of them strolled along the path.

"Can't you at least guess?"

"How could I possibly guess? I've scarcely noticed your suitors, Lucy."

Lucy flashed a little smile and linked her arm through Anna's. "Haven't you really? All right then, I'll tell you," she said as they paused to admire a showy stand of hollyhock. "I'm a bit partial to the Scotsman," she began, to which Anna rolled her eyes, "and Mr. Bradenton."

"Mr. Bradenton?" Anna repeated, a little taken aback. Mr. Bradenton had never called that she could remember, and had not been at any of the popular balls this Season.

Lucy smiled and nodded dreamily. "He's really so very handsome, and quite kind."

"Pray tell, Lucy . . . how could you possibly know if he is kind?"

Lucy shrugged. "I've heard tell."

"I've not met him that I recall," Mother said as they casually continued on.

"You can hardly expect to make a match with a gentleman who does not, at the very least, *call* on you," Anna reminded her.

"Really?" she said sweetly. "If that is the case, Anna dearest, how will you *ever* make a match?"

"Lucy!" Mother exclaimed. "Be charitable!"

Lucy smiled and fussed with her parasol; Anna looked heavenward for strength. "There is one more," Lucy said casually as her parasol opened, almost piercing Anna in the eye.

"*Is* there," Anna said, sighing wearily as Lucy swung her parasol up to block the sun over her and Mother. "Please enlighten us, for we are all aquiver with curiosity."

"Oh, Anna, how many times must I tell you that sarcasm does not become you?" Mother chided her.

Lucy slanted a triumphant look at her. "Mr. *Lockhart*," she whispered excitedly.

The blood rushed to Anna's neck; she quickly

looked away and shrugged nonchalantly. "Oh. Him. And when do you expect he'll return from Bath?"

"Good heavens, not *Nigel* Lockhart! Mr. *Drake* Lockhart!" Lucy shot her a heated look, but then smiled softly. "Mr. *Drake* Lockhart. Is he not impossibly handsome?"

"He is quite handsome, darling," Mother agreed.

"I really hadn't noticed," Anna lied, and did her level best to keep her expression stoic as she tried to keep down the myriad emotions bubbling to the surface.

"Can you keep a secret?" Lucy asked in a loud whisper.

"No," Anna said decisively.

"Oh, Anna!" Lucy whined. "Is it so difficult to humor me?"

"Yes."

"My secret is . . . that Mr. Lockhart rather fancies me, too!" When Anna did not respond, Lucy roughly elbowed her. "I'm *quite* serious!"

Anna couldn't help but look at her—for once, her younger sister looked rather earnest and wide-eyed. "Do you know that he wrote a poem, just for me?"

Anna's heart suddenly plummeted.

"He did! He wrote a poem, just for me!"

"Oh, how very romantic," Mother said dreamily.

Lucy eagerly nodded her agreement. "He recited it just last evening, in the Valtrain gardens. Would you like to hear it?"

No, Anna did *not* want to hear it, she was certain she didn't, but the sick feeling in the pit of her stomach prevented her from speaking immediately, and before she could utter a word, Mother said, "Of course!"

The three of them paused on the walkway. Lucy put the tip of the parasol on the ground, stacked her tiny hands atop the handle, and with a smile, lifted her face to the sky and said, " '*In the moonlight was her heart thus taken; a chaste kiss, another vow forsaken. And when the sun rose again on her lovely face, there she did lie in love's sweet embrace.*' " She lowered her happy gaze to her mother and sister.

"I had no idea Mr. Lockhart was a poet!" Mother exclaimed genuinely.

They turned twin smiles to Anna. But Anna's heart had stopped beating, and as she could not draw air into her lungs, she gaped at Lucy as she tried to grasp what Lockhart had done. Surely he had *not* given her poem to Lucy. *Surely not.*

"It's rather provocative, isn't it?" Lucy whispered excitedly.

But Anna was still gaping, trying to comprehend how Drake Lockhart could give *her* poem to Lucy.

Lucy's smile faded. She turned a frown to her mother. "Do you see, Mother? She takes the pleasure from everything!"

Mother frowned at Anna. "Darling, is there nothing you can say to Lucy about her lovely poem?"

Say? There was plenty she could say, all right, but her mother would be shocked by such vulgar language. "It's . . . grand," she made herself say. And it *was* a grand poem, especially grand when it had been for *her.*

Anna trailed behind her mother and sister, her disappointment mounting, her confusion about Lockhart and men in general steeping inside her. How could he do such a horrid thing? Did he think she and Lucy would not compare notes? When had he done it?

When he returned to her with the cider, he'd escorted them both back inside, and had left their side to dance with Miss Netherton. Maybe he had told Lucy of his poem for Anna and she had misunderstood. Oh yes, it had to be something as simple as a misunderstanding on Lucy's part, for what gentleman would create a poem and read it to *two* women?

Anna was so lost in thought that it took her a moment to realize that Mother and Lucy had stopped beside a handsome curricle. She started as she looked up to see who drove it.

Her traitorous lips formed a smile, completely independent of her. It was The Imposter, Ardencaple. And Mr. Fynster-Allen.

"Good afternoon, ladies," Ardencaple said, tipping his hat and smiling broadly.

"Good afternoon, my lord!" Lucy called. "May I introduce you to my mother, Lady Whittington? Mother, please meet my friend, Lord Ardencaple."

Anna watched as the Fraud of Ardencaple, charmer that he was, leapt from the curricle and landed lightly on his feet before Mother, leaving Mr. Fynster-Allen to climb down in a much less dashing fashion from the other side of the curricle. He took Mother's hand, bent over it with a flourish, and straightened again. "It is me great pleasure to make yer acquaintance, Lady Whittington."

"Oh, my lord, the pleasure is *mine,*" Mother said with a curtsey, then stepped back, gesturing for Anna to join them. "Might I introduce you to my other daughter, my lord?"

Ardencaple's gaze slid to his right, landing on Anna. His smile suddenly seemed frozen. "We've met. How do you do, Miss Addison?"

"Very well, thank you," she said, and turned a smile to Mr. Fynster-Allen. "Good afternoon, sir."

Bless him, but the man turned an appalling shade of red. "Good afternoon, Miss Addison," he muttered. "Lady Whittington. Miss Lucy," he muttered further, now bobbing so quickly and often that he looked a bit like a duck.

"Mr. Fynster-Allen! Why, we've not had the pleasure of your company all Season!" Mother declared.

"Ah . . . I beg your pardon, my lady, but we did indeed meet at the Davenport supper," he said, nervously taking his hat from his head. "Actually, we took a bit of cake together."

Mother's smile faded into a hint of confusion. "Did we?" she asked, brushing imaginary lint from her pelisse, then suddenly broke into another wreath of smiles. "Ah, of course we did, sir! You must forgive my abominable lack of memory!" she declared.

"Mother and I were enjoying the glorious weather," Lucy said, as if Anna was not present. "Perhaps you gentlemen would care to escort us for a time?"

"'Twould give me great pleasure, it would," Ardencaple said instantly, and smoothly moved in between Mother and Lucy, offering them both an arm, which they took as they beamed up at their handsome escort.

Anna looked at Fynster-Allen. He looked at her, too, his eyes wide with alarm. Anna laughed and held out her hand. "I promise not to bite you, sir."

"Oh! Of course not, Miss Addison, I never meant to convey that I thought you *would*," he said quickly, and after another moment's nervous hesitation, he thrust his forearm under her proffered hand. Anna did her best to smile at the poor man as she took it, and the two of them fell in behind her mother and sister and the insufferable Lord Deceit, following along like puppies.

As one might have guessed, Fynster-Allen was not much of a conversationalist, and Anna eventually tired of trying to gain more of a response than "Yes indeed" and "Can't rightly say." Besides, she was far too distracted by the gay laughter coming from the threesome ahead of her. Even her mother was beginning to look a little smitten, she thought with some disgust, and in a fit of pique for having been left behind—again—Anna asked of Fynster-Allen, "What is it, exactly, that brings Lord Ardencaple to London, of all places?"

Her question obviously startled her companion; he looked anxiously at her from the corner of his eye, his cheeks going red again. "Why . . . whatever do you mean, Miss Addison?"

Would that she had a pencil and a bit of vellum to spell it all out for him. "I *mean*, sir, what is it in London that draws the Scottish earl? Is he not missed at home? Surely he must think to return to Ardencaple, or whatever place he belongs."

"Why Miss Addison, I would never be so . . . so *bold* to pry into another man's affairs," Fynster-Allen said instantly, apparently shocked that she would.

Anna frowned at his appalled expression. *Oh why not?* she wanted to ask. *Everyone wants to know, and you really shouldn't pretend you don't!* But instead she said, "I did not mean to imply that you should *pry*, sir—I just thought that he might have offered his reason for being here, that's all."

He glanced uneasily at Ardencaple's broad back. "He's not said, really . . . I mean, other than his desire to find Amelia."

Find *who?* How intriguing! "*Who,* did you say?" she asked politely.

"Oh dear," Fynster-Allen said instantly. "Perhaps I've said too much—"

"Is it a secret, then?"

"Not a secret, I shouldn't think, as he has made several inquiries, really—"

"Of who?"

"Of who? Why, the Amelias, of course."

The *Amelias?* What was Fynster-Allen babbling about? In an effort to help him, Anna suggested, "Do you perhaps mean Miss Crabtree?"

A thin sheen of perspiration appeared on Fynster-Allen's brow. "Miss Crabtree. Yes. In a manner of speaking. But really *not* Miss Crabtree at all. Did she tell you so?"

"No. Did she tell you so?"

Fynster-Allen turned red. "She wasn't offended, was she? I'd regret it terribly if she were, since I pointed him to her. She's really a very kind girl and not experienced in the ways of the *ton*—"

"Mr. Fynster-Allen, of what are you speaking?" Anna demanded, a little too impatiently.

The poor man winced. "Oh all right, I can't suppose it would hurt, would it? Ardencaple is looking for the lost daughter of his uncle, and the only thing he knows for certain is that her name is Amelia. Oh, and that she was acquainted with Lady Battenkirk, and as I said to him, how unfortunate it is that Lady Battenkirk is in Wales just now, for I'm certain she'd clear it all up and point him to his cousin straightaway."

"Lady *Battenkirk?*" Anna exclaimed in disbelief. She knew the odd duck, had known her all her life.

As it happened, Lady Battenkirk was distantly related to her father's cousin. For years, upon the conclusion of the parliamentary season, her family would retire to the Whittington country house in Devonshire. Their estate abutted the estates of a number of loosely related relatives, and Lady Battenkirk, who resided somewhere there, had often been in attendance at family functions. Anna recalled that she was forever collecting strange little knickknacks and baubles of questionable taste. Worse, the woman talked so loud and long that one felt as if one could be blown clear across the sea with all the wind she generated.

As Fynster-Allen daubed his head with a kerchief, Anna tried to guess how Ardencaple, or whoever he was, could possibly *know* Lady Battenkirk.

And as to this ridiculous ruse about a long lost cousin named Amelia? It was preposterous! Patently ridiculous! And terribly, *terribly* intriguing.

Anna was not personally acquainted with any Amelia save Miss Crabtree, but she did recall that Lady Battenkirk's niece, Mrs. Merriman, lived near Hampton Court. If Lady Battenkirk was fast friends with anyone named Amelia, Mrs. Merriman would be certain to know it, wouldn't she?

"Anna, darling, come here, will you?" her mother suddenly called, startling Anna from her thinking. She glanced at Fynster-Allen, who, she couldn't help noticing, seemed rather relieved, and walked to where her mother and Lucy and the Lying Scotsman had come to a halt.

They were laughing at some tale; Mother's eyes were shining as she took Anna's hand and squeezed it playfully. "What a funny little thing to tell you! Do you recall, darling, the spaniel your lady grandmother had?"

"Of course," Anna said, looking at them all curiously.

"And do you recall that she used to call him Bo? 'Out the door with you, you little Bo,' she'd say."

"Yes, I recall."

"You will not guess what *bo* means in Lord Ardencaple's language!" Mother said, barely able to contain her laughter. "In the Scottish Highlands, it means . . . *cow!*" she cried, and she and Lucy doubled over with laughter.

Anna missed the point of all the hilarity, and looked again at Ardencaple. He was laughing, his green eyes flashing. "I beg yer pardon, Miss Addison," he said, his green eyes piercing her. "Do ye no' find it amusing?"

"Not particularly," she answered honestly.

"What's happened to your good humor, darling?" her mother chided her. "Just think of it—an old woman who thinks she has made up some precious name for her little dog. And it means 'cow'!"

The idea was so astoundingly funny a second time, apparently, that Mother laughed with girlish laughter all over again. Even Fynster-Allen was laughing a little. Slowly, Anna slid her gaze to Ardencaple again, watched one brow lift above the other, challenging her, daring her to laugh.

She merely smiled and thought that it was rather time she called on good Mrs. Merriman and inquired about her dear aunt, Lady Battenkirk.

Ten

That glorious day in the park was the last sunny one London was to see for a time, for over the next several days it rained relentlessly.

Grif, Hugh, and Dudley endured it like caged animals; Dudley's gout was inflamed again, and Hugh was developing a rather disconcerting habit of stealing away in the night to gamble away whatever amount of their funds he could get his hands on. Naturally, Hugh's behavior was a point of contention between Hugh and Grif, and in the passing of those few soggy days, they were locked in a battle of wills that eventually extended to fencing in the ballroom with swords taken from a decorative display.

The fencing solved nothing, however, and Grif knew he had to do something—Hugh's restlessness was growing. Not that Grif could blame him, what with all the sitting about. No one knew better than Grif that this was not the sort of life Hugh aspired to—he'd always imagined himself a man-about-town, not a lowly housebound servant. Grif's pleas that they stick to their plan were falling on Hugh's deaf ears. They had been in London two months now—a month longer than they'd hoped—and Hugh swore he could not abide the idleness a moment longer.

Grif suspected that if he didn't find an Amelia or the blasted beastie soon, he'd have the mutiny of one wretched valet on his hands.

But Grif's hopes were growing dim. He posted another letter to Liam, hoping that Liam would know what to do, perhaps where to look for Amelia. And, he hoped, he'd know something of what the devil was about.

The devil being Miss Anna Addison, of course.

Aye, between Dudley's worsening gout, Hugh's restlessness, Miss Addison's provocation, and what seemed like thousands of wrong Amelias, Grif was not having a very good time of it. In fact, he was beginning to fret that they'd run out of funds and be forced to return to Scotland before they ever found the blasted beastie.

And perhaps even without Hugh, by the look of it. Just this very morning, Grif had awakened to find him gone again and was brooding over it when he heard the pounding at the front door.

As Dudley was still recovering from the gout, Grif answered, pulling the heavy door open to see their neighbor, Lady Worthall, her cane raised to beat the door again, standing directly in front of one of her footmen, who held an umbrella over her head. Grif fought a grimace at the sight of her; her flaccid face seemed squeezed too tightly in the confines of that bonnet, and her gray ringlets were popping out.

"Good morning, Lord Ardencaple!" she said, and leaned to her right in an attempt to peer past him. "What a surprise to see you at your door, sir! Has your butler taken ill?"

"May I invite ye in?" Grif asked on a sigh of impatience.

"Why, *yes!*" she cried, and hopped up the entry and waddled into the foyer, her footman on her heels. "I've come to inform you that I've been delivered a letter from Lady Dalkeith."

Grif steeled himself and drawled, "Have ye indeed?"

"Indeed," she answered as she glanced curiously about. "She is rather determined to stay in Rouen until the end of the summer—"

That, at least, was welcome news.

"—at which point, she declares, she will return to London to open her house in time for the Little Season! I thought that a rather odd thing for her to say, don't you?"

"Odd?" Grif asked, raising a brow.

"*Odd,* as her house is already open, my lord!" Lady Worthall exclaimed impatiently.

"I donna find it odd at all, really," Grif said calmly. "The house is open for a time, 'tis true, but it willna be open as late as the summer."

"Oh *really?* So you will not be staying on?"

"I didna say as much as that, did I, then?" he asked pleasantly. "I havena determined my plans as of yet."

"Ah! I *seeeee,*" she said, nodding thoughtfully, and made a motion to the footman to open the door. "Then I suppose you won't mind in the least if I write to Lady Dalkeith and inform her that your plans are, at present, uncertain?"

Witch. Grif walked to the door and opened it. "My dear Lady Worthall, ye may write to Lady Dalkeith and inform her whatever ye like. 'Tis no' me affair."

Unfortunately, Hugh chose that precise moment to make his grand return from trawling about all night. His clothes were disheveled, his hair was a mess, and beneath the full shadow of a beard, Grif could smell whiskey.

It was obvious that the sight of Lady Worthall startled Hugh; he blinked several times, unable to find his tongue. Probably because it was still wrapped around a bottle somewhere. Actually, no one could quite find their tongue until Hugh gathered his sodden wits and bowed with a flourish before Grif. "Milord, I have done yer bidding and delivered the post," he said, rising with some difficulty. "Will that be all, then?"

"*Aye,*" Grif said through clenched teeth.

Hugh bowed again and strode quickly out of the foyer.

Lady Worthall turned a cold gaze to Grif. "As I said, my lord, I shall write to Lady Dalkeith straightaway and inform her that you and your . . . valet, is he? That you and your *valet* have not as yet determined your plans."

Now Grif could not even muster a smile. "Good day, Lady Worthall."

"Good day!" she said icily.

Her dull gray skirt had scarcely cleared the door before Grif shut it resoundingly behind her and her footman. He stood there, jaw clenched, staring daggers at the door. And then he turned that murderous glare to the staircase, his imagination already racing ahead to what, exactly, he might do to Hugh.

While Hugh and Grif were arguing loudly about what constituted "valetlike" behavior, across town, Anna had called for the coach and the family driver, Bentley, to take her to Hampton Court.

She'd vacillated about actually calling on Mrs. Merriman. But she was sick to death of listening to

Lucy go on about all the gentlemen who esteemed her, and when Bette and her husband had called to announce the happy news that they were with child for the third time, Lucy's bragging had been Anna's undoing at last.

Lucy, Anna, and Bette had been looking at gowns Bette could no longer wear when Lucy blithely announced Drake Lockhart had been to call *four* times since the Valtrain ball.

"And moreover," she'd said, clipping earrings on her ears and admiring herself, "he has kissed me rather passionately. And he has touched my breast . . . my *bare* breast."

"Lucy Addison!" Bette exclaimed, horrified.

"What?" Lucy asked innocently. "I should think that when a man touches a woman's *bare* breast, he intends to make the woman his own. Wouldn't you, Anna?" she'd asked, turning to look at her sister.

"I would never be so bold as to assume any such thing," Anna said quietly. "And I should hope I'd not be so easily seduced."

"What makes you think *I* was the one who was easily seduced?" Lucy asked with a wicked little laugh.

"Lucy!" Bette cried, putting a hand over her mouth.

Lucy laughed again. "Oh, Bette, really! I'm only teasing!"

It was true that Drake had called on Lucy, but Anna simply could not believe he'd kissed Lucy, or that Drake had touched Lucy in such a manner. She wouldn't believe it . . . all right, if it *were* true, she could only surmise that Drake had been momentarily distracted by Lucy's charm. At least that's what she told herself.

And really, in spite of the tiny little part of her that refused to believe what she'd told herself, certainly Drake had given Anna no reason to believe his esteem for *her* had wavered in the least. In fact, at the Sotheby tea, Drake had been quite complimentary of Anna, and had even shared some of his private thoughts with her. He'd confided that he worried so about Nigel, and how he hoped to make a good match for his sister, Barbara. He told her he'd rather like to be a physician, and found the study of human anatomy quite fascinating.

No gentleman ever spoke to Anna the way Drake did, as an equal, seeking her opinion. Anna could only believe that such intimacy of his thoughts was reserved for those whom Drake esteemed the most. And as Lucy had not mentioned it, Anna was certain Drake had not confided in her. He had confided in Anna. His attention to Lucy was a temporary blinding, that was all. After all, it happened to most of the gentlemen who met Lucy.

A temporary blinding . . . but still Anna tossed and turned at night, her mind full of conflicting thoughts and torrid images of Drake and Lucy, his hand on her breast, then his mouth on her breast, then the two of them, naked and copulating.

The disturbing dreams led Anna to believe that her only hope of holding fast to Drake's esteem was to learn the art of seduction herself, and at the same time, strengthen Ardencaple's suit to Lucy, which, she was sorry to note, had been less than vigorous of late. But Lucy adored the slightest amount of attention, and therefore, with even slighter provocation, Lucy would charm Ardencaple into her web.

Anna could make it happen.

Only one question remained, and that was if Anna was pushing an outlaw into her sister's embrace. While that had a certain scandalous appeal, she could not, in good conscience, see Lucy harmed.

The coach slowed, interrupting Anna's thoughts. She looked out the window, saw they had arrived at Hampton Court Palace.

The rain had stopped, which Anna took as a favorable omen. She bade Bentley to wait. "Are you certain I can't drive you, miss?" he asked with a worried squint.

"I'll be quite all right, Bentley," she assured him, and with her pelisse pulled closely around her, her reticule firmly in her hand, she set out in search of Mrs. Merriman in the clutter of village that surrounded the old palace.

It didn't take her nearly as long as she feared; the fishmonger in the marketplace was well acquainted with Mrs. Merriman. "Of course!" he said, delighted to be of some assistance. "Mrs. Merriman buys her fish here every Friday, as regular as rain."

"Might you have a direction? I'm afraid I've gone a bit daft and can't remember other than that she lives near Hampton Court."

"Oh, you'll find her on the row along the Thames," the man said jovially. "And if you would be so kind, tell her we've some right fine lampreys this morning."

"I will certainly do so," Anna said, and walked on, to the row of neat town houses along the Thames.

At the third door Anna tried, a daily maid opened. "I beg your pardon, but I am looking for Mrs. Merriman," Anna said politely.

"Aye," the girl said, eyeing Anna up and down. "And who shall I say is calling, miss?"

Aha! "Miss Addison," she said happily. "I should like to speak with her about her aunt, Lady Battenkirk."

"All right, then, please step in," the girl said, admitting Anna to the foyer. She left Anna standing there and walked down a narrow hallway, rapped lightly on a door, and at someone's beck and call, stepped inside. A moment later, a tall, thin woman with black ringlets about her face stepped out and came striding forward.

"Miss Addison?"

"I beg your pardon, Mrs. Merriman?"

The woman nodded.

"I am Anna Addison, Lord Whittington's daughter. My father is a distant relative of Lady Battenkirk's, and she often summered with us in Devonshire."

"Yes, I recall that she did," Mrs. Merriman said, regarding her suspiciously.

"I hope you will forgive me, but I have come to inquire as to Lady Battenkirk's whereabouts, as there is someone come to town to call on her."

"Oh?" the woman asked, clasping her hands at her waist as she assessed Anna. "Unfortunately, my lady aunt is in Wales just now. An archaeological dig of some sort and quite impossible to reach. If I may ask, who exactly is seeking her?"

"Ah, well . . . it's rather odd, really," Anna said, "but the gentleman in question is a Scottish earl—"

"A *Scottish* earl?" Mrs. Merriman repeated, clearly confused.

"Scottish," Anna nodded, "And he is quite desperate to find a woman named Amelia, who happens to be a friend of Lady Battenkirk—"

"Amelia? Surely you must mean Amelia Litton!

She and Auntie were fast friends until the day she died."

A rush of disappointment washed over Anna. "She *died?*"

"Yes, from bad meat, just last summer. Oh, you mustn't fret, dear. She was ancient," Mrs. Merriman assured her.

Anna looked curiously at Mrs. Merriman. "Ancient, you say? Not a girl, a young woman?"

Mrs. Merriman twittered at that. "Lord, no! She was an old spinster governess that once taught Auntie—I beg your pardon, forgive my manners, Miss Addison. Might I invite you in for a cup of tea?" she asked, gesturing to the parlor.

"That would be lovely," she said absently, her mind trying to reconcile what Mrs. Merriman had just said with what Mr. Fynster-Allen had told her about Ardencaple's quest.

Mrs. Merriman gestured toward the parlor. "My aunt never married, you know, as she is something of a Bohemian and could never stay in one place for very long. She and Miss Litton remained friends all through the years, although Miss Litton refused to travel with her, as she thought cavorting about quite unbecoming a lady. For thirty years, my aunt would bring Miss Litton a treasure from her travels. When Miss Litton died," she said, opening the door to the parlor, "I was the lucky recipient of all her treasures. I really must warn you—I've not quite determined what to do with it all, and I daresay my aunt's tastes run to the extreme," she said, and stepped aside, letting Anna pass into the parlor.

The sheer numbers of bric-a-brac and knickknacks in the room was enough to startle anyone. There were sculptures and plates and strange-looking objects Anna could not quite make out.

"I've been sorting through it all, trying to make some sense of it," Mrs. Merriman sighed.

It was the most bizarre and atrocious collection of objects Anna had ever seen in her life. She turned slowly, taking in the whole room as Mrs. Merriman began to recite some of the places Lady Battenkirk had been, and as she turned toward the mantel, she saw an object that literally took her breath away.

She had forgotten it completely, had not recalled she had seen it until this very moment—but she *had* seen that hideous thing, one night last Season, in a dimly lit room of the Lockhart mansion in Mayfair.

In that instant, she knew what Lord Ardencaple was about.

"How do you take your tea?" Mrs. Merriman asked as she walked to a bellpull, and Anna turned her most charming smile to the woman.

"Plain, thank you," she said, and wandered deeper into the room, her smile growing brighter as her mind raced ahead.

Eleven

A week after Anna's visit to Mrs. Merriman, the Seatons held their annual supper party for leaders of the House of Lords. This Season, however, the supper party had taken on a new mien; it was said that the supper party would include forty of Lord Seaton's dearest acquaintances . . . among them, the most desirable unmarried gentlemen of the *ton*, as the Seatons hoped to make a match for their daughter, Elizabeth.

And as there were so many guests invited to this intimate supper affair, the Seatons served sweet sherry in the grand salon while they waited for all their supper guests to arrive.

Miss Elizabeth Seaton took the opportunity to promenade about the room with Anna, along the edge of a large Aubusson carpet, past gilded hearths and torchères, damask-covered furniture, and ten-foot paintings of Seatons gone before them, gossiping about what she'd heard of Lord Ardencaple at the Hospital Society luncheon just Tuesday past.

"He's in London in search of a wife," she whispered to Anna. "His family has quite a grand fortune, and they despair of ever seeing an heir, so they have sent him to London."

"Is *that* what he's after?" Anna asked with a laugh.

"Yes!" Elizabeth exclaimed happily. "And he comes with the highest of recommendations."

"Really? Whose, exactly?"

Elizabeth blinked. "Who? I, ah . . . I don't know, exactly, but I heard Lady Paddington say so, and she's always quite aware of these things."

Lady Paddington also sat in her parlor making up gossip if she didn't have it firsthand—Anna would wager her dowry that Lady Paddington didn't know Ardencaple from her elbow and had made up every little thing, *including* his alleged recommendations.

But she wasn't going to have the chance to say so, for the Lying Scotsman himself was announced that very moment by the Seatons' butler. "His Lordship Arden-*caple*, Griffin MacAulay," he articulated, bowing low. And Lord Arden-*caple* swept into the room, smiling charmingly. Anna groaned as the debutantes, to a girl, swooned.

Not to be left out, Elizabeth immediately let go Anna's arm and asked to be excused, and nonchalantly made her way to the door and his exalted lordship, as did several other young women in attendance. What ridiculous creatures they were, rushing forward as if he were some prize.

All right, Anna thought as she turned away and wandered to the window, she could concede that he was indeed frightfully handsome, what with his long-styled hair, and his smoldering charm, and his dancing green eyes. And there was that lopsided smile, of course, and that lovely mouth, and all right, *yes*, that *body,* lean and hard, which naturally she could not help noticing the night he had kissed her so passionately on the veranda. And had imagined several times since.

But he was a fraud!

He was insinuating himself into the finest salons in London under false pretense! Rather charming and witty pretense, perhaps, but false nonetheless! And from what Anna had deduced, he intended to rob them all quite blind. The very thought of it made her angry all over again, and she turned around to face the room, saw that three young women were gushing around Lord Ardencaple as he tried to make his way around the room. Lucy, she also noticed, was chatting it up quite nicely with the elusive Mr. Bradenton, who, Anna had to admit, did seem captivated.

A bell was rung, and Lady Seaton stepped to the middle of the room. The din in the room slowly subsided; Anna's father suddenly appeared on her right arm, all smiles, and with his hand firmly on her elbow, he whispered, "Let's not be shy, shall we?" and led her into the middle of the large salon.

"We've a rather different arrangement this evening," Lady Seaton announced. Beside her, Ardencaple was smiling down at Miss Elizabeth, who looked as if she might melt into the floor at any moment.

"As we've so many guests, my lord husband and I have determined that we shall have *two* dining rooms, which will be divided on the basis of age."

"Oldest gentlemen with the youngest ladies, I should hope!" the ancient Lord Carsmith called out, and several of the older gentlemen laughed appreciatively.

"I should not be so careless as to let loose an old scoundrel such as yourself on the debutantes we are honored to have in our presence," Lord Seaton replied. A quiet little titter went through the hopeful young debutantes as they looked shyly at the unmarried gentlemen in the room, and Father squeezed Anna's elbow.

She felt absolutely ill with dread.

"If I may ask your indulgence as we seat our good friends in two groups," Lady Seaton said. She put on the reading glasses her butler offered her on a silver tray, and picked up the vellum, from which she read, "Lord and Lady Carsmith, if you would be so kind," she said, and thus began to arrange the promenade of the older guests to the first dining room.

Anna felt a bit like a spinster when her father kissed her cheek and joined her mother in their place in line.

The young ladies milled about, giggling as they stole glimpses of the gentlemen. The gentlemen, on the other hand, laughed with one another and smiled openly at the debutantes. The only one of them to see her, Anna thought, was Mr. Bradenton, and even that was a look of curiosity more than anything else. She felt hopelessly out of place, and when the sound of Lucy's gentle laughter rose above the others, she felt as if she would just as soon hurl herself out the window than proceed with this insufferable supper.

Unfortunately, Lady Seaton had other ideas. She returned shortly after the elder guests had promenaded their way into the first dining room, and with a clap of her hands, she said, "I daresay I shall miss the most fun! We've a dining table in the billiard room. I thought it quite lovely there, and I do hope you will find it to your liking."

Several of the young ladies quickly assured Lady Seaton that it was a wonderful venue.

"Well, then, shall we?" she asked, and with vellum in hand, she glanced at her paper. "Lord Ardencaple, would you do the honor of escorting Miss Anna Addison to the dining room?" she asked, looking about for her first arranged couple.

From where she stood, Anna saw his slight wince, which quickly melted to a pleasantly stoic mask. What a pity she couldn't reach the window and leap. She was reminded of why she despised social customs such as the promenade to supper, as if the prince regent were receiving them! Why couldn't they all just troop to the billiard room in one big pack? But she pasted a smile on her face as Ardencaple stepped into the center of the room and bowed toward her. "I'd be delighted," he said, and straightened, one hand behind his back, the other extended toward Anna.

With a moment's hesitation—which was ended with one look from Lucy—Anna quickly stepped forward and put her hand in Ardencaple's. "Good evening, Miss Addison. Lovely to see ye, it is."

"Oh, *likewise,*" she said, glaring at him as he brought her hand to his lips before dropping it unceremoniously.

He held out his elbow. Anna laid her hand on his forearm, let him lead her to the front of the room, where the butler indicated they should wait until the queue had been assembled for the procession to the billiard room.

"You mustn't strain yourself attempting to look so overjoyed by this turn of events," Anna muttered as Lady Seaton put her daughter, Elizabeth, with the highly sought-after Mr. Bradenton.

"'Tis no strain, I assure ye—I am quite adept at feigning pleasure," he muttered beneath his breath.

Anna could scarcely contain a snort at that understatement. "Yes, I imagine you are adept at feigning all manner of things."

"And I'll kindly spare yer tender feelings by no' telling you just how many things I must feign when I am near *ye*, Miss Addison."

Lady Seaton continued assigning the procession.

"And, Mr. Lockhart, would you do the honor of escorting Miss Lucy Addison?" Lady Seaton asked.

"I could not possibly be more delighted," Drake said, stepping forward to receive Lucy's perfect and dainty little curtsey.

Anna couldn't help herself; she immediately looked away, her gaze inadvertently landing on the Imposter again, who was actually smiling. "Foiled again, aye?"

"I beg your pardon, but do you *mind?*" she whispered hotly.

"No' at all. But I've a wee suggestion for ye, Miss Addison," he said amicably. "Ye might smile at the lad now and again, as ye really are quite a bonny lass when ye smile."

This time Anna could not contain her small groan of exasperation. "Do you take me for a fool, Ardencaple? Do you really think your flattery will induce me to find you agreeable? I shall advise you to try something else, for I will not, no matter how hard you wish it, become my sister."

The moment the words fell blithely off her tongue, she wanted them back.

Certainly her remark sparked something in his eyes; he looked at her so pointedly that she actually flinched a little. "I didna think for a moment that I should be as fortunate as that, ye wee *bana-bhuidseach.* I had every confidence ye'd remain sharp-tongued and entirely too vexing all yer natural days."

Whatever it was he called her, she felt his complete censure and did not think it a compliment. She inched away from him. "You may call me what you will," she said in a low voice, "but at least I can rest easy in the fact that I am honest, *my lord.*"

His face darkened terribly, but he said nothing as Lady Seaton called the last couple. "Mr. Fynster-Allen, would you be so kind as to escort Miss Crabtree? Lovely. And now, if you will all please follow me to the billiard room!"

They walked down a long hall, past the formal dining room where voices were already raised in merriment. Anna could feel the Lying Scotsman's body stiff beside her, could feel his loathing practically emanating from him, and while she shouldn't have cared in the least . . . she did. She was really quite bothered by it.

Fortunately, in the dining room, she was seated directly across from Lord Ardencaple, and next to Mr. Fitzwater, a gentleman of means who had offered for her two Seasons ago. Anna and Mr. Fitzwater made polite conversation through the first course of turtle soup while Lord Ardencaple, she couldn't help but notice, was charming the ringlets from Miss Daphne Dorchester's head.

As the footmen cleared the soup and began to serve the main course, Anna noticed farther down the table, Lockhart had eyes for only Lucy, seated directly across from him and gaily holding court with Mr. Bradenton on her right and Lord Nickson on her left. The whole room seemed to be having an extraordinarily gay evening; even Mr. Fynster-Allen and Miss Crabtree, perhaps the two shyest people in all of London, were actually tittering with one another as if they were old friends.

The single exception to the gaiety seemed to be Anna and Mr. Fitzwater, the latter continually mopping his brow with his napkin, as if she were somehow causing him distress.

It was Mr. Bradenton, surprisingly enough, who enlivened the affair by asking the Lying Scotsman about his estate. "Is Scotland your primary residence, my lord, or do you intend to make London your home?"

Ooh, excellent question, and one Anna wished she'd thought of.

"Ah," the Imposter said, lifting his flute of Madeira to Bradenton, "I canna deny London has her appeal," he said, shifting a smile to Elizabeth Seaton, "but Scotland has me heart, sir."

Elizabeth sighed.

"How poetic," Anna muttered.

"But you seem to enjoy your time abroad," a woman observed, and Anna snorted into her wine.

"Aye, of course," Ardencaple said. "In fact, I canna go abroad as often as I'd like, no' with me duties and all. Yet I suppose I travel enough to keep abreast of the news of acquaintances."

"Beyond England?" another guest asked.

"Oh, aye. The Continent, quite frequently."

Ah, so now it was the Continent, was it? If he'd been beyond the Strand, she'd be quite surprised. *"À quelle distance se trouve Ardencaple?"* she suddenly asked in French.

Lucy's head snapped up, and she openly glared down the table at Anna.

Ardencaple, however, seemed not the least bit disturbed and smiled cheerfully. "How far to Ardencaple? Why, Miss Addison, I confess, I havena measured it," he said, drawing a polite round of laughter.

"But you would put it very near the Highlands, wouldn't you?"

He glanced around at the others with a bit of smile as if he were patiently appeasing a child. "Aye, quite near."

"But the Highlands are so dreadfully large!" Anna blithely continued, smiling at the others. "Surely you can narrow its location for us?"

Ardencaple's smile was looking less and less charming. "If I said it was near Stirling, would that tell ye where she is, then?"

"Of course it would!" Lucy furiously insisted.

"Then my sister is a better student of geography than *I* am," Anna laughed. "I shall have to find it on my atlas," she said pleasantly, and picked up her fork. "And I suppose you must have a castle of some sort there at Ardencaple? One of those massive medieval structures?"

"Miss Addison!" Mr. Bradenton said, laughing. "Would you have us believe that you'd judge a man by the size of his *castle?*"

The gentlemen around the table laughed aloud at that, Ardencaple the loudest.

"Oh, I do beg your pardon, my lord," Anna said, nodding demurely to the Lying Scotsman as everyone began to eat. "It's just that I'm absolutely titillated by Scotland. I find it so frightfully interesting, what with all the old earldoms."

"Oh, me too!" Elizabeth Seaton avowed. "It seems a lovely place. Do you have family, Lord Ardencaple?" she asked, sparing Anna the necessity of doing so.

"Aye," he said. "Siblings and parents and even a dog. Miss Seaton, ye must send my congratulations to yer cook. The venison is delicious!"

Several agreed that it was and turned their attention to the dish.

Anna, however, was not the least bit put off and carefully laid her fork aside. "Come to think of it, I am quite certain I've heard the name Ardencaple," she said thoughtfully, tapping a finger against her bottom lip. "Ardencaple . . . isn't that a name closely aligned with the duke of Argyll?"

Ardencaple abruptly looked up. Surprisingly, Mr. Bradenton chimed in with a hearty, "Argyll! Yes, of course! I had occasion to meet his grace at a shoot just last autumn. Quite a lovely chap, really. Are you acquainted, my lord?"

Slowly, Ardencaple shifted his burning gaze from Anna to Bradenton and smiled. "I've had the pleasure of being introduced to his grace," he said amicably. "But I canna say we are close acquaintances."

"Really?" Anna said. "So there is no relation?"

"Perhaps his lordship has brought his family tree, Anna, so that we might all study it closely," Lucy said, to which several chuckled.

"That's exactly the thing we need!" Anna said brightly, and a few of the gentlemen laughed with her.

But not Ardencaple. If looks could kill, she'd be dead and quite deeply buried. Anna laughed, picked up her fork again, "I must beg your pardon, again, my lord. My curiosity has overcome good manners."

"No' at all," he said, for what else could he say? Anna smiled at him across the table. Ardencaple smiled back, but she could see the murderous glint in his eye.

She did not have another chance to goad him, for Bradenton began to talk about his family, which, Anna had to admit, was rather fascinating in and of itself, as no one knew much about him other than that he was quite wealthy and quite unmarried.

When the venison was cleared and the ices were served, the conversation deteriorated into little cliques, leaving Anna to try and make conversation with Fitzwater again. From where she sat, she could see Lucy and Drake in a deep tête-à-tête, and Ardencaple charming the silk drawers off Elizabeth Seaton and Barbara Lockhart. She was relieved when Lady Seaton reappeared and suggested the ladies withdraw so that the gentlemen could enjoy a smoke.

In the drawing room, Anna parked herself on a settee and watched as Lucy joined their mother and told her about Anna's behavior during supper. She knew exactly what Lucy was doing, because her mother kept looking aghast at her, and Lucy kept sneering.

When she saw Barbara Lockhart approaching her, she moved a little on the settee and made room. "Barbara, how well you look," she said politely as Barbara settled her large bottom on what was left of the settee.

"My father paid thirty pounds for this gown," she said as she attempted to straighten the feather in her hair that kept dipping over her eye.

"Shocking!" Anna obliged her.

Smiling, Barbara planted her pudgy hands on her

knees and looked about the room. "Wasn't supper lovely? I thought it was *lovely,*" she sighed.

"Yes, quite lovely."

"Ardencaple is lovely, too, isn't he?" she said. "So exotic, really."

"Mmm. Rather reminds me of Captain Lockhart."

"Does he, indeed? I hadn't thought of it!" Barbara said. Her brows knit in a frown. "He does rather resemble the captain, doesn't he?"

Yes, he did. Exactly how, Anna hadn't quite figured out. But she'd wager they were brothers. Cousins at the very least.

"He's quite taken with your sister, isn't he?"

What man in London wasn't? "I couldn't say, really."

"Well, I hope for his sake that he's not *too* smitten with her, for I think he shall be sorely disappointed."

Anna looked at Barbara. "Disappointed?"

Like a girl, Barbara covered her mouth and giggled. "Don't you *know,* Anna?" When Anna shook her head, she frowned. "Truly, you can't guess?"

Anna shook her head again.

Barbara playfully rolled her eyes, then grabbed Anna's hand. "Silly, Drake intends to offer for Lucy!"

Anna's mouth fell open. "No," she said low.

Barbara nodded fiercely. "I'm not to say a *word,* for I've been sworn to secrecy, you see, but really, what secrets can there be between two sisters? Well, *future* sisters," she clarified, nudging Anna a little. "You must promise me you won't mention a *word* to Lucy!"

"Barbara, are you *quite* certain?" Anna demanded.

"Of course! But it's not to happen for a fortnight, at the very least—Drake needs to tidy up some of

Nigel's affairs first. But as soon as he has, it's tickety-boo, off to speak with your father!"

When Anna did not react—other than to feel suddenly and terribly ill—Barbara giggled, nudged her again, and clasped her hand. "We're to be *sisters,* Anna!" she whispered happily.

Twelve

It was the most miserable affair Grif had ever suffered through in his life, thanks to the *diabhal* in the lovely dark green gown. If he'd been a little closer—say, within arm's reach—he would have happily wrung her neck.

Who in God's name did she think she was, questioning him like that? Did she think herself above the dictates of decorum? What exactly did she think gave her license to be so . . . so *unbearable?*

He'd taken his leave as soon as it was politely possible. Lady Seaton had been nonplussed by his quick departure, but Grif did not dare give the *diabhal* another inch, lest she expose him. And what was it, exactly, that the chit knew? Did she know more than that there was not, for all intents and purposes, an Ardencaple?

Disgusted, Grif arrived at Dalkeith House just after midnight. He stalked inside, wanting to express his anger to someone, but was met with cold silence. Growling beneath his breath, he tossed his hat and gloves and cloak aside and went in search of his compeers. A quick search of the ground floor turned up no one.

Grif's mood was growing blacker by the moment,

and he took the stairs two at a time. On the first floor, where he and Hugh had suites, he found no one. On the second floor, he found Miss Brody's room empty and moved on to Dudley's room.

Dudley was fast asleep, his snoring rattling the four walls. Striding to the bed, Grif put a hand on his shoulder and shook him. Dudley made a sound of disgruntlement, then rolled onto his side. Grif shook him again, only harder, and the old man came up like a shot, sputtering and grabbing at his nightcap. *"Chan fhaic thu na beanntan leis á cheò!"*

"Of course ye canna see the hills for the mist, Dudley! We're in *London!"* Grif said, shaking him again. "There are no hills, no mist!"

Dudley blinked. "Aye."

"Where is MacAlister?" Grif demanded.

Fully aware of his surroundings now, Dudley swung his skinny old legs over the side of the bed and stood gingerly, straightening his sleeping gown. "I canna say, sir. He departed shortly after ye did."

Mary Queen of Scots, he was going to kill Hugh with his bare hands one day—he could feel it in his bones. "And Miss Brody?"

Dudley blinked, looked up in surprise. "Has she gone?"

"Diah, how long have ye been abed, then!"

"I canna help it, Master Griffin! Me gout aches something fierce!" he said, grimacing.

God in heaven, his gout. Grif sighed, patted Dudley on the shoulder. "I beg yer pardon, Dudley. I'm a wee bit out of sorts, I reckon. 'Tis no' yer doing that MacAlister is a bloody rotten rogue!"

"Aye, sir," Dudley said, easing back onto the bed so that he could rub his knees.

With a wince of sympathy, Grif asked, "Is there anything I can do for ye, Dudley?"

The old man shook his head. "Fiona, *mo ghraidh,* she'd make a poultice for me joints, but I donna know how she did it."

Grif could hear the longing in his voice, and thought, for the first time since they'd come to London, that it was too much for the old man. "We must send ye home, Dudley," he said softly. "We didna intend to be gone so long, did we, more than two months now?"

Dudley smiled wryly, but shook his head. "Aye, I miss me Fiona, I do," he said. "But it's important that we find the beastie, sir. I wouldna feel right leaving ye to find it on yer own, I wouldna."

"Lay yer head down, Dudley, and donna think of it now," Grif said kindly. "There'll be enough fretting for us both on the morrow."

Dudley nodded and eased himself down.

Grif bade him good night and made his way downstairs, fetched a bottle of whiskey from the drawing room, then settled in the small parlor off the main entry. He removed his coat, his neckcloth, and waistcoat, and loosened the shirt at his throat. Then he settled onto a large, overstuffed chair, where he intended to wait all night if he must to have a word with Hugh.

As it turned out, it was all night and part of a day.

The sound of a female voice raised over a male voice woke Grif, and he came out of the chair, grimacing in pain at the horrible crick in his neck from sleeping in the chair. He staggered to his feet and to the door of the little parlor, blinking into the dim light where Hugh and Miss Brody were arguing something fierce, Dudley standing by, hopping from one foot to the next as he tried to stop them.

"God's blood, *MacAlister!*" Grif roared.

The three of them fell instantly silent and looked at Grif.

He glared at Hugh, who smiled unabashedly and pushed a hand through his hair. "Grif—"

"Save yer bloody breath," he said through clenched teeth.

Hugh started toward him, holding his hands up in innocence. "I've an explanation—"

"Aye, one that involves gambling and whoring, I'd wager."

"Now that's where ye are wrong, lad," he said pleasantly. "A wee bit of gambling, but no' whoring."

"How much did ye lose, then?"

Hugh shrugged. "A pittance. No' more than forty pounds."

Grif gave him a look of disgust, turned, and retreated into the foyer.

"Come now, Grif!" Hugh cried laughingly. "Surely ye'll give me a chance to explain!" He followed Grif inside, with Miss Brody and Dudley on his heels.

"Explain it, then," Miss Brody sniffed. "Tell his lordship how ye follow me about, sniffing at me skirts like a dog, then." She looked at Grif. "Yer lordship, I'm naught but a poor Irish girl. I'm only trying to earn a bit of money for me family in Ireland. I've a good reputation and I'll thank ye to help me keep it. Mr. MacAlister willna leave me be, what with his claims of love and devotion."

"Keara!" Hugh exclaimed, his arms wide. "Ye wouldna want to alarm his lordship with silly gossip!"

"I'm already quite alarmed, thank ye," Grif snapped. "I'd no' be even a wee bit surprised if Lady Worthall has sent for the constable by now!"

"*Ach*, that old bat's no' worth yer fretting," Hugh said dismissively. "I told her to mind her own affairs."

Grif lifted his aching head and glared at his old friend. "Ye did *what?*"

Hugh shrugged. "I've grown weary of her meddling, lad."

"Have ye lost yer bloody mind?" Grif exploded. "Have ye any idea what trouble she could bring if she were of a mind?"

"I havena lost me mind," Hugh shot back, his expression darkening. "I'm sick unto death of her! And how in God's name do ye expect me to sit about, waiting on ye hand and foot like yer bloody slave?"

"Ye agreed to be me valet!"

"Aye, but I didna agree to be a prisoner in this godforsaken house! I'll come and go as I please and I'll speak to whomever I desire!"

That was it, the last straw. Whether it was his fatigue or his general disgruntlement with the situation, Grif hardly knew. All he knew was that his feet were moving ahead of his brain, and he took a swing at Hugh without really thinking.

Hugh ducked his swing and lunged for him, but Grif easily sidestepped Hugh at the last moment, then fell on him. He heard Miss Brody cry out, heard Dudley plead with them to stop, but he and Hugh were upon one another, arms flailing, legs kicking, rolling about the carpet into furniture. He heard one crash, then another, felt a wooden chair as it fell onto his back, but his mind was wrapped around Hugh and his determination to kill him.

It wasn't until he heard Dudley shout, "Ye've a *caller*, milord," and felt a kick in the small of his back with another, desperately hissed, "*Caller!*" that he finally let go of Hugh's neckcloth, and Hugh let go his hair. For a moment, a very brief moment, the two men stared at one another, wide-eyed, as what had just happened sunk in. And then suddenly they were both desperately moving, clambering ungracefully to their feet.

Grif quickly wiped the blood from his mouth with the back of his hand and looked to the door.

And his heart stopped cold. *Cold.*

There, between a very angry-looking Miss Brody and a very frantic-looking Dudley, stood Miss Anna Addison, her bonnet dangling from her fingers, her parasol fallen to the floor in front of her, and her mouth agape.

There was nothing but a deadening silence, a silence that was filled with the sound of his heart pounding in his ears, as Grif could not seem to catch his breath.

Miss Addison was staring in horror at him. And at Hugh. And at Miss Brody, who had the cheek to eye her just as intently. It seemed like an eternity before Miss Addison at last dragged her gaze to Grif and said, rather unsteadily, "I beg your pardon, my lord, but the door was standing open."

Dudley, God bless him, was the first to come to his senses, and swooped down on her parasol. "It is I who must beg yer pardon, miss. Might I show ye to the drawing room where'd ye'd be a wee bit more comfortable?" he asked, inching toward the door. Miss Addison blinked up at Grif, and with a small nod fell in behind Dudley.

Grif looked at Hugh; Hugh looked at Grif. Grif slapped him on the shoulder. "What in God's name is the matter with ye? Mary Queen of Scots, we've done it now," he said, dipping to swipe up his coat. "Make yerselves scarce and I'll get rid of her," he said, and stalked out of the parlor, shoving his arms into his coat, then dragging his hand through his hair, trying to put some semblance of order to it.

As he neared the drawing room, Dudley stepped out, instantly withdrew a kerchief from his pocket, and thrust it at Grif.

"What the hell is she doing here?" Grif whispered.

"I couldna say, sir," Dudley said as he motioned to the corner of Grif's mouth where he had, obviously, missed some blood.

Grif swiped at it with the kerchief, thrust it back at Dudley, and put his hand on the door. "Stand by, then—I'll no' be long."

With that, he threw open the door, strode into the drawing room, and hands on hips, glared at Miss Addison. "What are ye doing here?"

Her spine stiffened and she lifted her chin. "I might ask the same of you."

"Ye might. But as ye are in *this* house, I suggest ye explain yerself."

"All right," she said, tossing her bonnet onto a couch. "I shall. I'll start with this: I know you are not Lord Ardencaple," she said, reaching into her reticule. "I know there is no such place as Ardencaple. I know what you've come for, and moreover, I know where it is."

She withdrew something from her reticule, walked to where he stood, and gestured for him to open his hand. In his upturned palm, she laid a tiny ruby.

Had the floor opened up and swallowed him whole, he could not have been more shocked. Speechless, Grif stared at the ruby, then slowly lifted his gaze. Miss Addison's chin was high, the spark in her eyes triumphant.

He was a proud man, and he'd as soon die than be bested by a woman. But by the same token, he was man enough to admit when he had been bested, and closing his fist tightly around the tiny ruby, he carefully closed the door behind him.

Thirteen

The moment he shut the door and leaned against it, staring at her like some enraged beast, Anna's heart twisted with fear. He was terribly disheveled, with a bruised eye and a cut lip. Some buttons from his shirt had been torn away and she could see the hair of his chest from across the room.

Worse, brutal fury had seeped into his green eyes.

"What is it, then," he asked in a horribly soft, horribly cold voice, "that ye think ye have, lass?"

Honestly, she wanted to tell him, wanted to explain that she really meant him no harm, but she was so fearful that she could not find her tongue.

Lord Ardencaple took one long, menacing step forward, his hands still clasped at his back, and Anna had the distinct impression it took some effort on his part to keep them there. "*What?*" he demanded, much louder. "What is it that ye will use to taunt me now? *Tell me!*" he commanded.

"I, ah . . . I have this . . . *thing*," she said shakily, and turned abruptly, walked to the other side of the room, as far away from him as she could get. "A, ah . . . *gold* thing," she clarified.

"And why would ye think this *gold* thing would interest me?"

Actually, that was the part Anna was hoping *he* could answer, but as he did not seem the least bit disposed to do any answering whatsoever, she pressed her trembling hands to her abdomen and said, "I don't know, really. But I also know you are not the first Scotsman to seek it."

That proclamation was met with a wintry silence, during which Anna pretended to be looking at the figurines on the mantel, but had closed her eyes to summon the courage that had been so damnably present not a half hour ago.

When it was apparent it had escaped her, she opened her eye, glanced over her shoulder—and jumped with a shriek. She'd not heard him move so close, but there he was, at her back, those glacial eyes boring through her.

"Describe this *thing,*" he demanded.

"I-I don't know what it is," she said, pushing down another lump of fear. "It's an ornamental gargoyle of some sort, but it's frighteningly hideous, with this gaping mouth," she exclaimed, gesturing wildly at her mouth, "and clawed feet, and a tail—"

Ardencaple moved so quickly that Anna could not react; with one lunge, he forced her against the wall, planted his arms on either side of her head, and glared down at her. *"Where. Is. It?"*

The veins in his neck and temple were bulging, his jaw was clenched, and Anna felt as if she'd been cornered by a raging beast. But as she was literally in a corner, there was nothing she could do but hold fast to her plan, or risk, by the look of him, certain death. "I won't tell you," she said low. "Not yet."

"WHERE IS IT?" he roared.

Anna shrieked, closed her eyes, and dipped her

head, hugging herself from his fury. "Put away for safekeeping."

He cried out as he slammed his fist into the wall. Anna twisted away, buried her face in her hands, and slid helplessly down the wall. But she felt him move away, and lifted her head as he turned back toward her, his chest heaving with fury. "Ye've no notion what ye *do!*" he railed at her. "Ye are a bloody fool!"

Her hand went to her throat as she tried to quell her panic, and she pushed herself up the wall.

Honestly, she didn't know what she had expected when she came here—but it had not been this. She had imagined he would be somewhat peeved, perhaps even ironically amused. She'd never expected such intense fury, not for a moment. He was always so . . . *cheerful.*

"On my word, I intend to give it to you," she said earnestly, and started again when he whirled about, pinning her to the wall with a pointed finger and a rabid glare.

"I don't mean you any harm!" she cried, darting to refuge behind a wing-back leather chair. "Truly, I don't!" she insisted as his eyes narrowed menacingly. "But . . . I am in need of your help, and I need that . . . that *thing* to assure you will give it to me!"

"Mo chreach—"

"If you will help me, Ardencaple, I will give it to you!"

"Help ye *what?*" he cried furiously. "Help ye torment me, aye? What could I *possibly* help ye with?"

"God in heaven," she said weakly, and in a moment of overwhelming regret, she covered her face with her hands. She wished she'd never been so foolish as to come here, wished she'd once, just *once*, listened to her practical nature.

"Diah," he muttered at last, and in a voice that was perhaps a tiny bit softer, he asked, "What sort of help is it that ye need, then?"

This had been a *horrible* idea, a wretched idea, but Anna had created an appalling quagmire from which she had no idea how to extract herself.

Except to go through with it. Walk on, as it were, into the fires of complete humiliation, for which she had no one to blame but herself. And it was the only course open to her, because she knew, looking at him now, in all his fury, that he'd *never* allow her to walk out of here now.

She drew a breath to steel herself. "I would like to, ah . . . sort of gain the, ah . . . *affection* of Mr. Lockhart," she stammered, and risked a glance at him. "And I would like for you to, ah . . . I mean to say that what I hope is . . ."

He was getting impatient. His hands were on his hips, his head down.

"I suppose there is no polite way to say it," she said, more to herself than him, and took another breath and said in a rush, "I would like you to teach me how to seduce him. A-And . . . keep my sister quite occupied."

The anger bled from Ardencaple's face and was replaced with a ghastly look of shock. He blinked rapidly, as if he were seeing something quite hideous. His mouth dropped open and he gaped at her for what seemed an eternity before he lowered himself into a chair, released his breath in one long *whoosh,* and dragged both hands through his hair. "Ye've lost yer bloody mind," he groaned.

Her fingers dug into the wingbacks so tightly that they cramped, but Anna could not move, could not even think.

"God blind me, lass," he said quietly, "but ye are indeed *às a chiall,"* he continued, and as he made a whirling gesture at his head, there was no need for him to translate that he thought she was impossibly daft, gone completely around the bend.

This was not exactly the way she'd pictured things when she'd imagined sailing into this man's home, imperiously informing him that she had determined what he was about, then smoothly suggesting she'd allow him to go scot-free (pausing there to laugh lightly at the *scot* part of that) in exchange for a little help.

Instead, she was standing behind a chair, feeling ridiculously childish and terribly spinsterish . . . so much so that she sighed and let go the chair, wearily walked around and fell into it, across from Ardencaple, sullen and gloomy.

He, too, had given up all outward appearances of decorum, and had turned in his chair, slung one muscular leg over the arm, and had propped his chin on his fist as he stared blankly into space. He looked rather ragtag, really, what with the blood and bruises, and his square jaw was shadowed by the growth of his beard. But he also looked potently masculine; his body, all long and muscular legs and arms, seemed almost animal-like in its strength, and now Anna wondered what in heaven's name she'd gone and asked this lusty, robust man to do. Perhaps she *was* mad.

A soft groan escaped her; like a wild animal, he jerked his head toward the sound. "How did ye find it, if I may ask?" he said, the shock and fury gone, replaced with something like surrender.

"I've heard you ask after Lady Battenkirk and someone named Amelia. And . . . I knew that Lady Battenkirk was abroad, so I paid a call to her niece . . . and that was when I saw it."

"Saw it," he repeated, shaking his head. "And how, then, would ye know what *it* was?"

"Because," she said quietly, "during the Season just past, I had occasion to meet Captain Lockhart—at the Lockhart ball, actually. I, ah . . . found him in a small study, where he was . . . well, standing before an open armoire looking at the contents, and . . . and I saw it then. And when I saw it again in Mrs. Merriman's house, I recalled it immediately, because it was really rather . . . grotesque," she said. "Mrs. Merriman had taken possession of it when Lady Battenkirk's good friend, Amelia Litton, died last year. She was more than happy to sell it to me for a few crowns."

Ardencaple sighed wearily.

"And I knew instantly what you'd come for—"

"And why, exactly, did ye ever think *I'd* come for *anything?*" he sharply interrupted her.

"Because," she said softly, "you resemble Captain Lockhart. And you wouldn't tell me where Ardencaple was—as if I were incapable of understanding . . . so I was quite determined to find it on my own, in my books. But I *couldn't* find it, and when I researched the name Ardencaple in my father's peerage papers, I discovered that the name was no longer in use—that it had been subsumed by the titles of the duke of Argyll."

For some strange reason, that made Ardencaple—or whoever he was—laugh. It was a bitter laugh, and he swung his leg off the arm of the chair and leaned forward, his arms braced on his knees, his hands dangling between his legs, and smirked at Anna. "Have ye any idea, then, how *hard* we endeavored to establish that name?"

"Who?"

He laughed again and stood abruptly, and walked to the window. "What, did ye no' determine *who* in all yer nosing about?"

"No," she said truthfully. "Not entirely, that is."

"And ye thought, did ye, that ye'd stroll into me house, and casually barter with what rightfully belongs to me and mine?" he asked, turning partially to see her.

Actually . . . in a word, yes. She nodded.

He was suddenly moving toward her, and Anna instinctively jumped up, tried to get away, but once again, he was far too quick, and grabbed her upper arm, jerked her around to him, and then grabbed her nape with his hand so that he could force her face close to his. "And ye thought, did ye, that ye'd practice yer bloody seduction on me, aye? Are ye so pathetic that ye must stoop to *this?*"

It sounded so contemptible, so reprehensible, that it sparked a flash of anger in her. What she'd done was ill-advised—all right—perhaps the most ridiculous thing she'd ever done—but it didn't change the way she felt about Drake, or her sense of desperation that he'd offer for Lucy if she didn't somehow prove herself to him, and she felt a shock of indignant outrage that this . . . this *liar* would judge her.

"Yes!" she cried, and tried to jerk her arm free of his grasp.

He tightened his grip on her arm as he moved her

head closer to his face. His gaze dipped to her lips and he whispered, *"Are ye certain ye know what ye ask?"*

That question stoked something wildly hot inside her; she looked into his glittering eyes and answered breathlessly, *"No."*

He laughed and put his mouth against her cheek. With a soft, long sigh, he held her tightly and moved, slowly and languidly, grazing her ear with his lips, flicking his tongue against her lobe.

Heat rapidly spread through her; Anna gasped at the sensation, but that only made him chuckle coldly, and he dipped his head lower as he forced hers to one side. His lips touched her neck—burned it, actually—moving slowly to the line of her jaw while Anna shuddered in his grasp. Her breath was coming faster, in little shallow pants, as his lips moved closer to hers, dangerously close to hers, and her head filled with the memory of that kiss on the veranda.

And then his lips touched hers, landing softly, full, and wet against her dry lips, and as he casually drew her bottom lip between his teeth, she couldn't breathe, couldn't catch her breath, and felt precariously close to collapsing.

"No, I think ye donna know," he murmured. "Ye've no idea what ye've done, Anna Addison," he murmured, and kissed her again, only deeper this time, dipping his tongue into her mouth and sparking an inferno within her. One hand slid up her rib cage to her breast, and he cupped it, kneaded it carefully, dragging his thumb over the thin fabric that covered her nipple and back again.

Anna felt as if she were floating beneath him, riding on some cloud of burning sensation, hurtling down some slope into debauchery.

Then Grif suddenly lifted his head and pushed her away.

His abruptness stunned her; she felt her pulse racing, felt her heart leaping in her chest.

He looked at her darkly, the glint in his green eyes hard. And then he pivoted about, strode to the door, and flung it open. "MacAlister!" he shouted.

The dark-haired man she had seen fighting with Ardencaple came striding in, eyeing Anna suspiciously "Aye?"

Hands on hips, Ardencaple shook his head and said something in his language. MacAlister's eyes bulged at whatever he said, and they had what sounded like quite a colorful exchange, Ardencaple's voice rising, the other man's brows going higher and higher, almost to his hairline.

When Ardencaple finished, a long moment passed before MacAlister could look fully at Anna.

And when he did, he burst out laughing.

Fourteen

That evening, a morose Dudley, a resigned Grif, and a highly amused Hugh dined on a delicious roast, arguing about what Grif was to do.

"Ye canna go through with it," Dudley pleaded. "'Tis no' right! 'Tis untoward, sir!

"What choice have I? If she is truly in possession of that accursed beastie, what can I do? We bartered Mared for it, Dudley! And we canna afford this charade forever—our funds run low as it is," he said, with a frown for Hugh. "What we've no' lost to Hugh's gambling—"

"Aye, rotten luck," Hugh muttered.

"We've spent on clothing and food and horses and appearances," Grif continued. "We pass each day in danger of being discovered and carted off to Newgate Prison to walk the treadmill. So I ask ye again, what bloody choice do I have?"

"None," answered Hugh without a moment's hesitation, and grinned. "*Ach,* but what a fortunate man ye are! She's a bonny lass—I'll teach her if ye like."

"Ye're a bloody scoundrel," Grif muttered. "But donna be fooled by her pleasing shape—'tis the shape of the *diabhal,* I swear it!" He pushed his plate aside, propped his face in his hands. "The worst of it is I've no' the slightest notion of how a woman seduces a man."

"Quite simple," Hugh opined, leaning back and casually clasping his hands behind his head. "'Tis all in the way she moves, lad."

"How so?"

"Ye know what I mean—the way she *moves.*"

Grif exchanged a look with Dudley; Hugh sighed and came to his feet. "Watch me, then," he said, and stepping away from the table, he proceeded to walk the length of the table, jerking his hips in a motion that looked almost painful.

"Mi Diah," Dudley moaned.

But Grif burst out laughing. "Mary Queen of Scots, ye look as if ye've something lodged in yer arse!"

"'Tis no' the walk," Dudley said, waving a hand at Hugh as he resumed his seat in something of a huff. "'Tis the voice. A woman's voice is soft and soothing as a sweet dream. And her laugh . . . so delicate, like the wee flowers that sprout after a spring's rain." With a sigh, the old man looked longingly into space.

Grif and Hugh exchanged a look of surprise.

Dudley suddenly seemed to remember himself, and looked sheepishly at the two of them before straightening up in his seat, tugging at his waistcoat self-consciously. "Aye, I'm an old man, that I am, but I'm a man nonetheless."

"As for me . . . I'm partial to the skin," Grif said, still grinning at Dudley. "Smooth like velvet, pale as moonlight."

"And her scent," Hugh added wistfully. "A woman's scent will make a man's blood boil, aye? And her shape, mind ye—there's naugh' more pleasing than the shape of a woman's bum. Or her bosom."

"Or her delicate hands," Dudley added.

"Aye, and donna forget her neck," Grif added in a

murmur. "And her smile. Ye'd think the sun rose in a woman's smile, ye would."

"What of the eyes?" Hugh asked, motioning absently to his own eyes. "A woman has a way of looking at ye that makes ye believe she can see all the way to yer toes, aye?"

All three men sighed then, lost in their individual thoughts, their contemplative silence broken only by the entry of Miss Brody, who walked through the service door only to stop dead in her tracks. She looked at the three of them. "What's gone on?" she asked in a lilting Irish brogue. "Did the roast no' agree with ye?"

The three men turned and looked at her, each of them smiling wolfishly.

Later that night, Grif lay awake into the morning hours racking his brain for a way out of his latest predicament with Anna Addison. And when no solution came to him, he lay awake until dawn trying to think exactly how he might go about teaching a woman to seduce a man.

It wasn't that he hadn't been seduced in his life, for certainly he had. But even in those instances he had been blatantly seduced, the complete seduction had been more of an air, an unspoken, impalpable aura of sex that engulfed him, than it was a single act.

And he could not, for the life of him, imagine that aura surrounding Miss Addison.

He was waiting for her promptly at three o'clock, the agreed-upon time, anxious to have it over and done with. Dudley showed her to the main drawing room, where they would commence this loathsome task.

Grif was seated in an overstuffed damask chair

when she came in, his legs crossed, his fingers templed when she entered.

She looked, he thought, remarkably improved from yesterday's unpleasant encounter—meaning, of course, the demon sparkle had returned to her copper eyes. She was dressed in a somber brown gown with sleeves puffed up at the shoulders and a demure neckline that hid her bosom. The gown was not quite floor-length, and he could see delicate slippers peeking out from underneath the heavily ribboned hem. In spite of knowing little about the art of seduction, he knew this—she did not look like a woman who intended to seduce a member of the opposite sex.

Nevertheless, he nodded curtly as Dudley shut the door behind her, and kept his expression carefully indifferent. "Miss Addison."

"My, ah . . . lord," she said, and tossed her gloves, bonnet, and reticule to a settee. "I beg your pardon, but now that we have embarked on a new arrangement, might you have another . . . perhaps *authentic* . . . name?" she asked.

"Ah," he said pleasantly. "I see ye've wasted no time in removing yer gloves, as it were. If ye feel ye have a need to address me at all, then ye may as well know me as Lockhart."

That prompted a narrowing of her eyes and she flashed a devilish smile like the spawn she was. "I *knew* it," she breathed, her voice full of self-righteousness. "I *knew* there was a resemblance!"

Grif shrugged. "Yer suspicions are thus confirmed."

"And your Christian name, might I ask?"

He sighed. "Griffin. Griffin Finnius Lockhart. Grif, as I'm known."

"You're the captain's brother, aren't you?" she

asked, grinning triumphantly at his nod. "And Drake Lockhart's cousin, then?"

"Aye," he said wearily.

Her smile faded into a puzzled frown. "I don't understand—why doesn't he know who you are?"

He debated what to tell her. "The Scottish Lockharts are estranged from the English Lockharts, and have been for a very long time. Now, then—"

"But even so, why should you hide your true identity? And why should your brother want that horrid gargoyle? And why—"

"Ach, ye ask too many questions, lass!"

She blinked. "Are you an *outlaw?*" she whispered excitedly.

"No, I am no' an outlaw," he said gruffly. "If ye must know, I have hidden me identity from Lockhart because we are engaged in something of a family dispute. So now ye might put yer imagination to rest."

"If it's a family dispute, why won't you just go to him?" she asked, brightening. "He's really very fair, and very thoughtful—"

"Did ye come to resolve me family's dilemma, or to learn the art of seduction?" he demanded.

She paused and seemed to debate that for a long moment. "The latter," she said at last.

"Very well, then, Anna—"

"Miss Addison will do," she said pertly.

"Ah, but if I am to teach ye to seduce a man, *Miss Addison,* it might be a sight easier if I knew ye by something a wee bit more . . . intimate."

She pursed her lips, considering it.

"Anna," he repeated softly, and pushed himself to his feet, clasped his hands behind his back, and moved toward her. "What a pretty name for the *diabhal.*"

She frowned. "That's hardly polite."

"I beg yer pardon, lass, but I believe we've gone well past *polite.*"

Anna folded her arms across her middle. "Then might we agree," she suggested in a sweet voice that belied the look in her eye, "that you'll not speak in your native tongue? I confess to feeling rather at a loss when you do."

"Do ye, indeed?" he asked, and slowly circled her, openly and honestly admiring her feminine form. "We canna have ye feeling at a loss, can we? After all, ye hold all the cards, do ye no'? I'll use the language of the Highlands only when I refer to yer body, so as no' to upset ye, aye?"

"I beg your pardon?" she demanded stiffly.

Grif laughed at her. "Come now," he chided her as he stepped up behind her, so close that his lips could, if he were of a mind, brush the crown of her head. "Ye canna ask me to teach ye how to seduce a man and no' imagine it would mean the involvement of yer body, could ye. . . . *Anna?*" he whispered, and casually, softly, brushed the hair from the nape of her neck so that he could see the smooth column.

She flinched at the touch of his hand. "You . . . you need not be so bold," she said, and stepped forward, walking away from him.

"Need no' be so *bold?*" He laughed incredulously. "*Mo chreach,* Anna! Ye've taught me the very meaning of the word, ye have!"

Her back still to him, she lifted a delicate hand to her nape, to the place he'd just touched. "You may think me bold, sir, but you cannot truly appreciate my situation." She dropped her hand and turned to face him. "And frankly, I don't understand why a woman can't ask to learn such things. It's not as if we are taught seduction along with geography or embroidery."

Grif snorted.

She sighed with exasperation. "Nor will I attempt to make you understand, for I fear it is beyond your capability, and we do have our sworn agreement, so if you please, might we begin?"

"Certainly," he said, and returned to the chair, irreverently fell into it, his legs sprawled before him, and tried to conjure up something—*anything*—to say.

She stood there rather anxiously, watching him, waiting for some signal.

Grif lifted one brow. "Well, then?"

"Yes?"

"A woman is seductive when she tends to a man's needs," he blurted, and thought it not a bad start, all in all.

It certainly flustered Miss Anna Addison. She glanced around the room, perhaps looking for a footman. "Ah . . . what is it you need?" she asked uncertainly.

Aye, this had the potential to be quite entertaining, Grif suddenly realized. "Do ye mean to imply ye canna recognize a man's needs, lass?" he asked, feigning shock.

She blushed and looked at her hands.

"A spot of whiskey to begin."

She glanced around again, as if she expected the footman to magically appear, and when he did not, she moved woodenly to the sideboard, studied the decanters there, and finally selected one. Not the whiskey he might have chosen, but there would be time for that.

She looked around for a glass, rattling the crystal glassware in the process, and found a tot, and poured the whiskey to the rim. With the tot firmly in hand, she turned round and marched toward him, her expression one of consternation, as if she had never served another human being in her life. Holding the tot as far away from her as she could, she placed it on the small walnut end table directly next to Grif.

A savory thought occurred to him—while he might not know the art of seduction, he had a much keener sense for the art of retaliation. And he saw an opportunity now, a chance to punish the strumpet for ever having heaped this predicament on him.

Aye, this *would* be entertaining.

Grif glanced at the tot, shook his head as he made a clucking sound of disapproval, and frowned up at her.

"What?" she demanded.

"Ye think that *seductive*, do ye? Ye bring a man his whiskey and put it away from ye as if it were a two-headed snake?"

She blinked, looked at the tot, then at him again, delightfully confused.

"Pick it up," he commanded her.

With a bit of hesitation and a bigger frown, she picked it up.

"Now, then," he said with a wicked smile, "come down on yer knees before me and put it just there," he said, nodding at the table.

Her mouth dropped open. "You cannot possibly be serious!"

Grif shrugged nonchalantly. "Very well, then. If ye donna want yer bloody English Lockhart, we might end this farce now, aye?"

At the very least, his suggestion had the desired effect of quelling her protestations. She stared at him, then the tot, then pulled a face as if it truly pained her.

"Kneel before me and put the tot there," he softly commanded her.

Judging by the murderous way she looked at him, Anna was having a difficult time making herself obey him, and Grif could not possibly have been more amused. With her eyes glaring daggers at him, she glanced down to where his legs were sprawled before him, then looked at the table. She tried to dip before his knees, but Grif moved his legs, indicating she should kneel *between* them.

With a bit of sidestepping and general wrangling, she at last knelt between his knees, put the tot on the table next to him.

"Is that all, then?" he asked.

"What could *possibly* be left undone?" she hissed at him.

"Yer kind and thoughtful inquiry as to anything else I might require," he suggested pleasantly.

"You're insane," she said through clenched teeth.

"No, lass, that would be ye. Go on, then. *Inquire,*" he said, his smile fading.

"Is there anything else you require?" she repeated through clenched teeth.

"Hmm . . . no' particularly pleasant, but it will do for the time being," he said. "Aye, lass, I should very much like ye to rub me feet."

Her shock was brief; her lovely coppery eyes suddenly flashed with anger, and she bounced to her feet, staggering back away from him. "You are a . . . a *blackguard!*" she cried. "You are *toying* with me!"

Her indignant fury made Grif laugh. Her little gasp

of rage at his laughter only made him laugh that much harder, and while he tried to contain himself, she whirled about, stalked to the settee where she'd put her things, and, grabbing them up, started for the door.

Somehow Grif managed to come out of his chair and reach her before she could escape. He grabbed her upper arm and forced her about. "Ye'll no' leave, lass," he said, still trying to swallow his laughter. "Ye'll no' fly off in such a huff."

"I did not come here to be humiliated!"

"No, no, of course no'," he said, the laughter in him dying. "Ye came to merely extort."

The woman had the good sense not to deny it, but she yanked her arm from his grasp. "As I said," she said to the floor, "I have reasons you could not possibly understand."

"I donna want to understand yer bloody reasons," he said coldly. "I just want to be done with this as soon as possible, claim what is rightfully mine, and return to Scotland." But that, he realized, was easier said than done, and he turned away from her, stalked to the table and the tot of whiskey, picked it up, and tossed it down his throat.

"I'm not trying to be indistinct," she said. "It's really rather a long and convoluted explanation, that's all."

He barely glanced at her as he went to the sideboard to help himself to more whiskey.

"I . . . I don't mean to be difficult, truly."

"Then donna *be* difficult," he suggested. "'Tis no' as if *I* wanted this," he reminded her, and poured another whiskey, tossed that down, and set the glass aside.

"I understand how you must . . . *perceive* this," she said, waving vaguely to the room. "But I am rather determined."

Grif shrugged at her absurd attempt to justify this.

"So if you would," she said, gesturing nervously at him, "kindly stop looking at me as if I am some sort of . . . doxy."

He said nothing, just watched her fidget with the watch pinned primly to her collar. When it seemed as if she might faint from nerves, Grif said casually, "Are we quite finished for the day, then?"

"I, ah . . . I don't . . . I suppose—"

"Good. If ye'd excuse me?"

Anna blinked big doe eyes at him, and looked, unbelievably, as if she'd been hurt. *Hurt!* The woman swam in an ocean of contradiction! She turned away, started for the door. He watched the way her gown moved around her shapely hips and a thought suddenly came to him.

"One thing, Anna," he said.

She stopped mid-stride, glanced at him over her shoulder.

"Yer appearance. . . . When ye return on the morrow, wear something a wee bit less"—he paused there, searching for the right word—"priggish."

"Priggish?" she exclaimed, looking down at her brown gown.

"Aye, priggish. Ye look like a vicar's wife, ye do."

"But this gown is the latest from Paris—"

"I donna care how fashionable or expensive it is. It doesna attract a man's eye."

She glanced up, her eyes wide with wonder for the first time since Grif had met her, as if she had no notion of what a man found attractive.

"On the morrow, wear something that allows a man to catch a glimpse of the promise beneath," he said gruffly, and looked down at his feet, waiting for her to be gone.

There was no sound, nothing but silence.

When he could no longer abide the silence, he glanced up, saw that she was rooted to the floor, staring at him with those lovely eyes, eyes which, for some reason, unnerved him. "Are ye still here, then?" he asked.

That seemed to wake her from her trance, and she unthinkingly put a hand to her bodice, dipped her head demurely. "No," she said softly. "No, I was just leaving." And with one last, curious glance at him, she walked out the door.

Fifteen

How Anna managed to survive the remainder of that day and evening in the company of her family, as if nothing had happened, was just short of miraculous—the encounter with the Lying Scotsman had left her breathless, almost feverish, and she could think of nothing but those cold green eyes, the way his breath felt on her neck and his hand felt on her skin.

As she sat in the drawing room, surreptitiously looking at her family around her, she wondered if any of them had ever known someone as unwholesomely prurient as Griffin Lockhart. What a pity for them if they hadn't.

Just thinking about him had her feeling hot again, and she absently fanned herself as she pretended to peruse the bookshelves of the drawing room while her mother and father played a round of cards, Lucy and Bette pored over the latest fashion plates from Paris, and David, Lord Featherstone, Bette's husband, sat quietly reading before the fire.

"By the bye," David said after a time, "Bette and I are planning a weekend affair at Featherstone Manor at the end of the month. A gathering of friends before it becomes unseemly for Bette to be about town."

"I've never understood why pregnancy is *unseemly,* my lord," Anna said. "It's not as if the miracle of birth is a secret. Practically all of us came into this world as the result of a pregnancy, save Lucy."

"Anna," her mother said, "it is impolite to speak of such things."

"What do you mean, *'save Lucy'?"* her younger sister demanded.

"Anna, love," her father said patiently as he dipped his head to have a look at his cards over the rims of his spectacles, "you mustn't tease your sister so. You know how sensitive she is."

"Why is it impolite, Mother?" Anna asked, ignoring Lucy. "It's perhaps the most natural thing in the world! Why should anything God gives us be considered impolite?"

"No matter the customs of our society," David interjected, "we are nevertheless determined to host an affair at the end of the month."

"We plan to invite all the bachelor gentlemen!" Bette added in a singsong voice.

"Why?" Lucy pouted as she flipped the pages of fashion plates. "I am forbidden to entertain even the smallest of offers until Anna is offered for. You might as well save yourself the expense."

"They will not be invited for *your* benefit," Bette said cheerfully. "But for Anna's."

Anna laughed at Bette's teasing; Lucy made a face.

"That's lovely they are invited for Anna's benefit!" Mother exclaimed happily. "After all, Lucy, you are the most determined of all of us to see her married."

"No one wishes it more than me," Lucy said with a huff. "But she'll not receive an offer from any of the gentlemen Bette shall invite."

"And why not?" Mother asked. "She's as accomplished and favored as you, and as they all can't offer for *you,* Lucy, it stands to reason that at least one of them might see their way to offering for Anna," Mother defiantly argued.

Lucy gave a very unladylike snort to that, and made a show of busying herself with the fashion plates.

Anna just shook her head and returned her attention to the books before her. Actually, a weekend at Featherstone was just the thing, really—just the image of Drake Lockhart sleeping nearby made her smile, and she didn't give a damn what Lucy thought of it.

But it was not the thought of Drake sleeping nearby that brought the peculiar heat to her face again. Not *that* Lockhart at all, and she absently fanned herself again.

The next afternoon, at quarter past three, Anna was at the back stoop in the mews of the house on Cavendish Street, still shaken after the spectacular misfortune of having run into Lady Worthall on the street. She had, of course, been forced to make up an excuse for being in this part of town on such a dreary and rain-soaked day. If she was discovered calling on a bachelor gentleman, unescorted . . . she'd be painted a loose woman.

"Calling on an old friend," she had answered politely when the meddlesome woman inquired.

"Who?" Lady Worthall demanded loudly, pretending she was deaf.

"A *friend,"* Anna said again. "But I think I am quite mistaken—I believe she must be on the *other* end of Cavendish Street," she said, and turned away, as if studying the other end of the street.

"If you tell me who, dear, perhaps I can help you," Lady Worthall insisted.

"Aha! I *am* quite mistaken!" Anna said gaily. "Thank you for your help," she said, smiling brightly as she reached out to squeeze the woman's hand. "Good day!" And with that, she pivoted about, went marching off in the opposite direction, and did not stop until she had gone at least a quarter of a mile. Only then did she circle around, using her umbrella as a shield, walking through the alleys and mews that meandered through the neighborhood.

When she at last had managed to slip into the mews undetected, she knocked frantically, watching the street entrance.

The old man who had seen her in yesterday opened the door with a frown. Anna paid him no mind, but quickly stepped past him into the dark interior and closed her umbrella. "I beg your pardon, sir, but there is a frightfully intrusive woman who lives somewhere close by."

"Directly adjacent, she does."

Anna glanced up at the old man in shock as the thought that Lady Worthall could be so close sunk into her brain. "Are you quite certain? Lady Worthall?"

"Aye, miss, I've naugh' been more certain of anything in me life," he said grumpily. "If ye will please follow me, his lordship awaits."

His *lordship,* such that he was, was waiting, all right, standing at the windows, his hands at his back, his legs braced far apart. He turned sharply when she was shown in the door by the old man, a frown on his face. "Ye're *late.*"

"I beg your pardon, but I was unavoidably detained by Lady Worthall."

"Lady Worthall!" he exclaimed wildly. "Did she see ye enter here, then?"

"Of course not!" Anna shot back. "Do you take me for a fool?" Instantly, she held up a hand. "I will thank you not to answer that," she added before he could speak, and angrily tossed aside her cloak, bonnet, and umbrella. "Honestly, Mr. *Lockhart,* I'm not any happier about this than you! I was forced to lie, and then it began to rain, and my slippers are near to ruined!"

"I donna give a damn about yer slippers," he said. "But if that old battle-ax discovers ye are here, there'll be hell to pay for it, mark me."

"I am quite accustomed to there being talk of me, sir. I assure you that if she is to mention seeing me abroad, it will not come as a surprise to—"

"God blind me, then, I'm no' speaking of *ye,* I am speaking of me!"

"You?" she said, pausing in her struggle to remove her gloves. "Why? I'm the only one who knows that you are not who you say!"

"Never ye mind *why,*" he said gruffly, and peered out the window before drawing the drapes shut. As that cut out what precious little light was left of this awful day, he went about lighting several candles.

Anna watched him as he moved about. He was dressed in a navy coat and gold embroidered waistcoat, his neckcloth expertly tied—a dashing figure of a man, the sort of figure that made her feel oddly light-headed.

When he had lit the last candle, he turned to face her again, put his hands on his trim waist, and studied her closely. "I told ye to dress in something less priggish, did I no'?"

Confused, Anna looked down at her gown. It was a pale blue silk, adorned with tiny pink rosebuds and gathered at her back into a long train; it had cost her father a small fortune to commission. "But I *did* dress less priggishly!"

With a shake of his head, Lockhart strode across to where she stood. "A man likes to see a *wee* hint of what is beneath." He frowned at her bosom, then lifted his hand as if he meant to touch her bodice. Anna froze. He hesitated. She let out a quick sigh of relief.

And then he did it. Just put his hand on the bodice of her gown—dug *into* her bodice, actually, his fingers curling around the fabric and his knuckles sinking into the round flesh of her breasts. She gasped; he frowned and forced the bodice of her gown down, so that it just barely covered her breasts.

"There," he said, more to himself, and pulled his fingers from her dress. "Aye, *there* ye are," he said again. He had not, as yet, lifted his gaze from her bosom, and in between her shock and the shaking of her knees, she caught her breath and held it.

He stood there like a mute, staring at her breasts for what seemed an eternity, but then suddenly stepped back and away from her as he lifted his gaze to her eyes. "There, then, do ye see, lass? A woman's bosom is to be politely admired . . ." His gaze flicked to her breasts again. "No' hidden away," he muttered, and abruptly turned away.

Anna released her breath.

"Perhaps ye should bring a slate and take notes of what I tell ye. When ye are in the presence of a man ye admire," he said, his back to her, "ye'd do yerself well to use such a . . . bonny bosom to yer advantage."

"Use it?"

"Aye. To catch his eye."

"By exposing myself?" a perplexed Anna asked.

"No' expose them—*Diah!* A man doesna want to *see* them until he has the lass in his bed. But he very much wants to *imagine*, and he needs a wee bit of help in that regard!" He glanced at her over his shoulder. "Ye've no idea what I mean, aye?" he asked, frowning a little, and pivoted about, once again closing the distance between them.

And once again, before Anna could determine what he was about, he grabbed her hand in his, then snaked an arm around her back so that hand was on the small of her back, and pulled her into his chest as if they were dancing.

"*What* are you doing?" she demanded.

He grinned, a boyish, devilish grin. "I'm pretending to stand up with ye, lass. And ye may pretend ye coerced me into doing so, if ye prefer—"

"I did *not* coerce you!"

"*Uist!* Ye complain too much!" he said, and stepped backward, awkwardly dragging her with him. "All right, then, pretend ye are dancing with yer dandy Mr. Lockhart, will ye, light as a fairy on yer pretty little feet, and ye'd like him to pay close attention to what ye say. How, then, do ye drag his attention away from yer bonny sister across the room?"

She frowned as he moved backward, dragging her along. "It's quite impossible to pretend anything without at least the hint of music."

"*Ach,* Anna! Can ye no' use just a wee bit of yer imagination? We've only begun to dance!" He smiled; his gaze dipped to her bosom again. "Go on, then," he said, his voice softer. "How do ye gain his attention?"

"Oh, I don't know," she said irritably. "I suppose I should kneel between his knees."

He smiled lopsidedly at that. "That would undoubtedly gain his attention. But no' the sort I think ye want."

"Ah. So that lesson only applies in the delivery of a whiskey, is that it?"

"That is no' the only thing it applies to, but ye will require many more lessons ere we broach the other arts for which yer knees are useful."

Anna blushed furiously at that, and he laughed. "Shall we try again, then? How do ye gain a man's attention?"

"Oh all right!" She tried to find her feet without music, stumbling a little as he shifted directions and forced her backward. "I suppose I'd say something like . . . 'You seem to enjoy dancing, sir.'"

Grif suddenly paused in his strange little dance, looked at her as if he expected her to say more. "Is that the best ye can do, then?"

She thought about it. "Yes," she said with a firm nod. "If I make polite conversation with a gentleman, he should respond in kind."

Grif sighed heavenward, as if she were intentionally taxing him. *"'If ye make polite conversation, a gentleman should respond?'"* he mimicked her. "If ye want a man to *see* only ye, to *think* of only ye, then ye must do more than make polite conversation!"

"Really?" she said uncertainly. "What more should I do?"

"Mary Queen of Scots," he groused. "Mind what I do now. Do ye see how far away I hold ye from me?"

"Yes. A proper distance."

"Aye. 'Tis a proper distance for grandmothers and spinsters. But if ye want him to hold ye close like a lover, then ye will move just so," he said, prompting her with a hand at the small of her back, pushing her closer to him. Anna took one step. Then two, at his urging, and a third, so that now her bosom was brushing against his coat.

He grinned appreciatively. "*Now* ye have me undivided attention. And ye say . . . ?"

"I say . . . 'Do you enjoy dancing?' "

"No, no! Ye look up into me eyes, through those lovely lashes . . . lean forward now, lean forward . . . aye, there ye have it! And say, *'Ye're a bloody fine dancer, Mr. Lockhart,'* " he said in a falsetto voice while batting his lashes. " *'What other talents might ye be hiding from me, then?'* "

Anna couldn't help herself. She burst into laughter.

"What?" he demanded.

"What other talents might you be *hiding?*" she repeated, and laughed again.

"Then give me one better!" he challenged her. "Show me how ye'd gain yer love's attention, and God blind me if ye mention the bloody weather!"

She laughed again, laughed deeply at her situation, which suddenly seemed ridiculously absurd.

With a dangerous grin, Lockhart yanked her into his chest, holding her so tightly that she could scarcely catch her breath. "Ah, there ye are," he said low. "A bonny laugh ye have, Anna."

That was the moment Anna felt something inside her trip and fall, something come clean away from all the snares and traps and tangles of the propriety in which she'd been steeped all these years. And as he began to move, she pressed into him as he had shown her, looked up at him from beneath her lashes as he'd directed, and said, in a purring voice, "My, *my*, sir, how well you move us about the dance floor! One can't help but wonder if you move as well in other, more intimate circumstances," she said, and let her lips stretch into a soft smile.

It worked. Grif's grin faded; he slowed his step a little and blinked down at her for a moment. But that dangerous smile slowly appeared again, starting in his eyes and casually reaching his lips. "If ye were to pose such a question to me, lass, I'd say, 'As fast or as slow, as soft or as hard as ye'd want, *leannan.* Pray tell, how would ye want?'"

The tingling in her groin was a signal that she was on perilous ground. Anna looked into his green eyes, so dark and so deep that she couldn't quite determine if this was a game they were playing or something far more dangerous. And her good sense, shaped and controlled from years of living among high society, quietly shut down, allowing the real Anna, the Anna who yearned to be loved, to be held and caressed and adored and know all manner of physical pleasure, to slide deeper into the circle of his arms.

"I don't rightly know *how* I'd want, sir, other than to say . . ." Her voice trailed away as she let her gaze roam his face, the perfectly tied neckcloth, the breadth of his shoulders, his thick arms. And then she lifted her gaze to his, saw something smoldering there, and recklessly whispered, " . . . that I'd most definitely *want.*"

He said nothing. The muscles in his jaw bulged as if he refrained from speaking, and she realized that they had come to a halt. But then his hand spread beneath hers, his palm pressed to her palm, and he laced his fingers between hers, one by one, and with the last one, he closed his hand, gripping hers tightly. *"Tha sin glè mhath,"* he whispered hoarsely.

Anna smiled, lifted a curious brow.

"I said, that's very *good*, lass. Very good indeed."

Sixteen

A dreary afternoon and an erotic, musicless dance cast Anna Addison in a whole new light. Grif had always thought her rather exotic, but now he saw her as someone who was . . . desirable. Captivating, in her own unique way. Sultry. *Bloody* sultry.

Not that she didn't need work, for that she did, and quite a lot of it, actually, owing primarily to an annoying little habit she had of speaking.

But when she *wasn't* speaking . . . *ach*. . . .

As that dance went on, he had thought to kiss her again, for after all, what was more seductive than a lass's tender kiss? But as he might have expected, Anna had a completely different notion, and put her hands on his chest and laughingly pushed him away, reminding him that he was merely acting a part and that she did not desire to kiss him in the least, nor did he desire to kiss her.

She had something of a point in that. Truly, he did *not* want to kiss her, and the fact that he had remained awake half the night thinking of how badly he did not want to kiss her he hoped had more to do with a particularly bad batch of beef than anything else.

Nevertheless, he at last arose from his bed and

drank quite a lot of whiskey to numb the smoldering burn that dance had left behind in him, particularly in all those places where they touched each other. Like his hands. And his knees. His thighs and chest. His groin.

Diah!

All that smoldering had made him particularly anxious to get on with the lesson the following day.

Unfortunately, Dudley's gout had flared up again, and it was Hugh who showed Anna in.

She glided into the room ahead of him, removing her bonnet. Hugh stood there watching her in a way Grif understood all too well. Anna looked up; Grif said, "MacAlister was just leaving, he was."

"No, I wasna," Hugh responded, and walked across the room, hand extended. "I beg yer pardon, miss, but we've no' had the courtesy of a *proper* introduction—"

"Hugh MacAlister is me valet, Miss Addison," Grif quickly interjected.

"Oh! How do you do?" she asked politely as Hugh took her hand.

"Quite well," he said, bowing over it.

Grif cleared his throat. Hugh dropped her hand, but did not leave. In Gaelic, Grif said to Hugh, "What in God's name are you doing? You're a valet! You should be gone from here to wash clothing or some such thing."

"Your valet?" Hugh spat, his eyes still on Anna. "It's not as if you need to hide anything from her any longer—she knows what you're about."

"No, all she knows is that she has something I want, but she has no idea *why*, or how deep our lie runs. The less she knows, the better, ye canna argue."

Now Hugh looked at Grif. "You're the only one to have any amusement, is that it? Dudley and I are to waste away in some darkened parlor while you connive the beastie out of her?"

Anna cleared her throat. Both men stopped their argument and glanced at her cautiously. "Perhaps . . . I should come another time?"

"No!" they exclaimed at the same moment, and glared at one another again.

"We've almost done what we came to do, lad," Grif reminded him softly in their native tongue. "Be patient, will ye?"

"Patient! And perhaps you might hurry it along," Hugh snapped, but he looked at Anna and smiled, and said sadly in English, "I beg yer pardon, miss, but I've a . . . ah, a wardrobe . . . to, ah . . . tend," he said, and with a very lackluster bow for Anna, he dragged himself to the door and through it.

Anna watched him go, her expression curious. When the door had closed, she shook her head as if confused and removed her pelisse. "Isn't that the man you were fighting with? You were fighting with your valet? On my honor, I've no idea what you're about, sir, but I am quite certain it can't possibly be good!"

Never mind that—Grif was extraordinarily pleased to see she had taken his advice to heart. She wore a rose-colored walking gown trimmed in earth brown.

"I shall probably find myself in Newgate for somehow abetting you in whatever scheme you're involved in," she continued, oblivious to Grif's admiration.

Her bodice, he noted happily, was suitably draped in sheer silk, and cinched so low that her breasts were luscious mounds of creamy flesh, waiting to be freed.

"I must have quite lost my mind to have come here," she said, smoothing her hair, then looked at Grif.

He smiled. Her eyes narrowed in an expression he knew quite well in spite of their brief association, and he instantly threw up his hands. "I'm admiring yer good work, lass! Ye've taken yer instruction well."

Her expression softened a bit as she looked down at her gown and reached behind to shake out the train. "Really? Do you like it?"

Like it? He was tempted to lick it off her body. "It is indeed quite lovely," he said in all honesty.

She smiled demurely, clasped her hands behind her back. "Thank you," she said, blushing a little. "I thought . . . well, given what you said yesterday, I thought . . ." Her voice trailed off and she shrugged. "So? Shall we carry on with the lesson?" she asked.

Grif held out his arm to her. "Aye. Let's be done with it."

Anna looked at his arm. "You . . . don't intend more dancing without music, do you?"

As appealing as that sounded, he shook his head. "Today ye learn to speak with a man."

"*Speak* with him?" she exclaimed. "Oh, I can well imagine! Speak only when spoken to, and never speak too much, for women should leave the thinking to me. Something like that, I suppose?"

"As usual, ye are quite wrong. I should like to see ye laugh. And smile. There's naugh' more appealing to a man than a woman's bonny smile," he said, and indicated she should take his arm.

"I smile!" she insisted. "And I laugh when there is something clever or amusing!"

"Ye donna smile or laugh nearly enough in the company of men."

"*I do!*" she argued, her brows dipping into a frown.

"No," he argued pleasantly. "On me word, ye have a tendency to be the most humorless woman about. Always frowning, always seeking a way to deride—"

"That isn't true!" she protested, putting her hands to her hips.

Grif raised one brow, asked calmly, "Did ye no' make yer deal with the devil, Anna? I am honoring this end of it . . . will ye no' honor yours?"

She glared at him. Bit her lip. "Blast it," she muttered beneath her breath.

"Come, then," he said, reveling in her defeat. "Pretend we're having a walkabout."

Anna sighed skeptically, put her hand on his arm, and didn't flinch when he covered it with his hand. "Where shall we walkabout?" she asked, sighing impatiently.

"Here," he said, and began to stroll, walking the length of the room. "Imagine ye are strolling with the object of yer great esteem, Mr. Rake Lockhart—"

"*Drake.*"

"Drake, Rake . . . 'tis all the same to me. Imagine he has ye on his arm. 'Tis a lovely spring day, without a hint of rain. There are flowers here and there. And he says, because he wishes to impress ye, 'Miss Addison, ye look as fresh and green as a daisy,'" Grif said, using an effeminate voice. "What do ye say?"

She rolled her eyes. "Oh, I don't know . . . perhaps something about daisies not being green, but white and yellow?"

"*Mo chreach,* ye are a thick student! A man likes to know that his efforts to compliment ye are appreciated!"

"But that compliment makes not the least bit of sense."

"*Especially* if it makes no sense. Most men are no', by their nature, poets."

"All right . . . I suppose I should say, 'Thank you kindly, sir.'"

"Good," he said, smiling warmly. "But have ye more? Perhaps a wee bit of a smile?" he asked, nudging her with his shoulder.

She smiled. A wee bit of a smile, to be sure, but a smile all the same.

"And can ye no' look me in me eyes?" Grif pressed her.

With a snort, she turned her face up to his, looked him squarely in the eyes, and smiled charmingly, all white teeth and coral lips.

Better still, Grif saw something flicker behind those coppery orbs, and grinned at her. "*Excellent*. Perhaps ye might practice this smile at night, before ye sleep. Corners of yer mouth up, corners down, and then repeat."

What was that? A hint of a *genuine* smile?

"Shall we try it again?" he asked pleasantly.

Anna nodded.

"Very well." He made a show of drawing a deep breath. "Will ye look at the glorious day about us, Miss Addison? And it is made infinitely brighter by yer beauty."

Anna smiled, nodded demurely. "Thank you kindly, sir."

"Aye, but ye look as bonny as a purple moon, ye do."

She glanced at him from the corner of her eye.

He grinned, daring her to argue his metaphor.

"Why, Mr. Lockhart, I do not believe kinder words were ever spoken!" she said, and laughed gaily.

She was perfect in that moment—her smile beautiful, her laugh beautiful—and Grif wondered where this Anna had been hiding. "Oh my, I'm afraid you really *have* gone round the bend!" she cried gleefully.

She could not possibly have been more appealing.

Around the room they went, several times more, and Grif discovered, in the course of making ridiculous conversation that afternoon, that Anna was well-read on a variety of subjects, and her opinions ventured far outside the usual debutante's reply of paying no attention to this or that important event. She did pay attention to the world around her, and she seemed to have many different interests, which made her far more interesting in comparison.

"Thank you," she said, after his thorough examination of the rituals of the Season, from which she was still unable to catch her breath from laughing. "I believe I do understand what you mean about smiling and laughter and will endeavor to do more of it." She pulled her hand from his, and still laughing, walked around to the divan where she'd laid her pelisse.

"But . . ." Grif said, watching as she picked it up. "What are ye doing, then?"

"Oh! I really must be on my way. We've a tea we're to attend," she said as she put one arm in the coat.

"But we've no' finished our lesson yet!" he exclaimed, feeling oddly perturbed that she would deign to end their lesson so soon.

She laughed, put her other arm into the coat. "If I didn't know better, sir, I would think you desired me to stay!"

Grif shoved his hands in his pockets. "No. Of course no'," he muttered.

She smiled, fastened her pelisse, and picked up her bonnet. "Shall you call on Lucy tomorrow? It's been three days now, and I am certain she's wondering why you haven't called."

Lucy? The *last* thing on his mind at the moment was Lucy.

She paused in what she was doing and looked at him. "Shall I see you on the morrow?"

This agreement was beginning to grate for reasons Grif did not really understand, had him feeling a bit rudderless, and he scowled. "How can I know ye actually have what ye say it is ye have, Anna?"

She blinked as she fit the bonnet on her head. "Because I gave you one of the rubies."

"Aye, that ye did, but for all I know, ye've gone and sold the blasted thing."

She laughed roundly at that. "Of course I haven't! First, where could I *possibly* sell something as hideous as that, and second, why should I? I'm certainly not in need of money. And third, as long as I have it, you will do what I ask, isn't that so?"

Grif glared at her, his lighthearted feelings for her having suddenly evaporated.

Anna smiled, tied her bonnet in a bow beneath her chin. "Very well, then. On the morrow, you will call on Lucy, and perhaps we might meet in Hyde Park afterward, at Rotten Row. Lady Worthall makes me terribly anxious. She'd ruin me if she saw me coming here unescorted."

"What a tragedy that would be," Grif drawled, and got a dark frown for it.

Seventeen

Anna wasn't certain if she was imagining it or not that Grif had seemed rather perturbed when she took her leave, instead of being entirely happy to be done with her, as was typical.

But she had no time to dwell on it, for today the family was calling en masse on the Lockharts for tea.

She arrived home in just the nick of time; her family was gathered in the drawing room, waiting for her as she came breathlessly through the doors, a smile on her face.

"Darling, where have you been?" her mother cried. "We shouldn't want to keep the Lockharts waiting!"

"I'm sorry, Mother. I was detained at the milliner," she said quickly, and fussed with the buttons of her pelisse to avoid her mother's gaze.

"The *milliner?*" Lucy asked, her voice full of suspicion. "I had no idea you were interested in millinery! Honestly, I always thought quite the opposite."

"I'm as interested in millinery as any young woman." Anna lied.

"What does it matter?" Father politely interjected before Lucy could question her further. "She's here now, and I do think we must be going or be late. Shall we?" He gestured for the ladies to quickly precede him out the door.

The ride to the Lockhart mansion was filled with Father's chatter about the goings-on of Parliament, for which Lucy could not have possibly cared less, and therefore she stared out the window. And Anna was a bundle of nerves, having convinced herself that she *could* stop Drake from offering for Lucy, with just the right smile and the right amount of laughter. Exactly as Grif had said. *Grif.* An image of him popped into her mind, an image of him smiling that devilish smile as he spoke of purple moons. She smiled a little—she couldn't help admiring him on a certain level, for it took a different sort of man to smile when his back was against the wall.

When they arrived at the Lockhart mansion, the family was in the grand salon, where a very elaborate tea service had been laid. They looked idyllic, the four of them, as if someone had arranged them for a portrait. Drake was standing at the mantel, looking majestic, his sister Barbara seated at a writing desk, laboring over some sort of missive, and his lordship and lady seated together on a settee.

"Ah, here they are!" the elderly Lockhart called out, waving a hand at a footman. "Now we might have a spot of whiskey, eh?" he exclaimed, and gestured to an underbutler to pour one.

Everyone exchanged the usual pleasantries—Mother and Lady Lockhart pairing off instantly, Father and Lord Lockhart each with a tot of whiskey. Drake came forward straightaway, all smiles. "Miss Lucy," he said, beaming. "Miss Anna. How good of you to come."

"We wouldn't have missed it," Anna said, smiling

brightly. Drake smiled warmly, and then turned to speak to Lucy.

"*Aaaaaaaana!*" Barbara trilled with delight, forcing Anna's attention away from Drake. She leaned in, kissing the air near Anna's cheek.

"Good afternoon, Barbara."

"It looks as if we'll be partners once again!" Barbara cried happily, and grabbed Anna's elbow and turned her slightly, as she put her head next to Anna's and whispered, "As those two shall undoubtedly be together, then so shall we!"

Anna's heart sank; in the moment that she had turned to greet Barbara, Drake had taken Lucy by the arm to escort her to a seat, then, flipping out his coat, he took the seat next to her.

Barbara linked her arm through Anna's and pulled her closely into her doughy side. "We've the most delightful biscuits today! I confess I sampled one when no one was looking." She pulled Anna to the tea service, away from Drake, and Anna was forced to politely listen to Barbara babble on about Nigel's stay in Bath until the tea was drunk, at which point, the Lockharts were keen to hear sweet Lucy play the pianoforte. They were not, notably, so keen to hear either Anna or Barbara play.

Anna was standing behind the settee where the Lockharts were seated, and as Lucy daintily took a seat at the pianoforte, Anna was delighted to see Drake moving casually toward her, smiling and nodding as Lucy began her performance. It was with even greater delight that Lucy peeked up just as Drake reached Anna's side.

"Anna," he whispered below the admittedly lovely chords of Lucy's playing. "You look lovely."

A rush of heat filled her instantly. "Thank you," she whispered back.

"That gown makes you particularly . . ."

He paused; she glanced at him from the corner of her eye as he boldly let his gaze dip to her bodice.

" . . . radiant," he said in a near growl.

Anna did what Grif had taught her and laughed softly. "It's not the gown that has made me radiant, sir."

Drake smiled and lifted a brow as he stole a glimpse of Lucy and the others. "Pray tell, then, what has?"

"A friendly smile," she whispered coyly.

Drake chuckled appreciatively as a polite round of applause went up when Lucy ended her song. "I shall keep that in mind," he said, and with a nod, he turned and walked around the couch, applauding louder than anyone.

Blast it! She'd had him here and had lost him, and now he was sitting next to her mother, laughing and holding court. Laughing and smiling were alluring, Grif had avowed! A hint of flesh was impossible to resist, he'd claimed! A more likely truth was that Lucy had not been lying when she said Drake had touched her breast. Perhaps he wanted to touch more of it. Well, then, perhaps Anna would redouble her considerable efforts.

The next afternoon, Anna was waiting for Grif, secreted away in the small drawing room when he came striding through the front door, hat in hand, on his way to make a call to Lucy.

As he followed the butler down the hall, Anna stepped out of the small parlor, clearly startling him, as he exclaimed his surprise in his native tongue, along with the butler, who was likewise startled.

"I beg your pardon, if I may, sir," she said politely, "but if you've come to call on my sister, she is taking the sunshine in the garden. I'd be happy to walk you there."

"I beg your pardon, miss, but Miss Lucy is—"

"Ah . . ." she said quickly, holding up a finger, "Actually no, Duckworth. She . . . moved." This much she knew to be true, since she had sent a parlormaid to tell Lucy that Drake was in the gardens. She flashed a dazzling smile at Duckworth. "I'll show Mr. . . . ah, Lord Ardencaple to the garden."

Duckworth colored slightly, but had the good sense to click his heels and bow. "Of course, miss," he said, and instantly turned and strode away.

Anna grabbed Ardencaple-Lockhart-whoever by the arm and yanked him toward the small parlor. But he was stronger than she and resisted her attempts as he looked down the corridor toward the sitting room.

"We are to meet at Rotten Row," he reminded her through clenched teeth, "*after* I call on Miss Lucy."

"Yes, but there has been a change of *plans*," she said, tugging at his arm. He reluctantly allowed her to pull him inside the small parlor, but once inside, he refused to move from the open door, so Anna had to push him.

"What in God's name are ye about?" he asked, hands on hips as she shut the door and leaned against it.

"*Sssh!*" she hushed him, waving her hand at him anxiously, and turned so that she could press her ear against the door, listening for any sound. After a moment, she heard the familiar click of Duckworth's shoes on the entry's marble floor.

She whirled around, her back pressed against the door. "We haven't much time. All right, then, I know what you've done! Mr. Lockhart—the *real* Mr. Lockhart—oh, blast it all, shall I call you Grif?" she demanded in a near fit of hysteria.

He blinked. "Aye. Grif."

"All right, then . . . *Grif,*" she said carefully, unaccustomed as she was to calling men by their Christian names. Particularly, tall, handsome . . . green-eyed men who frowned quite a lot. "You *promised* me that smiling and laughing were perfectly sufficient to entice him, but as it happens, when we attended the Lockhart tea yesterday, and I smiled and I *laughed,* he paid me not the least bit of mind!" she cried.

"What did ye say to him, then?"

"He said the gown I was wearing made me radiant. And I said, 'It's not the gown that has made me radiant, sir, it is a friendly smile,' or some such nonsense."

"Aha," Grif said, and put his hand to his chin, and looked very thoughtful.

"Aha . . . *what?*"

"And what did the rake say to this?"

"*Drake* said he'd keep that in mind!" she exclaimed, punctuating the air with her hands.

"Ah. Well, then. I think it quite obvious. He's really rather obtuse, isn't he, then?"

"Stop that!" she insisted. Grif opened his mouth to respond, but Anna was not quite finished. "So it would seem now that I really haven't any time, as Barbara *avows* he will offer for Lucy soon, before the

Season's end, and in spite of my parents' words to the contrary—they promised they would not accept an offer for Lucy until *I* had been properly offered for, but as that seems to be an impossibility that grows more and more certain with each day, I suppose they shall accept it!" she cried, the words coming out of her in such a rush now that she couldn't stop them. It panicked her, and she suddenly darted to the window overlooking the street and drew the sun shades closed.

"All right, then, calm yerself, lass," Grif said soothingly, although he watched her warily. "I think it is time that ye consider the game is lost."

Anna's mouth dropped open in stunned disbelief. "*Lost?* How could you say such a thing? Lost! I haven't even *begun* to try for his attentions! I've only just started these blasted lessons, which, I might add, you hardly seem adept at providing—"

"I never claimed to be!"

"And you proclaim my chances lost?" she continued, ignoring him. "You sorely misunderstand me, sir, if you think I shall give up at the least bit of adversity, for *I*—"

He startled her out of her rant by grabbing her elbow, and only then did she realize he had crossed the room. "All right, then, Anna," he said softly but firmly, "take a bloody breath ere ye go flying across the room."

She took a breath.

"Now, then. Before we are discovered and create the Season's most infamous scandal, what is it ye want at this particular moment, pray tell? For if it is to tell me that I've failed ye miserably when it was *ye* who sought *me* out, I believe I will bloody well excuse meself and call on yer sister!"

Anna released her breath and glared at the door. "All right," she said, her voice low and calm. "I have a rather important question. And I beg you, sir, for once, please be truthful."

"Mary Queen of Scots! *Aye,* I think he'll offer for Miss Lucy!" he said angrily.

"NO!" she cried, slapping away his hand from her arm. "That is most certainly *not* what I intended to ask! I want to . . . I would like . . ." She couldn't say it. She couldn't bring herself to string the words together to ask the question on her mind.

But then Grif looked impatiently at the door. "Anna—"

"Is it true, do you think," she blurted, squaring off, "that if a man puts his hand on an unmarried woman's bare breast, he will, in all likelihood, offer for her?"

The question stunned him into silence. Grif did not move. The clock did not move, the air did not stir, nothing—it was as if the entire world stood still for a moment, and Anna couldn't help but bite her lower lip as myriad emotions skimmed across Grif's green eyes. He stared at her for an interminable moment, his expression turbulently confused, as if he didn't know who she was, could not quite seem to place her, did not know what to make of her.

And then his brows dipped low over eyes that flashed with an expression so hard she could not name it. "Have ye lost yer bloody fool *mind?"*

He suddenly whirled away from her. "*Criosd,* what have I done to deserve this?" he exclaimed. "What bloody curse brings *this* on me head?" He pivoted around to her again, his expression gone very dark. "What *is* it about this man that has ye so enamored?"

he demanded. "Will ye tell me what it is, then? For the *life* of me, I canna see why a lass as bonny as ye are would toss away all that she has for the likes of *him!* He's a rotten bastard, Anna! He cares no' a wit for ye—how can ye no' *see* it?"

Although the truth in his words jolted her, she lifted her chin and folded her arms defensively. "You've no idea what you are saying!"

"Aye, but I do!" he said sharply, striding to her again. "He doesna *care* for ye, Anna! What allure does such indifference as his have for ye, then?"

The question burned her, for it was a question that had taunted her from the fringes of her consciousness, whispering answers like *jealousy, salvation, fear.* And now, the question spoken aloud, brought to life by a man who would just as soon see her die a spinster as marry a bastard, burned in the back of her eyes. "Just *tell* me!" she demanded hotly.

"All right, I'll tell ye," he said roughly, and suddenly grabbed her on either side of her head, forced her to look up, so that she'd have to look him square in the eye. "If ye present yer *breast* to him and invite him to touch it, he will take ye for a *whore.* Do ye understand what I say to ye, lass? Ye will have carried yer silly game too far!"

She angrily shoved against his chest and out of his grip, and said imperiously, "*Thank* you."

He reared back, still staring at her, obviously appalled. "Ye are a bloody fool," he said quietly, thoughtfully. "For a woman as intelligent as I think ye are, ye're a bloody fool."

His censure knifed her, and she looked at her hands, which, she couldn't help noticing, were shaking slightly. But she lifted her head and smiled, walked to the door. "It is not necessary to meet at Rotten Row. I shall call on you on the morrow, as we previously planned."

Whatever he might have thought, she would not know, because she opened the door and stepped behind it. She heard him mutter beneath his breath and stride to the door and out, his boots echoing down the corridor.

She shut the door behind him, walked to a chair, and fell into it, feeling all at once ashamed for having let him see the strange desperation she was surprised to realize she felt, ashamed for having asked such a bold question.

Ashamed for having *asked* it . . . but not for having thought it.

Eighteen

When Grif entered the room where Lucy was receiving, he was filled with so much fury that he scarcely heard her usual litany of platitudes. It was one thing for Anna to impose herself on him as she had, but it was quite another for her to impose herself and then have the absolute *gall* to ignore his advice! And frankly, he wasn't certain what made him more furious—that she ignored his advice or that she intended to offer her body, or any part of it, to the likes of Drake Lockhart.

This he mulled over until he thought his head might very well explode from his shoulders, and when he merely nodded at Lucy's insufferable remarks about the bloody weather, she cocked her head and studied him prettily. "Would I be mistaken in perceiving you to be a bit out of sorts, my lord?"

Grif turned a startled glance to her—was it so obvious? He drew a breath, pushed his irritation down, and forced a smile. "*Ach*, no, Miss Lucy. Please forgive me ill manners."

"Lord Ardencaple!" she exclaimed with a smile. "You could not possibly be ill-mannered! Why, you're always so marvelously cheerful that I credit you with bringing the sunshine whenever you call!"

Aye, and he could credit her sister with bringing black clouds and thunder and lightning—

"I am quite appreciative of your cheerfulness," Miss Lucy added primly.

"That is a compliment I shall hold dear," Grif said, his smile coming easier as he tapped his heart.

"I believe that if one enjoys another's company, one should say so," she said with a pert little nod of her head.

"And do ye likewise believe that if one *demands* another's company, particularly the company of the opposite sex, that she—or he, certainly—should also express at least a wee bit of gratitude for *receiving* that company?"

Lucy blinked. "I beg your pardon? Have I demanded—"

"*Diah*, certainly *no'*, lass!" he exclaimed with a little laugh. "I inquire in general."

"Oh," she said, and cocked her head to one side, pondering it. "I can honestly say I have no opinion," she happily concluded. "Speaking of company . . . my sister, Lady Featherstone, intends to host a weekend at Featherstone Manor in the very near future, and I know that she intends to extend you an invitation to join the festivities."

"Does she?" Grif asked, his mind still racing around the many ways Anna mercilessly annoyed him.

"I am certain *I* shall attend. Do you think you shall, too?"

Not if he had the blasted beastie in hand, he wouldn't. He'd leave this town and that ridiculous creature to become the spinster that was her self-imposed destiny. What man could abide her?

"My lord?"

"Aye!" he said, straightening in his seat like a guilty child. "Do ye think I'd miss the opportunity to spend an entire weekend in yer presence, Miss Lucy?"

Lucy smiled at that and coyly batted her eyes.

"If such a coveted invitation is extended to me, I'll certainly move mountains to attend."

Lucy's smile went deeper, and she smoothed the lap of her gown, stole a glimpse of her chaperone. "That's lovely. I do hope the weather holds."

Grif fixed his gaze on her throat. Perhaps if he looked at her throat, he'd overcome the urge to strangle it every time he heard the word *weather* on her lips.

"In the past, at such weekend soirées as my sister plans, I know that more than one gentleman has determined the course of his future," she said softly, and looked at him from the corner of her eye. "Do they do the same in Scotland?"

Grif nodded. To what, he really didn't know or care, as he was far more interested at the moment in the curve of Lucy's neck, or rather . . . actually, he hadn't noticed until just this moment that Lucy's neck was shorter than Anna's. And a wee bit thicker.

"I would hope that if any*one* desired to proclaim the course of his future, he might do so at my sister's house, when all his friends could join in good tidings. Wouldn't you?"

"Aye," Grif said, having no idea what one was to say to such vague rambling as this, and wondered absently if he might be able to steal more than a kiss from Lucy in the course of that bloody weekend, whenever it might be. Perhaps *he* would touch *her* bare breast. His gaze dipped to the décolletage of her gown, such as it was, as he pondered that extraordinarily appealing thought . . . and remarked to himself that her bosom did not seem as plump as Anna's. A pity, that.

Apparently, however, his answer had not been sufficient, for Lucy suddenly leaned forward and whispered adamantly, *"My lord Ardencaple!* What I am *attempting* to say is that if *you* have any desires as to *your* future, you should express them, and that it would be a perfectly well-suited weekend for you to *do* so, and quite frankly, in some circles, it would be expected!"

It took a fraction of a moment for him to understand what she was implying, and Grif almost gasped like a girl with shock. And he *was* shocked, absolutely dumbstruck by the notion that she thought *he* would offer for her. He'd not once, not *once* hinted at such a ridiculous thing! He'd never given her cause to believe he wanted anything other than . . . well, the obvious. But *marriage?* To an Englishwoman?

And what of his cousin Lockhart? Everyone in this blasted town was talking about the match between Drake Lockhart and Miss Lucy Addison!

"What is it?" Lucy whispered hotly, a frown marring her lovely face. "Why are you looking so appalled?"

"Appalled?" he echoed dumbly, his mind still racing. "No, no, lass, ye misunderstand me. I merely . . . I hadna thought . . . that is to say, I hadna considered . . ."

Her brows dipped into such a glower that he actually felt a small shiver run down his spine.

"That ye'd even . . . *entertain* . . . such a notion," he managed to get out.

She blinked and straightened slowly. Her cold glower softened to a composed countenance, and she smiled prettily again. "Not *me,* my lord. Offer for *Anna!"* she said sweetly.

Whatever he was about to remark was lost for all time—his mouth dropped open and he found himself completely speechless. As mute as a tongueless beggar.

"You *do* esteem her, do you not?" Lucy demanded.

"But I . . . I thought . . . I mean to say that I—"

"Yes, well," she said, prim and very cool. "I am quite certain you did. But the truth is, my lord, that I have promised my intentions to someone else."

"Ah . . . aha," he managed.

"Do we understand one another?" she asked sweetly.

"Quite," he said, and sat a little straighter, wondering how quickly he might quit this room. His palms were damp and his collar felt impossibly tight. "All right, then!" he said abruptly and far too cheerfully. "I shall look forward to the invitation."

She gave him a nod of her head, signaling her pleasure that he had come round to her way of thinking.

Grif put his hands on his knees and looked at the door. "It is with great reluctance that I must bring me call to an end. Alas, I've another engagement."

"Of course," she said, and after Grif made the customary departing proclamations, he strode out of the room as quickly as he dared.

He did not, however, manage to get out of the house, and, in fact, he did not manage to go very far at all, for he heard Anna's familiar warm laugh. The sound of it unnerved him, and he paused mid-stride. It seemed to be coming from the foyer. He walked quietly to the edge of the corridor, and paused there, leaning to one side to peer into the foyer.

He should have known.

It was Lockhart. Anna was laughing at something he'd said, her face upturned to his the way Grif had taught her, her smile bright and sparkling, just as he'd instructed.

With one hand on her elbow, Lockhart was smiling down at her bosom; Grif could plainly see the man was enjoying Anna's attention. He said something in a low voice, and Anna leaned into him, her bosom grazing his arm. If nothing else, she was an excellent student. She laughed again, then went up on her tiptoes, cupped her hand, and whispered something in Lockhart's ear that caused him to throw back his head and laugh loudly.

That was the moment Grif made his entrance, striding into their midst.

Both of them started at the sound of his boot on the marble floor, and both turned round to see who it was. Anna's smile did not fade at all—if anything, it grew brighter.

Lockhart, on the other hand, lost all good humor at the sight of Grif.

Grif smiled. Clasped his hands behind his back as he came to a halt before them. "Sharing a bit of jest, are ye?" he asked pleasantly.

"Yes," Anna said. "A *private* jest."

"Ardencaple," Lockhart said coolly. "Making the rounds of the debutantes' parlors again, are you?"

"As a matter of fact," he said pleasantly, then feigned concern. "Does it displease ye, Lockhart?"

"Not in the least, my lord. Your activities matter

not to me. Or to anyone else, I should suspect. I will admit, however, to giving over to wonder from time to time . . . how long will we be graced with your considerable presence in London?"

"Have ye wondered, indeed?" Grif asked, and left it at that. He had no intention of answering any question put to him by the rake.

He'd almost forgotten the helpful *diabhal* next to Lockhart. "Did you not say, my lord, that you'd be leaving by Season's end?" she asked sweetly.

"Did I? I canna recall."

"I'm certain you did," she said, clasping her hands behind her back and rising up on her toes, and down again, smiling so sweetly that she looked like a bloody angel. "I'm really rather certain that you *did.*"

"I beg yer pardon, Miss Addison, if I gave ye the wrong impression," he said, inclining his head apologetically. "I couldna possibly depart ere I finished what I came to do."

That retort seemed to delight her. She smiled so broadly that she had to bite her lower lip in an apparent attempt to keep from laughing.

Lockhart, on the other hand, was looking more and more perturbed. "And what is it, exactly, my lord, that you came to do?"

Grif shifted a cold gaze to Lockhart. "I wouldna bore ye with the details of it all," he said. "'Tis a bit of old family business."

"Sounds rather tedious," Lockhart said with a smirk.

"Ye've no idea how tedious, sir. Now, if ye'll excuse the intrusion, I'll take me leave now," he said, and with a bit of a pointed look for Anna, he proceeded to the front door, received his hat and gloves from the footman, and was walking out when he heard Anna call a cheerful good day after him.

Aye, have yer fun, he thought. He'd deal with her later. And frankly, he'd delight in imagining how exactly he would deal with her until that happy opportunity was upon him.

Nineteen

Anna's step was much lighter the next afternoon as she hurried to her lessons. Her "impromptu" encounter with Drake Lockhart the day before had renewed her hope that all was not lost, that she might indeed one day find herself in the enviable position of being Mrs. Lockhart.

She snuck into the mews from Cavendish Street and ran to the side door where Mr. Dudley usually met her. She gave the door three quick raps, waited excitedly for him to answer, and when he pulled the door open a crack, she leaned in, smiling. "Good *afternoon,* Mr. Dudley! Glorious day!"

The old man's eyes narrowed suspiciously, and he pulled the door open a little more, stuck his head through.

"Oh, I'm quite alone!" she said gaily, and putting a hand on the door, pushed it open, hardly noticing that she had inadvertently pushed Mr. Dudley back, too, as she stepped inside the dark entrance. "You should really see about putting some sconces here," she offered helpfully. "It's dreadfully dark, don't you think?"

The old man blinked up at her as she pulled her gloves from her hands, finger by finger. "I suppose he's in the usual spot, pouty and cross because I'm calling? He shouldn't fret in the least, for I think our lessons will come to a desirable end shortly." She turned a beaming smile to Dudley and held out her gloves.

"Aye," Dudley said, and stuck out his hand, grimacing slightly, fingers curled uncomfortably, to receive them.

Anna hesitantly deposited the gloves, then untied the ribbon of her bonnet as she eyed the butler. "Are you quite all right, Mr. Dudley?"

"Aye. Bit o' gout, 'tis all."

"Oh dear. My grandmother suffered terribly from it. She often made a remedy for her gout from the flowers of an autumn crocus plant. Shall I bring you a tincture?"

Dudley grimaced in pain again. "I'd no' ask for such favor, I swear I wouldna, miss, but we've precious few medicinals, and I do seem to be suffering unusually so."

With a sympathetic smile, Anna carefully patted his arm. "We can't have that, sir. Consider it done," she said with an adamant nod before removing her bonnet and placing it on a small console. "I'll bring it round on the morrow."

"Thank ye kindly, Miss Addison," he said, still grimacing as he laid the gloves next to her bonnet.

"Shall I go on?" she asked, motioning to the rest of the house. "I know the way. No need for you to suffer the walk," she said, and without waiting for an answer, carried on, humming a little tune.

"Something smells *delicious!*" she called over her shoulder to Dudley, and lifting her skirts, she ran lightly up the servants' stairs to the first floor, where her lessons were held. As she strolled down the much brighter corridor, she passed an open door, and noticed Grif's valet standing at the window that overlooked the street. "Good day, Mr. MacAlister!" she called.

The man whipped around, held up a finger to his lips, and motioned for her to come inside.

Anna was instantly at his side. He pointed to the street. Anna peeked out through the crack between the sheer drapery liners. She could see Grif on the sidewalk below, speaking with Lady Worthall, whose abominable little dog kept hopping up and nipping at his trousers.

"Aye, *that's* trouble," he said with a frown, and pulled the drapes shut. He turned to look at her; his gaze boldly wandered the length of her. "Aye, he's turned ye out quite well, has he no'?"

His perusal made her feel self-conscious, and Anna nervously put her hand to the nape of her neck.

"I intended no offense, Miss Addison," he said, clasping his hands behind his back. "It was meant as a compliment of the highest order, it was."

Anna looked at him again, noticed for the first time that he was wearing only boots, trousers, and a shirt with a plain neckcloth. His waistcoat and coat were God knew where, but the effect was rather dashing.

He, however, was looking at her feet. "Has he told ye about the ankle, then?"

Unthinkingly, Anna glanced down at her feet, encased in dark burgundy high-heeled shoes that matched the burgundy of her day gown. "The ankle?"

"Aye. A gentleman enjoys the turn of a lass's ankle. See what I mean," he said, and walked to the mantel, struck a peculiar, feminine pose, and thrust out one leg to the side, so if he had been wearing a gown, she might have seen his ankle.

Anna gaped at him standing there with his leg so artfully turned out. She could not help herself—she burst into laughter.

Mr. MacAlister's grin broadened charmingly, and he straightened up. "If he's no' told ye of the ankle, then I suppose he's no' gotten round to the walk, aye?"

"No sir, he has not."

"Then allow *me.*"

Before Anna knew it, she was learning to walk provocatively, using the natural swing of her hips to propel her.

And while she practiced walking, Hugh, as he insisted she call him, regaled her with tales of his own unrequited love for one Miss Keara Brody. He had an infectious, engaging way of telling his tale that had her laughing so much that he felt compelled to put his arm around her waist and guide her through their walking lesson.

They moved slowly and with a bit of flounce. "There ye are, lass. Just a wee bit more in the hip," he said. They went again and gave it a bit more in the hip.

Hugh clucked his tongue. "No, *no,* no' like that—'tis too obvious. Watch me," he said confidently, and proceeded to strut across the carpet, turn at the corner just as Anna had done, and come to a halt at the mantel, where he thrust one hip to the side and turned out his ankle perfectly. Were he not wearing a boot, that is. "Come on, then, we'll try it again, aye?" he asked, gesturing to Anna.

She slipped beneath his arm, put her arm around his waist.

"Dé tha thú dèanamh?"

The boom of Grif's deep voice startled them both badly enough that they instantly jumped apart. Hugh whipped around, thrust his arms akimbo, and frowned at Grif, who was striding in from the entrance at the other end of the room. "What are we doing? We're no' *doing* anything!" Hugh scoffed. "I was merely showing Miss Addison how to walk. Hurrying things along for ye, then."

"Thank ye kindly, MacAlister, but I'll conduct the lessons, if ye donna mind," Grif said.

Hugh sighed, flashed a warm smile at Anna, and then strode to where Grif stood, clapped him on the shoulder, and said, "Aye, then I've warmed her up for ye." And with that, he walked out the door, whistling.

Grif shut the door at his back and turned around, leaned against the door, arms folded, as he considered Anna, much like, she thought, a hungry lion might consider a rabbit. It felt exactly as if she'd been caught misbehaving in the nursery, and she smiled tremulously. "He was helping me," she said, but Grif's cat-like expression did not change. "You neglected to mention the ankle, after all."

"Aye, that," Grif said, nodding thoughtfully.

"And you did say I was to use my, ah . . . body . . . to its best advantage, did you not?"

He pushed away from the door, casually strolling toward her, his head down. "I did indeed. But when I said to use yer body to advantage, I intended that ye should use it to *yer* advantage, not his. 'Tis a fine line a woman must walk, between using her body to have what she wants and letting a man use her body to have what *he* wants. Ye'd best learn the difference now ere ye make trouble for yerself."

For Grif, an imposter, to threaten her with scandal was really too rich. Anna lifted her chin and reminded him, "It is *you* who should be afraid of scandal."

"Me?" he asked, coming to a halt, looking incredibly surprised. "Why?"

"*Why?* Is it not obvious? You've come to London posing as someone you are not, you have told more than one falsehood in seeking some hideous little gargoyle, you travel with a man you would call your valet, but who is obviously *not* your valet—"

"He would that it were so!" Grif interrupted irritably.

"Do you call him a liar?" Anna demanded.

"Aye. And on most occasions, to his face."

That silenced her. That *confused* her. What, exactly, was the situation between these two men?

"*Mo chreach,*" Grif said impatiently at her bewildered look. "All right, then, here it is. MacAlister is in fact me dearest friend, and has been since we were but wee bairns bouncing on our fathers' knees. He's come to London to help me. But he is no', nor shall he ever *hope* to be, a *valet.*"

"That's not all of it, is it?" Anna demanded, her eyes narrowed. "What of poor Mr. Dudley? Have you impressed him into your service?"

"Poor . . . ?"

"Have you the slightest notion of what is happening in your very own household?" she exclaimed with much superiority. "Mr. Dudley's gout bothers him terribly, if you hadn't noticed!"

He annoyed her further by smiling. "Oh, *aye,* lass, I've noticed it, all right. I've noticed it all me life, for Dudley is me family's butler. It happens that he has come to London to help me as well."

"Help you . . . *what?"* she tried.

He just laughed, his gorgeous lips sliding over his white teeth. "*Ach,* Anna!" he laughed. "I wouldna tell ye if ye were the last soul on this earth, and well ye know it! Ye are hardly to be trusted, are ye now?"

"*You,* an admitted imposter, would speak to *me* of trust?" she cried, incensed. "I am the only one in this room who can be trusted!"

He snorted his opinion of that.

"I *am!*" she insisted, pacing now. "Just because I've—All right, well, I've really pushed you into a bit of a corner, I'll grant you that—but not because I wish you harm! Because I am rather in need of assistance!" she said earnestly. "And quite honestly, Grif, it is I who shouldn't trust *you,* isn't it? You are the one parading about as some Scottish earl when in fact you are . . . well, you are . . ." God in heaven, what was he?

Anna paused and sighed irritably to the ceiling. Truthfully, she had lain awake more than one night wondering why he was in London, why he wanted that dreadful little gargoyle so much that he would bargain for it. "Frankly, I've no idea who you might be, although a number of nefarious thoughts come to mind."

"Aye?" he said, brightening. "Such as?"

"Such as murderer. Thief. Spy."

"I beg yer pardon? No' statesman? Earl? Perhaps even the bloody king of Scotland?"

"I was making a *point.* Why do you want that wretched gargoyle so badly that you'd come to

London with a false identity?" she demanded. "Why shouldn't you address your cousin directly?"

He laughed darkly. "Come, now, what could I possibly tell ye, given the circumstance? What assurances do I have that ye will no' use it against me? Or repeat what I say to yer sister, or a friend—or the very person who would bring me harm?"

At the suggestion of someone besides her harming the pompous man, Anna's curiosity was piqued so dramatically that she almost burst with it, and she quickly crossed her heart. "On my honor, you have my word. I will not breathe a word of it to another living soul!"

He chuckled and reached out to untangle a curl of her hair from her earring. "I've no' seen such glee in a woman's eye," he said quietly.

That served only to pique what was now an insatiable curiosity. Grif seemed to read her mind, and, still chuckling, he dropped his hand and fell, unceremoniously, onto the settee. "No. I canna say," he said cheerfully.

Anna was instantly beside him, sitting as close as she dared, her hands clutched tightly together on her knee, facing him. He grinned proudly, and his green eyes danced with the childish delight of having a secret.

But Anna was completely undeterred and inched closer to him. "I swear, I cross my heart, that I shall not breathe a word of it!" she promised, crossing her heart again.

"No," he said again, casually shaking his head, and yawned, just like a lion—big and long and terribly nonchalant. "I canna trust ye—"

"But you *can!*"

"No."

"Grif!" she exclaimed, and leaned forward, so that her head was in front of his and he *had* to look at her. "Whyever not?"

He grinned at her effort, caressed her cheek with his finger. "Because, lass, the secret involves the object of yer adoration and his family."

"Really, what could Drake Lockhart possibly have done to *you?*"

"What the English have done to the Scots for centuries. Stolen what is rightfully ours."

She scoffed at him. "Drake Lockhart would never steal!"

"Ye donna believe me? Then hear this," he said, his voice going quiet. "Centuries ago, the Lockharts were split by civil war. One half—the cowardly half—fled to England. The other half—the true brave souls—remained in Scotland."

Anna edged a little closer, all ears.

Grif suddenly sat up, so that his face was just inches from hers, and glanced around as if he expected someone to be nearby, listening. "When the cowards fled, they took something that was quite precious to the Scottish Lockharts. So precious that, decades later, the Scots came to London and took it back. But the English Lockharts could not bear to let the Scots have it, so they returned to Scotland and took it *again.*"

Anna nodded eagerly. "What? What did they take?"

He snorted. "The *beastie,* lass!"

"You mean they went back to Scotland for that *gargoyle?*" she exclaimed incredulously.

"'Tis a beastie!"

"But . . . why would they steal it?" she demanded, wrinkling her nose in disgust.

"Because of its value. But the Scottish Lockharts, they took back what was rightfully theirs. And the English came again, only this time, they didna know about the *curse,*" he whispered ominously.

"The curse?" she whispered excitedly.

"Aye. It was during the Jacobite War of '46 . . . do ye know it?"

"Yes, yes," she said hastily, inching toward the edge of the settee. "Those loyal to the deposed King James sought to restore his successors to the throne."

Grif blinked with surprise. Anna frowned. "I *told* you that I was a student of Scotland."

"Aye, that ye did. All right, then, when Cromwell and his murderers came to Scotland, among them was an English Lockhart. He came to Talla Dileas under the guise of friendship, but he stole the beastie, for he was an Englishman and, therefore, a bloody rotten bounder. But the laird of Lockhart was angry," he said, ignoring Anna's gasp of indignation, "and he went high into the Highlands to call on Donalda."

"Donalda?"

"Aye, Donalda the henwife."

Anna shook her head.

Grif sighed at her ignorance. "A *magic* woman, aye?"

"Oh! Yes, yes," Anna said, and gestured for him to go on.

Grif grinned lopsidedly. "The laird called on Donalda and beseeched her to put a curse on the English Lockharts, which of course she was proud to do, for no self-respecting Scot can abide the English—"

"And?" Anna interrupted him.

"And she did."

"So . . . what is the curse?" Anna asked, leaning forward.

Grif looked over his shoulder again, gestured for Anna to lean forward even more. She leaned so close that she could smell the balsam in his cologne, could feel his breath on her ear as he whispered, "The curse is that the Sassenach who takes possession of the beastie will forfeit possession of his . . . or her virtue."

It took a moment for Anna to understand that he teased her, but she let out a cry of frustration and reared back. "What is the *matter* with you?"

Now he was laughing. "Ah, if ye'd seen yer eyes, lass!" he exclaimed through his laughter. "Big as moons, they were!"

"You're not the least amusing!" she cried. "It's absolutely *wretched* of you!"

"Aye, right ye are—'tis wretched of me, for ye will lose yer virtue without the help of the beastie, will ye no'?"

His implication shamed her, and she raised her arm, intending to slap him, but Grif easily caught her wrist and twisted her arm so that she fell against the back of the settee.

"What has angered ye, lass? That ye heard the truth? Or that ye will believe anything a man tells ye?"

"You *bastard!*" she hissed, but Grif just laughed irreverently and tightened his grip on her wrist.

Her eyes were shimmering with wrath, and Grif unexpectedly and uncharacteristically took sensual delight in them. Anna struggled to free herself, but he easily pushed her back, trapping her with one arm against the settee, letting her squirm.

"You're a liar!" she hissed at him.

"What, did ye think I'd confess *all* to ye, then?" he asked. "Did ye believe that holding me beastie hostage somehow gives ye the *right* to know me and mine?"

"I should think that having agreed to our arrangement, you might at least act the gentleman!"

"God blind me, why should I do that?" he asked, stopping her attempt to slide off the settee by pressing one knee on top of her leg. "Did ye no' come here to learn how to seduce a man?"

That riled her to furious indignation and she struggled much harder.

"Ah, but its no' a gentleman ye want, Anna. Ye want a *man*—a man to touch ye like ye desire to be touched."

Her indignation turned to a shriek of pure fury, and she struggled violently now, managing to push his leg off of her and almost escaping him. But Grif was too strong for her—she could not prevent him from twisting her arm around her back and pushing her into him. They were half on, half off the settee; he dragged her across his lap, so that they were face to face, her body against his.

He could see Anna's rage in the harsh rise of her chest. "You are a scoundrel," she bit out through clenched teeth. "A blackguard, a *rake*—"

"But ye like that in a man, *leannan*."

She floundered frantically like a large fish in his arms, but Grif was not of a mind to let go, and, in fact, he clamped his free hand on her shoulder. He was angry, too, had been for days, even weeks now, and worse, he *enjoyed* seeing the rabid flush of her skin, the fury filling her eyes. It was a taste, he thought, of her own medicine, a well-deserved call to truth.

"I should have gone to the authorities," she hissed at him. "I should have handed them that blasted thing!"

"But if ye'd done so, ye'd no' have had the opportunity to torment me!"

"Do you think I *torment* you?" she cried, incredulous, and threw back her head, shouting her laughter like a madwoman. "You've not even *begun* to know my torment!" And to prove it, she tried to kick him, but Grif pressed her leg against the settee with his thigh, effectively trapping her again. "What in God's name is *wrong* with you?"

"I merely do as ye bid. And here is the last of today's lesson," he said, breathing harder from the exertion of restraining such a wild banshee. "Always make yer conversation engaging, for above all else, that will draw a man to ye. A keen wit and a pleasant way with words—*no' vitriol!*"

"Vitriol!" she cried, ceasing her struggles for the moment to argue with him. "I have *tried* to converse with you, you blasted scoundrel, and I can say with all confidence that you'd not recognize a keen wit and pleasant way with words if they should rise up from the ash and poke you in the bum!"

Grif grinned at that. "Aye, ye're quite the clever one, are ye no'? If ye could manage to be clever without being so bloody vile, and do so with an enchanting smile, there is naugh' that would draw a man faster to yer side. A *real* man."

"A *real* man does not appreciate either wit or conversation," she said, panting. "His interest is drawn only to the palest of skin!"

"Ach," he grunted, dropping his gaze to her bosom,

enjoying the closeness of such a lovely pair of breasts. "'Tis no' entirely true. A woman's fair skin will indeed draw a man, but a man is equally drawn to vibrancy and intelligence in women."

"Ha!" she scoffed. "Then what is it that draws you to my sister? For she is frightfully pretty, and perhaps even clever, but she does not spend as much as a *moment* practicing the art of conversation!"

"I'm attracted to her beauty—a liar I'd be if I said otherwise," he admitted, moving his hand from her shoulder to her neck. "But I am drawn to more than beauty—I am drawn to a woman who can think on her own, who can parry with me, word for word."

"Are you indeed?" Anna asked hotly. "Naught else?" she spat. "Not *this?*"

That was the moment she abruptly and rudely astonished him, threw him completely off kilter and sent him tumbling head over heels down a dangerous slope he had not seen until that moment.

She kissed him.

Mary Queen of Scots, but the wench lurched forward, pressing her lips to his in such a swift and violent manner that it toppled them both backward, so that she was lying partially atop him on the settee.

It was no sweet and chaste kiss meant merely as a flirtation, either. It was a kiss that was brimming with fire—unbridled, unfulfilled passion to which Grif could scarcely respond as her tongue was darting quickly into his mouth, her teeth grazing his lips as if she enjoyed some delicacy. And furthermore, he was keenly aware of her body on top of his, her breasts pressed firmly against his chest, the scent of her skin and hair, the sweet taste of her mouth, the succulent flesh of her tongue.

The sensation was so naked and pure that it poured like molten gold into his groin flaming sensations he had not felt more than once or twice in his entire life.

And then, just as surprisingly, she cried out against his mouth, pushed with both hands against his chest—he'd not even realized he'd let go of her—and rose above him, staring down at him, one side of her hair having come undone and drifting between them, disbelief filling her eyes as it must have filled his.

They stared at one another like that for a moment, a single moment in time that seemed, impossibly, more alive than all the moments he had ever lived put together. He saw the tears of fury welling in her eyes, and grabbed her head between his hands before they could fall, pulling her down to him again, returning her kiss with one as full of desire as he'd ever known.

Lord God, he was lost, lost in the feel of her body against his, the taste of her on his lips. They were wild; passion was flowing out of her and into him, and it seemed to Grif that she was trying to drink him in, much as he was trying to devour her. She moved, shifting, her hands running down his torso, then his arms.

They lost their precarious balance and fell as one off the settee, Grif grabbing her around the waist to stop her fall and bracing himself with his other arm so as not to crush her when they landed on the carpet.

Now she was beneath him, and her arms went round his neck, pulling herself up to him, feverishly devouring his lips as he was hers, in spite of the silken strand of hair that had somehow come between their lips. Grif eased them down onto the carpet, caressed her side, feeling the ribs of her corset beneath her gown, and moved higher, until his palm rested beneath the plump shapely globe that was her breast.

The moment he touched it, the moment he felt its weight in his hand, she panted into his mouth and suddenly arched her neck, let her head fall back to the carpet while her body rose up against him.

With frantic longing, Grif dropped his head to her bodice, mouthing the ripe mounds of flesh, burying his lips in the crevice between them, inhaling the sweet scent of lavender on her skin. He could feel her body swell and pulse beneath him, could feel himself spiraling down that golden path of desire, hard and throbbing with the hunger to be inside her.

And he might have found his way there, might have known that bliss had Anna not suddenly bucked beneath him, abruptly toppling him over onto his side.

She scrambled to her knees, looked down at him, wild-eyed. Her gown was twisted on her body, her hair a dark sweeping mess. *"Sweet Jesus!"* she whispered frantically, and dragged the back of her hand across her mouth before struggling to stand up.

Slowly, a wee bit stunned, Grif came up on his elbow as she shook out her skirts, tried to soothe the thick strands of hair that had tumbled loose from their coif.

"This is . . . this is *insupportable,"* she said quietly, in something of a daze.

"Insupportable?" he echoed as he tried to catch his breath. "I rather enjoyed it."

She jerked a horrified look to him. "No, *no!* You mustn't say that!"

"Why no'?" Grif asked, coming easily to his feet and straightening his own clothing—his trousers being the more difficult item as he had a terribly large erection. "Why should I deny that I enjoyed kissing ye?"

"Because—" She stopped there, her eyes going wide with fright—or perhaps awe, Grif hoped—at the sight of his erection pressing against his trousers. "Oh my God. Oh—it's not proper!" she cried, whirling away from the sight of him and darting to the window. She took a deep breath, tried to adjust her sash. "Dear God, I've already pushed the bounds of propriety to come here at all! I've risked everything by doing it and now . . . now to have . . . *kissed* you like a strumpet—"

"No' a strumpet," he quickly interrupted her as he attempted to retie his neckcloth, which had mysteriously come quite undone. "Ye are a woman filled with passion—"

"Yes! I won't deny it! I am filled with passion—but not for *you!*" she cried over her shoulder.

"Indeed?" he snapped irritably. "Yer actions would suggest otherwise!"

She whirled around at that, opened her mouth to speak, but saw his struggle with his neckcloth and quickly closed the distance between them and pushed his hands away to tie it for him. "My actions were ill-advised and born in a heated moment of . . . of *anger!*" she insisted as she quickly and expertly tied his neckcloth. "And you must take your share of responsibility, sir, for you held me against my will—"

"Only because ye moved to strike me!" he sharply reminded her as she smoothed the ends of his neckcloth so that they hung properly. *"Mi Diah,* but ye are the most *vexing* lass!" he said gruffly, pushing a strand of hair from her temple and behind her ear before trying to soothe the rest of it. "Ye donna listen!"

"On the contrary, I *do* listen, but frankly one can make very little sense out of the things you say!"

"Why make sense of it at all, *leannan?*" he demanded, trying to comb his fingers through her hair. "My life is no' yer concern, is it, then?"

Anna frowned more deeply, folded her arms tightly across her middle, and stared up at him, studying him closely, as if trying to read something in his expression or his eyes.

He dropped his hand, stared right back, letting her see whatever she thought to see.

"No," she said at last, shaking her head resolutely. "It is no concern of mine—you are quite right. My only desire is to learn how to gain Mr. Lockhart's complete affection—nothing more," she said pertly, and turned away from him, walking to the middle of the room where she'd left her things.

What? She would just up and leave, pretty as you please? "I beg yer pardon, but where do ye think to go?" he demanded.

She looked up in surprise. "Home, of course! We've completed our lesson, have we not?"

Grif couldn't help himself. He grinned lopsidedly at the woman's unabashed cheek. "And what lesson have ye learned, may I ask?"

She snorted at that. "To make witty and engaging conversation, and to . . . oh! To not believe anything a man says. I believe that was the sum of it." She flounced to the other end of the room, intending to leave. "I really must be on my way," she said primly as she pretended to casually study a few of the porcelain figurines on the mantel. "Given that Mr. Lockhart and I enjoyed quite a lovely exchange yesterday—"

"Did ye?" Grif asked, suddenly feeling perturbed.

"Yes!" she said brightly, and smiled happily at him. "He was *quite* felicitous in my company and expressed a desire to call on *me* this afternoon."

"Oh?" How odd that his perturbation was, inexplicably, growing at the mere thought of that scoundrel actually calling on Anna.

"Yes! There, you see? The lessons are working just as I hoped! You've done me an invaluable service, sir!"

Bloody well, he had, and with hands on hips, he gave her a stern look. "If that is so, then where is me bloody beastie, may I ask?"

"Oh, the gargoyle," she said indifferently, flicking her hand dismissively at him.

"No' a gargoyle, a *beastie!* Where *is* it, Anna?"

"In my room, in a secret place for safekeeping," she said as she examined her fingernails.

"And when shall I be presented with it, then?"

"Why, when the lessons are complete!"

"But they *are* complete. Ye just said so yerself, did ye no'?"

"No, I did *not*," she said, as if that was the most preposterous thing she'd ever heard. "I said you've done me an invaluable service. But I have not yet received an offer from Mr. Lockhart, have I?"

"Ye said naugh' of an offer!" he blustered heatedly. "Ye said, *seduce*—it was yer very word, it was!"

With a sweet smile, she glided to the door, put her hand on the porcelain knob. "I may very well have said *seduce*, but I certainly meant *offer*, for I will *not* lose possession of the beastie before the fate of my virtue has been clearly sealed! Good day, Griffin Finnius Lockhart! I shall send a tincture round for poor Mr. Dudley on the morrow!" And with that, she blithely sailed out the door.

Twenty

The morning of the highly anticipated Garthorpe soirée, Grif woke in a loathsome humor. He'd grown very weary of London, and even wearier of the *ton*.

It did not help matters that he lunched with Hugh, who was restlessly pacing about Dalkeith House (or, as he had recently dubbed it, London Tower) like a caged animal, ruthlessly teasing Grif about the lessons as he went from window to window, staring out at the street.

He was growing weary of Hugh, too.

So Grif sought to escape his valet's attentions with a walkabout, but on his return to Dalkeith House, he had the misfortune of encountering Lady Worthall, who informed him that she was still anxiously awaiting a reply to her letter to Lady Dalkeith, in which she had explained his lordship's early arrival and indefinite plans.

Short of responding with a "bloody grand for ye," Grif tipped his hat, wished her a good day, and walked on.

When he entered the foyer of Dalkeith House, he was met by Miss Brody, who was holding a cup of something that smelled foul and was a rather putrid shade of green.

"What in God's name are ye carrying about?" he asked, waving a hand in front of his nose at the smell.

"A tincture, sent by the lass who comes round to see ye," she stoically informed Grif. "For Mr. Dudley and his gout, it is. He's abed again."

"Then by all means, do take it to him," Grif said gruffly. It was increasingly obvious that an ailing Dudley needed to be home with Fiona, who knew how to care for his old body.

Miss Brody shrugged, shut the door behind him. "The lass left ye this as well," she added, and pulled a small vellum from her pocket and thrust it at Grif as she walked on.

Grif glanced at the vellum she had given him, and was rather surprised by Anna's flourished handwriting. He would have thought it uneven and carelessly blotted with ink. He took the note to the small library, sat at the writing desk, and opened the missive.

There was another piece of vellum within; the first was an invitation to a weekend affair at the home of Lord and Lady Featherstone in Yorkshire. The invitation touted a Friday evening supper party, lawn games on Saturday, and culminating with a ball that night. Behind that invitation was a smaller piece of folded vellum. He unfolded it and read:

To the esteemed Lord Ardencaple, Greetings and Salutations:

My sister, Miss Lucy Addison, will be in attendance at the Garthorpe soirée tonight. I should very much appreciate your efforts to converse with her about Scotland, for she is quite keen on learning more about the north of Britain. I know that you enjoy conversation and I think you will find her company very pleasurable indeed, as she is a most attentive companion.

Sincerely,
Miss Addison

He could feel the heat rising in his face; he crumpled the damn thing and hurled it halfway across the room. Her impertinence was astonishing—now she thought to instruct *him?* Aye, it was part of the bloody agreement he'd struck, and if he wanted the blasted beastie, he'd do as she asked. But her insolence was unbearable.

The thing that angered him most about Anna's reminder and made matters worse . . . *far* worse—so much worse that he was of half a mind to hie himself over to London Bridge and plunge his arse into the Thames—was that he could not stop thinking about *her.*

Aye, her, the *diabhal.* The vexing, perpetually annoying and highly offensive and terribly alluring *her.*

There could not have been a person more surprised or astounded by this change of heart than he. Not a fortnight ago, he would have sworn on the Stone of Destiny that he'd never esteem that woman in any way. And while he wasn't entirely certain he was *esteeming* her, precisely, she had certainly somehow managed to get under his skin.

The *last* thing he wanted or needed at this point was to have some ridiculous enchantment of Anna. Just as the wench had said yesterday afternoon when she had rolled to her knees, dragged her hand across her mouth, her hair wildly mussed, her skin pink: It was insupportable.

He'd been so bloody confident in his ability to

fetch the beastie and have a bit of sport while he was in London. Nothing could have prepared him for this unfathomable turn of events.

Aye, he'd do well to push her into Drake Lockhart's arms and have his beastie and be done with this.

Which is precisely what he intended to do this very evening at the Garthorpe soirée. If he could, by some miracle, bring himself to do it.

At the Garthorpe soirée, Grif found Lucy early on and made himself a fixture at her side, regaling her and the other debutantes with tales of Scotland: "The heather is so thick, one feels as if one is floating on a cloud when walking," and "The sky is as blue as a robin's egg, and clouds as white and thick as lamb's wool."

When one of the debutantes remarked that she had always had the opinion Scotland was dreary, Grif bristled. "Dreary? Why, Christ and his saints slept in Scotland, lass!"

That had earned several tweets of laughter from the young ladies. Lucy merely smiled.

Later, when Grif escorted her to the sideboard for a cup of punch, they stood to one side, hardly making conversation. Not that Grif didn't try—when he brought up the latest news from Parliament, Lucy looked at him blankly. When he expressed his opinion of a popular travel novel that was making the rounds of various parlors, she seemed confused, and asked if he read very often, then declared she did not, for she found it quite tedious.

Grif thought Lucy had no inkling of true tedium. As politics and popular fiction did not interest her, Grif began speaking of the guests, and inadvertently his gaze fell on Anna, who was, he was chagrined to see, deep in conversation with Lockhart, her face alive with her effervescent smile. Lockhart's smile was likewise bright, but more akin to a burning flame. And he had not, as far as Grif could see, taken his eyes off Anna's very delectable and very exposed bosom. He would speak to her about that straightaway—he'd meant *enticing*, not exposed.

"Vulgar," Lucy muttered next to him.

He glanced at her, saw that she was looking at Anna, too. "Beg yer pardon?"

She sighed, handed him her empty cup. "My sister. She's vulgar." She said it so easily, and with such a sneer, that it made Grif's skin crawl with revulsion. That she would remark on her very own sister in such a way to a gentleman . . .

He casually stepped away from her. "I'll just put yer cup away," he said coldly, and strode away.

He found Fynster, who invited Grif to a glass of wine, and the two of them broke away, making their way to another sideboard, where there were decanters of wine and whiskey.

As they stood chatting, Grif noticed that two young dandies had quickly swooped down on Lucy in his wake, and he thought that splendid, wished them well in their endeavors to speak with the lass.

"Quite lovely, isn't she?" Fynster remarked, and Grif nodded out of politeness, but he was beginning to think he'd never seen a less attractive woman.

"A remarkable change, really. I've always admired her, mind you, but she's not been readily accepted."

Grif looked at Fynster and realized he was not looking at Lucy, as he had assumed, but at Anna. He was watching Anna laugh gleefully at something Mr.

Bradenton had said to her, tossing her head back, exposing her lovely neck to the bloody bastard.

"She seems rather . . . uplifted, does she not? Happier somehow," Fynster said thoughtfully. "Rather a lightness of being I had not remarked before now."

Aye, a lightness of being *he'd* taught her. And was it his imagination, or were the men swarming around Anna tonight? "Aye, lovely," he muttered into his wine.

"I always considered her an Original," Fynster went on, "but no one else seemed to notice."

"It would seem the entire population of London has noticed," Grif said, and sounded, apparently, so grudging that Fynster gave him a look.

"You should wish her good evening," Fynster prodded him.

"And what of ye, Fynster?" Grif asked, forcing a smile. "Ye esteem the lass, do ye no'? Or do ye prefer Miss Crabtree? Ye've spent quite a lot of time in her company these last few weeks, aye?"

He might as well have declared for her then, for instead of answering, Fynster turned quite red and looked at Anna again. "Shall we pay our respects to Miss Addison?" he asked, and put aside his wine.

Anna could not believe what was happening to her. Grif had been so right—a smile, a laugh, a bit of conversation that went beyond the weather, and suddenly she was surrounded by gentlemen. She'd speak to one, turn round, and there would stand another waiting to be introduced. She spoke with Mr. Bradenton about her dogs, those kenneled at Whittington Park, her family's seat, which she had trained to hunt fowl. He seemed rather taken by it, professed to being quite a hunt enthusiast, and was profoundly interested when she mentioned she took second place at the Sussex dog trials the past year.

She laughed at Sir Farley's tale of a particularly long night spent in New York before returning to England, and was able to share with him some anecdotes about New York she had gathered through years of faithful correspondence with her mother's cousin. She longed to go there one day, she told him. Sir Farley said that henceforth he would long to take her there.

And then she regaled Lord Prudhomme with a tale of three sisters, who had, one dark, sultry night when their parents lay sleeping, determined to swim in the lake. Except that they could not find the lake in the dead of night, and could scarcely find the mansion from whence they had begun their journey, and returned exhausted and dirty and wishing earnestly for bed, but went straightaway to classes lest their parents learn what they had done.

At that point she heard a gentleman clear his throat behind her, and she turned round to see Drake smiling down at her once more. He had already spent a considerable amount of time in her presence, laughing at her stories, whispering little things in her ear that made her blush, and then stepped away, saying there was someone he wanted to introduce to her.

"Mr. Lockhart!" she exclaimed happily, and glanced at the man who was standing beside him—but that man startled her out of her gaiety. It was his brother, Nigel Lockhart, obviously returned from Bath, and looking renewed and invigorated.

"Mr. Lockhart!" she cried happily, offering her hand. "I had not heard you had returned!"

"Just this morning," he said, bowing gracefully over her hand.

He was decidedly thinner. And his cheeks looked slightly pink, not the dark, ruddy color she had associated with him all these years. Most remarkably, his eyes were clear. "You are looking quite well, sir! I dare say Bath agrees with you."

"It is I who agrees with Bath," he said. "But I've been quite a long time from London, and I am rather relieved to be home again. How marvelous to find that the beautiful ladies I left behind are even more beautiful than before."

Dear God, was this really Nigel Lockhart? The man who could scarcely tie two coherent sentences together was making such a compliment? What an astonishing change! So remarkable, in fact, that she did not even notice that two more gentlemen had come into her circle until she heard Mr. Fynster-Allen speak to Drake.

She turned slightly to see Grif, who was looking at her with an expression that was at once amused and wistful, such an odd mix of emotion that it made her laugh, and she extended her hand. "Lord Ardencaple, how do you do?" she asked, curtseying deeply.

"Quite well," he said, instantly lifting her up and pressing his lips to the back of her hand. "*Quite* well," he said again, his gaze meeting hers.

Beside him, Mr. Fynster-Allen cleared his throat. She laughingly withdrew her hand from Grif's and turned to greet him.

"What a delight you should join us now!" she said to

Grif and Mr. Fynster-Allen, as those two men nodded curtly to Drake. "Lord Ardencaple, may I present to you Mr. Lockhart's brother, Mr. Nigel Lockhart?" she asked, and saw something flick across Grif's green eyes.

Nigel instantly offered his hand, but looked perplexed. "A pleasure, my lord . . ." he said, peering closely, "Lord Ardencaple."

"And of course you know Mr. Fynster-Allen," Anna added.

"Yes, yes, of course," Nigel said, greeting Mr. Fynster-Allen, but instantly turning his attention to Grif again. "I beg your pardon, my lord, but have we previously met?"

"I am certain we have no', sir, for I am just come to London."

"Just come? You've been in London *weeks* now by my count," Drake drawled.

Grif turned a cold gaze to Drake. "I didna realize ye were counting, sir."

The atmosphere had gone from bright and warm to very chilly, and Anna was suddenly desperate to put the men apart. "There, now, we've all met!" she said, trying to garner the attention to herself, and tried to think of what Lucy would do in this situation. "I'm quite parched—"

But Nigel was still staring at Grif and said again, rather insistently, "I beg your pardon, I do not mean to stare . . . but I am *certain* we've met before."

Now Drake was scowling at Grif. "Mr. Lockhart, you have surely confused his lordship with someone else!" Anna said brightly, tapping her fan against his arm. "How could you have possibly been introduced to him? Unless, of course, you might have had occasion to meet in Scotland?"

"Oh no," Nigel said, instantly shaking his head, and then paused, laid a finger against the side of his nose. "But still . . . there is something rather familiar . . ."

If she'd had a cane, she would have bounced it off the top of Nigel's very thick skull, and she blurted, unthinkingly, "You are undoubtedly reminded of another Scotsman who attended the Lockhart ball—"

"Ah! Of course!" Nigel cried happily, the memory lighting his face, and he clasped his hands together and levitated to the tips of his toes. "Cousin *Lockhart*, of course!" he cried happily as he floated down to his feet again. "I do beg your pardon, sir, for I *am* thinking of someone else."

Grif nodded tautly. "Aye. Someone else entirely."

Oh God. Oh dear God. Anna realized what she'd so stupidly just done, and tried frantically to step into the breach she had created, to think of something, *anything*, to move the conversation forward, but Nigel laughed happily and looked at Drake before she could speak. "The resemblance is *uncanny*, really! One would think all Scots look alike!" he exclaimed, and laughed roundly.

Drake, however, did not laugh, but was suddenly looking very intently at Grif. Grif did not shy away from Drake's stare, but steadily returned it, even though Mr. Fynster-Allen was also peering at him as if seeing him for the first time.

"Are you acquainted with him? Captain Lockhart?" Nigel asked Grif.

"Never heard his name before in me life."

In a desperate attempt to salvage the situation, Anna stepped into the middle of the four men, flipped open her fan. "Mr. Lockhart," she said to Nigel, "you simply must tell me *all* about Bath. Are the waters truly as medicinal as they say?" she asked, shoving her elbow at him. "Perhaps you might help me to a cup of punch and tell me all!"

"Punch?" Nigel asked, startled.

"*Punch,*" Anna repeated, a bit more firmly.

"Yes, yes, certainly, Miss Addison!" he crowed. "I'd be delighted!" He took her elbow, escorted her away from Drake, Grif, and Mr. Fynster-Allen, his gaze locked firmly on her bosom.

Anna's gaze was locked firmly ahead, for she could not bring herself to turn and look back at the three men she'd left in her silly, girlish, ridiculously chatty wake.

Twenty-one

In spite of her blunder, Anna was all smiles when Dudley showed her into the main salon at Dalkeith House the next afternoon.

Grif was waiting for her, had been waiting an hour or more, his mind racing around so many wild and ambiguous thoughts that his head was aching.

He could no longer deny that strange things were happening to him. Feelings were surfacing he'd never really experienced, his thoughts were turning increasingly to Anna, and he had convinced himself that he had lost his mind, for he was, he realized, extremely jealous of Drake Lockhart.

Or rather, jealous of Anna's fondness for him.

So when she appeared smiling and flushed from her walk, looking absolutely beautiful in a green and gold walking gown that brought out the gold in her hair and her eyes, and smelling like a veritable rose garden, he lost all sense of humor and immediately sprang to his feet, walked briskly to the door and locked it, then turned around, glaring at her.

Naturally, being the *diabhal*, Anna just laughed and then held a smile that was startlingly bright.

Grif clasped his hands at his back to keep them from

touching her. "Did ye enjoy yerself, then?" he asked as he walked slowly toward her.

"Would you mean my walk across town? Or the soirée?" she asked coyly.

"The soirée," he said, inclining his head.

"The soirée," she said, tapping a finger against her bottom lip. "Let me think on it. Hmmm. . . . Ah yes. I enjoyed it *enormously!*" she cried, and impetuously whirled about in a moment of exuberance. "I daresay I've never had quite so much *fun* at a gathering! It seemed as if the stars and moon hung above me the entire night!" She laid a hand on her heart and beamed at him. "I really must thank you, Grif. You've been a great help to me."

"I'm so grateful I could be of service," he said snidely, which, of course, did not affect her grin in the least. "But if ye think to trap me, ye willna succeed."

"*Trap* you?" she exclaimed happily. "Whatever do you mean?"

"I *mean,* ye wee *diabhal,* that ye reminded Lockhart the Younger of the captain's visit. I canna help but wonder why ye'd do such a thing. Did ye hope he'd discover me?"

She winced, seated herself on the very edge of a chair. "*That* was an unfortunate mishap—"

"*Mishap? Diah,* lass, ye sound as if ye did no more than twist yer ankle!" he exclaimed, stealing a glimpse of said ankle.

"Oh, please, don't be cross," she said cheerfully. "I inadvertently blurted it without thinking. But surely then it was obvious that I was *attempting* to move Nigel along. I'm quite sorry for the whole thing, truly," she said, looking hopefully at him. "But I gave you my word that I'd not reveal your identity, and I did not."

He considered her, sitting there, eyes as bright as the stars that blinked over Loch Chon, skin as smooth as butter cream. She must have read his doubt, because she crossed her heart in silent promise and arched a perfect brow.

Still, Grif shook his head and wearily pushed a hand through his hair.

"And I *did* attempt to smooth it all over."

That brought Grif's head up. "Ye did what?"

"Drake had just one tiny question, that's all."

"*Criosd!* What question?"

"It was nothing, really," she said, flicking a hand at its insignificance before fussing with her gown. "He merely inquired if I'd had occasion to meet the captain, and when I said that I had, he wondered aloud if there were truly a resemblance between you and he, and of course I said not that *I* had particularly noticed, and then he made some mention of things gone missing last summer and wondered if I had, perchance, heard of a bit of thievery among their staff, to which I replied straightaway I had *not,* even if that were not entirely true—"

"What are ye saying?" Grif demanded. "What has any of that to do with whether or no' I resemble the captain?"

She shrugged very lightly. Looked at the window. Then at the carpet.

"Anna?"

"I suppose he thinks that the items went missing about the same time your brother took his leave of London."

"Mi Diah!" he cried. "What was it he said had gone missing?" he demanded, horrified now, frantically trying to grasp what Lockhart thought he knew.

Anna looked at the clock on the mantel, shrugged again. "Just a few little things that led them to believe a parlormaid and a footman were stealing from them. They were dismissed straightaway, of course, and the thievery stopped—" She glanced at Grif. "So I *hear.* Naturally, I have no firsthand knowledge."

"What things?" Grif demanded.

She held out her hand and studied her fingernails. "Silver candlesticks. Two silver spoons, I think. And . . . well, I believe there was something about a horrid little gargoyle thing made of gold and rubies."

"Ach, for the love of Christ!" Grif exploded to the ceiling.

"Honestly, Grif, they can't *possibly* put it all together! How could they?" she cried, springing to her feet now. "I certainly didn't, and I was there! Of course I will not tell them. I promised you! I gave you my word!"

"All right, then," he said, calming himself. "And now perhaps ye will see yer way clear to returning what belongs to me and mine. Ye canna deny I've held me part of the bargain, and now it is yer turn, Anna! Return it to me! Return it to me ere yer Lockhart discovers what I'm about and bloody well ruins it all!"

"I promise I will," she said quickly, but held up her forefinger. "But perhaps not quite yet."

He let loose a string of Gaelic curses that would have sent even the most hardened of Scotsmen running.

Not Anna. She was holding out both hands now, waving them in a desperate attempt to quell his anger. "I don't mean to keep it forever!"

"Ye donna understand the urgency!"

"Of course I do!"

"No! Ye donna understand what ye do, Anna!"

She recoiled a bit, but kept on. "But . . . but there . . . there is the Featherstone weekend, and it's just a week away, and if everything should go according to plan—"

"Bloody hell," he muttered.

"If I am successful in wooing him to me, I should know it then, shouldn't I? And then . . . well . . ." Her voice trailed off and she lowered her gaze.

"And *then?* What then? And God help ye if ye have come up with some reason no' to honor yer part of the bargain—"

"I will!" she snapped, frowning, and folded her arms defensively.

"Then *what?"*

"Then I suppose I should give the thing to you!" she all but shouted, and suddenly she sank into the chair, her head down, as if it pained her to say that.

He was immediately suspicious and took two or three halting steps closer to her, cocked his head to one side, and had a look at her. "If Lockhart suspects me, I willna have as much as a week, lass."

"That's absurd! Even if he suspects, he can't possibly prove anything!"

"I have yer word on this?" he asked, his voice softer.

"Yes, of course!"

"Ye'll return it to me, then. The beastie," he added, to make doubly sure she knew what *this* meant to him.

She sighed and looked away. "Straightaway."

Grif took another step toward her. "So we are in

agreement, are we? At the conclusion of this grand Featherstone ball, ye'll return what rightfully belongs to me and we'll be done with all this, aye?"

She nodded again, and then she . . . *sniffed*. Not as if she were suffering from a spring malady, but a sniff that sounded as if she were on the verge of tears. Grif instantly took a step backward, hopelessly confused, but then stepped forward again, reaching for her—

Anna was suddenly on her feet, walking quickly to the window to peer out onto Cavendish Street. "My sister's ball will be quite the event!" she said brightly. "They've determined to extend the dance floor onto the terrace, and my sister has hired a small orchestra. Lord Featherstone has *always* hosted a mid-Season ball, as he believes a reprieve from the happenings at Parliament is imperative to the well-being of his peers and his friends, and there will be billiards and cards, although I think after Sir Herman's unconscionable loss last year, they shall wisely limit the amount the gentlemen may gamble."

She put her hand to her nape in the way that Grif had come to learn meant she was nervous, and he recognized that she was babbling now.

"And of course *all* the debutantes will be in attendance, as well as the most eligible of gentlemen, including, naturally, Mr. Lockhart and Mr. Lockhart—although one might argue whether Mr. Nigel Lockhart is particularly eligible, given that Mr. Drake Lockhart is older and stands to inherit the fortune, with a smaller stipend going to Nigel, and then there was the rather unpleasant business of Bath—"

Lockhart again. His emotions were high, and in a fit of frustration he abruptly demanded, "Why him?"

"What?"

"Lockhart! I would like to know—why *him?"*

"Why him indeed!" she snorted. But at Grif's frown she puffed out her cheeks in exasperation and cried, "What should you care? It's just the way of things, and has been since the moment I came out. To marry well is all that is really left to a woman highborn who is out, and now that I . . . now that . . ."

"Aye, lass, now that ye are a woman highborn and out, ye admire a bloody rake! But ye are far better than him!"

"He's *not* a rake—"

"He's a goddam blackguard!" Grif exploded. "He speaks from both sides of his mouth! He promises ye one thing, yer sister another, and God knows what else he promises to the other debutantes!"

"Oh *stop,* will you please just stop! That's entirely untrue—"

"'Tis bloody well true, and ye know it is, Anna. Ye know it well, for ye are a frightfully clever woman. What I canna understand is why a woman as . . . as *bright* as ye are, as . . . vivid and alive and deserving of so much more as ye are . . . would be smitten by the likes of him!" he roared.

His opinion clearly surprised her, and for once she said nothing for a very long moment, just blinked at him. "You . . . you think I'm bright and vivid?"

God in heaven. Exasperated, feeling all at sixes and sevens, Grif could only shake his head and glare at the carpet. He had no idea what he meant anymore, why it should matter to him, given the circumstance. The only thing he knew was that he felt completely at odds with himself, as if someone else entirely had suddenly inhabited his skin. "What I mean to say," he said quietly, "is that ye are deserving of a better man than Drake Lockhart." *Ye are deserving of me . . .* "And I canna understand why he's caught yer eye as he has," he said. "'Tis pure folly."

That left her quite speechless; she just stared at him with those big copper eyes until Grif began to feel terribly self-conscious.

He started to turn away, but she stopped him by saying, "You can't possibly hope to understand it, Grif, because you're a gentleman. There really, truly is nothing left to me but marriage, and the only free choice I have in my life is *whom* I marry. I'm not a fool—I know the time is quickly approaching that I will be labeled a spinster and will be forced to live under my parents' roof for the rest of my days. And truly, that wouldn't be so horrible, for at least I am allowed to pursue my interests. I train hunting dogs, I paint, I read, and I play the harp—rather badly, really, but nevertheless . . . I am free to play it. As long as I am content to be alone."

How rudely that reminded him of Mared, who had been sentenced to a similar life at the moment of birth by some ridiculous and ancient curse. No one in his family believed in the curse that haunted her, that a daughter born to a Lockhart would never marry until she faced the devil himself. But the rest of Scotland did, and they had made the poor girl something of a pariah.

Aye, he understood what Anna was saying, and looked at her, quietly assessing her. "All right. I understand yer desire to be married—"

"No," she said, interrupting him as she instantly and adamantly shook her head. "No, it's not the desire to be *married.* How can I explain it? I would that my life had been different, that I had fallen in

love. But now . . . now it's more a desire not to be left behind. Although I'd enjoy some freedom in my parents' house, I . . . I would be left behind," she said earnestly, her expression pained. "There is a difference, do you see?"

Yes, he understood the difference, and nodded thoughtfully. "All right, then . . . yer desire is to . . . belong," he said softly. "But why him?"

Anna moaned, walked to the chair she had vacated, and sank into it again, only this time like a rag doll. "I honestly can't say why him. I suppose because I admired him above the rest. And I feel rather strongly that I cannot sit idly by and watch my sister marry him. I cannot live knowing that the man I have admired for so long is sharing my sister's bed. So . . . I've done the only thing I knew to do. I sought help from the one person who would not judge me." She looked up. "I sought you."

A wave of desire washed through Grif, a desire to show her that she could have so much more, to make her understand there were men who *deserved* her esteem.

But how could he show her? He had nothing to offer her, nothing to recommend him, unless she fancied a man who had perpetuated a fraud and came from a family that was almost as penniless as a beggar. Moreover, as long as she held the beastie, she held his family's future in her hands. What could he do?

He smiled sadly. "I understand ye well, I do, *leannan.* I willna judge ye. I will help ye as much as I can. But donna hold the treasure that belongs to me family. Just . . . give me the beastie ere it is too late. Please."

She looked up at him with such gratitude that it made his gut wrench. "I will," she promised.

He walked to where she was sitting, and looked down at her. "By the bye, did I teach ye to wear yer gown so that ye reveal everything ye have to a man?"

"What?" she asked, her brow dipping in confusion as she looked at her gown.

"No' yer day gown, then. Yer evening gown—the one ye wore last night," he managed, unable to think of a word that described how lovely she had looked last night—as captivating as any woman he'd ever seen.

"But you said—"

"I said to give him a *hint* of what lies beneath, and let his imagination see the rest of ye. Last night, ye left naugh' to his imagination, and it's a wonder ye didna wipe his spittle from yer breast."

That caused her to laugh, and she cocked a brow at him. "I must be confused, for I thought I dressed exactly as you instructed."

"No," he said calmly, shaking his head as he eyed her, sprawled enticingly in that chair. "Can ye no' understand how a man will desire to take ye when ye are so revealing in yer dress?"

"Take me?" she laughed. "What do you mean? He can't *take* me."

"Can he no'? Are ye certain of it?"

"*You* may hold no esteem for Mr. Lockhart, but he'd not do . . . *that*," she said, flicking a hand at him and turning delightfully pinker. "He's too much a gentleman to besmirch a woman's good name!"

"*Ach*, how ignorant ye are when it comes to men."

"I'm hardly ignorant," she said with a tedious sigh. "I suppose I rather knew *your* mind, didn't I?"

Now Grif raised a brow. "Did ye indeed? And ye know, then, that there are men who are quite good at giving a woman pleasure without ruining her good name?"

He paused there and worked to keep from smiling. She turned quite red, but brave and curious girl that she was, she merely shrugged, examined the frill on her sleeve as if he were boring her.

"Do ye know what I mean, Anna?"

"I scarcely care, for you are speaking of men with whom I would certainly not consort."

"Ah," Grif said as he shrugged out of his coat and carelessly tossed it onto a divan. "Ye believe there are gentlemen who'd no' do so, is that it? Perhaps I should say it another way, then," he said calmly, divesting himself of his waistcoat. "What of instances such as now, aye?" he said as he removed his neck-cloth and let it dangle from his fingers. Anna peeked at him through the corner of her eye, but quickly averted her gaze. "When a woman as bonny as yerself enters a room, and a man . . . any man . . . shall we say *me* . . . catches her scent . . ."

He suddenly leaned over, bracing himself on the arms of the chair, putting his head next to hers, and slowly breathed her in.

Anna did not move, did not breathe, just held very still.

"He catches her scent . . ." he murmured, moving to the other side of her, taking another deep breath, "and it goes through him like the streams that run down the Highlands, racing along, smooth and clear, crashing into a deep pool of desire in the very pit of him."

Anna drew a shaky breath at that, and he slowly, surely pressed his lips to her neck, to her warm skin.

"Aye, but 'tis no' all," he said, nipping at her ear.

"He'll touch her skin, and it feels as soft to his hand as a baby's belly, as warm as fire," he said, and he moved his hand to caress her neck and collarbone. "*Now* do ye understand?"

"Hardly a seduction, sir," she said, although there was a wee catch in her throat.

"But then I notice the light in yer hair," he continued, "and when a strand falls across yer brow, I imagine that it's as pure as newly shorn wool, just as soft . . ." he murmured as he lowered himself to one knee before her, reaching for a strand of dark auburn hair that had fallen across her temple, and pushed it behind her ear.

Anna looked at him, her eyes large and luminous, flecked with gold that reminded him of the moonlight reflected off the top of the Highlands. He moved his hand to either side of her neck, held her there, gazing into her face. How had he missed the beauty of this face for so long? How had he missed her luster?

"Do ye see, then, how easily I might kiss ye if I were of a mind?"

She nodded.

"And ye know that if I were to kiss ye, it wouldna end there, aye?"

She smiled, a little lopsidedly, her gaze dropping from his eyes to his lips. "You make it seem as if I'd have no say in the matter."

"I wouldna take advantage of ye, of course no'. But I'd have ye *begging* me to go on, lass. Ye'd beg me to give ye all I have."

Anna laughed, wrapped her hand around his arm. "I don't think I'd beg you for anything."

He grinned confidently. "Oh, *aye*, lass. Ye'd beg me."

"Shall we place a small wager on it?" she asked, and lifted her face. "Kiss me."

As aroused as he was at the moment, Grif chuckled and shook his head. "I'll no' be commanded. *Ask* me nicely to kiss ye, and I may."

With a throaty little laugh, Anna smiled seductively. "*Kiss* me?" she whispered, and lifted her face a fraction more, so that her lips skimmed his like a breath of air.

Grif's good sense told him it was a mistake, but the rest of him reacted to the carnal enticement, and his hand was moving around the nape of her neck, pulling her closer.

She opened her mouth beneath him and he delved deeply into the sweetness of her mouth, his hands caressing her shoulders, her hair.

Anna kissed him just as hard, dropping her hands to his thigh, then feeling his chest, slipping her hands into the open collar of his shirt to feel his neck. And then, just as suddenly, she pushed him away. Her eyes were glittering and her chest heaving. "There, you see? I have the power to stop you," she said in a husky voice.

Grif laughed low—he adored her curiosity and the many ways he could teach her the lesson she was begging to be taught. "There, ye see, then, do ye, that ye have a wee bit of the *diabhal* in ye," he said, and reached down, caught her foot. Anna leaned forward, balancing herself on the arms of the chair, her face only inches from Grif's.

"Is that your response? To hold my foot?"

"*Ach,* now ye're being impudent. When ye beg for mercy, I willna be of a mind to give it," he said, shifting forward so that they were, literally, nose to nose. "Now that I have followed yer blessed scent to the gates of heaven, ye think I canna go farther. But I am made delirious by yer scent, and the purity of yer skin, and the silkiness of yer hair, and *now,* lass, now that ye have so boldly challenged me, I think that I might have a wee taste of ye . . ."

Anna laughed wickedly. "Do you intend to gnaw on my ankle?"

"The ankle is merely the door," he said, encircling her ankle with his fingers as she sucked in a breath. "A door to yer leg," he added, his hand riding up her calf, slipping beneath her drawers.

She sucked in another breath, but kept her gaze steady on his face, the glimmer of amusement shining deep.

"And yer knee," he added, pausing there to push up her drawers so that he might slip his hand beneath them and caress her knee.

A sound of unmistakable delight escaped her. "Is that all, sir? Master Stephen Throckmorton performed a similar maneuver on my knee when we were both twelve and hiding behind the dog kennels."

"Did he?" Grif asked pleasantly. "And did he remark that yer thigh was as soft as a goose-down pillow?" he asked, his hand moving upward, to the fleshy part of her thigh.

Her breathing, he noticed, was coming faster. "Actually, no," she murmured.

"And I suppose he was much too shy," Grif said, withdrawing his hand from her drawers, "to have dared to touch ye here, eh?" he said in a low voice, as he slipped his hand between the slit of her drawers to feel the springy curls that covered her sex.

"*Ooh,*" she whispered, and slipped, falling back onto her elbows on the arm of the chair, her gaze still steady on him.

Grif did not falter; he watched her eyes closely as he played with the curls, then slipped his fingers deeper inside her drawers, between the wet folds. He grinned; she was warm and wet, and now her lower lip was trembling slightly as he casually, methodically stroked her, his fingers glancing against the tip of her lust, then sliding slow and long to the bottom and back and again.

After several moments of that, Anna gave in to the pleasure. With a moan, her eyes slid shut and her head dropped back. "What are you *doing?*" she asked breathlessly.

"I'm teaching ye a lesson," he murmured, and with his free hand, abruptly caught her around the waist and yanked her upright, so that her breasts were at eye level. "I'm showing ye what could happen if ye are foolish enough to believe a man willna have his way with ye, with only a wee bit of encouragement," he said, and buried his face between her breasts for a moment, inhaling deeply before letting her slip from his arm, back against the chair. "I'm showing ye how a man might find his pleasure in giving ye pleasure," he said, and withdrew his hand from her thighs.

Sprawled against the chair back, Anna silently watched him, her hooded eyes following his every move as he casually moved first one leg, then the other, so that he could kneel between them.

"You mean to take advantage of me," she said hoarsely, but made no move to stop him. "You call Lockhart a rake, but you are worse than he," she added as he grasped the edge of her gown, and incautiously, deliberately, began to gather the material, pushing it up, rolling it up over her bent knees, along with her chemise, until she was sprawled in that chair, her legs apart, nothing between her and him but her frilly drawers. "You are seeking revenge for that horrid gargoyle," she said, her voice nothing but a husky whisper now.

He laughed low, put his hands on the insides of her thighs, stroking them, watching the copper color of her eyes deepen to oak as he shook his head. "'Tis a *beastie.* And I've no desire but to show ye exactly what ye asked, *leannan.* And now that ye have, I'll move Buckingham Palace if I must to have a taste of ye." To prove it, he moved his hands to the apex of her drawers, grabbed the opening, and in one fluid yank ripped it open.

Anna gasped.

"Ye'll tell yer maid ye met with a wee accident," he said, and with a wink lowered his head to the flesh between her thighs.

The moment his lips touched her, Anna cried out and began to squirm at the feel of his breath against the most vulnerable part of her. When he flicked his tongue against her, she moaned, her hips moving earnestly against him. He grabbed her hips to steady her as he began to explore the untouched recesses of her body, his tongue flicking into every crevice, feasting on her flesh, his senses awash in her earthy scent.

When he drew the small pearl that was at the core of her desire in between his teeth and lips, her hands flailed against his shoulders and head, her fingers in his hair, grabbing fistfuls, then snatching at his shirt, the chair—anything to ground her as he brought her to the edge of the abyss, then happily pushed her into that dark, bottomless hole with all the male strength in him he could muster.

She cried out with her climax; her fingers sank into his hair, pulling him to her, her hips riding up and up and up against his mouth.

And then she lay still, the only sound her labored breathing. With a chuckle, Grif sat back on his heels, found the neckcloth he had dropped beside him, wiped his mouth, then wiped her. Still, she did not move. Her head lolled on her shoulder; one arm was curled above her head, the other lying lifelessly down the side of the chair. Her hair was a terrible mess of ringlets come quite undone. She looked like a woman who was completely and thoroughly satisfied.

It wasn't until he lowered her skirts that she opened one eye and peeked at him, a soft glow in her cheeks and a lovely smile on her lips. "You're horrid, Grif. I shall never forgive you." But she was smiling as if she wanted more, wanted all of it.

That was the moment that Grif thought it possible he actually loved this woman.

Across town, Drake Lockhart was seated in his study, quietly studying the Bow Street man, Mr. Winston Garfield, as he reviewed his credentials.

Over the last few weeks, as Drake's attention was drawn more and more to Anna, he couldn't help notice that Lord Ardencaple was never far away. It had aroused his suspicions, and he had been quite keen to know who, exactly, was Lord Ardencaple.

But his suspicions had been raised to new heights when Nigel had mentioned a resemblance to Captain Lockhart, their cousin. From what Drake was given to understand, Captain Lockhart had arrived in London soon after the end of the French war, and had quickly reacquainted himself to Nigel with some tale of a family dispute. Unfortunately, Nigel and their father had been too fond of drink at the time to remember anything but the vintage of their port.

Nonetheless, it was a well-known fact about town that after attending the Lockhart ball, when Nigel and Father had retired to Bath for a time, the captain had mysteriously disappeared.

The only reason that fact had stayed in Drake's mind at all was because Barbara had mentioned that the removal of the parlormaid and the footman for thievery occurred just after the ball. She had naturally assumed that when all the silver was brought out for the ball, the two servants had helped themselves. Drake believed that was probably true. But it was the disappearance of the family heirloom from an entirely different place that gave him pause.

Just when their cousin, Captain Lockhart, went missing, the family heirloom went missing, too. While he had nothing on which to base his suspicions, he could not help but believe that their long-lost cousin was somehow involved with the family heirloom, particularly given its value.

Drake's suspicions of Ardencaple were flamed in part by his disdain. From the moment the Scot had made his splash about town with Mr. Fynster-Allen, it seemed that whenever Drake was enjoying the attention of a debutante, Ardencaple found a way to interrupt it. That seemed especially true of the Addison sisters. But it wasn't until an evening at Almack's, where he'd watched the bloody rake move between Lucy and Anna quite freely, that he realized the man might offer for one of the sisters before he was able to. And now that Nigel had mentioned the resemblance . . .

Mr. Garfield completed his review of his credentials.

"You quite understand, do you, Mr. Garfield?" Drake asked again, to assure himself. "I want to know everything you might learn of Lord Ardencaple. What is his fortune? From where does he come? What are his intentions in London?" Drake asked as he pushed an envelope containing several banknotes across the desk to him.

Mr. Garfield picked up the envelope and slipped it into his coat pocket. "I quite understand, sir," he said, and removed his monocle, placing it in his pocket. "If there is something to be learned about this man, I shall find it."

"Very good," Drake said. "I'm to travel to Featherstone in a few days. Perhaps you might have a bit of information for me when I return next week," he suggested, leaning back in his chair.

"I shall endeavor to do so," Mr. Garfield said as he rose to his feet and extended his hand. "Your private matter shall have my undivided attention."

Drake did not stand, merely reached for the man's hand and shook. "Very well, Mr. Garfield. You know the way out?"

Garfield nodded; he quit the room, leaving Drake to stare at the long row of windows in the library, hoping that Garfield would indeed give this matter his undivided and expedient attention. Certainly Drake had.

Twenty-two

The drive to the Featherstone estate, while a relatively short journey, felt interminable to Grif.

Not on account of the roads, which were remarkably passable due to an unusually dry spring—this Grif knew because of Lucy and her preoccupation with the weather. Nor was it the coach, as Grif had hired the best in order to maintain the appearance of a well-to-do Scottish earl, which the old Lockhart coach did not convey.

It was made interminable on account of Hugh, the would-be valet, who whined the entire two-hour journey along the Thames about Keara Brody, who refused, even under Hugh's constant duress, to appreciate the numerous and considerable qualities that Hugh believed he possessed and made him irresistibly attractive to the fairer sex.

Even Dudley, who this very morning had given in to Grif's pleadings to return to Scotland, where Fiona might look after his gout, had snapped at Hugh like a turtle as they had put him in a public coach bound for Glasgow, imploring Hugh to kindly put his mind to being a valet instead of an arse, to which Hugh had replied, very hurtfully, that this was a matter of the heart, and therefore he could not simply stuff it away to be forgotten. And then Hugh had sulked instead of preparing the coach they'd hired for the journey to Featherstone.

Grif tried to ignore him, tried to block out his complaining by thinking of something else, but his thoughts inevitably wound their way around to Anna again, and his mood turned correspondingly dark, for that afternoon in the drawing room had sent Grif privately reeling.

It seemed that for a time all he could taste or hear or see was that moment, that incredible moment when he had wanted her to feel pleasure more than he wanted it for himself. That fantastic moment had been followed by a thousand moments more, all tangled together, in which he hungered to touch her again, to feel her skin, to feel her body surround him and draw him in.

Yet in the days that followed, he dared *not* touch her, no matter how badly he desired it, for fear that he would slide deeper into an enchantment with the one woman in all of Britain he could not have.

Oh, aye, of that he was convinced, notwithstanding the remarkable sentiments stirring in him. The sentiments terrified him, for he had not the slightest notion what to do with them—he was not a man to yearn for a woman. All his life, he'd left the pining to the ladies, and this was the first time that the tide had turned. What made it so horribly frustrating was that she was—for him, at least—unattainable.

Flirtations aside, Grif was quite certain that there was nothing in the world that could entice her to leave her prominent family for the likes of him and Scotland.

In the last few days, he'd felt as if he'd somehow

slipped into a quiet space between the dreams of Anna that had began to haunt him at night and the harsh reality of his days, in which he lived an outrageous lie. But it was a small space in which he could believe that he might be quite content in the company of one woman all his days. That wasn't something he'd ever really believed of himself—he'd always thought that sort of devotion was reserved for better men than him, men who had the capacity to put others before themselves.

Grif had never believed he was more than a perpetual gentleman caller. He'd always assumed he'd be the Lockhart to keep the estate books and keep the family from ruin while enjoying the flesh of many. He'd assumed his brother, Liam, would provide the family heirs. It had never occurred to him that one woman might fulfill him completely and make him question his assumptions.

He had come to believe that Anna could have been that woman, had the circumstances been different. But they weren't, and he could sense his heart's impending doom. So Grif did the one thing he knew to do in those long days as he reluctantly prepared Anna—and himself—for the weekend at Featherstone Manor. He removed himself from her charm, forcing his heart and mind away from her, piece by piece, until there was nothing left of the old Grif in her presence.

Diah, but she made it tough sledding! Every day her countenance seemed to lighten. She'd laugh, her eyes sparkling up at him, leaning into him provocatively as he'd taught her, while he clenched his hands into fists behind his back. She'd engage him in some lighthearted debate, and the more Anna tried to engage him, the harder it became to resist her, especially as he watched her transform into a delightful, delectable woman whose every move had the capacity to captivate.

It was enough to make a man bloody well miserable.

And now, as they turned through the massive stone pillar gates that marked the entrance to Featherstone Manor, he'd face his toughest challenge yet—watching her secure Lockhart's offer of marriage.

The thought of it made him so angry that Grif cuffed Hugh on the shoulder, and none too lightly. "Snap *out* of it, ye donkey's arse! We've only a short drive until we reach the main house, and if ye alight from this carriage sobbing like a bairn for an Irish lass who has no regard for ye, our hosts will think I've lost me mind hiring ye on, and bloody hell if I havena!"

Hugh scowled at Grif and sat up from his lounging position across the forward bench to straighten his neckcloth. "I never knew ye to be so cruel, Lockhart. I'm hardly the reason yer Miss Addison prefers yer English cousin to ye, am I now? There's no call for ye to take yer frustration out on me."

"Ye've no idea what ye say," Grif growled.

"I've no idea?" Hugh repeated incredulously, then laughed roundly. "Bloody hell, it's a wonder the whole of London doesna know it as well as I! Ye think me blind, Grif? Ye think I've no' seen how ye mope about after she's gone, or seen ye staring out the window after her? Ye've been smitten, but ye are too stubborn to admit—"

"Shut yer gob, MacAlister, or I'll shut it for ye, I will," Grif snapped. "If there's any moping about, 'tis because I am fearful of someone discovering our perfidy, something ye obviously pay no heed the way ye flit about London chasing after Miss Brody's skirts!"

"I pay it heed!" Hugh shot back. "But I willna spend each waking hour fretting—"

The coach suddenly lurched to a stop; Grif and Hugh surged as one toward the small window, their argument forgotten.

"Diah," Hugh breathed as they looked out at a massive Georgian house, built of sandstone and stretching for what seemed a mile. It was three stories tall, with row upon row of sparkling windows reflecting the sunlight. There were at least a dozen chimneys, and in the front of the house, a large wide staircase led up to two huge oaken doors. Down those steps, three footmen and a butler came running to greet them.

"Mind ye now," Grif said quietly as he straightened his coat. "Ye're a valet, not a lovesick fool."

"Aye, and ye're an earl, no' a miserable old goat," Hugh muttered, just as the door of the coach was swung open. He quickly went out.

"My lord," a man said, bowing deep, as a footman hastily put a stepping stool beneath the door.

Grif climbed down, looked at the man. "MacAlister here will see to me things," he said, nodding casually toward Hugh, and with one last glare at his old friend, he followed the butler to the entrance hall, leaving Hugh to ride around to the servants' entrance to unload the baggage. That, at least, put a small smile on his face.

While Grif was attended by the Featherstone butler, Anna was upstairs in the room she was to share with

Lucy, lying very still, her head aching as thoughts of Grif bedeviled her.

From the moment they had shared such intimacy in his drawing room, her life had changed irrevocably, and in some sense had only just begun. There was a certain power in the knowledge of what went on between a man and a woman—perhaps not in *all* its physical forms—but at the very least, the emotion that could bridge the gap between the sexes.

Indeed, that long-past afternoon Anna had felt the stirrings of something mysteriously profound for Grif. It was not what she'd felt for Drake Lockhart—this seemed so much more meaningful. It was the Scotsman's image she took to her dreams each night, his image that stayed with her throughout each day. He was why she kept the ugly gargoyle in her wardrobe, for it was the only reason she had to see him and feel those stirrings each day.

Stirrings *she* felt. . . . But since that day in the drawing room, Grif seemed changed somehow, and no amount of her trying to engage him could move him.

It was not from a wont of trying. Naturally, they continued their lessons because Anna insisted upon it, insisted she hadn't learned everything she would need to seduce Drake. Grif obliged her, coaching her each day to turn the head of a man.

But he was detached, indifferent, instructing her much as her old tutor, Master Burton, had once instructed her. She'd attempted to lure him by doing all the things he'd taught her, but to no avail. She tried to make him laugh, regaling him with the antics of her family, or her hunting dogs, or, in desperation, the *ton*. But he'd do nothing more than smile thinly and remind her of their purpose, then continue her lessons.

Yet Anna was not deterred, no matter how dry his response, because something else was happening to her. She could feel the transformation in her, could feel the very core of her turning over like soil, and the rich, multihued part of her coming to the surface. With Grif's instruction, she could feel the layers of the child and the debutante peeling off, revealing the woman she was inside.

It was an experience that was quite staggering.

Whatever was happening to her was being noticed in drawing rooms around town, too. It seemed as if overnight she had garnered a handful of gentleman suitors, all of them clamoring for her attention. And where Anna once might have frowned, or refused to engage, she now laughed, engaged in discourse, challenged the gentlemen to a game of wits, and enjoyed herself immensely.

The change in her was not lost on Drake, either. He attended her more often than he had before, called on her with equal enthusiasm as he called on Lucy, and made certain promises to Anna that she could not help believing meant that he intended to offer for her.

That pleased her enormously, of course it did. It had been her dream for so long, hadn't it? And when he finally kissed her, fully and passionately beneath the arbor of her family's garden, Anna had walked away quite breathless from it . . . with just one tiny little problem.

Her breathlessness was the direct result of her horror at having discovered he had absolutely no flair for that function whatsoever. The man possessed no art of kissing!

He simply did not inspire her as Grif did with nothing more than a look, and she lay in her bed at Featherstone believing that if Drake were to offer, she'd never in her life be so physically inspired again.

So lost in sorrow at that thought was she that when Lucy came bursting through the door, Anna was badly startled.

Not that Lucy noticed; she flew to the vanity to pinch her cheeks, breathlessly announcing that the Messrs. Lockhart had arrived. "Drake gave the footman a note to be delivered," she quickly informed Anna. "I saw him do it, and I'm certain it is addressed to me." She stole a glance at Anna's reflection in the mirror. "I don't mean to hurt you, Anna, because it's quite obvious you hold him in high regard," she said absently, and leaned in a little to have a closer look at her face. "By the bye, Mr. Fynster-Allen has arrived, as has Northam, although I am at quite a loss why Bette would invite *him* . . . and Ardencaple, of course."

Anna's heart did a funny little flip in her chest.

A knock at the door earned a squeal from Lucy, as Anna sat up and gained her feet. The door opened; Bette stuck her head through and smiled happily at her sisters. "Might I come in?" She slipped through the door and coyly withdrew a piece of vellum from her pocket. "I have a note," she said, waving at the two of them as she walked into the room. "From Mr. Lockhart."

Lucy instantly whirled about on her stool. "I *knew* it! Give it, please!" she said, her hand out, her smile bright.

Bette laughed. "It's not for you, Lucy! It's for *Anna*," she said, and handed the note to Anna, beaming as if she'd already sealed a match.

"For Anna?" Lucy repeated, sounding baffled.

"For me?" Anna asked, taking the vellum.

"Is this some sort of jest?" Lucy demanded testily as Anna hastily turned her back and opened the vellum. The note read:

Dearest Anna, forgive me this letter, but I have counted the days since I last laid eyes on your lovely face, and believe I cannot mark the hours until this evening when I might once again gaze upon your beautiful smile. I quite look forward to your company.

Yours faithfully,

Drake

Anna folded the vellum and glanced sheepishly at her sisters.

Bette looked curious, but Lucy looked so hopeful. "What has he written?" she asked, her eyes on the piece of vellum in Anna's hand.

"Ah . . . well . . . it was a private message," she said uncertainly. "For, ah . . . for my eyes only, as it were."

Lucy's expression dissolved into dejection. She brought a hand to her face. "But . . . what could he possibly have to write, for your eyes only?" she asked, her voice smaller and, amazingly, her amber eyes dark and tinged with sadness.

That surprised Anna. She could hardly look at Lucy when the girl looked so unexpectedly wistful and vulnerable. "That he . . ." *Was it possible that Lucy really did esteem Drake so very much? Was it possible that she really did desire a match with him as much as Anna?*

Lucy blinked up at her, waiting. Anna cleared her throat. "That he, ah . . . *ahem!* That he hopes I shall impress on you his many good qualities," she said softly.

For a moment, it seemed as if Lucy had not heard her, but then in a blink of an eye she whirled around to the mirror on the vanity and resumed her primping. Behind her, Bette looked at Anna skeptically, but Anna shrugged slightly, tossed the vellum into the fire, and picked up her wrap.

"How do you suppose he'll offer?" Lucy asked excitedly. "Before everyone at the ball? Or do you think he shall speak privately with Father?"

"Really, Lucy!" Bette said, but she was looking at Anna, clearly puzzled.

"I suppose he'll speak to Father—wait!" Lucy cried into her mirror at Anna's reflection as she moved quietly to the door. "Where are you going?"

At the door, Anna turned around and looked at both of her sisters. Bette was looking at her as if she pitied her, and Lucy, who had twisted around on the vanity bench, was all smiles, her eyes bright with excitement. Anna's predicament was feeling heavier, and she forced a smile as she pulled the door open. "I think I should like a walkabout before the gathering this evening," she said, and with a less-than-cheerful wave, she quit the room before either sister could call her back.

She slipped into her green pelisse and took the servants' stairs down, lest she encounter anyone she'd rather not encounter, and walked through the kitchen with a terse wave, not even hearing the many "G'day, misses" tossed out to her.

Outside the kitchen, men in various liveries were milling about around a mound of baggage that might have been ten feet high if it were one, waiting for the

Featherstone underbutler to assign them to their rooms. Anna walked on, through the stone gates that led through the kitchen garden and laundry quarters, where some maids were still cleaning chamber pots.

She was oblivious to the bustle, for it was as if her mind were rearranging itself altogether, moving things about that had been in place so long that they left deep grooves. This was an awfully foolish feeling, to have wanted something for so long and on the verge of achieving it to realize it wasn't what she wanted in the least.

As she entered the quiet space of the east lawn rose garden, she realized that all her life she'd believed in that old saying that if she wanted the fruit of life, she'd have to climb the tree to get it. She'd set out to do just that, to chart her future and control her destiny instead of giving into the social forces around her, reaching for something just beyond her grasp.

It was exactly what she'd done with Drake. She had wanted him—she had thought him the most beautiful man in all of London. And she had reached for him, disregarding all societal rules and proprieties in her quest. Now that he seemed to want her, too, she had no idea what she wanted. She was horribly confused, particularly since the *only* thing she knew with certainty was that she had fallen in love with Grif, a man who was beyond her capacity to reach—far, far, beyond her grasp.

"Anna!"

The whisper of her name startled her out of her wits; she whirled around, hoping it was Grif . . . but it was Drake who stepped out from the roses to stand before her, smiling warmly. "Anna," he said again, reaching for her hand. "You received my note?"

She nervously tried to collect herself. "I, ah . . . I *did,*" she said, and suddenly smiled. "How *silly* you are, sir! I've not been gone more than a few days."

Drake's gaze greedily swept her body. "Think me silly if you will, Anna, but it has seemed an eternity since last we met."

She took a small step backward. "Mr. Lockhart!" she said gaily. "You flatter me."

"I do not," he said earnestly, matching her small step with a forward step. "I have come to admire you dearly, Anna. I esteem you greatly—can't you see that I do?"

"Indeed? Then your opinion of me has changed." She took another small step backward. "There was a time when you could not seem to recall me at all, sir!" she said laughingly.

He cocked a brow and smiled. "Do you believe a man cannot change?"

"Would you have me truly believe you've changed?"

"Indeed I have. I have come to esteem you in a way I did not think possible," he said, his smile fading, and he laid his hand tenderly against her cheek.

His response astounded her—Drake had flirted with her, kissed her, but he'd never spoken as earnestly as he did now.

Anna's mind was racing wildly, her cheek growing warm beneath his palm. "But . . . w-what of Lucy?" she stammered helplessly as he drew her to him. "She . . . she holds you in the highest esteem, sir."

Drake chuckled and kissed her forehead. "I hold your sister in high regard as well."

"What I mean to say," Anna said, trying again, as he nuzzled her neck, "is that she holds you in . . . *great* esteem." And she laid a hand on his chest, pushing a little, to impress on him just how much Lucy esteemed him.

Drake looked down at her hand on his chest and sighed. "Pray tell, what am I to do? I will admit that I had come very close to making an offer for her, but then something rather remarkable occurred. I was quite blinded by you, Anna," he said, and lowered his head, kissed her chastely on her lips.

This was it, her prize. She was supposed to feel triumphant, the victor with the spoils. But she felt nothing but a vast emptiness and a sorrowful feeling, because she never wanted to hear those words from anyone but the one man she could not possibly hope to hear them from. Yet how could she possibly push away the man who would offer for her because of her feelings for a man she could never marry?

Her head was aching with confusion, and she forced a smile, pushed lightly against Drake's chest again. "Lucy's feelings are very tender on the subject, and I suppose she is wondering about your intentions."

Drake gave her a dumbfounded look, then abruptly laughed. "I don't understand. You would have me tell your sister that my affections lie with you, is that it?"

"No, no," Anna said, uncertain what she wanted him to say. "But you should set it to rights with her."

Drake slipped his arm around Anna's waist. "If I . . . set it all to rights with her, might I assume, then, that I should pay a call to your father to inquire as to my suitability as a future son?"

"What?" she exclaimed. His opinion of her may have changed, but she could not believe he'd reach this conclusion so soon, before any real courtship.

She must have looked shocked, for Drake laughed. "You precious child! I'm asking you if I should inquire as to the availability of your hand?"

A hot rush of panic flooded her brain; her heart was twisting with all the wrong emotions. "*Should* you?" she echoed, and all she could seem to think of was Grif, and frantically searched her mind for the right thing to say.

"I thought this was what you wanted, Anna."

For the love of God, what had she *done?* "I would think that . . . *you,* Mr. Lockhart . . . you should not make a . . . *hasty* . . . inquiry?"

"And would that be a *hasty* inquiry?"

"Umm . . ." Dear God, what should she say? That she couldn't decide how, exactly, she felt about him any longer, if indeed she felt anything—other than that it would be a good but standard match of fortunes and she would gain some respectability in the eyes of the *ton* for having made a match at all—but that her heart would always be with another? Or that she was fairly certain, given the events thus far, that she did not feel the heart-pounding eagerness to see him or touch him any longer, but, in fact, felt a bit of revulsion when he touched her?

"Everyone believes you intend to offer for Lucy," she suddenly blurted. "*Including* Lucy. And Father . . . Father will believe there has not been a, ah . . . proper . . ."

Drake lifted a brow.

Proper, proper . . . ". . . proper amount of courting!" she exclaimed with a bit of relief for having thought of something.

It worked. Drake smiled. "I understand. I shall wait before I inquire. I should think the end of this affair would suffice," he said, and smiled.

Dear God, she had the space of two days to think of a way out of the wreckage she'd created.

Drake put his hands on her shoulders and pulled her close to him. "I shall wait to speak to your father," he said low, "but I shan't wait to kiss you." He planted his mouth on hers, and Anna tried not to grimace too terribly.

It was an overall uneasiness that had Grif searching for an exit from the Featherstone mansion in the waning hours of the afternoon, somewhere outside, away from all the bustle of guests arriving and settling in, just somewhere he might at least draw a breath when he thought of Anna.

But the direction of the gardens was not readily apparent in a house of such size, and he was soon wandering about the ground floor of the spacious mansion, peeking through doors, marveling at the wealth of the English *ton.* It far surpassed anything he'd ever seen in Edinburgh, and frankly, most anything he'd seen during his Grand Tour of Europe.

He had heard in one of the gentleman's clubs that Lord Featherstone, a viscount, had inherited part of his wealth, but had gone on to double it by investing in the East India Company. Featherstone was perhaps an example of the very best match an Englishwoman could hope to make, and Grif rather imagined Lord Whittington, Lady Featherstone's father, would want to make similar matches for his remaining two unmarried daughters.

The bar was set so high that were he of a mind, Grif could not possibly ever hope to meet it, not even in his wildest imagination.

When he found his way into the gardens by chance, he turned and looked back at the massive structure. How terribly puny Talla Dileas looked in comparison.

He turned and walked, head down, into the garden with that knowledge piling onto the vague uneasiness that had rooted in him the day he'd touched Anna so intimately, and he felt his heart growing heavier and heavier with the weight of his desire for a woman he could not have.

He started badly when he saw them, Lockhart and Anna, entwined in an embrace on the path ahead. With her back to him, she shone like an exotic bird, with her long green pelisse drifting behind her, the flutter of ribbons in her hair.

Grif stepped quietly behind a stand of rosebushes and watched them. Their voices were carried away by a light wind that rustled the trees behind him, and he could not hear what they said. But he didn't need to hear them, for it was painfully obvious—this was a lover's meeting.

He shouldn't have been surprised—after all, this was what Anna had wanted, had worked so hard to gain.

Nevertheless, when Drake Lockhart took her in his arms and kissed her with the passion Grif felt for her, Grif's heavy heart snapped clean and plummeted into a pit of loathing. He pivoted about, walked out of that garden, his breath coming in furious pants, his fists clenched tightly at his sides.

This may have been what Anna had wanted, but she'd used him unconscionably to get it. She had practiced her feminine sorcery on him, drawing him into her flame until he was burning for her. He loved her. He could not bear to see her with Lockhart, he could not bear to think of her in another man's arms, and at that moment he hated her with every fiber for having forced this on him.

But what he hated more than her was the situation that could not be altered, could not be made any different than what it was. There was no way out of the bloody quagmire.

Twenty-three

As the guests began to filter into the grand salon to greet their hosts before supper, Drake Lockhart moved through the room with a bright smile. Years of bachelorhood had taught him that one of the great joys of life was moving among a sea of pretty women such as this, where a man might carry on to his heart's content, and on occasion find a young woman willing to play more mature games in the privacy of his carriage house than the childish games played in drawing rooms across Mayfair.

He'd always believed Anna Addison could be one of those women. She had the reputation of being an adventurous sort, not one to put much stock in all of society's rules for women. And she had let Drake know, on more than one occasion, that she could be seduced. After that torrid kiss in the Featherstone garden, he believed he was well on his way to having her.

There was a time Drake had not been so inclined, but then Anna had gone and shed her sharp exterior by some miracle; she'd come out of her cocoon to be the Season's most surprising butterfly. Now she was a bit harder to please—she did not seem to long for his attention all the time, and, in fact, there were many times she seemed not to want it at all.

That was something of a bother, for Drake was discovering that the more she did not want his attention, the more he wanted hers.

On the other hand, there was Lucy—sweet, beautiful Lucy. She'd been a willing participant in his games, but in private moments, when he thought to act on their fierce flirtations, he had discovered Lucy was rather prudish. She was not willing to explore her desires, as he rather imagined Anna was willing, but nonetheless, Lucy's renowned beauty made it impossible for him to ignore her. Since the darling had made her debut, Drake had amused himself on more than one occasion with the fantasy of debasing her perfect flesh, driving deep into that virginal womb and watching her eyes flutter shut with the ecstasy of it.

In recent weeks, he'd begun to have the same sort of fantasy about Anna (although in those particular fantasies he envisioned instructing Anna to impale herself on him).

And there were various assorted other fantasies involving most women of the *ton*, but none that could elicit so sharp a response in him as those about the Addison sisters.

He realized he was enjoying the game far too much. It amused him—Lucy needed adoration, Anna needed a battle of wits. There was just one small distraction—the bloody Scot was mucking up his fun.

To Drake's way of thinking, the man had no more business being in London than he did in turning the heads of the two most desirable creatures in town. And as he watched him now in the crowded salon, making love to Lucy with his smile and his eyes, Drake smirked a little. When he returned to London, he'd have a full account of the man from Mr. Garfield. He'd be pleased to expose him to the *ton*. Just thinking about that happy occasion prompted Drake to smile and move to interrupt an intimate discussion between Lucy and the scoundrel.

He bowed deeply before Lucy. "Miss Lucy, you are as radiant as ever."

She smiled in that superior way she had, lifting her chin. "Good evening, Mr. Lockhart. I wasn't aware you had arrived."

Little liar. He'd seen her up on the first-floor balustrade, leaning over to have a peek when he and Nigel had arrived. "Then I was remiss in not sending word to you straightaway."

That earned him a cold look, which told Drake she knew about his note to Anna. Sisters! They were not to be trusted in the least. "I shouldn't like to interrupt," Drake said, sparing Ardencaple no more than a glance, "but I was having a look at the globe in the corner, and I found that I could not locate exactly where your lady mother's family hails from. I wondered if you might be kind enough to assist me."

Lucy's gaze narrowed. "Is it so very hard to find England on the globe, sir?"

Ooh, she was angry with him, and Drake could not help his smile—he'd very much enjoy bringing her round to adoring him again. "I'm afraid I'm entirely unaccustomed to viewing the world on a globe."

The Scotsman snorted into his drink.

Lucy sighed with great tedium and glanced at the Scottish bastard. "Would you please excuse me, my lord? I shall endeavor to point out Great Britain to Mr. Lockhart."

"By all means," he said with a smile, and Lucy smiled back at him with every feminine inch of herself.

Drake took her by the elbow and steered her clear of the bastard. "Come now, Miss Lucy," he admonished her. "Would you give all your attention to a foreigner?"

"He's hardly a foreigner, sir, and I can't possibly understand what difference it makes, given that *your* attention recently has been directed elsewhere."

"Directed elsewhere? Is that the thanks I am to have for courting you all Season?"

"*Courting* me? How odd that I should think you've been courting my sister! But what can I think, what with all the private notes of affection hurled her way?"

"There now, sweetheart," he said soothingly as they reached the globe. "I fully expected you'd be pleased when she came crying to you with the news that I've determined my heart's inclinations lie elsewhere—but not with her."

His insinuation had the desired affect; Lucy came to a sudden halt and peered up at him.

"Didn't she tell you?" he asked, acting terribly surprised.

"No . . . she said she was to impress your good qualities on me, but I didn't believe her. I thought you'd written something rather provocative, just for her."

"My sweet little bird, you assumed to know the bent of my devotion instead of hearing it from mine own lips? Have I been untruthful or unfaithful to my word?"

She thought about that for a moment, then shook her head.

"You know how I feel about you . . . why should I ever want to jeopardize your good opinion of me?"

Lucy smiled a little then and impudently tossed her head. "I really wouldn't know," she said with mock disdain, and put her hands on the globe. "No more than I would know why you can't seem to find Great Britain, Mr. Lockhart. It is quite plainly here."

Drake looked up; she was smiling warmly. He returned that smile and carefully leaned over her shoulder to have a look at Great Britain.

Anna's intolerable day bled into an intolerable night, particularly given Grif's attention to Lucy. When he'd arrived at the gathering before the supper was served—a little later than most, she noticed—he'd gone to Lucy's side immediately, smiling gorgeously, his eyes crinkling in the corners. He was doing his part quite well, Anna thought petulantly. Yet she didn't think it necessary that his smile be *that* bright.

That smile . . . she desperately wanted it for herself, and the brighter it shone for Lucy, the harder her heart wrenched. She couldn't bear to see that smile shining on anyone but her, really, and turned away from him, made her presence known to Mr. Northam.

It seemed forever before they were called to supper, and fortunately, Anna was seated next to Mr. Bradenton, who was quite interested in the hunting dogs she trained, as well as, she sensed, her. She should have been thrilled with the attention of one of the *ton*'s most eligible bachelors, but she wasn't. She was perturbed that Mr. Bradenton was seated at the opposite end of the table from Grif, so that in the course of supper she had little opportunity to see Grif at all, for Mr. Bradenton kept her quite engaged.

But she could hear his deep, lilting voice and laugh, and it scored her, over and over again.

Through seven dining courses and three wines, she sat on pins and needles, and when Bette finally announced that the ladies would adjourn to the main salon while the men enjoyed their port, she had to repress the urge to leap from her seat and run.

In the salon, the ladies were treated to sweet wine. Anna sat beside Miss Crabtree, who smiled at her cup of wine as if she enjoyed a secret, while Barbara Lockhart regaled the ladies with her latest foray onto Bond Street, where she claimed to have purchased an astounding twelve pairs of shoes.

When at last the men rejoined the ladies, Anna made her excuses to Miss Crabtree and offered her seat to Mr. Fynster-Allen, who had rather suddenly appeared by their side, and who sheepishly accepted her place on the settee next to Miss Crabtree. Anna moved to the far end of the salon, away from Drake, away from Mr. Bradenton, and anyone else who looked as if they might wish to speak with her.

And away, unfortunately, from Grif. He strolled in well after the others with a glass of port in hand, casually surveying the crowd. As he looked about the room, his gaze met Anna's. She didn't move, just smiled quietly and held his gaze for a long moment. Until Grif lifted his port glass in a silent toast to her . . . and then to Drake.

Sickly warmth fluttered in her belly, and Anna dropped her gaze to her lap. The cacophony of voices seemed to crowd all rational thought from her head, and she suddenly needed air, a breath of cool night air. She abruptly stood and went to the doors leading onto the terrace, and walked outside.

There was no one about. She walked to the edge of the terrace, gripped the stone railing, and closed her eyes, breathing deeply of the cool night air until the bit of nausea passed. Slowly, she opened her eyes and looked out over the landscape lit by a full moon. Her gaze drifted down to the white rose garden, directly below her. White roses glistened everywhere beneath the moonlight, and Anna had the overwhelming desire to touch them.

What possessed him to follow Anna, Grif could not say. All evening, he kept seeing her in Lockhart's embrace until he was crazed with it, but he had nevertheless slipped out the terrace doors, away from the laughing voices in the salon and the mangled tune coming from the pianoforte, which some good soul was determined to play.

Anna was not on the terrace. Grif lit a cheroot and walked to the railing. He caught sight of her below, moving languidly among what seemed like hundreds of white roses, pausing here and there to take in their fragrance. In the moonlight Anna looked like one of the flowers—she was wearing a white gown with an overlay of sheer gold silk that shimmered in the milky pale light, strangely illuminating her.

Grif tossed aside the cheroot, and thrusting his hands in his pockets, he headed down, ignoring his conscience shouting at him to turn around.

The gardens were silent but for the sound of the night breezes and crickets, and he could hear her slippers crunching the gravel path. He caught up to her as she reached the bird fountain in the middle of the white roses, where her fingers idly skimmed the edge of the stone bath.

He must have made a sound, for she suddenly turned around. The moment she saw him standing there, something seemed to pass over her eyes, and she broke into an enchantingly warm smile. "Lord Ardencaple!" she said, gliding forth.

"Anna," he responded quietly. Her hair, dark with glints of gold, was done up in soft curls. The white and gold gown went well with her complexion and her eyes, and Grif thought she never seemed lovelier than she did at that moment, standing there in the glow of the early summer moon.

"What a surprise to find you wandering about the gardens at this hour. I rather supposed you'd be inside, enjoying the company."

"I rather supposed the same of ye," he said, and clasped his hands behind his back as he was accustomed to doing when near Anna.

She cocked her head to one side, absently toyed with the sash of her dress as she considered him. "You seem rather pensive, sir. Has my sister treated you ill?"

"I am certain neither of yer sisters would treat me ill."

Anna laughed. "I daresay Bette wouldn't," she said with a bit of a wink, then gave him a smile that raced through his veins like fire. Grif grit his teeth and glanced down at the flowers, silently berating himself for having followed her out here like a fool. Her smile, her gaiety . . . his helplessness—anger and hopelessness rose up in him like an illness, sticking in the back of his throat.

But Anna blithely moved toward him and peeked up at his face. When he did not return her smile, she touched his arm.

Grif flinched away from her touch.

Her smile faded; she dropped her hand. "Dear Lord, what irks you? I've not seen you in such ill humor!"

Perhaps because he'd never been in such ill humor, had never felt as if he was turning inside out. "I would have this over and done," he said curtly.

"Over and done?" She tried to laugh. "Goodness, Lord Ardencaple! The Featherstone event is one of the premier events of the Season! Have you any idea how coveted an invitation to this gathering is?"

"*I* didna covet an invitation, ye will recall," he said sharply. "And I donna refer to this affair, but the fact that I am here so that I might entertain yer sister and thereby fulfill me part of the bargain for the beastie."

"Well, you needn't be so cross, Grif," she said quietly. "I can't possibly imagine how one silly weekend might harm you."

"That has been the problem, Anna. Ye canna possibly imagine. Ye havena *tried* to imagine. Ye've thought of no one but yerself."

Anna gasped, but truly he could no longer stand by, gazing at a face he loved without feeling the anger bursting inside of him. He would do well to just endure this interminable weekend so that he could possess the beastie and leave London as quickly as possible. Then he could forget Anna, forget everything that had happened. He'd *make* himself forget.

"*Really?*" she asked coolly. "And I suppose *you've* had the good of your fellow mankind at heart all this time?"

He should have turned away from her, standing so regally before him, but he let his gaze drift down her body, to where her perfectly matched, embroidered silk slippers peeked out from beneath her gown, and up again, past long legs covered in the finest silk, past the flare of her hips and the curve of her waist and bosom, to her lush, full mouth, and her glistening eyes, eyes that *always* glistened with a devil-may-care glee.

"Frankly, one might argue that you've thought of no one but yourself as well," she haughtily continued. "Duping innocent people!"

Grif couldn't help himself; he smiled lopsidedly. "Ye're wrong, lass. I've good reason for what I do, and well ye know it."

Anna lifted a sculpted brow. "Ah. And I suppose my reasons are trifling?"

"That is the kindest thing I might say of them."

"Why *is* it," she said, taking a step closer to him, "that gentlemen always assume the reasons for their abominable behavior are infinitely more important than those for a woman's honest behavior?"

"Because they *are*," he said.

"And you think your gargoyle—"

"*Beastie*—"

"—is more important than the sum of my life?" she asked, thumping him on the chest.

Grif cocked a brow at her boldness. "Aye. I do. The beastie is for me family, for the future of the Scottish Lockharts, whereas *yer* quest is naugh' more than a game to ye."

"A game. That's what you believe this is to me?"

"Aye. A bloody rotten game," he said, his smile fading.

She sighed with exasperation. "You may call it what you like, but it's just as much a matter of my future as it is yours, for I have no choice but to marry, lest I be put on the shelf. I'm in my third Season, Grif—have you any idea how crippling a *third* Season is for an unmarried woman?" she exclaimed. "If I don't make a match, I will be put out to field at

Whittington Park like an old used-up dog! This is very important to me, and I will thank you not to pretend you haven't liked playing this so-called game along with me!"

He snorted his disagreement at that, and Anna's frown deepened. "You *have!* But you mustn't be so cross, for it's almost over, and you will never have to lay eyes on me again," she said, and incongruently reached for the pearl buttons of his waistcoat.

He looked down at her hand on his waistcoat. "What in heaven's name do ye think to be doing?"

She pressed her lips together, toyed with the buttons of his waistcoat for a moment. "It's almost over, Grif, and . . ." She paused, staring intently at his buttons. "And will you kiss me?" she asked in a whisper as she lifted her gaze to his. "Will you kiss me once more like you did that afternoon in the drawing—"

"*No,*" he said roughly, and pushed her hand away as he stepped back. "God blind me, but I've fulfilled me part of this bloody agreement, and now ye may save yer kisses for yer Lockhart and leave me be!"

"But why not?" she rashly insisted, moving forward so she was in front of him again, her body boldly touching his, burning him. "Once I give you the blasted gargoyle, I'll not ever see you again, will I?" she asked earnestly.

The question made him feel remarkably empty, as if the life had gone out of him. "No," he said honestly.

She rose up on her toes, so that her lips were just beneath his, almost touching his. "I rather like your kisses, Grif. If I'll never see you again, where's the harm?"

He could smell the sweet scent of roses, could all but feel the soft surface of her skin, and suddenly grabbed her arms, his fingers digging into her bare flesh. "Where's the *harm?* Are ye so careless with yerself, Anna?" he asked, yanking her close. "Have ye no more regard for yer virtue than this?"

She smiled, but her eyes were suddenly glistening with tears. *"I don't care,"* she whispered, her breath warm on his lips. "One day I shall be married and I shall never again know . . ."

"Know what?" he demanded angrily. "*What* will ye never know? Another man? That's the way of life, *leannan.* Ye make yer choices and ye live with them. Ye donna seek a man's kiss when ye love another, aye? And ye donna risk losing everything for just a bloody kiss, no' when ye are on the verge of winning everything ye've desired!"

A single tear slipped from the corner of her eye, and Anna closed her eyes, tilting her face up to his, her lips almost touching his. "I don't care!" she said again, and collapsed into him.

The warmth of her body and the desire raging through him clouded his thoughts and knocked him off balance. Grif went down on one knee, pulling Anna down to her knees with him. "*Criosd!* I canna understand ye, lass—have ye no' dreamed of being held in some esteem by Lockhart?" he demanded angrily, shaking her. "To know his lips on yer lips? His hand on yer body?" His gaze roamed her lush, full lips, the milk-white flesh of her bosom, and he imagined his own hand on every part of her body. On her breast, on the flat plane of her belly. Between her legs. "Is that no' what ye've wanted?"

Anna closed her eyes and let her head fall back, exposing the smooth curve of her neck to him.

"Is it no' what ye wanted!" he demanded again, shaking her.

She opened her eyes, abruptly caught his head between her hands, and touched her lips to the corner of his mouth. "What I want, above all else, is for you to kiss me."

Fury and desire exploded within the wall of his chest, and Grif crushed her to him in the circle of his arms, his mouth wildly seeking hers, filling her with his kiss. Anna's hands cupped his face, and she eagerly drank him in, her body lithely arching into his, molding to him. He surged upward, to his feet, pulling her with him, then hoisted her up in a tight embrace so that her feet dangled just above his, and moved deeper into the rose garden, around the fountain, and into the arbor.

Anna's hands flitted across his temples, his shoulders, his neck. She kissed him deeply, kissed him like a woman who enjoyed and desired the many pleasures of the flesh, and Grif's body hardened quickly in response. He stopped somewhere beneath that glorious moon and let her slide down his body while his hands explored her every curve, dipping down so that his mouth could seek the creamy skin of her bosom. With his hand, he freed her breast from the low décolletage of her gown, and took it into his mouth. Anna sucked in her breath above him, and leaned limply over him as her breath began to come in pants. Grif ravaged her breast, teething the rigid nipple while his hand slid down to her bottom and kneaded her flesh, pushing her into him.

They drifted onto the bench beneath the arbor, Anna leaning against the latticework, her hands in Grif's hair, Grif at her breast, his hands wildly roaming the curves of her body. *"Leannan,"* he murmured against her skin. "God help me, but I canna resist ye, *mo ghraidh."* He rose up and roughly caught her face between his hands, caressed her hair, and looked into the copper of her eyes. *"Boidheach,"* he murmured.

She smiled, wrapped her hand around his wrist. "I don't know what you are saying, but it sounds sweet on your lips."

"Beautiful," he said with a smile, kissing each eye. "Ye are beautiful, lass."

"Beautiful," she echoed softly, and surged forward, throwing her arms around his neck to kiss him. Grif dragged his lips to her cheek, her neck and shoulder, her bosom. His hands swept down her sides, to her waist, to her hips, and lower.

"God in heaven . . . *Grif,"* she moaned on a whisper as he took her in his mouth again. "Let me feel it all again," she whispered plaintively above him. "Let me feel you again, your hands on my body. *Everything."*

How he wanted to give her that, how he wanted to fill her completely, let her feel everything that was inside him. His hand slipped to her knee, down to her ankle, and gathered the silk fabric of her gown, pushing it up so that he could slip his hand beneath it. His hand found a smooth velvet-soft leg, and he followed it up, past her knee, to the pliant flesh of her thigh, and onward, between her legs, to her damp core. She sighed longingly into his hair, and Grif felt himself straining to the point of bursting, feeling the overpowering need to be inside her.

He loved her. He realized that it was love filling him, bursting within him, and he loved Anna more than life. He moved between her legs, pressed himself against her, his wish to respect the sanctity of loving her fading in the heat raging through his body.

"I would know love at your hand," she whispered

into his hair, and desire surged like a rough wave through him. "I don't want to marry without knowing what it is to love—"

The desire in him bled out so quickly that it shook Grif, and he sat up. Anna blinked up at him, obviously confused, ignorant of the power of her words.

He angrily shoved away from her—the magic of the moment, the depth of his feeling for her shattered into tiny shards by the mention of marriage to another man.

Stunned by his push, Anna fell against the lattice.

"Ye want me to love ye while ye plot to wed yerself to another man?" he demanded acidly. "God in heaven, but I canna abide the way ye use me!"

"*Use* you?" she cried. "I haven't *used* you—we had a bargain!"

"We didna have a *bargain!* Will ye no' admit it? Ye've made me a hostage!"

"That's a lie!" she cried, and angrily adjusted the bodice of her gown as she sat up. "You didn't have a choice? *I* didn't have a choice! I didn't know what else to do! I don't know what to do even *now,*" she cried.

Grif moved forward and cupped her cheek, forcing her to look at him. "Forget this folly, Anna! Forget Lockhart!" he blurted.

Anna gasped softly and reared back, her eyes belying her disbelief. She shakily dragged the back of her hand across her mouth. "What are you saying? You know I can't do that," she said quietly.

"Why no'?" he demanded furiously. "Ye've no' agreed to anything—"

"And do *what,* pray tell? Run off to Scotland with a liar and a thief?" she angrily exclaimed.

Something twisted violently inside him; a shot of

pain sliced his chest. He sat back, pushed both hands through his hair. "Bloody hell, then."

"Grif . . . I didn't mean that—"

"Congratulations, Anna. Ye've all but succeeded in yer quest—"

"Grif!" she cried, moving toward him, but Grif instantly stood up and put up his hand to stop her.

"No, Anna. Ye have what ye wanted—but I'll no' pleasure ye like a whore," he said sharply, ignoring her indignant gasp. "I've done me part of it. Now it is time for ye to do yer part and give me the goddamn beastie! I only hope to God ye finish this business sooner rather than later, before it is too late for us both," he said, and turned away, striding away from her and crossing the chasm that had opened between them and spread as long and as wide as an ocean.

Twenty-four

Grif wanted to be as far away from the Addison sisters as he could reasonably get, for he could not bear to be near Anna without exploding in fury, and he could not, on his honor, make any more conversation with Lucy. If he was forced to spend another moment in her presence, he thought he might be driven to madness.

He retired at a time that was unfashionably early, but his charade was wearing very thin, and the evening had been irreparably marred. He fell into a fitful sleep, haunted by dreams of Anna.

The next morning, he rose early. Fynster, who had come in quite late, was still snoring peacefully across the room. Grif donned a dressing gown and rang for Hugh. And rang again. And twice more.

Were it not for the kindness of Fynster's valet—Gregerson, he thought he said his name was—Grif would have appeared to all in his nightshirt. Gregerson managed to find Hugh and rouse him from his slumber, and was even able to find Grif's clothes when Hugh was unable to rise.

"He's got a bit of the ague, I should think, sir," Gregerson politely explained.

"He's a fondness for drink," Grif said roughly as the

man handed him the clothes. He thanked Gregerson, and once he was dressed, he skipped what breakfast might have been left, and made his way up to the third floor, where the servants were housed.

He found Hugh easily enough—he was the only scoundrel still abed, a pillow covering his head, a sheet scarcely covering his body. With a well-placed boot, Grif brought him up, sputtering and squealing like a stuck pig. "Ye'll behave yerself, MacAlister, or ye'll return to Scotland without yer fool head."

"Aye, aye," Hugh said wearily, waving him on.

Luncheon was a quiet and boring affair—most of the ladies refused it, since they had breakfasted so late, and most of the gentlemen had breakfasted early so that they might have a ride about the manor grounds and into the village. Grif sat with an elderly gentleman from a neighboring estate who wanted to talk about sheep, of all things, while Grif brooded about Anna.

Shortly after luncheon, a very restless Grif wandered outdoors and saw that the ladies and the few gentlemen who had remained at the estate were gathering for various lawn games. There was lawn bowling, battledore and shuttlecock, archery, and even target shooting. A smattering of tables and chairs had been set up under awnings so that the ladies who were not inclined to exertion could watch the games around them.

That was where he saw Anna for the first time today, looking invigorated by the fresh air, with a rosy flush in her cheeks. Apparently, she had slept rather well. He intended to avoid her completely, to join the gentlemen who preferred to target shoot, but Lady Featherstone stepped out from beneath the awning and waved to him. "Lord Ardencaple!" she cried happily. "We were just to begin a game of battledore and shuttlecock and need a fourth. Would you be so kind as to join them?"

He was on the verge of declining, but Anna turned around, and in her hand was a battledore, a racket. And her eyes were shimmering with that devilish glint.

"I'd be delighted," he said, abruptly changing his mind, and marched forward to receive one of four battledores and the shuttlecock.

Anna walked out from beneath the awning, tapping her battledore against her palm as she glanced up at the sun. "Splendid day for games, don't you think?"

"Splendid," he said coldly.

She glanced at him from the corner of her eye. "Are you adept at *these* games, sir? Or do you find these games not to your liking, either?"

"Predictably, ye misunderstand me, Miss Addison. I'm always eager to indulge in fair sport."

She rolled her eyes heavenward.

"You must be quite careful of Anna, my lord!" he heard Lucy call from somewhere beneath the awning. "She's ruthless in sport." As if he needed to be told as much.

Anna merely shrugged. "She's far too frail. I enjoy physical activity."

"Aye, it's quite apparent that ye do."

"Apparently, I'm not the only one," she murmured, and squinted at the sun again as Lady Featherstone hurried forward with two more players.

She introduced Grif to Lady Killingham, who was to be his partner. And then he turned to the other woman who had joined them, a tall, older woman, with a bonnet so outlandish and large as to require its own lawn, not to mention her collar made of a starkly familiar tartan and a day dress adorned with the oddest assortment of bric-a-brac he'd ever seen.

When Lady Featherstone introduced them, Grif felt the earth shift beneath his very feet. He was so startled that he had to ask the hostess to repeat the woman's name.

He could honestly attest that Lady Battenkirk did not appear at all how he'd pictured her.

Anna wanted to laugh—Grif looked as if had Lady Battenkirk so much as breathed, she'd have toppled him right onto his bum. But somehow he managed to remain standing, to smile and nod as Lady Battenkirk spoke breathlessly.

"I've only just arrived, you know," she announced, as if Grif could possibly care. "It's quite far to travel, all the way from Wales, my Lord Ardencaple. *Ardencaple.* Is that Welsh, perchance?" she asked, her eyes lighting up at the prospect.

"He's Scottish," Anna replied helpfully.

"Scottish! How fortunate for *you* sir, for Welsh is a frightfully harsh language with a lot of *achs* and *grrrs.* Nevertheless, the Welsh are a very clever people, what with their pottery. I found the most *delightful* figurine of a lion spirit. You call them beasties, I believe. I've seen them."

"Shall we play?" Anna asked gaily, her spirits immeasurably improved with the arrival of Lady Battenkirk, who provided a welcome relief after last night's crushing blow to her heart. Oh yes, it had been crushed, all right. It was small wonder it hadn't left a horrid stain beneath the arbor, he had trampled it so badly.

"Oh yes, please, let's," Lady Battenkirk exclaimed. "I'm *quite* good, you know. I was rather spry in my youth," she avowed as she marched forward to the small lawn where the net had been set.

Lady Killingham dutifully followed, as did Grif, but not before casting a murderous look at Anna, who lifted her chin and marched on, too.

At the net, Grif shrugged out of his coat, tossing it onto a shrub, and followed that with his waistcoat.

"I've had the pleasure of playing battledore and shuttlecock with the duke of Langford," Lady Battenkirk was saying. "I twisted my ankle rather violently!"

Anna nodded, surreptitiously watching Grif roll up the sleeves of his lawn shirt—but he caught her watching him and turned his back to her.

Dear God, she was angry with him, *exceedingly* angry . . . yet she had spent the entire night feeling his body next to hers, hearing his whispers in her ear. *Boidheach* . . . She longed to touch his back now, to place her hands side by side across the breadth of his shoulders and rest her cheek against him. It was a desire so resoundingly loud within her that she lost track of Lady Battenkirk's story of her violent ankle twist until the poor woman tapped her on the crown of her head with her battledore to gain her attention.

Anna gasped with surprise; Lady Battenkirk smiled. "Mind that you watch for rabbit holes. That is the advice I'm trying to impart."

"Are we all quite at the ready, then?" Grif called as Anna rubbed her head. "Mind the shuttlecock," he advised them, and very lightly sent the thing across to Lady Battenkirk.

She swung at it with such force that it was a wonder the poor thing didn't lodge permanently in the net instead of dropping directly to the ground. One lone feather drifted helplessly behind it.

It was quickly apparent that the only two persons who had a knack for the game were Anna and Grif. Lady Killingham never lifted her racket, and Lady Battenkirk swung frequently, but rarely hit the shuttlecock.

When Anna batted the shuttlecock to Lady Killingham, Grif sprang, gazelle-like, in front of her, and hit it back, catching Anna off guard and thereby forcing her to lose sight of the thing. It hit her in the shoulder and floated to the ground.

"You must have a *care,* Miss Addison!" Lady Battenkirk admonished her.

They bandied the shuttlecock back and forth, Grif hitting with enviable ease, considering he was covering his entire half of the lawn. Anna grew terribly frustrated at his penchant for playing each and every turn.

At last the shuttlecock was hit to Anna, and in a fit of frustration she purposely hit the bird directly at Grif, but he misjudged her direction, and was lunging toward Lady Killingham to recover the shuttlecock when the thing hit him square in the side of the head and floated to the ground.

Grif looked at the bird, then at Anna. "I believe ye intentionally meant to hit me head."

"What a perfectly unsporting thing to say!" Anna snapped.

With a dark frown, he stooped to pick the thing up,

and when he served it across, it seemed to Anna to be a bit more forceful than before, and she decidedly aimed for his person again, managing to ping him on the shoulder.

She laughed triumphantly and strutted to the net, let her fingers trail across it as she pinned Grif with a look. "I believe that ties our score, does it not?"

"Aye," he growled.

She returned to her place on the lawn. Grif smiled wickedly, tossed the shuttlecock into the air, and swiped it hard. The thing sailed across the net and hit Anna on her hip, as she turned from the projectile at the last minute. She gasped and jerked around. Grif was smiling and bowed over one leg stretched before him, his arms splayed wide.

Furious, Anna pounced on the fallen shuttlecock. "You really shouldn't have done that, my lord!" she cried, and served it with as much force as she could marshal.

The final battle was begun.

The ladies beneath the awning had turned their chairs to face the court and began to call out helpful suggestions. "A bit on your toes, Lady Killingham!" one suggested. "Miss Addison, do take care to keep from wrenching your back!" called another.

But for Grif, they had nothing but words of encouragement. "My dear Lord Ardencaple, shall you have my favor?" one lady cried, waving a white kerchief at him. "Oh my lord, what marvelous skill you have!" another assured him when he managed to save another shuttlecock from its demise on Lady Killingham's battledore.

As the game neared its conclusion, Anna and Lady Battenkirk were dangerously close to being eliminated. "Go on, then, let's not dally," Anna said irritably, preparing herself to receive the shuttlecock.

Grif smiled dangerously, pointed his battledore at Anna, tossed the shuttlecock in the air, and slapped it to Lady Battenkirk. She returned it hard to Lady Killingham, who shrieked and turned away in fear. Grif easily retrieved it and batted it to Anna. She swiped at it with great force, but her battledore caught nothing but feathers, and the bird sailed into the net. She watched in horror as the thing fell to the ground.

"Oh dear, you've lost the game!" Lady Battenkirk cried.

"W-what?" Anna asked, gasping for air.

"But never you mind, Miss Addison. A bit of practice, that's all you require! Oh *dear*, I'm really quite parched! Come, Lady Killingham, shall we have a lemonade? This warm weather brings to mind the time I was in York. Have you been to York? They have such lovely textiles there . . ."

Lady Battenkirk dragged Lady Killingham along. Anna looked at the fallen shuttlecock, then at Grif.

His gaze was cold as he shoved one arm into his discarded waistcoat, and then the other. "It would seem we had time for one last lesson, aye? Never challenge a man at his own game," he said, and picked up his coat. Without another glance at her, he walked to the awning to join the others while Anna stood alone, staring at the lot of them.

Twenty-five

Grif finally broke away from the ladies and spent the better part of the late afternoon pacing his room, his thoughts in turmoil with the unexpected appearance of Lady Battenkirk.

Everything had fallen into place so easily before this—he'd never imagined he'd face something so daunting. What would Fynster say about Lady Battenkirk's arrival? He'd tried so hard to help Grif find her friend Amelia. He'd undoubtedly be anxious to introduce him to Lady Battenkirk and ask after her friend Amelia, a question that would lead to disaster.

Even worse, what if Lady Battenkirk mentioned the beastie, or the Englishwoman from whom she had bought the blasted thing? She'd already mentioned the beastie once, and he feared she had almost mentioned it again—he would never know for certain, because he had stopped her by changing the subject when, after the game, she had begun to catalog all the goods from Scotland she'd ever purchased. It was obvious Drake Lockhart was suspicious of him—the slightest suggestion from Lady Battenkirk might aid him in putting all the pieces together.

This was a bloody nightmare.

Grif was still pacing when Hugh appeared, carrying the formal suit of clothing Grif was to wear to the evening's ball, which he carelessly tossed on a bed. He put his hands on his hips, glared at Grif. "Have ye any idea how the English treat their servants, then?"

"I've a feel for it, aye."

"It's abominably inhumane!" Hugh groused, and walked across the room, fell into one of two leather wing-back chairs that faced the hearth. "They've forced me into a room with a bloody valet," he said disapprovingly. "*Mi Diah,* what these fops expect to be done to their clothing!"

Grif shrugged, looked absently at the clothes Hugh had tossed aside, his thoughts elsewhere.

Hugh frowned at the window. "And to add insult to me injuries, I lost two hundred pounds to the English bastards."

That certainly caught Grif's attention. "Ye did *what?*"

Hugh waved a limp hand, and dropped his head back against the chair. "Cards," he said simply.

"*Cards!*" Grif bit out, incensed. "Bloody hell, MacAlister, how do ye suggest we return to Scotland if ye lose every coin we have?"

"*Ach,* we've coin enough to return home, Grif. Dudley's already gone—"

"How dare ye gamble it away?" Grif spat, stalking to Hugh's side. "That is money me father borrowed!"

"*Diah,* I'll repay ye with me share of the beastie!" Hugh said angrily. "And as to that, when is it that we shall possess the wretched thing? I am sick unto death of living like a bloody prisoner!"

Grif sighed. "Sooner than ye think," he answered morosely.

"*How* soon, then?"

"I donna know precisely. But we've a wee spot of

trouble," he said, and proceeded to explain the dilemma they suddenly found themselves in with Lady Battenkirk's arrival.

Hugh listened thoughtfully. "There's no more time," he said at last. "Ye must demand the lass return it at once."

"Aye," Grif said. "Aye."

Hugh cocked his head, looked at Grif a long moment. "Ye donna want to demand it."

"Of course I do," Grif said with a disdainful shake of his head.

But Hugh clucked. "Aye, 'tis just as I gathered, then. Ye *are* in love with her—"

"*Diah,* but ye are a man of enormous exasperation!"

"And ye think ye are no'?" Hugh returned. "At the very least, admit what's true! Ye love her, ye do!"

Grif groaned to the ceiling and shook his head wearily. "I'll speak to her tonight," is all he would say.

It was true: the Featherstone ball was plainly an event that was not to be missed. Nothing had been left undone; the ballroom was lined with giant vases of yellow and white flowers—wood sorrels, daffodils, primroses, cowslips, daisies, and coltsfoots. Beeswax candles, cut to uniform height, were lit and glittering against three crystal chandeliers. The carpet had been rolled away and the pine dance floor polished with beeswax to a high sheen. Embroidered armchairs lined the walls, and in a far corner an impressive eight-piece orchestra played.

There were, Grif guessed, almost three hundred people already in attendance that evening, and still more arriving.

He and Fynster had made their way down, were standing in the ballroom watching the dancers who floated past on the strains of music. Along with Fynster, Grif admired the women who filled the ballroom; mostly in pale pastels and varying shades of white and ivory, they blended well with the delicate flowers.

And there was the brightest of all the flowers, the one in pale green. Anna was engaged in a quadrille with a ruddy-cheeked young man who could not stop smiling.

She looked, Grif thought, absolutely radiant. Her green brocade gown was cinched tightly beneath her bosom, covered with the sheerest of silk, and gathered in folds high on her back. Her dark auburn hair was affixed artfully to the back of her head, and it appeared as if she had helped herself to some of the flowers in the ballroom and put them in her hair. Her arms, encased in gloves, were slender and long, and her smile . . . he could feel the force of it from where he stood.

From his vantage point, Grif could quietly watch her and manage to avoid Lucy's gaze altogether, as she was caught up in conversation with two young gentlemen who looked as adoring of her as a pair of puppies. Lockhart was across the room with his smiling brother, who was holding a small crystal glass. His sobriety, Grif thought, would be short-lived.

It seemed to Grif that Fynster was always watching the dancers. "What is it, man," Grif asked him, "that keeps ye from joining the others?"

Fynster smiled ruefully. "I'm a dreadfully horrid dancer, Ardencaple," he said cheerfully. "I would trample a lady's feet black and blue!"

"Come on, then," Grif said, nudging him lightly on the shoulder. "Ye canna be so clumsy as that."

A sheepish grin spread across his friend's face, and he shrugged. "If you must have the truth, I'm afraid that my heart's attached itself to someone and there it has remained, steadfastly unchanged in its devotion. But I've not found the courage to declare my esteem . . . or to dance." He glanced at Grif from the corner of his eye. "You'd not understand the feelings of a man such as myself in this regard, I'm afraid."

"Aye, but I would, Fynster, more than ye can know."

"*You?*" Fynster snorted. "A man who enjoys his reputation as a libertine, who toys with debutantes as if they were mice and he the cat? Come now!" he laughed. "You've no regard for matters of the heart, Ardencaple."

That frank assessment startled Grif. "Do ye truly believe this of me, Fynster?" he asked in all earnestness. "That I have no desire to love or be loved?"

Now Fynster laughed and shook his head. "You are teasing me, sir, for it is plainly obvious to all who know you that your desire to love or be loved would not extend beyond the linens of your bed!" He laughed again, shaking his head, as if he enjoyed a good joke.

Grif supposed he could hardly blame Fynster for that: he'd not really had an affair of the heart before now. How trifling he must have seemed to a man of integrity such as Fynster, how very cocksure and unrepentantly randy.

He sighed wearily and shifted his gaze to the dance floor again. "I'll have ye know, Fynster, that I have greatly appreciated yer friendship. By any measure, ye are one of the finest acquaintances a man could hope to have."

With a sound of surprise, Fynster looked at Grif. "Why, how very kind of you, sir! I very much appreciate the sentiment, and the feeling is entirely mutual—a better Scotsman I've not had the pleasure to meet."

"There are better Scotsmen, lad, far better than me," Grif said, trying to smile. "My only hope is that one day ye'll know one."

Fynster chuckled fondly and clapped him on the shoulder. "I *do* know it. Why, I've—"

"Mr. Fynster-Alll-*len!*" a familiar voice trilled behind them.

Grif groaned beneath his breath, but Fynster turned with a start, his face breaking into a wide grin. "Lady *Battenkirk!*" he exclaimed, surprised. "But I was given to understand you were in Wales!" he said, taking her proffered hand.

"Oh, Wales, how lovely it is, sir." Lady Battenkirk sighed. "I discovered some very *interesting* artifacts there. They're quite unique. I don't know how to describe them, really—do you recall the pieces I purchased in Cambridge last year?"

"No," Fynster said, trying to turn her toward Grif.

"No? Oh dear, I must have given them all to Amelia before I showed you—"

"Lady Battenkirk, forgive my interruption, but I'd very much like to introduce my friend, Lord Ardencaple," Fynster managed to squeeze in.

"Oh!" Lady Battenkirk exclaimed, seeing Grif now. "Lord Ardencaple, we meet again!"

"What? You've met, then?" Fynster asked, confused, his gaze darting between the two of them.

"Aye, in a game of battledore and shuttlecock," Grif said, taking her hand and bowing deeply over it.

"In*deed!*" Fynster exclaimed, obviously delighted.

"Oh yes," Lady Battenkirk said, folding her hands over her belly. "Lord Ardencaple is a formidable opponent! Would that you had joined us, Mr. Fynster-Allen."

"But . . . I was not aware you'd come from Wales. I was quite assured you'd not return until the late summer," Fynster said, clearly confused. "In fact, I explained to Lord Ardencaple that you'd not be back to London for quite some time, as he desired an introduction—"

"Which I have been fortunate to receive," Grif said quickly, and bowed over Lady Battenkirk's hand. "It was indeed me great pleasure."

"Oh?" Lady Battenkirk trilled, clearly pleased as Grif let go of her hand. She coyly patted her ringlets. "You sought an introduction, my lord?"

"Aye. I'd heard of yer interest in old . . . cathedrals," he said, trying desperately to ignore the frown of confusion on Fynster's face.

Lady Battenkirk's face beamed with delight. "A fellow enthusiast! Indeed, my lord, I attended an *archaeological* dig," she informed him, putting her hand to her bodice, which, he noticed, was a peculiar shade of green, particularly against the burgundy cuff of her sleeve.

"I am certain it was fascinating."

"Oh, indeed, it was *quite* fascinating. They found some pottery of some sort, which I suppose was all well and good for the men of science, but I have rather a lot of pottery and didn't see the significance of it, really. I was so hoping for something a bit more exciting. Bones, perhaps."

"Bones would be far more exciting," Fynster politely agreed.

"I rather suppose that at the end of the day I much prefer traveling about and picking up trinkets here and there," Lady Battenkirk said gleefully. "I do adore a bargain, my lord. Speaking of bargains, I have traveled as far as Scotland and found some *very* interesting trinkets."

"Did ye find any bones?" Fynster asked with a wink.

That made Lady Battenkirk laugh in a sort of wheezing guffaw. "Nary a one!" she cried through her laughter before catching her breath. "But there truly are such wonderful knickknacks to be had from Scotland—not at all like the markets in London. Frankly, England's north country has quite interesting pieces, too, and many of *them* are from Scotland. All those border wars, I suppose, back and forth and back again."

Grif smiled thinly.

"Oh!" she cried, laying a finger next to her nose as she peered into space. "I know something that might interest you, my lord! One day last year, I happened into Cambridge and I had the chance to meet a lovely young woman from London, who was selling a gold statue of a *beastie* of all things!"

"A *what?*" Fynster asked, wrinkling his nose a little while Grif felt his heart sink right to his toes.

"*Bea-stie,* darling," Lady Battenkirk said, articulating carefully. "A creature of some sort. Reminds me of an angry lion with his great gaping mouth and red glass eyes. I honestly can't say what it is, but it made for such an unusual piece of art! Well, I paid the poor miss for it, as it was clear she desperately needed funds, although I would have sworn by the look of her that she was Quality. Nevertheless, my mission in life is to help those who cannot help themselves, and I helped that poor dear by purchasing her statue and giving it to my friend Amelia. And do you know that Amelia faithfully displayed that unique creature on her mantel until the day she died?"

Grif had the overwhelming urge to put a finger in his collar and loosen it for some air. He risked a glance at Fynster who was looking at Lady Battenkirk in confusion.

"You'll not find such unusual art in London, I assure you," she said with a snort and a shake of her head. "Southern England has her treasures, too, you understand. Once, in Cornwall, I found the loveliest amulet. Do you know what an amulet is?" she asked Fynster.

"I can't say that I do, really," he answered absently, and frowned curiously at Grif.

"I beg yer pardon," Grif said, quickly interrupting before she could pin him in with another long-winded tale, "I am certain I promised the next dance."

"Then you must run along, my lord! You'd not want to keep a pretty young miss waiting. Perhaps you might like to view my various treasures when we are next in London?"

"I would indeed. I shall call on ye, if I've yer leave."

"Of *course* you do, sir!" she said, beaming happily.

Grif smiled at a clearly perplexed Fynster, wishing that he had the luxury of truth to explain to his friend what he was about. But there was nothing to be done for it—a man of Fynster's character could not rest without telling the truth to the Lockharts, Grif was certain—so with a bow for Lady Battenkirk, Grif took his final leave of his good friend.

He walked outside onto the terrace so that he might breathe some air and get his thoughts together. Between a pair of torchlights, he gripped the railing and stared out into the black night, his insides as jumbled as his mind with nerves and regret and a whole host of things he could hardly name. He'd never bargained for this. He'd never thought his journey would result in such an upheaval in his life, of lies and betrayals and even love . . .

"Ah . . . there you are."

Speak of the devil, Anna's voice drifted behind him, and Grif closed his eyes. The good Lord was punishing him, surely. He opened his eyes, made himself turn around. Anna leaned forward and peered up at him. "Are you quite all right? No bumps or bruises from the game?"

"No' from the game," he said evenly.

Anna lifted a brow, walked to the railing and looked around. "I thought perhaps you might do me the honor of standing up with me," she said, lifting her arm and jiggling her dance card. With a conspiratorial look about, she whispered, "I know you don't approve, but I'm anxious to demonstrate that I have indeed learned quite a lot from you, sir. I no longer feel compelled to lead." She smiled softly.

In spite of himself, in spite of his anger, Grif couldn't help smiling a bit. "I donna believe you."

"It's true," she said, nodding. "I'm quite cured of it. Come, and I'll show you."

Grif shook his head.

Anna touched his hand. "Come, please come, Grif. I don't want to leave things as we did last night," she said softly. "Come then, just a waltz. And then you may hie yourself to whomever."

In the ballroom, the orchestra began to play the waltz, and Anna smiled warmly at Grif. "They're starting."

He knew he shouldn't do it. He didn't *want* to do it. He should have told her then and there that he had to leave, leave tonight, but as usual he felt powerless to resist her, and the thought of holding her once more . . .

"I've yer word ye'll no' lead?"

Anna laughed and crossed her heart. Grif offered his arm, escorted her to the dance floor, and stood back, bowing deeply as she curtsied. "Oh my," she said as she carefully placed her hand in his, "how very formal of you."

He said nothing, just swept her into the rhythm of the waltz, pulling her closer with each turn, closer than he should, as close as a man would hold his wife. She felt so perfect in his arms, so right, and he had a small, treacherous desire for that dance to go on forever.

"Will you go on dancing without so much as a smile?" she asked him. Her head was tilted back so that her face was upturned to him like a flower to the sun. "You handed me a rather sound beating at battledore and shuttlecock, and here you are, given the pleasure of leading this dance, and still you frown."

"Do I?" he asked absently, momentarily lost in the copper depths of her eyes.

She laughed, her lips full and dangerously kissable. "You do! All right, then, you really must smile. You'll be done with me soon."

A feeling of sadness swept through him and he put his mouth near her head, taking a breath of her. "Sooner than ye know, lass. I must go," he whispered.

"Honestly, Grif, it's only a dance!" she said with cheerful exasperation. "As soon as it ends, I swear I'll leave you at peace, for I shouldn't want to stand in the way of your many admirers."

He smiled sadly, pulled her closer to avoid a collision with another couple, let his hand slide up her trim back and down. "No, Anna . . . I mean that I must *leave* here. Before dawn's light."

The smile instantly faded from her face. *"Tonight?"* she gasped. "What are you saying? You *can't* leave tonight! There is the ball, and they've gone to great lengths to have chess on the east lawn on the morrow, and what shall Bette think, and besides, *everyone* is leaving tomorrow afternoon, so why must you hurry away?"

She looked so confused and so hurt that he couldn't help but pull her closer and hold her there, propriety be damned. "I canna remain here, Anna. Lady Battenkirk has returned, and surely ye can understand the potential jeopardy she brings. She has already mentioned the beastie and her Amelia. It's only a matter of time ere I'm found out," he said, his voice dropping to a whisper.

"But . . . but won't they suspect something is amiss if you just up and leave?" she demanded frantically. "Why must you go now?"

"What is this, now, Anna?" he asked, dipping his head a little to have a look into her face. "Ye have what ye want, aye? Ye must fulfill yer end of our agreement and bring me the beastie. I canna leave

England without it, and I must leave England as soon as possible."

Anna said nothing, just pressed her lips together as they twirled about. But she could not keep silent for long. "I don't understand why you must rush away!" she insisted. "Even if Lady Battenkirk says something about the silly thing, what has it to do with you?"

"*Ach*, lass, donna be childish, now," he softly admonished her. "My offense is a hanging offense. Ye must honor yer word, and as soon as possible."

"But I . . ." She dropped her gaze to his neckcloth. "I don't want you to go," she whispered, and Grif felt insupportably heartened by it. But then she added, "I can't possibly do this all by myself!"

Lockhart. Always Lockhart! The waltz ended; Grif instantly dropped his hand, stepped back, and bowed.

Anna dipped a stiff curtsey, put her hand on his arm to allow him to escort her from the dance floor, her gaze on the floor ahead of them.

When they reached the seating, Grif removed her hand from his arm. "Donna look so forlorn, then," he said impatiently. "Ye donna need me—ye *never* needed me. It was never more than a matter of simply believing."

Anna made a sound of disagreement that Grif ignored.

"Ye return to London tomorrow night, do ye?" he asked, and she nodded reluctantly. "Monday, Anna, do ye hear me, then? Ye *must* bring it Monday."

She sniffed disdainfully.

Grif leaned down so that she could not mistake him. "If ye donna bring it, I will come for it and I will tell yer father the bargain we made for yer bloody trinket. Donna believe for a moment I willna do as I say, *leannan*. I'll remind ye one last time that the beastie is what will keep me family from certain poverty. *I must have it!"*

"Fine," she said, turning away. "Monday, then." She walked away from him.

Grif watched her go, the tail of her gown sweeping behind her, her head held high. And then he turned and disappeared into the shadows of the corridor.

Twenty-six

The news that Lord Ardencaple had left in the night was indeed discussed at breakfast the next morning. There were a handful of guests in the room, Anna among them.

It was Lord Killingham who remarked he had left, and that he was sorry for it, for he wanted to congratulate him for having taught Lady Killingham to enjoy a sport. Any sport. He seemed quite amazed by it, actually.

"Oh, he was a splendid competitor," Lady Battenkirk said as she helped herself to a plateful of eggs and black pudding. "Scots are, you know, quite good athletes."

"Scots?" Drake scoffed. "Quite good with the whiskey, you mean," he said, and gained a laugh for it.

"I rather like the Scots," Lady Battenkirk said. "They are quite a creative people, just like the Welsh. You should see the gold creature I bought from a young woman in Cambridge. She was English, but she said it was made by a Scot centuries ago. It's a very fine piece—exquisite in detail and rather monstrous in appearance."

Nigel, who was seated across from Anna, blinked and looked strangely at Lady Battenkirk. "Eh, what? What was that you said about a monster?"

"Oh, it was absolutely stunning!" Lady Battenkirk said, clearly pleased with the attention. "About so high, and really rather heavy, and covered with quite a lot of red glass baubles. And it had a gaping mouth, as if it was screaming. Excellent craftsmanship."

Nigel looked at Drake; the two of them looked at Lady Battenkirk. "And how did the lady come to sell it to you, if I may ask?" Nigel asked.

"Oh, that was merely a coincidence," she said. "It was a quaint little shop in Cambridge, and the merchant there refused to even *consider* it, can you imagine? So *I* offered, for it was just the sort of thing Amelia loved, God rest her soul, and the young miss seemed quite relieved to be rid of it."

"A Cambridge woman?" Drake pressed.

"Oh no, I shouldn't think so," Lady Battenkirk said thoughtfully. "Too finely dressed for Cambridge! I assumed she was from London."

"And what of the brooch you wore last evening, Lady Battenkirk?" Anna interjected. "Where did you say you found that lovely treasure?"

"Oh, now, *that*," she said, putting down her fork. "That was *truly* a find!" she exclaimed, and launched into a tale of finding the black pearl brooch. Anna found it quite difficult to follow the story, for she could see the change in Drake's expression at the mention of the gargoyle.

Grif was right; suspicions had been raised to dangerous heights.

It was clear to her now. She had to give it back. As much as it pained her, as much as she did not want any of it to ever end—or to *begin*, she thought, stealing another glimpse of Drake now, she could tell by his expression that he knew something. And she rather thought he was the sort of man who would not stop until he knew it all.

With that on her mind, the day passed interminably, what with the giant chess party on the east lawn, where guests and servants were coerced into actually playing the various chess parts while teams of guests moved them about in a rather fantastically sensational match. Anna played with Drake, but he was very distracted, hardly caring of their moves. They lost badly.

When it finally came time to return to London's Mayfair, Anna was fortunate enough to find a seat in her mother's carriage, in spite of all the baggage and her mother's widowed friend who had journeyed with them. Father was returning a bit later with Lucy, he eagerly explained, for Drake Lockhart had asked for a moment alone with him. "I can only imagine what this might mean," he said excitedly.

Lucy smiled brilliantly at Anna. "I had so hoped there'd be news for you, too, Anna," she said. "At least from *some* gentleman."

Anna smiled thinly and climbed into her mother's carriage.

Her mother crowed to her friend about Lucy's prospects for a match with Lockhart all the way home, having forgotten in all the excitement, it seemed, her vow to see Anna wed before Lucy.

Anna wondered how very surprised her parents would be when Drake spoke of his desire to wed *her*, and not Lucy. She wished she would be anywhere but Whittington House when Father and Lucy returned later this evening.

Once they arrived home, and a footman had delivered her two trunks to her rooms, Anna sent her maid away with the excuse of a blinding headache and locked the door behind her. She peeled off her gloves and tossed them aside, and walked to a large oak wardrobe in her room. Hands on hips, she glared at it, debating. Then, in a moment of frustration, she threw open the doors and looked up at the ugly gargoyle sitting atop the highest shelf. "Bloody wretched creature!" she said aloud. "What trouble you've caused!" She whirled away from it, stalked across the room, and threw herself, facedown, onto the bed in a flood of tears.

She must have cried herself to sleep, for the next thing she knew it was early morning. She wearily stripped off her clothes and crawled beneath the linens and bed coverings wearing her chemise.

Later that morning, she awoke with a headache. She rose, washed and dressed, and went down to the breakfast room.

Her father was within, frowning down at his breakfast on the table before him.

"Father? Is everything all right?" She obviously startled him; his eyes went wide, and Anna stopped midstride. "What is it, Father? Has something upset you?"

"Oh no," he said. "No, no, nothing has happened, darling," he repeated, and began to fold his napkin, carefully smoothing each fold. "And what have you planned for the day, Anna?" he asked loudly, looking up with a forced smile.

"I . . . I thought I would call on a friend," Anna said, walking to the sideboard and helping herself to toast. "Perhaps make a day of it."

"Splendid idea. Splendid," Father muttered, and pulled his timepiece from his waistcoat and squinted. "Nine o'clock, is it? I should go on with it and walk down to the club, do you suppose?" he asked, coming quickly to his feet just as Anna reached the table.

"Father . . . what's wrong?"

He looked at her then, his lips working but no sound coming forth, until he blurted out, "Frankly, darling . . . there's nothing wrong!" he said, and shook his head as if to clear it. "Everything is very fine. But I suppose there are times when life hands you a bit of a dilemma, aren't there? Not anything that can't be overcome, I should think, yet . . ." He suddenly walked to her and kissed her on top of her head. "I rather think this an excellent day for calling on friends. Be abroad as long as you like."

"Thank you," she said, looking at him curiously. Father tried to smile, but was not completely successful, and walked out of the breakfast room, his head down.

All right, there it was. She'd never seen her father quite so agitated and surely he might have mentioned his meeting with Lockhart had everything gone as he'd hoped. And if Drake had offered for *her*, wouldn't her father be happy to present it to her? It was all starting to feel very odd—Anna couldn't make heads or tails of it, and honestly, she thought, wrinkling her nose at her toast, she would have no appetite until the deed was done.

As there was no avoiding it, she really ought to go on and do it. No matter how badly she preferred not to.

While Anna was bathing and dreading handing over the gargoyle, Drake was meeting with Garfield, who had come with some very interesting news. "It seems, sir," he was saying, "that Lord Ardencaple does not exist. He's a fraud."

The news was not altogether unexpected, but nevertheless it hit Drake squarely in the jaw. "What do you mean, he does not *exist?*"

"That particular title was consumed by the duke of Argyll decades ago. Ardencaple, as it were, no longer exists. Nor is it possible that Argyll granted the title to anyone; it was abolished by the duke."

Something snapped in Drake's head, and he put a hand to his temple to rub it. "But to what end does he perpetrate this fraud?" he demanded of Garfield. "What could possibly possess him to come to London and parade about as some Scottish earl?"

"I can only imagine his intent is to defraud further."

"But what of the house on Cavendish? How did he manage that?"

"It belongs to Lady Dalkeith, who is in France, presently. When I inquired, a cook or some such servant showed me the letter of introduction that gave Lord Ardencaple leave to use the house for a time."

"Is it authentic?"

"No one can tell us but Lady Dalkeith, sir, and I've sent a formal inquiry to France. Nevertheless, I should think the man is here to do something far more serious than impersonate an earl. Theft, perhaps."

Theft . . . The thing snapped in Drake's head again, and this time he knew without a doubt. He hadn't quite connected all the pieces, but he knew the Scot had something to do with the missing heirloom. The missing heirloom Lady Battenkirk had, inexplicably, bought in Cambridge. He looked at Garfield. "I want to know about the house as soon as possible," he said. "If you have to send a man to France and inquire of Lady Dalkeith herself, do so at once. I hardly care about the expense."

"As you wish, sir. If there is nothing else?"

"There is. Have a bit of a chat with Lady Battenkirk about a piece of art she bought in Cambridge. I want to know where it is," he said, writing down her whereabouts and pushing it across the desk to Garfield.

Garfield took the paper, bobbed his head in understanding, and quit the room. Drake walked to the windows, and clasping his hand behind his back, he stood staring out at the gardens. "Bloody rotten scoundrel," he muttered at last. "I shall have your goddamn head on a platter, I shall." But first he would have a conversation with his father about the items gone missing last year.

With the gargoyle safely stuffed into a small satchel, Anna took one last look at herself. She was wearing her favorite day gown—the rose muslin made by London's finest modiste and cut to enhance her figure, as well as shoes fashioned in the same color. Unfortunately, her best gown could not detract from the dark patches under her eyes. She looked quite drawn, but it was the best she could do given the circumstance, and with a heavy sigh she shrugged into the matching pelisse.

Then Anna picked up the satchel with the heavy gargoyle and departed for Cavendish Street.

Bentley drove her to Tottenham Court, where she had asked him to leave her. "My friend's father will send me home in his carriage," she said.

"Are you certain, miss? I can return," Bentley said, looking a little concerned.

"I'm certain, Bentley. I may be quite a long time. My friend is, ah . . . sick," she said, and stepped up onto the street and waved him on. Bentley eyed her satchel for a moment, but drove on, leaving her to walk a half mile or more to Cavendish Street.

By the time she arrived at Dalkeith House, she was certain she had a bruise on her leg where the blasted gargoyle had banged against her with each step. As usual, she slipped into the mews and knocked on the servants' entrance, and waited for what seemed an eternity, shifting the bag from one hand to the other. Odd that no one came to the door, she thought, and tried to push it open, but found it locked.

"All right, then, if you *want* your bloody gargoyle, the least you might do is come to the door and *fetch* it," she muttered beneath her breath, and glanced toward the street. It was a rather gray and blustery day; there were few people about. Certainly she could risk walking up to his front door. Of course she could. For goodness' sake, she had done it before, and how many would remark it, really? And what if they did? Was it so awful, really, for a woman to call on a man?

The wind was picking up; Anna pulled her pelisse tightly around her and made a decision. She marched up the mews to the street, and walked boldly up the steps to the front door. Lifting the brass knocker, she rapped three times, let the knocker fall, and glanced anxiously about. Aha, just as she suspected—not a soul in the street on such a blustery day.

The door swung open so suddenly that it startled Anna, and she gave out a little shriek. The Irish cook was on the other side of the door, one brow cocked. "Aye, miss?"

"I, ah . . . is Dudley ill?"

"No, miss. He's gone home, he has," she said, wiping her hands on her apron and looking rather impatient.

"Home!" Anna cried, feeling a surge of sorrow. She had rather liked the old butler. "I had no idea."

"Aye, and have ye come to speak to his lordship, then?" she asked, cocking that brow even higher.

Anna felt herself color slightly. "Ah, yes. Yes, I have," she said, straightening her spine.

"This way, then," she said, and stepped back, giving Anna access. She led Anna up the grand staircase to the first floor and pointed in the direction of the drawing room, the last room at the end of the corridor, where their lessons had been held. "He's there, as usual," she said, and turned, gliding down the stairs before Anna could speak.

Not that there was anything left to say, really. Just as she'd told herself—she'd had her moment of excitement and adventure, had actually obtained what she had wanted, and no matter how her heart ached, it was time to fulfill her end of the bargain and bid him a fare-thee-well.

She took a breath, adjusted the satchel in her hand, and marched purposefully down the corridor.

The door to the drawing room was closed, and she rapped softly, straining to hear any sound from within. A moment later, she heard his footfall, and the door swung open. When he saw her standing there, an expression passed over his face of something she felt deep in herself, something she could not name, but that reached to the very pit of her soul.

It passed quickly; he coldly gestured for her to come in.

"And a jolly good morning to you, sir," she said smartly as she strode into the room and heaved the satchel onto a chair.

Grif quietly shut the door and leaned back against

it, his arms folded across his chest. He was wearing only his waistcoat, and Anna could see the faint outline of his arm in the fabric. It reminded her of the feel of his arms and shoulders beneath her hand as they had kissed in the garden.

The memory angered her, and she jerked off her gloves and flung them on top of the satchel.

When she looked up, Grif was smiling a little sardonically. "Is that it, then?" he asked, nodding at the bag.

"What else would it be?" she asked peevishly.

He shrugged lightly. "Any number of things. A rock, although I wouldna recommend it, as that's been done before. All Scottish Lockharts know to be vigilant of rocks."

Anna gave him a snort as she untied her bonnet, and threw that, too, on top of the bag. "It's there; your precious gargoyle is there."

"*Beastie,*" he calmly corrected her. He pushed away from the door, strolled across the room to the bag. "May I?" he asked as he reached for it.

"By all means. Assure yourself that I am not a thief and that I honor my word," she said, folding her arms tightly across her middle.

He grasped the leather handles of the satchel and pulled them apart, then quickly undid the buckle. He reached inside, pulled out a white bundle with tiny blue bows and lifted a brow. "What is this, then?" he asked, clearly amused.

"I had to have something to wrap it in!" she exclaimed, blushing at the sight of her drawers.

Grif chuckled again, unwound the drawers from the beastie, and made a sound of surprise as he held it up. "*Diah,*" he said, wrinkling his nose.

"It's quite ugly, that thing. I can't possibly imagine why it should hold such a place of honor in your family."

"Legend has it that Lady Lockhart's lover had it commissioned for her. She and her lover were executed when their affair was discovered by the laird of Lockhart."

"Really?" Anna asked, dropping her arms and moving closer to view it. "Why should he have such a horrid thing made for her?"

Grif shrugged as he touched the ruby eyes. "No one knows, really. Our great grandfather speculated that the beastie held some sort of meaning for them. Whatever its meaning, it is cast of gold and boasts two dozen rubies. 'Tis priceless, and has been highly desired by the English and the Scottish Lockharts for centuries. But it rightfully belongs," he said, carefully wrapping it in her drawers again, "to the Scottish Lockharts."

"Well, there now, you have it," she said with a dismissive wave of her hand. "You may happily trot back to Scotland with your booty."

"Aye . . . thank ye, Anna."

"Why? Why are you thanking me?" she demanded, feeling cross again. "We had an agreement, you and I, and you, well . . . I suppose you held your end, and naturally I did the same."

"And thank ye for holding yer end of it. Women canna always be trusted," he said, as if it were a scientifically documented fact.

"That's absurd!" she exclaimed. "Women are no more or less trustworthy than men!"

"Ach, do ye truly believe that?" he asked as he stuffed the statue into the satchel.

"Of course I do!"

"Then I can trust that ye will honor yer word and marry Lockhart when he offers for ye?"

Why in God's name *that* should make tears spring to her eyes, Anna could not say, and horrified by them, she abruptly whirled away from Grif and stalked blindly to the window.

"What is it now, Anna? Why should this make ye sad?"

"I'm not sad," she insisted, squeezing her eyes shut to keep tears from leaking.

"Ye should be happy. Ye've earned his affection. Why, I can see ye now, bouncing a wee bairn on yer knee, yer new sister, Barbara, at the pianoforte, yer dear husband quietly reading. What a lovely portrait it would make."

"Stop it," she said through gritted teeth.

"But why? *It is* a lovely portrait, is it no'?"

She realized she was clenching her hands into fists, and her nails were biting into her palms as she tried to maintain her composure.

"Ah, ye *are* sad," he said, at her back now, and put his hands on her arms, let his palms glide up to her shoulders, then down to her wrists. "Tell me, lass, are ye the sort of woman who enjoys the hunt but not the spoils?"

Whatever possessed her, she couldn't say, but she abruptly twisted about and threw her arms around his neck, burying her face in his collar. *"Yes! I don't want him!"* she cried into his collar. "I don't love him!"

"Anna," Grif said sternly, wrapping his hands around her arms and trying to pull them free of his neck. "I shouldna have—"

"But it's too *late!* I think he's already spoken to my father, and I can't go back, I can't refuse him!"

"W-what?" The surprise in his voice trickled into her ear and down to her heart, and rashly, boldly, Anna seized her last opportunity to know the man she loved. She raised her head, grabbed his face between her hands, and pressed her lips to his—hard and unyielding—and then, as tears began to slide from the corners of her eyes, she kissed him softly, her tongue feeling the seam of his mouth, her teeth grazing the flesh of his lips.

Grif's hands stopped fighting her. They went round her, pulling her into him so tightly that she could barely breathe. His tongue swept inside her mouth; he began to caress her back, her arm, then, coming to her face, he cupped her chin and angled it toward him.

Anna knew nothing but the pleasure of his body against hers as he moved her away from the window, moved her backward, toward the settee. His arm held her easily as he lowered her onto the settee and moved over her. His mouth was everywhere—on her lips, her neck, the swell of her bosom. She could feel his erection hard between them, a pulsing, moving thing that awoke a throbbing in her.

He caressed her breast, molding it and shaping it to fit his palm, his thumb grazing her nipple, sending little pulses of fire down her spine and into her groin. The more he kissed her and caressed her, the more Anna's body ached to have him. Caution flew out of her head; she could think of nothing, could see nothing but Grif, and in her eagerness she groped at her gown, pulling it up, up, and up, squirming beneath him, moving so that she could feel his hardness pressed against her.

But Grif suddenly broke the kiss and grabbed her wrist, stopping her from pulling her gown any higher. "No," he said through clenched teeth. "I hold ye in too high regard to ruin ye, Anna," he hissed.

"You want me, I want you," she whispered, her fingers moving featherlike across his eyes, his lips. "Let's not leave it like this, please?"

"No," he said again, his hand squeezing her wrist. *"No."*

His rejection, no matter how justified, and so soon on the heels of what had happened in the arbor of Featherstone, humiliated her, and the days of frustration and fear seemed to all bubble up in her. She suddenly bucked beneath him, shoving her knee between his legs.

With a yelp, Grif let go of her hand, and Anna bucked with both knees, knocking him off of her and onto the floor.

She quickly stood up, shook her gown loose. "Very well," she said, as Grif lay there, flat on his back, his arms splayed wide, blinking up at her. "You have your blasted gargoyle, so I suppose there is nothing left to say."

She took a step, but Grif caught her ankle in a viselike grip. "No' so fast, *leannan.* First, for God's sake, it is a *beastie,* and second, ye willna leave thus!"

"Ha," she said, kicking her leg out. "You can't stop me!"

He gave her a hard yank and a twist that pulled her foot from beneath her and sent her sailing to the floor. She landed with a thud right on her bum, and before she could move, Grif had, by some miracle, popped up and over her, had grabbed her arms and pinned them on either side of her head. "Ye wee *diabhal*," he said with a dark grin. "How capricious and peevish ye become when ye canna have yer way."

"Get off of me," she warned him.

Grif laughed, lowered his head so that his lips were just a moment from hers. "I'll get off ye when ye apologize."

"Apologize! For *what*, pray tell?" she snapped, and tried to wiggle out from beneath him, but Grif held firm.

"For being so bloody cantankerous."

"Oh!" she cried, fighting again. "There was never a more cantankerous person than *you*, and how you could *possibly* say that of *me*—"

"Uist, now, lass," he said, smiling down at her. "I canna kiss ye when yer tongue is wagging so. We've a saying in Scotland: *Binn beal, na chonai.*"

She stilled, looked at him curiously. "What? What does that mean?"

" 'The mouth that speaks no' is sweet to hear,' " he said, and laughed when she shrieked her disapproval as he lowered his head until she could feel his breath on her lips, could smell his skin . . . she took a deep breath, closed her eyes . . . but she heard the knocking, and her eyes flew open. Grif's head was raised; he was as still as the night, his eyes on the door.

The knocking was followed by shouting.

Grif groaned with aggravation and bellowed, "God blind me, is there never a moment's *peace* in this town?"

Twenty-seven

Drake Lockhart was uncertain as to which house belonged to Lady Dalkeith and had walked up Cavendish Street twice, looking at the distinctive window fans above the door for a clue. A shell of some sort, Garfield had said. As he didn't see anything that looked like a shell, exactly, he turned round, retracing his steps.

He might have walked over Lady Worthall had it not been for her little dog, which attacked his boot as if it were a cat.

"Mr. Lockhart, is it?" she asked, peering inquisitively through her monocle.

"Lady Worthall, how do you do?"

"Quite well indeed, sir. And how is your lady mother?"

"Very well, thank you," he said, trying to kick the dog off of him.

"Sirius! Stop that at once!" she cried, but the dog ignored her. Lady Worthall peered up at Drake again beneath the long bill of her bonnet. "No doubt you are in search of Lord Ardencaple," she said.

He jerked his gaze up in surprise. "How did you know?"

"Why, it would seem the entire town is in search of him!" she exclaimed.

Drake forgot about the dog. "Does it seem so, indeed? Are you acquainted with him?"

"Acquainted!" she spat. "Hardly! He has taken up residence in my dear friend's house. Of course I wrote straightaway to Lady Dalkeith in France and expressed how happy we were that her dear friend, Lord Ardencaple, had come to reside! And do you know that she wrote me in return and claimed to have no knowledge of a Lord Ardencaple, and that, in fact, the only Scot she had any contact with at all was her grandson, Mr. MacAlister, but neither had he written to request the use of her house!"

"Are you certain?" Drake asked.

"Of course I'm certain!" she snapped. "At last look, there are no bats in *this* belfry, sir!"

"Of course not—it's just that I find it quite hard to believe that a man would simply steal someone's home."

"As do *I*, sir, which is why I took it upon myself to inform Lady Dalkeith. And she has written that she will return by the end of this week to have a word with Lord Ardencaple."

"Which house is it, if you'd be so kind?" he asked.

Lady Worthall pointed to one in the middle of the block. "And best you call now, sir, for Miss Addison has been within far too long!" Lady Worthall sniped.

Drake's blood ran cold. "I beg your pardon?"

"Oh, that impertinent Miss Anna Addison!" Lady Worthall said, and paused to stop down and pick up her awful little dog, which struggled to be set free. "She's called on several occasions without benefit of escort! I shudder to think what unspeakable things must be going on behind closed doors!" she said, and closed her eyes and shuddered.

Drake couldn't think. He could not *think*. It was impossible to believe that Anna would risk so much by coming here. It was impossible to believe that Anna would have desire or reason to come here! His cold blood was boiling now, and he turned sharply toward the house. "Which one again, that one?" he asked, pointing, wanting to make doubly sure he had it.

"Yes indeed, sir, that one," Lady Worthall said, nodding furiously. "You'd best pay your call. I think well of Lord Whittington, and I would not like to see his name tarnished!"

"Quite right." With a tip of his hat, Drake turned and strode purposefully toward Dalkeith House.

He took the steps in twos, banged loudly on the door. And when it was not immediately answered, he banged again, only harder. It was at last opened by a pretty woman with golden red hair, wearing an apron. She cocked one hip as she took him in. "Aye?"

"Lord Ardencaple. You may say Mr. Lockhart is calling."

"Beg yer pardon, sir, he's engaged just now."

"Then I suggest you *un*-engage him, miss, for I will see him *now!*"

The woman moved to shut the door, but Drake slapped a hand against it.

"Ye canna come in here like this!" she cried. "Ye've no call to do it!"

"I've every call, and if you don't do as I ask straightaway, I will have the authorities at your door before you can drop a hen in your kettle, wench."

The woman gasped with shock, then suddenly whirled and went running into the house, shouting, *"Milord, milord!"*

Drake was on her heels, following her up the grand staircase and down the corridor to the last door on the right.

"Lord Ardencaple!" she screeched as she tried to reach for the doorknob.

Drake was too quick; he shoved past her, threw the door open, and strode into the room.

Ardencaple was standing in the middle of the room, his arms folded, his legs braced far apart. He was wearing buckskins and boots, but no coat, only a waistcoat and a neckcloth that was partially untied.

"What in God's name do ye think ye are about, Lockhart?" Ardencaple roared. "How dare ye push yer way in here!"

"I should ask the same of you, sir," Drake said, forcing his way into the room. "It would seem you have commandeered a house as well as a title."

"He forced his way in!" the wench behind him cried.

"That's quite all right, Miss Brody. I apologize for his abominable behavior," Ardencaple said calmly. "Ye best go on about yer work now."

"Are ye certain, milord?"

"Quite," he said, and walked to the door, held it open so that she might exit. She reluctantly quit the room, eyeing Lockhart with daggers in her eyes.

Ardencaple quietly shut the door and turned to regard Drake. "How dare ye come into me house like this," he said low.

"How dare *you* come to London and masquerade

as an earl! You don't have permission to use this house!"

"I beg yer pardon! I've proper letters of introduction—"

"Spare me your bloody letters of introduction!" Drake shouted. "Lady Worthall has a letter from Lady Dalkeith in which she writes she has no knowledge of you or anyone like you, and that she will return by the end of the week to set the matter to rights! What will you say to *that*, I wonder?"

"Lady Worthall is sadly mistaken," he said, very calmly. "And so are ye, Lockhart. Ye have no reason—"

"The hell I don't, sir! I think it quite a remarkable coincidence that a precious family heirloom would disappear from my family's home the last time a Scot was in London!"

Ardencaple lifted a brow and chuckled with amusement. "Now what could that possibly have to do with me? Would ye accuse me of stealing, sir?" he laughed again. "How ye must despise me."

"I more than despise you. I desire to see you behind the bars at Newgate before the day is done."

"Donna be ridiculous," Ardencaple scoffed.

Drake was about to tell him that he was quite serious, but the door flew open and another man burst into the room, looking first to Ardencaple, then to Drake. "Is everything all right, milord?" he asked, eyeing Lockhart. "Cook was quite distressed."

"And well she had reason to be. Mr. Lockhart has shown her an uncommonly vulgar side of himself. But I believe he was just leaving . . . are ye no', Mr. Lockhart?"

"Not without Miss Addison," he said through clenched teeth.

For a split moment Ardencaple seemed to freeze. He exchanged a look with the other Scot, then shifted his gaze to Drake. "I donna care for the implication of that, sir," he said through clenched teeth.

"I'm not implying anything, you goddamn rogue! Miss Addison has been plainly seen entering this house on more than one occasion and *including* this morning, without proper escort! Do you think to make whores of our women while you plot your thievery?"

"Mind yerself, sir!" the other Scot exclaimed hotly. "Ye willna impugn the reputation of Lord Ardencaple!"

"I will do as I bloody well please. If he takes issue with it, then he may call me out," he spat.

Ardencaple laughed derisively at that. "Ye'd welcome it, would ye no'? But there is no need for yer bravado, Lockhart. Miss Addison is no' here. She's never been here. Lady Worthall, for what it's worth, is a doddering old bird with naugh' more to do with her days than create scandals. Why, do ye know that she claimed The Prince Regent was paying uncommon court to a lass in the house on the corner, who hasna even come out? If there is no scandal to speak of, our Lady Worthall will create it. Only a bloody *fool* would believe her mutterings."

That gave Drake pause—it was indeed possible that Lady Worthall was a mad old bird. He scarcely knew her, and what Ardencaple said made some sense, for he could not believe that Anna would come here, unescorted, and risk her reputation. But then again, there was nothing he wouldn't put past this scoundrel.

What he needed was a constable who could cart the bastard off as he so richly deserved.

He pointed a finger at Ardencaple. "You had best prepare yourself, sir, for I will bring the full force of the magistrate down on your head!"

Ardencaple laughed. "Be our guest, Lockhart. Bring whomever ye must. But be forewarned that everyone in London will know what a bloody goddamn fool ye are ere it's all over."

Drake turned sharply and shoved the other Scot aside as he strode out of the room and then out of that house.

He could have a constable here by late afternoon.

His head lowered, Grif looked at Hugh as he slammed the door behind the departing back of Lockhart.

"I should have put him on his bloody arse," Hugh said. "What are we to do? He'll return shortly, ye know he will."

"Aye. We leave," Grif said. "Just as we planned. I have the beastie."

"She brought it round, then?" Hugh asked, his eyes lighting up. "Bloody hell, then, we'll go! I've brought the coach out; we can be away from London by nightfall."

A noise, much like a disembodied shout in the far distance, came from behind the bookcase. Hugh looked at the bookcase, then at Grif. "Right. But we've a wee problem yet," Grif said, cringing a little.

"*Diah,*" Hugh groaned. "Miss Addison?"

"Aye. Do ye recall the hidden wall space Dudley discovered? I put her there when we heard Miss Brody's shouts."

Another muffled cry, which both men ignored. "Send her home, then," Hugh said.

"What? To certain ruin? No."

"*Ach,* Lockhart!" Hugh exclaimed, narrowing his gaze. "What do ye think to do? Ye canna take her to Scotland, of all places! That'd be *kidnapping.*"

"I bloody well know what it'd be, thank ye," Grif muttered.

Another muffled shout was accompanied by some sort of scratching noise, which Grif assumed was a bit of kicking.

"Ye canna think to do so!" Hugh continued heatedly. "We must run for our *lives* now, do ye no' realize that? We've already done enough to be hanged, and the English will certainly hang us if ye add kidnapping a lord's daughter to our crimes. Do ye think yer cousin willna make good on his threat to see us in Newgate Prison? Ye *canna* bring her along, for we'd no' go as far as Charing Cross before they were upon us!"

"But I canna leave her!" Grif exploded. "Lady Worthall has told this man that she's come here many times without escort! Do ye know what life will be left to her once the whole bloody *ton* knows she's called on me, a thief and a scoundrel, without chaperone or escort? She'll be labeled a whore!"

"*Ach!*" Hugh cried, throwing his hands up in anger. "She brought it on her own head! She came here seeking ye, Grif, no' the other way around!"

Another loud bump and scratch, and both men looked at the bookcase.

"I willna ruin her," Grif said again.

"For the love of *Criosd!*" Hugh roared to the ceiling, then dropped his head and his shoulders and sighed. "*Ach,* love! It makes a grown man as barmy as a bloody bean!"

"We'll split apart," Grif suggested, ignoring him.

"They'll be looking for two men. Take one of the horses, and I'll take Anna in the coach. We'll meet in Scotland in a fortnight."

"What, you think to arrive on yer mother's doorstep with the woman ye stole from England? If ye love her, lad, at least do what ye must!"

Grif nodded, considering that. "We'll meet in Gretna Green, then, in a fortnight. And if, for whatever reason, one of us doesna arrive in a forthnight, the other will wait a week, no more, then carry on, to Talla Dileas. Can ye do it, then?"

"Me?" Hugh cried, as the scratching and shouting got louder. *"Ye* are the one to contend with that!" he said, pointing impatiently at the bookcase. "I'll be waiting for ye in Gretna Green, I will. But I'll need a wee bit of coin."

Grif strode to a small table at the end of the room, pulled open a drawer, and withdrew a leather pouch, from which he fished out several banknotes. "There ye are—half of what we've got left, then. What of Miss Brody?"

"I'll give her a week's wages," he said, extending his hand for more money, "and send the lass home." Grif looked skeptically at Hugh. Hugh gestured impatiently. "I've no' lost me fool mind, lad. Only ye can claim that. I'll send the lass home."

Grif pulled a few more banknotes from the pouch; Hugh took the money and pocketed it. "Where is it, then?" he asked, looking around. "I'd have a look at the thing that will see me hanged."

Grif walked across the room, picked up the satchel. "They say the beastie is cursed, that she'll slip through the fingers of any Scot who tries to possess her, for she's truly English at heart."

A sharp crack on the other side of the bookcase startled them both. Grif quickly removed the beastie from the satchel and held it up. Hugh recoiled. "I'd leave it to the bloody English were I ye. She's hideous."

Grif nodded and quickly wrapped it again, stuffed it in the satchel, and put it aside. "I'll meet ye in Gretna Green in a fortnight. Godspeed to ye, lad."

Another muffled scream and Hugh shook his head. "I wish ye Godspeed and the protection of the saints, for ye'll need it all yer days."

"Aye, that," Grif sighed, and looked at the wall. "Ere ye go, would ye lend a hand?" he asked, nodding at the wall.

Hugh snorted.

Grif removed his neckcloth, frowning at the sound of her muffled shouts. "God in heaven, have mercy on me soul," he muttered, "and forgive me for what I am about to do." With a look at Hugh, he walked across the room, pushed the panel that sprung the bookcase.

As it swung open, Anna came tumbling out of the old wall safe, her pretty gown mussed with dust in a few places, a cobweb in her hair. But her eyes were on fire, and she whirled around, glaring at the two of them. "I beg your pardon, but it was rather close in there! Nevertheless, I am *certain* I heard you say you intend to kidnap me! Did you say as much?"

Grif wound the neckcloth partially around one hand.

Anna glanced at the neckcloth, then at Hugh, who stood casually before the open door. "You can't carry me off like a bit of chattel!" she cried, backing up. "My father is a very powerful man, I'll have you know, and he will look for you *everywhere*, and he *will* find you, and *then*, you bloody fool, you'll be hanging by your neck!"

Grif walked toward her; Anna instantly backed up. "What are you *doing?*" she cried.

"I must do it, *leannan,* and pray that one day ye might see yer way to forgive me."

Anna opened her mouth to shriek, but Grif had been trained by the best—his brother, Captain Liam Lockhart. He managed to get the neckcloth into her mouth and twirl her about while Hugh grabbed her arms.

And the fight was begun.

Twenty-eight

Anna had no idea where they were, or how long she'd been on the floor of the coach wrapped in some sort of carpet, which, incidentally, smelled as if a dog had once called it home. The least he might have done was to find a clean carpet.

Her hands, tied behind her back, hurt awfully, and her shoulders ached. She desperately wanted to sleep, but she was terribly uncomfortable. They'd been traveling a while; she had bumps and bruises from every rut to prove it.

She hoped that he had at least remembered her pelisse and gloves in this ridiculous abduction.

Anna was angrier than she'd ever been in her life. She was mortified, a little frightened, and desperate to escape this unconscionable attempt to kidnap the daughter of an important lord!

But there was no possibility of escape—not like this, not wrapped in a carpet with her hands bound behind her back. Images of her parents kept flashing in her mind, horrified at the news she'd been abducted, or worse, horrified, if anyone suggested it, that she'd gone off willingly. When she got out of this bloody carpet, she'd tear Griffin Finnius Lockhart limb from limb and feed him to her dogs.

And really, what in God's name did he intend to do with her? If only he'd stop and let her out of this horrid carpet, she would *ask* him what he intended and, furthermore, suggest a few things.

Until that happy moment, apparently, she'd be forced to endure the agony of bumping about the interior of an old coach that had not even a single spring as far as she could tell, and feeling absolutely faint with hunger.

She must have fallen asleep; the next thing she knew, she was being abruptly tossed back and forth between the two benches, rolling like a log as the coach made a series of sharp turns. But then the coach came to a complete halt. At last! She hoped it was an inn of quality, where they might have a hearty dinner. And a bath! Oh *yeesss,* a hot, steaming, scented bath.

The coach Lounced a little with the weight of someone climbing down from the driver's bench. Anna tried to move herself around so that she could see out the top of the carpet tube she was in. But she couldn't budge—it seemed as if part of the carpet was stuck somehow. There was more jostling about, and she could hear one of the horses neighing. At last, the door opened after what seemed another eternity. She couldn't see him, but she could hear and smell the rain.

"Quite awful out," Grif said, climbing into the coach and, apparently, stepping over her as he took a seat on one of the benches.

And then she felt the weight of something on her hip. What was *that,* his bloody *boot?* Anna wriggled furiously, trying to knock his boot off her hip, but he pressed down.

"Stop that, Anna."

And what in heaven's name did he expect? She was trussed up like a Christmas pig! *"Uuuh,"* she shouted against his neckcloth that was bound around her mouth.

He nudged her, annoying her to no end. "Aye, I know ye are quite alive and *quite* vexed, and *Diah,* I can hardly blame ye, can I? 'Tis no' every day that a lass is taken from the bosom of her family."

Certainly not, and if he'd just let her out of this carpet—she jerked hard again to indicate that he should free her, and he instantly put a foot on her hip again, stilling her. "Calm yerself, Anna," he said sternly.

She would strangle him. Squeeze his neck until his head popped off—

"Now, then. As to where we are . . ." He paused then, and Anna shrieked against the neckcloth for him to let her up, but he only increased the pressure. "We have passed through St. Albans, which means, of course, that it would be near to impossible for ye to find yer way home were ye of a mind to escape."

Oh, honestly! All right, but what about *food?* And an inn? If she couldn't escape, why couldn't he let her out of the carpet? Anna bucked with all her strength again against his foot, and succeeded in dislodging it and rolling onto her stomach. But then he was suddenly on top of her, straddling her, squeezing his muscular legs tightly around her, and stifling what little breath was left in her after her monumental struggle.

"We'll no' have another round of scuffling and squabbling, do ye hear me, lass? I'm right tired, I am, and soaked through to me drawers, for 'tis raining like the end of all time. The fact is, Anna, ye are in a wee bit of a predicament, and the best ye might do for yerself is to act a lady and make the most of it, aye?"

A lady. A *lady?* After kidnapping her and putting her in this wretched carpet with his neckcloth in her mouth and something terribly stiff and scratchy around her wrists and ankles, he would think to lecture her on *decorum?* Fury renewed her strength to that of ten men, and she was suddenly kicking and squirming all at once, trying again to dislodge him, to get *out* of that ridiculous carpet and explain to him that *yes,* she did indeed understand she was quite kidnapped, but that the least he could do given his unconscionable crime was to untie her and *feed* her, for Chrissakes!

"Ach, did ye hear a word I said, then?" he exclaimed, and put his hands on her back, pressing down, holding her still. "Give me yer word ye'll behave and I'll free ye from the carpet. If I've yer word, wiggle yer bum a wee bit."

She'd die before she'd wiggle anything for him, the rotten bounder.

He sighed, then abruptly lifted off of her. There was a bit of grunting and moving about, and suddenly she was shoved up on her side, and then rolled onto her belly again. She heard the coach door open, heard the rain falling, and suddenly the carpet was pulled free of her body.

Still on her belly, she screamed through the gag at him, but Grif ignored her and struggled to pull the carpet out of the interior. Then there was more bouncing around as he obviously put it on the back running board.

More important, she saw no evidence of an inn. She could see no evidence of *anything.* It was absolutely pitch-black outside the coach, and it seemed as if they were miles and miles from any sort of life.

No *food!* No lovely country inn where they might dine. *No hot bath!* Her fury pounded like a drum in her chest and ears.

Grif appeared in the doorway and climbed inside, closing the door behind him. He leaned over Anna, slipped his hands beneath her arms, and easily hoisted her up like a sack of grain, propping her up on the bench across from him. A thick strand of hair had fallen from her coif and was lying, annoyingly, over her eye. And her gown, her perfect rose day gown, felt oddly twisted about on her body. Worse, as she looked down at her shoes, she noticed one of them had a horrible gray stain that covered the toe. Her specially made shoes.

That was the last straw. He might have kidnapped her, but he didn't have to be so intolerably crude about it. She slowly raised her gaze and glared daggers at Grif.

He smiled a bit impishly. "Kidnapping, it would seem, is no' exactly tidy."

"Not exactly tidy?" she screamed against her gag with such force that she actually levitated off the bench, and then fell back against the squabs.

Grif leaned forward, propped his hands on his knees. "That willna help, all the squiggling about," he said, gesturing in what she assumed was a squiggly way. "There's naugh' that can be done for it now. It is what it is."

Oh, how very profound, Anna thought, glaring at him still, and tried to twist around and show him her hands, hoping to make him understand she wanted to be untied.

"I know ye want me to untie ye now," he said, surprising Anna. "But I must explain something to ye first, about the beastie."

Oh no, not that bloody gargoyle! Was he blind? Could he not see how uncomfortable she was?

"The beastie, as I told ye, is worth a fortune. A fortune large enough that the thing has been stolen back and forth across the Scots border many times, and has been since the days of Culloden."

Anna groaned to the ceiling of the coach. This was *hardly* the time to review the history of that blasted thing!

"I tell ye this, lass, so I might defend why I kidnapped ye. Our family is in rather dire financial straits, what with all the sheep . . . 'Tis quite complicated, really, so we'll just leave it at this—the beastie rightfully belongs to us, and we desperately need the money she'll bring to save our home, Talla Dileas. But the beastie, ye see, she was in England when we needed her. So me brother, Liam, came to retrieve her last Season."

Had he heard even a word she'd ever said? She *knew* this. She'd told him so and tried to kick him now with her bound feet for not listening to her.

"Aye, but he was distracted by a woman, he was. Perhaps ye know her, then . . . Ellie Farnsworth? And she has a wee lass, Natalie."

Ellie Farnsworth? Anna stopped squirming, her eyes wide. How exciting and how romantic that it was *true*—Miss Farnsworth had run off with the captain!

"Aye, I can tell by the look of ye that ye've suspected the truth. There was a wee bit of wrangling for the beastie between them—Ellie needed it to escape her father, and, well, she stole it from Liam, she did, and sold it to Lady Battenkirk for a paltry sum." His face darkened for a moment, but then he leaned back and said, with a flick of his wrist, "*Ach,* she didna understand what she did—nevertheless, the only thing the lass knew in all certainty was that Lady Battenkirk intended it as a gift for her friend Amelia."

Yes, yes, she had discovered who Amelia was, how could he have forgotten? She tried to express her desire to speak by inching forward on the bench until her knees were touching Grif's, but he did not seem to notice, was too determined to prattle on.

"So then Hugh and I came to fetch it . . . Well, there are quite a lot of details I'll spare ye, but the point is, ye found it ere I did, which left me with no choice but to endure yer demands because of how important the beastie is to me family. Ye must understand, Anna—had the situation no' been so bloody important, I wouldna have agreed to help ye seduce a man, aye? That's a very wicked thing to do—but then ye held me captive with that bloody beastie!"

She felt an ugly twist in her belly at the word *captive.* Well, then, they were quite even on that score, weren't they? she thought, and lifted her chin.

But then Grif bowed his head, dragged his hands through his hair, and said, low, "It was a wicked thing to do, aye, because ye also held me bloody heart captive."

Anna's heart stopped pounding for a moment. Then started again in earnest. She screamed against her gag.

"Aye, 'tis true!" Grif said crossly at her scream. "While I was teaching ye to seduce me cousin, I was falling in love with ye, damn it all! I donna know how it happened, for I didna care for ye in the least in the beginning—I thought ye *impossibly* bold," he said, waving his hand at her. "And then, as if by magic, one day I was . . . well, I was bloody well staggered by yer grace and beauty, I was. Just like that, it seemed. And it's only gotten worse."

Staggered. By *her.* A tear trickled from the corner of Anna's eye. If that was what he'd felt, why, then, had he kept such a distance from her?

"I couldna say as much, could I?" he said, reading her thoughts. "I couldna offer ye the sort of life ye had or deserved. I couldna offer ye even a fraction of what Lockhart could provide. I had nothing, really, but me heart to give ye. Aye, but I'm no' fool, Anna. A heart is no' the tender used to win a lady's hand."

Yes, yes, yes it is, you stupid, stupid man! she screamed against her gag.

"Calm yerself, lass. I was set to let ye go, I was, but then that bastard Lockhart called, and he knew ye had come to me, and more than once, thanks to that meddlesome old cow, Lady Worthall. I knew then and there that there would be no end of it for ye. The *ton* would never forgive ye—they would label ye a whore."

Anna tried to kick him, to make him look at her and understand she wanted to speak, but he put his hands on her knees and held her there.

"Regardless of what ye might think of him, Anna, I believe Lockhart would have seen ye ruined. I couldna leave ye to that fate, no' having put ye in it."

When would he stop speaking? In a desperate fit of frustration, she threw herself back against the squabs as tears slid down her face.

" 'Tis no' happy news, I understand," he said sadly, his voice trailing off. "I know how confused ye must be. But I give ye me word that I'll do all in me power to make it up to ye. I *swear* it, Anna."

Then, by some miracle, he leaned across the coach, his hands slipping behind her back and pulling her up. He pushed her up to the edge of the bench, helped her to turn partially, and untied her hands. The moment the ties were off, Anna grabbed her wrists, rubbed them tearfully for a moment, then reached up behind her head, untied the blasted neckcloth, and spit it from her mouth. "You . . . you are such a *fool!*" she sobbed, and angrily shot forward, striking him in the chest with her fist as hard as she could.

Grif did not even flinch. "Aye," he said sadly.

His reaction infuriated her. "Dear *God*, how could one man be so . . . so *ignorant?*" she cried, and struck him again, but this time he caught her by the wrist.

"I'll take it once, but no' twice," he warned her.

Anna ignored him and kicked him hard in the shin. With a yelp, Grif let go her arm to grab his shin. "You'll take it until I am quite done, you bloody fool!" she shouted at him.

"Anna!" he shouted, and deftly grabbed both her wrists.

"A bloody *fool!*" she sobbed. "And blind! I think you should see a physician straightaway about your sight, sir, for only a blind man or an imbecile would not be able to see how much I love you, and *have* loved you! Could you not deduce that I kept that wretched gargoyle in my wardrobe for as long as I did just so that I'd have an excuse to see you?"

"What?" he asked, lifting his head, his eyes wide.

She yanked her hands free of his grasp. "And how could you have botched this kidnapping as badly as you have?" she cried, throwing his neckcloth down.

"Botched this kidnapping?"

"Yes, *botched!*" she cried, slapping his hands away.

"You wrapped me in a carpet that . . . that *reeks* of dog, and you drove all the way out here and there is no *inn*, and there is no *food*, and there is no *bath*, and I am certain you forgot my pelisse and my gloves!"

Judging by Grif's blank look, he certainly had, and Anna wailed.

But Grif caught her by the arms again and shook her lightly to make her look at him. "Why did ye no' tell me, lass?"

"Because," she said, pushing against him. "You had me all trussed up like a pig! How was I to speak?"

"No, no, I mean . . . ere *today!* Why did ye no' tell me what was in yer heart? Ye spoke of no one but Lockhart!"

"I don't know!" she cried. "I was afraid! You . . . you staggered me, too, Grif—but you were a scoundrel and a liar and the good Lord only knew what else!" she said, the tears flowing now. "And you were so distant, and so enamored of Lucy! What was I to do?"

Grif grasped her jaw and tilted it upward so that he could see her tearstained face. "Hear me," he said softly. "I wasna enamored of Lucy. I wanted to stuff a sock in her mouth, aye, but I wasna enamored of anyone but ye, Anna." He shifted his hand, put his palm against her cheek. "I understand now, *mo ghraidh* that I didna speak me heart, either . . . but what matter? It's all changed now, has it no'?"

Anna unsteadily wiped the tears from beneath her eyes with her fingers. "Yes. Everything," she whispered, and looked at him.

They reached for each other at the exact same moment; Grif pulled her onto his lap and kissed the path of her tears from one cheek. "I'm neither a thief nor a scoundrel," he said. "I canna offer ye great wealth, but I can offer ye unending love," he vowed, kissing her eyes, the bridge of her nose.

"I don't care about wealth," she said. "I don't care about anything but you, Grif—just to be with you, by your side, part of your life . . ."

"I'll no' let ye go, Anna. The king's men couldna take ye from me now. I'll keep ye safe, I'll keep ye warm, and I'll love ye until I draw me last breath, I swear to God I shall."

Anna closed her eyes as his earnest vow seeped into her heart. Suddenly, nothing else mattered—not the kidnapping, or the scandal that was sure to follow, or the lack of food—nothing but his arms around her. She opened her eyes and unconsciously lifted her hand to touch his face. He leaned into it, kissing her palm.

"Ye'll come with me, aye, Anna? Ye'll be with me." His voice had grown rough, his green eyes glittering with the strength of his emotion. "Ye'll be with me for many long and happy years, aye?"

Her heart rose and swelled to fill the cavity of her chest. "*Yes,*" she whispered. "Yes, yes, yes . . ." Her dream had come true—she would marry for love . . . wouldn't she? "Then . . ." her voice trailed off.

"Then?"

"Then will we . . . I mean, what I'd ask, is whether . . ." She paused again.

"Whether . . . ?" He looked confused.

She frowned. "Whether those . . . long and happy years, as you so eloquently put it . . . would result in something perhaps a bit more . . . formal than . . . *this,*" she said, gesturing to the two of them and the coach.

"Formal," he repeated, looking around at the coach. "Aye, of course . . . ye'd want it formal."

She blinked at him, her mind unwilling to accept what she was hearing. "Don't you want . . . *formal?*"

He looked at her from the corner of his eye. "I . . . want, I suppose, whatever . . . ye want," he said uncertainly.

Anna stared at him for a long moment. "I can't *believe* you!" she cried, pushing against his chest and off his lap. "Do you mean to say that you have kidnapped me and will convey me all the way to Scotland to be your *mistress?*" she exclaimed hotly, and punched him square in the arm.

"Ouch!" he shouted. "I didna say *mistress!*"

"You didn't say *anything!*" she shouted back at him. "You never said a bloody word but *kidnap!*"

She saw a spark in his green eyes, and Grif threw his head back with a shout of laughter as he caught her fully around the arms and clasped her to him. "Ye are the most impossible woman God ever made!" he exclaimed. "Of *course* I mean to marry ye! Do ye think I'd have endured so much for anything *less?*"

Her frown instantly gave way to a smile. "Really?"

"*Ach,* lass! I suppose I thought it was understood. Why would I kidnap ye, then? How else might I keep ye from harm? Aye, aye, we'll *marry, mo ghraidh,* my love. In Gretna Green."

"Gretna *Green!*" she gasped.

"Aye," he said, cringing a little. "I know ye must be disappointed, but we canna arrive on the steps of Talla Dileas without having married, aye? And I canna promise ye a big fancy formal wedding such as they have in Mayfair—"

"Gretna Green is wonderful!" she exclaimed, throwing her arms around his neck and squeezing him almost to death. "I can't wait to write home and tell them that *I* was married at Gretna Green!"

Grif seemed a little confused by that, but he smiled broadly all the same, a smile that warmed her to her toes, wrapped around her heart and held it. She kissed him passionately on a surge of raw emotion, and Grif responded, his fingers in her hair, his tongue stroking deep into her mouth.

God help her, but Anna was on fire. She had never ached like this, had never hungered for another living soul as she did at that moment. She loved him desperately and he loved her. He wanted to marry her. She would, by some miracle, marry for love.

Grif's hands eagerly swept her body, traveling down her arms, her legs, and up again, to her breasts, and around, fumbling with the tiny buttons of her gown. The rain drummed against the coach, matching the tempo of their beating hearts. Anna sought the strength of his body, thrusting her hands deep inside his waistcoat, feeling his spine, his rib cage, and the corded muscles in his neck and shoulders, the hard plate of his breast, the hardened nipples.

But suddenly Grif caught her hands and pulled them free of his body. "No, Anna, no," he said breathlessly, shaking his head. "*Diah,* I want ye, lass," he said, caressing her hair. "I want ye . . . but ye deserve far better than this," he said, looking around at the old coach. "I'll no' make love to ye until I've married ye, for ye deserve to have a name, and a castle, and a warm, soft bed . . ." he said as he slowly leaned back against the squabs, holding her to him.

She didn't argue, but pressed her face against his chest. "It wasn't supposed to be like this," Anna said dreamily. "I'm so very happy."

"Ye willna regret it. I'll spend every moment of every day making certain ye donna ever regret it, *leannan*."

"How could I regret something so beautiful?" she asked, smiling. "Life has been so exciting since you came into it, Grif. I would rather have an exciting life than an intolerably dull one in London."

Grif kissed her forehead. "I canna lie—I am relieved and happy to hear it."

They lay together a while longer, listening to the rain and enjoying the freedom the truth had at last given them, until Anna's body made a groan. She put a hand on her belly and asked, "What of food?"

He sighed wearily and stroked her hair. "I didna exactly think of food."

She moaned and pressed her face to his shoulder, whimpering. "You really are a deplorable kidnapper, Grif."

"Aye, and I suppose ye'd do better?" he asked with a grin.

"Of course I would," she said in all sincerity.

Grif quietly smiled into her hair as she began to enumerate the many ways his kidnapping skills might be improved.

Twenty-nine

Over the course of the next several days, Grif and Anna made it to within miles of the Scots border, to Carlisle, without serious incident, managing to dodge two Englishmen who appeared woefully out of place in Nottingham's market stalls as they walked through, peering closely at all the women. They were certain the men were looking for Anna.

Grif determined that they must travel faster and off main roads, and deeper in the countryside to avoid being spotted. He bought a pair of boy's trousers for Anna and left the old family coach behind so that they might continue on horseback. Anna became quite an equestrian in those few days, and arrived in Carlisle with her face a bonny shade of brown, what with all the sun.

It was remarkable to Grif how quickly she adapted to any surroundings. One day she was a debutante from one of the finest families in London's Mayfair. Today she was little more than a peasant, riding across England on horseback eating apples and cheese and the occasional trout, all without complaint. And she enjoyed pointing out various flora and fauna she had obviously studied under the tutelage of some very expensive tutor. She loved the adventure of their flight, loved the freedom.

But she wasn't entirely free. They had some unfinished business that weighed heavily on Grif's mind.

Grif took a room at an inn in Carlisle, posing as a man and his boy, so that Grif might buy some provisions. He purchased two suitable gowns for Anna as well as some shoes. Anna insisted she loved the shoes, but he could not help noticing that she could hardly bring herself to look at them. Perhaps study black walking shoes had not been the ideal choice, but he had thought them rather practical.

Grif also purchased two saddles for the long ride to Talla Dileas. The gowns, shoes, and saddles put Grif near the end of his funds. But he was certain that Hugh was already in Gretna Green. He fully expected to marry Anna properly and continue on to Loch Chon the very next day.

He fully expected that, and nothing else.

There was nothing left but the unfinished business, for which Grif had also purchased vellum, so that they could, together, write a letter to her parents.

Anna labored long and hard over her portion of the letter, writing a few words, then putting down her pencil to rub her temples, then writing a few words more before she would stand and pace restlessly. When at last she finished, she put the epistle in the pocket of her trousers.

"Have ye done it, then?" he asked.

"I suppose I've done most of it," she said with a frown. "It's rather hard to do, actually. It doesn't seem as if the story is quite finished, does it?"

There was nothing but a small cross at the border to signal the fact that they were free.

The afternoon they crossed into Scotland, Anna impulsively looked over her shoulder and felt tremendous relief. Although they had not seen the men from Nottingham again, she had never felt free of them. It was as if some invisible person were watching her, following her every move, waiting for the perfect moment to snatch her from this dream.

But there was no one to snatch her, nothing but green rolling fields and sheep.

"Anna? Are ye all right, then?"

She loved the sound of his Scottish burr, so familiar to her now, so much a part of her. She turned toward him, smiling. "Quite," she said, reaching for his hand. "Better than I've ever been in my life."

He brought her hand to his mouth and kissed it.

On the outskirts of the little village of Gretna Green, they stopped in a heavily wooded area so that Anna might don one of the gowns Grif had given her. In the village, they stabled the horses and walked about, deciding at last to inquire within the dry goods shop as to where they might find a vicar. Neither of them wanted to wait a moment more.

The shopkeeper was busy counting what looked like licorice candies. "Blacksmith," he said without looking up from his count.

"The smithy?" Grif repeated, exchanging a glance with Anna.

"Aye, the smithy. Round the corner just there," the shopkeeper added with a nod of his head.

"Perhaps he's having his horse shod," Grif said reassuringly to Anna's worried look as they walked out of the shop.

But the vicar was not having his horse shod. The vicar

was shodding the horse, as he was the smithy. He looked up as Grif and Anna entered the wide barn doors and gave them a quick once-over. "Wedding, is it?"

"Aye," Grif said, taking Anna's hand.

"Two pounds."

"Very well," Grif agreed. "Is the vicar within?"

"Here, lad," the smithy said, rising to his feet and pointing to himself. "*SEAMUS!*" he roared.

An elderly man instantly shuffled through a back door, wiping his hands on his apron. The smithy said something to him that Anna could not quite catch—it sounded a bit like English, and maybe a bit like Grif's language. Whatever it was, Seamus seemed to understand it, and disappeared to the back room.

"Ye'll stand there," the smithy said, pointing with his poker to a large cold anvil near one of several thick posts that held up the roof. "I'll be but a moment." And as he went about putting away his implements, Seamus reappeared, carrying the Book of Common Prayer and a dirtied white ecclesiastical stole, which he handed to the smithy.

The smithy draped the soiled stole around his neck and opened the Book of Common Prayer.

"Ye'll be needing a proper witness, aye?" a familiar voice asked from behind them, and Anna and Grif both whirled around to a grinning Hugh.

"MacAlister!" Grif cried, grabbing his hand and clapping him on the shoulder.

"I rather imagined ye'd make yer way here above all else," Hugh said with a wink, and took Anna's hand and kissed it warmly. "Miss Addison, what a beautiful bride ye are," he said gallantly.

"Have you been here long?" Grif asked.

"A day or two."

"Did ye meet with any trouble?"

"No, of course no'," Hugh scoffed, still smiling at Anna. But then he shrugged a bit. "Perhaps a *wee* spot of trouble. Never mind that now, lad. I'll tell ye all, but at the moment I'd be honored to witness yer marriage, I would."

"Thank you," Anna said.

"And I'll have ye know, lass, that I stand before ye now as a gentleman and a friend, and most certainly *no'* as Lockhart's bloody valet."

Anna laughed. "I am right thankful for that, for I understand that you were not a particularly *good* valet."

Hugh laughed roundly and fondly patted Grif on the back. "On me life, the worst valet in all of England for the worst lord!"

"Shall ye turn round now?" the smithy asked loudly. "I've too much work to dally. If ye would, sir, take her hand," he instructed Grif.

Beaming, Grif took Anna's hand; Hugh moved to stand beside him. The smithy flipped through several pages of the Book of Common Prayer. "Ah, here we are, then," he muttered.

Grif squeezed Anna's hand and flashed her a handsome smile.

The smithy cleared his throat, and began in a theatrical voice, "'Dearly beloved, we gather today in the sight of God to join together this man and this woman in holy matrimony.'" He paused, looked up at them. "I'll just hurry it along a bit, if ye donna mind," he said, and held the book out before him. "'The holy estate which Christ adorned and beautified with his presence . . .'"

He paused again, squinting at the book.

"Aha, here we are," he said, and straightened again. "'Tis no' to be taken in hand, unadvisedly, lightly or wantonly; but reverently, discreetly, advisedly, soberly, and in the fear of God. It is ordained for the increase of mankind according to the will of God, and it is also ordained for the mutual society, help, and comfort that the one ought to have of the other, both in prosperity and adversity. Into this holy estate ye come now to be joined. Will ye . . .'" He glanced up and pointed at Grif. "Yer name, then, lad."

"Ah . . . Griffin Finnius Lockhart."

"Will ye, Griffin Finnius Lockhart, take . . . ?" He looked at Anna, cocked a brow.

"Anna Louise Addison."

"And will ye love her, comfort her, honor and protect her, forsaking all others, and be ever faithful to her for as long as ye both might live, then?"

"I will indeed," Grif said, smiling at Anna.

"And, lass, ye will do the same, will ye no'?"

"I will," Anna avowed.

"Any objection?"

"No, sir!" Hugh said grandly.

"Then as hammer and anvil join metal together in the heat of the fire, I hereby join ye together in the heat of this moment!" he said, and made the motion of a cross. "Two pound, if ye please," he said to Grif, "and will ye put yer names to the register. Yer witness, too."

Grif let out a whoop, grabbed Anna up, kissed her hard on the lips as he twirled her around. "Mrs. Griffin Lockhart," he said with a broad grin, and kissed her again, until the smithy tapped him on the shoulder, wanting his two pounds.

As Grif fished the money from his pocket, Hugh grabbed Anna and kissed her fully on the lips, and showed no inclination of letting go until Grif playfully slapped the back of his head, at which point he let go of Anna and grabbed Grif in a big bear hug. "Aye, and the luck of the Scottish with ye, Grif," he said genuinely. "May ye be blessed with many wee bairns that have their mother's beauty and their father's stubborn determination."

His wish caused Anna to laugh giddily. How remarkable that she'd come so far in so short a time, to this, to her heart's desire. She had married Grif and she loved him, and they were happily and forever married. As if to seal it, Grif took her hand, and together they signed the register, their full names and their ages, alongside Hugh.

When the three of them turned round again, Seamus had disappeared, the smithy had already divested himself of the Book of Common Prayer and the ecclesiastical stole, and was back at work.

"Come on, then. We must hold a proper celebration," Hugh insisted. "Ye must have a wedding supper at the Queen's Head Inn."

Hugh insisted on making the arrangements for a wedding supper, which Grif and Anna were happy to let him do, for they were far more interested in one another and the very new and exciting notion that they were, indeed, husband and wife, and free to enjoy all that entailed.

Hugh called the innkeeper to them at once. "I introduce ye to Griffin Lockhart," he said, bowing toward a beaming Grif, "who traveled as far as London to find his bride, and now they've just come from the vicar and would request a wedding supper."

The innkeeper's ruddy face lit with delight. "Aye,

of course, sir! Ealasaid!" he shouted, and a girl with the same ruddy face appeared from a door leading toward the kitchen. "Show his lordship and his bonny bride to a private dining room, aye? And bring round a bottle of Scots whiskey!"

"Aye, bring the best Scots whiskey ye have," Grif said. "I would introduce me English bride to one of many fine qualities of Scotland."

"Whiskey!" Anna cried, laughing. "Good English ladies do not drink whiskey, sir!"

"Then be thankful that ye are now a Scot," he laughed, and kissed her to the great delight of the serving girl and the innkeeper.

"Ye must drink whiskey, milady," the innkeeper said sternly. "It will bring ye health and many bairns."

"As to that, sir, they'll be needing a sleeping room for the night as well," Hugh said, winking at the innkeeper as he pulled a roll of banknotes from his pocket and peeled off several. "A fine room, too—one befitting a lady on her wedding night."

Anna blushed furiously, but the innkeeper quickly pocketed the banknotes. "I've a fine one, indeed, if ye'll follow me."

Grif and Anna started after him, but Hugh stopped them with a hand and a grin. "Be patient, lad. Give me yer things, then," he said, winking at Anna. "I'll make certain it is made ready for ye. But first we celebrate."

"Hugh," Grif said, handing over their satchel. "I'm right touched, I am. I didna know ye to be so sentimental."

Hugh laughed. "Ye'll save me a tot of that fine Scots whiskey, will ye?"

"Ealasaid! Come along, then!" the innkeeper bellowed over his shoulder as he hurried alongside Hugh's determined stride to inspect the sleeping room upstairs.

"Aye, milord, it's just here," Ealasaid said, smiling broadly as she showed them to a small private dining room, well appointed with a table and six chairs upholstered in leather. "I'll come round with yer whiskey," she said as Grif and Anna entered the room, and pulled the heavy drapes behind them.

It was their first moment alone since they had wed, and Grif took Anna in his arms. "*Ach,* lass . . . it wasna the most fashionable of ceremonies—no flowers, no wedding breakfast. No ring on yer finger and yer family so far away. I pray ye are no' disappointed."

"How could you even suggest it?" she asked, rising up on her toes to kiss him. "I'm too happy for words, Grif. I love that ours was such an exciting wedding! Think of it, married in Gretna Green, by a smithy! Imagine the stories we'll tell our children!"

"Aye," he said kissing her neck. "I would that we'd have our celebration so that we might carry on with a more pleasurable and private—"

"Yer whiskey, milord," Ealasaid announced at the drapes.

Anna laughed at Grif's look of disappointment as the girl stepped in and placed a decanter of whiskey and several small glasses on the table. She glanced shyly at Grif as she poured the whiskey. "Ye look quite happy, milord," she teased him. "The world smiles with ye this day, no?"

"The world smiles with me every day, lass," Grif said, grinning at Anna. As Ealasaid slipped out of the room, he poured a tot and handed it to Anna, and gestured for her to hold it up in a toast. "To me heart, which heretofore hadna awakened," he exclaimed, lifting the tot. "*Slainte mhath*—Good health, *mo ghraidh.*"

"To our hearts," Anna said, and watched Grif toss back the amber liquid, then did the same. But as she'd never drunk whiskey, she was not prepared for the burn of good Scots whiskey, and instantly erupted into a fit of coughing.

"*Ach,* Anna, ye must *sip* it until ye've been in Scotland a wee bit longer," Grif suggested, rubbing her back.

Anna was still coughing when Hugh stuck his head between the drapes. "Are ye ready for a wee celebration, then?"

Grif grinned and gestured for him to enter. "We are learning the art of drinking Scots whiskey," he said laughingly. "Come, then, Hugh, and tell us about yer journey out of London."

Hugh smiled roguishly, but he did not move. "Ye will recall I said I had a wee spot of trouble, aye?"

"Aye," Grif said, frowning lightly, gesturing him in. "What trouble?"

"It wasna exactly easy, fleeing London, aye, Grif?"

Grif frowned darkly. "God blind me, what have ye done, MacAlister?"

"*Ach,* I've done naugh' wrong, Lockhart! Well . . . that is to say, at least no more than any man in our situation might have done."

"*Diah!* What—" Grif started, but Hugh suddenly threw back the drapes, and standing just behind him, her hand in his, was Miss Brody.

Both Grif and Anna gasped with surprise. Miss Brody colored slightly and frowned at Hugh for a moment. "Good wishes on yer wedding day," she muttered, clearly uncomfortable.

"Hugh!" Grif cried, but Hugh waved a hand at him as he pulled Miss Brody into the private room. "'Tis no' what ye think, lad! Miss Brody—*Keara*—she and I met with a bit of a problem leaving London, and I couldna leave her there in harm's way."

"Oh dear God," Anna said, gaping at Miss Brody, who frowned at the table. "Miss Brody, are you quite all right?"

"Oh, aye, miss, I'm quite fine, I am."

"What happened, then?" Grif demanded.

"Lockhart returned just after ye left," Hugh said with a smile, anticipating Grif's question. "He wanted yer head on a platter, he did." He laughed and looked at Miss Brody. "And he'd no' take no for an answer," he added with another laugh, and even Miss Brody smiled.

He went on to tell them that Keara had been out that afternoon, to see her brother, and Hugh wouldn't leave Dalkeith House or London, not without explaining to her what had happened and giving her a week's wages. But Hugh felt uncomfortable in his grandmother's house—he claimed to have had a very strange feeling about it, as if he were being watched. So he moved the horses to the public stables, along with his bag, and returned to Dalkeith House under the cloak of darkness.

It was that which saved them, he reckoned.

He waited for Keara in the kitchen, in a darkened house, and when she returned, he told her what had happened. He'd just provided her wages when they heard several voices on the floor above them. They quickly hid in an old, unused larder, listening as the men made their way to the kitchen. It was Lockhart, returned with a constable and his men to search the mansion for Grif, cursing the fact that he'd apparently escaped.

The men were in the kitchen, not a foot away from Hugh and Keara, when the constable assured Lockhart that Grif would indeed hang were they to find him.

It was all Hugh and Keara needed to hear, and fearing for their lives, the moment the men left the kitchen they escaped the house via a window, ran to the public stables, and rode out of London in the night.

"But . . . why didn't you seek refuge with your brother?" Anna asked Keara.

She exchanged a look with Hugh. "He was angry with me, me brother Kevin. He didna think I was bringing him all me wages," she said softly. "He'd threatened me when I'd gone to him that afternoon, and I was afraid to return for fear he'd beat me."

Anna reached across the table to take Keara's hand.

"So then . . ." Grif said, looking at Hugh, "ye and Miss Brody came to Gretna Green. And I suppose ye made yer own call to the smithy—"

"Keara and I will go our separate ways when the beastie is sold," Hugh interrupted, looking at Keara. "I've promised her half of what I receive so that she may go home to Ireland, as she desires, to her family."

"Aye," Keara said, shifting her gaze to Grif. "I'll return to Ireland just as soon as I am able. I've sisters and brothers who need me."

"So we shall toast our escape, then, aye?" Hugh lightly suggested, sliding his arm across the back of Keara's chair. "No' a one of us left our head in London after all."

"Aye," Grif said. "That's worthy of a toast." He poured four tots of whiskey. *"Slainte mhath!"*

As the four of them drank to their collective health, the innkeeper pushed aside the drapes and announced grandly, "On this happy occasion, milord, I've a Highland roast beef for yer wedding supper!" Two women carried in heavy trays, and the smell of the Highland beef was enough to make them swoon with pleasure.

They celebrated with dinner and whiskey, laughing at the tales of their flight from London, and toasting Grif and Anna's happiness over and again.

When the food had been taken away, Grif glanced at Anna. He could see the flush of a bit of whiskey in her cheeks, the sated look in her eye. He put his hand on her knee and squeezed it, gave his thanks to Hugh and Keara for a wedding celebration they would not otherwise have had, and putting his hand on Anna's elbow, he helped her up.

"Just a moment more, lad," Hugh urged him. "Let us see to it that all is at the ready for ye," he said, and hurried Keara along with him, quitting the private room.

"Come, lass," Grif said gently, putting his arm around Anna's waist. "'Tis time I took me wife to her wedding bed," he murmured, and kissed her cheek.

"Mmm," she said dreamily, and allowed him to languidly lead her from the private room, across the common room, pausing briefly to thank Ealasaid and her father, and up the stairs, to the room at the end of the corridor where Hugh was standing, grinning proudly.

"'Tis all as we'd hoped. Mind ye have a care with her," he said, and threw open the door to the room.

Anna gasped. It was filled with flowers, Scottish primrose and bluebell. A fire roared at the hearth, a pair of candles blazed on either side of the bed, and primroses blanketed the bedcover.

"How?" Anna asked, clearly taken aback by the room.

"I'm a Highlander. And now I'll take me leave—Keara is waiting," Hugh said, and with that he clapped Grif on the shoulder and sauntered down the corridor and the stairs, disappearing into the common room below.

Grif laughed softly. "Bloody sentimental fool."

"It's *beautiful*," Anna said softly.

"No' as beautiful as ye are, lass," Grif said sincerely, and swept her up in his arms, surprising her.

"What are you doing?" Anna cried, laughing.

"*Ach*, what do ye think I'm doing? Carrying me bride across the threshold, of course!" he said, and walked into that room, kicked the door shut, then put Anna down, turned to lock the door, and then turned around again, divesting himself of his coat and waistcoat, all the while smiling at Anna.

She shyly returned his smile and wandered to a vase full of primroses next to the basin. She selected one and put it in her hair as Grif tossed his neckcloth aside. He moved to stand behind her, wrapped his arms around her waist, and kissed her neck. "Ye canna know how I've longed for this night," he said. "I've longed to show ye just how much I've come to love ye."

"How long?" she asked, smiling, and took another primrose from the vase.

"A lifetime," he muttered. "A bloody lifetime." He ran his hands up her arms to her shoulders. "Come on, then, and lie down, will ye, so that I might show ye just how much I do," he said, and pressed his face to her hair, inhaling her scent.

"Shouldn't I remove my gown?" she asked, falling back against him and tucking her head under his chin. "Or would you prefer to imagine what lies beneath?"

He laughed. "The time for fancying ye has passed." He moved his hands to her back, began to undo the tiny buttons, moving deftly down her back. Anna lifted her arms and let down her hair as he did.

When he had finished, she let her hair fall, and turned around to face him, her gaze roaming his face. "You must tell me what to do."

He smoothed her hair, kissed her forehead, and carefully pushed the gown from her shoulders, watching it slide to the floor and pool at her feet. He offered his hand to her; she put her hand in his, slipped out of her shoes, and stepped out of the gown, moving gracefully in nothing but a thin chemise.

They moved to the bed; she tossed the primrose she held onto the bed with the others, and Grif gathered her in his arms, kissed her gently. "Are ye frightened?"

Anna laughed lightly and shook her head. "I'm not the least frightened."

"Is this what ye want?" he asked, caressing her face.

She laughed again, slipped her arms around his waist. "Do you recall the night in the garden at Featherstone? The night you asked me what I wanted?"

He nodded solemnly.

"I want you to kiss me, Grif. I want to know how it feels to love."

Diah, but he loved this woman! He gazed down at her now, her face between his hands, her coppery eyes glinting with a delightful, devilish glint, and wondered how he'd come to be such a lucky man. No woman had ever evoked such passion in him, good or bad, and he marveled at how he might have gone on, never feeling such depth of emotion for another human being, had it not been for that wretched beastie.

He'd cherish her because of it, for he never wanted to be without this feeling again. "I want ye to feel how I love ye, Anna," he said with great emotion, and lowered his head to kiss her.

Anna instantly pressed against him, lifting her face, her tongue seeking his. Grif made a sound of approval, and Anna's hands were on his back, pulling his shirt from his trousers, seeking to touch his skin, her hands on his bare back, sweeping up to his shoulders, then around to his belly. Then she broke away from him and focused on the buttons of his shirt until she had undone them all. She pushed the fabric of his shirt aside and caught a breath as she looked at his chest.

And she slowly released that breath as she lifted her hands to his chest, let her fingers slide down, over taut nipples, to the flat plane of his stomach, and to the fine line of hair the disappeared into his trousers. She stared down at his trousers, at his thick erection, and then lifted her gaze to him. "I want to feel it, Grif. All of it."

Grif had never been more aroused than he was in that moment, and he unfastened his trousers, guided her hand to feel the strength of his desire for her. When her small hand closed firmly around him, Grif was lost.

He was suddenly feverish, working to loosen her chemise, seeking her bare breasts with his hands while her fingers squeezed him, sliding down his shaft, then deeper, to his heavy testicles. With a moan, Grif grabbed the hem of her chemise and pulled it up over her head and tossed it aside.

She stood naked before him, wearing only a flower in her dark tangled hair, her breasts full and ripe, her belly smooth, the dark patch of hair flowering above trim, long legs. He put his hands on her hips, pulled her into him, kissed her deeply, and lowered her onto the bed. She fell onto her back and smiled up at him as he removed his trousers.

Grif couldn't take his eyes off her. She was beautiful, perfectly made, a shape that could drive a man wild with desire. He lay beside her, put his hand on her belly, and just gazed at her, unable to fully absorb that she was his wife.

Anna touched his brow, traced his nose with her finger, then pressed it against his lips. It was so innocently seductive that Grif found it impossible to resist. He bent down, took the rigid peak of her breast fully into his mouth, and she lifted to him, openly indulging in the ravishing of her breast.

For Anna, the sweet sensation of his mouth on her breast was intoxicating, burning deep inside her and building a fire in the pit of her stomach.

With his mouth and hands, he exalted in her, and Anna received his caresses with pure elation. He moved with his mouth on her breast, his shaft pressed against her hip, and his hand skimming up her leg, sending a thousand shivers through her. She propped herself up on her elbows so she could see him naked, could see his magnificently masculine form—the curve of his hip, the power of his legs, and the thickness of his arms.

Grif suddenly lifted his head, frowning a little.

"Anna, *m'annsachd,* my beloved, how did I find ye?" he softly demanded. "What did I do to deserve ye?"

She did not answer, but smiled wantonly as he pressed her down into the flowers. She buried her face in his neck as her hands anxiously roamed his body. When her fingers grazed the tip of his erection, Grif drew a long breath through his teeth.

"Bloody hell, I want ye, lass," he said gruffly. "I want to possess ye as a man will possess his wife, the woman he loves."

Anna responded to that with a smile and by taking him fully in hand. His eyes darkened; he pushed himself up, balanced on his muscular arms, and looked at her, his gaze reverently sweeping her body.

Never had she felt so beautiful as she did in that moment, as Grif gazed so longingly at her. He sighed, kissed her mouth, then her breast, moving lazily to kiss her belly. "Me wife. Me beautiful, bonny wife."

Anna grabbed Grif's hair as he put his hands on her hips, his fingers digging into her flesh, and pulled her forward. He buried his face in her belly, pushed her right leg and lifted it, putting it over his shoulder. "*Grif,*" she whispered, smiling as his lips traced a warm, wet path across her inner thigh, toward her sex, and she absently lifted her hand, let if flutter across her breast.

His breath brushed the apex of her thighs. When his tongue dipped inside her sex, she grabbed his shoulders, suddenly terrified by her own desire. She was gasping for air as he flicked his tongue in the valley, her body moving against him. But Grif held her firmly, his mouth closing in on the point of her desire, nibbling, sucking, licking.

She was spiraling down again, into a dark pool of

ecstasy, clutching desperately at his head, moving instinctively to meet the caress of his tongue. Unable to contain her desire, her body was quickly shuddering, and just as she began to cry out, he caught her breast, holding it, kneading it as she fell into paradise.

Her cries sounded delirious; she writhed beneath him, her arms flailing, her hair covering her face as the extraordinary sensations washed over her in wave after wave of stunning delight.

She forgot everything but Grif, could think of nothing but returning that remarkable pinnacle of delight, and having no idea how to do it.

Grif moved between her legs, softly caressing the damp curls. "Anna," he said hoarsely, and she opened her eyes, rolled her head to look at him. "Come to me now as a wife, as I will come to ye as a husband." He came over her, pressed his thick erection into her sex. He found her hand, guided it so that she could feel how much he wanted her. "*Grif,*" she murmured helplessly.

He smiled, reached between them, felt her slick opening, and slowly, carefully slid into her.

Anna gasped softly as the tip of him entered her, but felt the discomfort ease as her body adjusted to him. And then he slid a little farther, the clench of his jaw the only outward sign of his restraint. Anna closed her eyes, let her head fall back, let her body feel her husband inside of her.

"*Diah,* I canna wait," he said, his voice sounding as if he struggled to remain calm. "I want to be inside ye, to show ye how a man will give his wife pleasure so that he may know his own."

With a smile, Anna opened her eyes. "Show me, husband."

Grif slipped an arm under her back and lowered his mouth to hers. And as he kissed her, he thrust powerfully with his hips, breaking the barrier. Anna cried out, a mixture of pain and sheer ecstasy enveloping her, and she had the sensation of Grif sliding slowly into her depths.

"Uist, m'annsachd," he whispered. He waited a moment, allowed her body time to adapt to him, then slowly, carefully, began to move inside her, sliding and plunging, sliding and plunging.

The sensation was astoundingly lurid and beautiful all at once, a strangely pleasurable pain, and when Anna began to move to meet his thrusts, Grif moaned into her flesh, his breath hot. She could feel her body tighten around him, drawing him in, just as she could feel the strength of his desire growing and the power of his body.

But then his strokes began to take on a new urgency, and she met him in perfect harmony as his body bucked beneath her. He slipped his hand between their bodies and began to stroke her in time to the stroking inside her. The fires began to build in her again, raging, white hot, and she realized she was whimpering with the sensational mix of pleasure and pain. Then, suddenly, she felt an overwhelming wave of fire flash through her and cried out.

Grif cried out, too, with one last powerful surge inside her, and she could feel his member convulsing, spilling into her, his life's blood to hers. Panting, he collapsed onto her, his face in her hair. He gathered her in his arms and rolled to his side, holding her tightly to him, until he had caught his breath.

"I love ye, Anna," he said at long last. *"Diah,* but I love ye."

She smiled into the curve of his shoulder. "I love *you*, Grif."

In the privacy of that room, their desire for one another sated for the time being, they lay naked together in candlelight, their bodies entwined, and on a bed of primrose and bluebell, watching the flames at the hearth slowly die, naming their future children, in complete peace.

And when Anna fell asleep in Grif's arms, her lashes dark against her sun-drenched skin, he recalled what he'd once seen on a tombstone: "Here lie Leslie MacBeth and his loving wife, Aileen, together in conjugal felicity in death as in life."

At the time Grif had thought it a rather odd thing to put on one's tombstone. But tonight he prayed with all his might for conjugal felicity with the woman beside him, in life and into death.

Thirty

The next morning's light, bright and warm, streamed in the small window of their room at the inn. Grif had already arisen, was washed and dressed when Anna awoke. She sat up, stretched her arms high above her head, and yawned with pleasure. "My husband," she said, smiling prettily.

"Wife," he responded, grinning like a happy man as he walked around to the side of the bed to kiss her.

"You've risen so soon," she pouted, her arms around his neck. "I had rather hoped you would show me again," she said, smiling wickedly.

He was only a man, and he laughed as she tugged at his neckcloth, at last untying it himself in the interest of obliging his bride. It wasn't until a maid knocked on the door that he extracted himself from the bed and her and reluctantly rose.

Grif dressed quickly. "I'd best find MacAlister," he said, and kissed the top of her head. "We should press on, *mo ghraidh*, as soon as ye are bathed and dressed."

She fell back against the pillows, looking marvelously sated. "I don't ever want to leave here."

"Aye, but we must. We've no money, lass," he said, unable to resist the urge to kiss her again. "I'll have a bath sent up and come for ye after a time, aye?"

"Very well," she said, twirling a length of hair around her finger. "But go now, will you, so that you may soon come back to me."

He laughed, kissed her once more, and grabbing up his hat, walked out the door.

He found the innkeeper and inquired after Hugh. The innkeeper, still flush from what Grif assured him was a successful wedding supper, seemed confused by Grif's question. "Yer man, milord? Oh no, he didna keep here. We had only the one room, aye?"

That surprised Grif—he'd assumed Hugh had taken a room here. "Then where might he have gone?"

The innkeeper shrugged. "There's a small public inn at the end of the high street," he said. "Perhaps he's there."

Grif started in that direction, but paused and looked over his shoulder at the innkeeper. "Might there be gaming in the village? Somewhere a lad might find a bit of sport?"

The innkeeper shook his head. "Perhaps a game now and then at the smithy, milord," he said, "but no' more."

The other inn, then. Grif walked on, ignoring the knot of discomfort in his belly. It was ridiculous to believe something had happened. What would Hugh have done with Miss Brody? If the Queen's Head Inn had no rooms, of course he'd gone to the smaller inn.

He walked down the main village thoroughfare to the opposite end of the village, where the other, smaller inn was located. The innkeeper at this rather sordid establishment, a woman, grimaced when he asked after Hugh.

"Aye, I know of him. A friend of yers, is he?"

"Aye," Grif said.

"Then ye be the same bad ilk!"

"I beg yer pardon?" Grif asked, taken aback.

"Yer friend and his Irish whore left without paying!" she spat.

Grif felt a knife of panic. *"Left?"* he exclaimed. "That's impossible!"

"Impossible, is it?" she hissed. "The rotten bounder left in the middle of the night like a bloody thief, owing me six crowns!"

Stunned, Grif dumbly reached into his leather purse and handed her a five-pound banknote. "That should take care of yer troubles," he said angrily, and left, stalking back into the village, feeling terribly confused. Nothing made sense—Hugh had left London with no more money than Grif, and probably had much less after last night's celebration. Unless he'd been gambling . . . still it made no sense that he'd leave without the beastie—

He stopped mid-stride. *No.* No, no . . . Hugh was many things, but he was not a thief! Still . . . Grif hurried on, the panic taking hold.

Shop after shop, he inquired, and received the same answer. No one had seen a man resembling Hugh this day. Grif's last call was to the smithy, and there he felt the deep, sharp pang of fear.

"Aye, he was here," the smithy said, eyeing Grif. "He took his horses, he did, without bothering to pay for their keep."

"When?" Grif asked, reaching for his leather purse again.

"In the dead of night," the smithy said, snatching the banknote Grif held out.

"The lass too, aye?"

"Aye."

Grif nodded, and walked to the edge of the smithy's

barn. He put his hand on a post there, and tried to draw a breath.

He knew, of course. He knew what Hugh had done before he could even reach the inn and confirm it. The lad had betrayed him in the worst conceivable way.

Somehow he managed to stumble out of the blacksmith's barn onto the main thoroughfare, his mind racing with sickening thoughts. Twice he had to pause and put his hand to the wall, and lean over, eyes closed, trying to catch the breath that had been snatched clean from him.

Grif staggered toward the inn, attempting to convince himself that he was jumping to conclusions, that it might have been someone else altogether. He even tried to believe Hugh was waiting for him now.

Yet his gut fear roared louder than his common sense, telling him that last night Hugh had used the excuse of readying their wedding room to take the beastie, and once Grif and Anna had gone up to their marriage bed, he and Keara Brody had taken the beastie and ran, making Grif to be a bloody fool.

When he returned to the inn and the room where Anna was waiting for him, he leaned against the door, fearing he might be sick. He had just *married* this woman—and now he would tell her that their future was *ruined*? That he had taken her from the lap of luxury to certain poverty?

"Grif!" she cried happily from the basin, where she was winding her hair into some sort of coif, wearing a chemise. "I didn't expect you so soon! I finished my letter home this morning, and told them everything. Well," she said batting her lashes coyly, "perhaps not quite *everything*." She laughed.

He looked at her, feeling nothing but a growing ache. What of his parents? *Dear God,* what of *Mared?* How could he possibly disappoint them all?

"And where is your valet this morning, hmm?" she asked gaily.

"Ye've no' seen him, then?" he managed to ask.

She paused in the styling of her hair and looked over her shoulder at him. "Seen him? I should hope not sir, for I would have seen him from my bath!" She laughed again, and when Grif did not smile, she lowered her arms. "Grif, what's wrong?"

"He's gone, Anna. He and Miss Brody are gone."

"Oh! Well, then," Anna said, her bright smile returning. "They seemed rather comfortable, did they not? Perhaps they have sought the vicar—"

"I've just come from the vicar. And the innkeeper. And every bloody shop in this village. He left in the dead of night without paying his debts," Grif said, and forced himself to shove away from the wall, to look in the satchel.

Anna stood there, watching him. "What are you doing?"

"The beastie," he said, choking on the word, and tore open their small satchel.

"*No,*" Anna said sternly. "He'd not betray you so!"

But he would and he had. Hugh had brought their things to the room, and in his happy delirium Grif had forgotten to be vigilant. He'd forgotten the bloody beastie, and Hugh knew he would.

Grif tossed the empty satchel aside and turned around to face his bride. "'Tis gone."

Her eyes widened with shock, and she looked wildly about, then suddenly ran across the room, pouncing on the bed, pawing through the linens. "No, *no!* I will not believe he betrayed you!"

Grif said nothing. She caught his hand, pulled him to the bed. "Think! Where would he go? Talla Dileas?"

Grif clenched his jaw and shook his head. "He's stolen it, *leannan.*"

Anna collapsed onto her heels on the bed. "But . . . but *why?*"

Grif pressed a fist to his forehead to stave off the blinding headache he felt behind his eyes. "Money, I'd wager. He's a gambler, Hugh."

"But what of Miss Brody?" Anna demanded, near to tears. "She's not a thief!"

"She'd have had no choice but to do what Hugh demanded," he said with a shrug. "And she needed money for her family in Ireland, aye? Perhaps they thought of it together."

Anna gasped softly; she sprang off the bed, began looking around. "I can't just *sit* here! We must have another look about."

Grif halfheartedly helped her, because he knew in his heart of hearts that they'd not unearth Hugh or the beastie. Nevertheless, they searched the room, top to bottom, and then went out, Anna vainly hoping that there had been some mistake, that Hugh was wandering the village.

But there was no sign of him or Miss Brody. And, in fact, they encountered the one person who had seen the couple after Grif and Anna had retired. Ealasaid.

Ealasaid brightened considerably when Grif asked if she'd seen Hugh. "Oh, aye," she said, smiling broadly. "I saw them both," she said, looking a little dreamy. "Looking into one another's eyes and whispering sweet things. 'Twas a night for love, milord."

"Did they retire?" Anna asked.

"Oh, I donna know, milady. They left, picked up their bags and left."

"Left? And did ye see them leave town, lass?" Grif asked.

"No, milord, just the inn. I thought it'd be too dark to start a journey, but they took horses and rode on."

Anna covered her face with her hands.

"Oh, there now, miss!" the girl said kindly. "There's no shame in it, truly, for they seemed very much in love!"

Anna and Grif rode out that morning after posting Anna's letter home. When Grif paused to look back at Gretna Green, Anna put her hand on his. "It's no use," she said softly. "He's gone."

"Aye," Grif said, and looked north, toward Talla Dileas, wondering what in God's name he would tell his parents now.

Thirty-one

Mared, Ellie, and Natalie had taken it upon themselves to repair the old gazebo down by the loch. They had hammer and nails and a bucket of whitewash, and wore, over their worn spring gowns, old aprons. While Ellie and Mared hammered strips of maple they had lathed themselves, Natalie calmly painted one section of railing they had completed yesterday.

The gazebo was perched on a soft hill overlooking Loch Chon, and from the gazebo one could see portions of the road wending its way from Aberfoyle. It was a movement on the road that caught Natalie's eye, and she glanced up, shielding her eyes from the sun with her paintbrush. "We've callers, Mother," she said calmly.

Ellie and Mared both jerked their gazes to her, then looked to where she pointed. Mared instantly gasped and tossed aside her hammer, marching across the gazebo to have a better look. "Mary Queen of Scots, it's Grif! I'd know the lad anywhere," she said. "Dudley was right—he said they'd be less than a fortnight behind."

"Grif!" Natalie squealed, running to Mared's side as Ellie walked to the railing.

"Is that Mr. MacAlister, too?" she asked. "He looks rather small."

"Aye," Mared said, squinting a little. "*Too* small."

"Perhaps he brought his wife home, too, Mother, like the captain brought you," Natalie suggested.

Ellie and Mared both laughed heartily at that suggestion. "I think no', Nattie," Mared said, running her hand over the girl's head. "Liam, well, he's always had a soft heart, he has. But Grif . . . he prefers the company of many to one."

"Then who might it be?" Ellie asked, and exchanged a look with Mared.

The three of them quickly put away their things and hurried off to the main castle, to warn Aila and Carson that Grif had come home.

It was therefore the reason that the entire family had assembled (Dudley included, for he was, thanks to his dear Fiona, quite improved) in the old great hall, nervously pacing, waiting for the riders to come all the way to the top of the mountain where Talla Dileas had once reigned supreme.

"He's here, he's here!" Natalie shrieked, running in from her post at the front entry.

Carson nodded at Dudley.

"Aye, milord," Dudley said, and with a nod and a click of his heels, he strode smartly from the great hall.

They waited nervously for several moments, each of them stealing glimpses of the other, Natalie with her face pressed to the windowpanes. And then they heard the voices. Nothing they could make out, of course, but enough that they gasped collectively and looked wildly at one another.

"It canna be," Aila whispered.

"The hell it canna," Carson said gruffly, and suddenly, as if they were one, the six of them were pushing one another out of the great hall and to the front door.

"They'll think me a tart," Anna groaned as Grif helped her down from her horse. "Will you *look* at me? It's as if you dragged me behind all the way from London," she moaned as Grif helped her adjust her clothing.

"They'll think ye a bonny lass and they will love ye as I do," he said, and tried to give her a reassuring smile, but his stomach was in knots. He could recall all too easily his own feelings of anger when Ellie had arrived on their doorstep in place of the beastie, but he put his arms around her and hugged her. "It will be quite all right, *m'annsachd*. Ye'll see."

"I wish I were as confident," she muttered as he turned her around and gave her a bit of a push out of the way so that he could tether the horses.

Anna moved, walking into the middle of the green, looking up at the huge monolith of an estate. "My God," she said quietly, peering up at it, and Grif laughed.

"Talla Dileas is no' a fancy English estate, but she has part of every wee bit of Scottish history, both the good and the bad. Aye, she's no' bonny, is she? But she's as strong as the mountain on which she sits!"

"It's the most . . . fantastically bizarre thing I've ever seen in my life," Anna said, almost reverently.

Grif tethered the last horse, walked to where Anna was standing, and slipped his hand around hers. "Ye donna have even a ring," he said.

"I have no need for a ring, darling," she said with a smile. "I have you."

If his family didn't love her instantly, he would be forced to seriously consider severing all ties, for who could not love this woman?

Together, chins up, squeezing one another's hand for strength, they walked forward. When the door of the main entry swung open, Grif heard Anna catch her breath . . . and then release it in a huge *whoosh.* "Mr. Dudley!" she cried, and let go Grif's hand to run to the old butler. At least, Grif thought, himself quite relieved, Dudley had made it home all right. He was happy to see him well.

Dudley, however, looked rather shocked. He gaped at Anna, then at Grif, then at Anna again as she threw her arms around him, hugging him tightly. "You did arrive safely!" she cried. "And your gout. How does it fare?"

"Quite well, miss," he said. "Me wife, Fiona, she has the special herbs."

"Dudley, lad! How grand of ye to make it home alive," Grif said, reaching for his hand.

"Thank ye, sir. Oh dear, sir," he said, shaking his head. "Oh *dear.*"

"Aye," Grif said sheepishly.

"I hate to be a bother, Dudley," Anna said, "but . . ." She stepped closer, whispered conspiratorially, "Do you think you might find us a bit of food? We used our last coin somewhere near . . . actually, I'm hardly sure where, but it has been quite a long while, and we are rather famished."

Dudley never got a chance to answer, because Liam came striding out the door behind him with a look that would have frightened a troll. Grif reared back, half expecting Liam to punch him, but he grabbed Grif, squeezed him tightly in a bear hug, then let him go. "Ye're alive," he said. "I always believed they'd kill ye, I did."

"Aye, they'd certainly like to see me dead," Grif said. Liam grinned proudly, then turned to Anna—and his jaw dropped. *"No!"* he bellowed.

"What a pleasure to make your acquaintance again, sir," Anna said, curtseying deep in her riding trousers.

Liam looked at Grif. Grif shrugged helplessly. *"Mi Diah,"* Liam cried, slapping his hand to his forehead. "Did ye no' get me letter, then, Grif? I told ye to stay far away from this one!"

"No, I didna receive any letter—"

"No! Miss *Addison?"* Ellie cried behind Liam.

"Miss *Farnsworth?"* Anna shouted, and the two women shrieked simultaneously, running to one another's arms, whirling around with pleasure as Liam groaned helplessly and the rest of Grif's family spilled out onto the grassy lawn.

"What is it, what is it?" Carson cried, looking from Grif to Anna and back again.

"I think Grif brought his wife here, too," Natalie offered helpfully.

"*Ach,* for the love of God!" Aila cried, looking as if she might faint.

"But where is MacAlister?" Carson demanded. "What have ye done with him?"

"Perhaps we should all go inside and sit down," Grif suggested.

"Oh no," his father said, and closing his eyes, he leaned his head back. "God in heaven."

No one would sit, of course. Grif and Anna stood, hand in hand, at one end of the old great room. Grif's family stood on the other end of the room, all eyeing him like the devil, with the exception of Ellie, who beamed like sunshine and continued to assure Anna that their bark was far worse than their bite.

"Ye may as well begin with yer . . . friend," Aila said, looking at Anna. And her trousers.

"Actually, Mother . . . she's me wife," Grif said, and instantly threw up his hands at the cries of glee and despair. "Mother, Mother!" he shouted, gaining her attention. "I love her, more than me very life. We married in Gretna Green."

"Oh no, oh *no* . . ."

"It's quite all right, Lady Lockhart," Anna said. "We wrote my parents and explained everything."

Aila sank into a chair and threw a hand over her eyes.

"I suppose we'll have yer story soon enough," Liam said, "even though ye swore ye'd no' hie yerself home with a wife—"

"Liam!" Ellie chided him.

"But what of the beastie, Grif?" Liam demanded. "Dudley said ye had found it. Where is it, then?"

Grif and Anna exchanged nervous glances. "With MacAlister," Grif said.

They all leaned forward.

Grif shrugged.

"I'll ask," Carson said. "Where, then, *is* MacAlister . . . and the beastie?"

Grif cleared his throat. "I, ah . . . I wouldna rightly know, Father."

There was a moment of stunned silence. "Wouldna *know?*" his father echoed incredulously.

"All right, here it is, then," Grif said, and set Anna away from him, lest there be any hurling of objects.

"We had the beastie, we did, in Gretna Green. But then . . . then there was the matter of our wedding," he said, flashing a smile at his bride. "And MacAlister, well . . . he wasna alone."

All eyes widened; no one as much as blinked.

"He, ah . . . he saved an Irish lass," he tried to explain delicately.

All eyes went wider.

"Which I didna know, for we'd split apart, aye? For I was . . . well, essentially, I was kidnapping Anna—"

"*Aaah!*" his mother cried.

"I had no choice, Mother," Grif hastily explained. "There were certain to be rather dire consequences if I was found with Anna and the beastie—probably a hanging, it would seem, as our cousin Lockhart suspected foul play, and then all would be lost, aye? So Hugh and I . . . we agreed to go our separate ways and meet in Gretna Green in a fortnight, and he arrived with a lass."

"And?" Carson roared.

"And . . ." Grif sighed. There was no getting around it. "And he stole the beastie on our wedding night, and he and Miss Brody fled with it."

The *thunk* they heard was Mared keeling over. With twin shrieks of surprise, Ellie and Aila were instantly at her side, and a wail unlike anything Grif had ever heard rose up from his sister.

"What have ye done, Griffin?" his father roared. "What in the bloody hell have ye done but bring us another mouth to feed?"

Everyone gasped with shock and looked at Anna. She looked at Grif with fear in her eyes.

Natalie walked calmly across the room, slipped her

hand into Anna's. "You mustn't worry about Grandfather," she said. "He often says things he doesn't mean in the least."

"Aye," Carson said with a weary sigh, and walked to Anna, his arms open. "I'm sure ye'll grow on us, lass. The last one certainly did," he said, and hugged her, welcoming her into their fold.

Thirty-two

It took less than a month for the family to cherish Anna as one of their own, particularly when she announced that she was with child. Nothing might have endeared her as quickly as that.

Aila and Carson, after much consideration, penned a letter to Anna's parents, to inform them that she was indeed quite well and cared for and the love of their son's life. In a month's time, they received a reply from Lord Whittington, who, surprisingly, expressed his great relief and pleasure that his Anna had found happiness, and that he'd been rather fond of the Scot—far fonder of the Scot than his English cousin, who, it seemed, would become his son-in-law by marrying his youngest daughter, Lucy.

But Lord Whittington further wrote that while *he* was happy for his daughter's good fortune, and had always wished a match that would suit her uncommon spirit, the same could not be said for his lady wife, and it might be some time yet before that rift was healed. He mentioned in passing the scandal Anna's flight had caused, and sent a bit of money for her keep as his wife refused to send Anna's dowry, given the circumstances. It wasn't much, but it was a welcome relief to the Lockharts.

And last, but not least, Lord Whittington reported that Mr. Fynster-Allen had surprised everyone by offering for Miss Amelia Crabtree. The two were to be married at the Christmas season. Grif was quite pleased to hear it.

Most evenings, the Lockharts played a game in which they tried to determine where Hugh might have gone with the beastie. His father, Carson's old friend, had not heard from his son, nor had Hugh's friends in Edinburgh. And with the exception of the day Grif had come home, Mared had remained remarkably serene about the whole thing, worrying her parents and delighting her brothers.

But on one very sunny afternoon, as Ellie and Anna continued work on the gazebo, Mared sat and stared at the mountain that separated Talla Dileas from the Douglas estate.

"In truth, Mared," Ellie said carefully, "Douglas seems a good man."

Mared snorted.

"It won't be so very bad, marrying him," Ellie added. "He seems to rather esteem you. He'll make a fine husband."

"Ye're quite right, Ellie, he shall undoubtedly make a good husband to one of the ladies from Edinburgh he seems to enjoy so very much."

Ellie exchanged a look with Anna. "But . . . what of the terms of the loan? I meant for *you*, Mared."

"Oh that!" Mared said gaily. "There are six months until our year is through! And one canna guess what might happen in that time." With an enigmatic smile, she strolled out of the gazebo. "I think I shall pick some berries for supper," she called over her shoulder, and walked into the woods, leaving her sisters-in-law to wonder if perhaps the strain of it all had caused the poor lass to lose her mind.

Enjoy the following excerpt from

HIGHLANDER IN LOVE,

Julia London's

next tantalizing historical romance,

now available in paperback
from Pocket Books

The music started up in earnest; Payton grinned, twirled Mared into the rhythm of the music, pulling her close to his body, his hand going around her waist. This close to him, she could smell his cologne, which reminded her of that kiss in Glen Ard, the feel of his body against hers, and his thigh between her legs. Much to her horror, she blushed.

He smiled knowingly. "What are ye thinking?"

The question startled her—could he read her thoughts? Could he know how vividly she recalled that day and that kiss? Flustered by his smile and the gleam that went deep in his gray eyes, Mared did what she always did when she felt threatened. She assumed a certain nonchalance.

"Can ye no' guess, then? I was wondering why ye would have Lockharts to a silly ball. 'Tis no' the Douglas way."

"Aye, 'tis no' the Douglas way, because the Lockharts, particularly when they travel in a pack, can be a wee bit . . . *fiadhaich.*"

Mared laughed, for the Lockharts thought the same of the Douglases—that they were a wild, unruly lot.

Her laughter pleased him and he smiled, one of his knee-weakening smiles that somehow had her feeling completely outside of her body, and he pulled her closer, so that their bodies were touching.

She did not resist him. "What are ye doing? Ye'll create quite a scandal dancing so close to the wretched daughter of Lockhart."

"Hush," he said low. "I enjoy the feel of ye in my arms, and I'll no' abide any derision of ye, no' even from yer own lips. They will think what they will, but let them know that ye will be a Douglas soon enough."

A Douglas . . . Mared reacted to that by suddenly rearing back, pushing against the arm that firmly anchored her to him. "Let me go," she said sharply.

The warmth in his eye evaporated. "What is it, then?" he demanded. "Do ye still foolishly deny what will be?"

"Stop it," she said, looking away. "Ye willna provoke me into making a scene."

"Bloody wee fool," he muttered, and easily pulled her closer. "I've courted ye, I've tried me damnedest to make it easy for ye—"

"'Tis no' a matter of *trying*," she said, as a feeling of helplessness began to rise in her throat. "'Tis a matter of being forced against my will—"

"Then I suggest ye no' be so free with yer word of honor, Mared."

"Ye think I was *free*?" she insisted incredulously. "Do ye think a woman is ever free? I do as every woman I know must do—I bow to the will of my father and my brothers!"

"For God's sake, will ye stop yer complaining!" he said irritably. "Ye will do as yer father wisely decides because ye are too foolish left to yer own devices! I offer ye a good life, but ye are too stubborn to see it."

"Ye donna offer, ye command," she shot back.

His expression grew dark, and he tightened his hold on her hand. "Donna provoke me, Mared. My patience is at an end and I'll no' stand for yer impertinence and willful disdain once we are married."

"Indeed? And pray tell how do ye think to stop it?"

He clenched his jaw tightly shut and jerked her closer. He refused to look at her, just twirled her one way, then the other, until the music thankfully drew to an end and, at last, he stepped away from her and bowed. She inclined her head, turned to walk stiffly next to him.

But he was not through with her—he put an unyielding hand to her elbow and guided her none too gently toward the doors that opened onto the terrace.

Mared opened her mouth to protest, but he quickly cut her off. "*Ach*, no, donna speak! Ye despise me, ye've made it perfectly clear, but ye are to be me wife, whether or no' either of us can abide it," he said tersely. "I've always thought ye a bonny lass, a bird with a lively countenance, but this evening I find ye shrill."

She gasped indignantly and tried to wrench her arm free of his grasp, but he held firm. "Then let go of me!"

"Stop acting the child! I've a gift for ye, Mared. In a moment of weakness, I had a gift made for ye."

"Oh *no*," she moaned heavenward.

He made a sound of disapproval, but dropped his hand from her elbow when they reached the balustrade that overlooked the expansive gardens below.

He pulled something from his pocket. "I had this small token of my esteem made so that ye might come to understand that I intend to honor ye, Mared," he said, and holding out his hand, he opened his fingers.

The gift knocked her back on her heels. Mared put her hand to her throat as she stared down at the luckenbooth. It was shaped like a thistle, cast in gold and studded with emeralds around a diamond, the Lockhart colors. Along the bottom it was inscribed with the Lockhart motto, *True and Loyal*. It was exquisite, intricately carved.

She'd never owned anything like it and was incongruously touched by his thoughtfulness, yet angered by his extravagance, too, and wondered how long a valuable piece of jewelry such as this would feed her entire family.

"I'd no' take ye from the Lockharts," Payton said gruffly. "I mean ye to stay close to yer family's hearth. I quite clearly understand that while ye may be Douglas in name, ye'll always be a Lockhart at heart."

"Oh," she murmured, lifted her gaze, and saw a shimmer of hope and affection in his eyes that made her heart tilt a little. She looked at the luckenbooth again.

"Take it, lass," he said, his voice noticeably softened.

Mared wanted to take it, she wanted to hold it in her hand, to feel the weight of it and the warmth of his sentiment but, somehow, taking it seemed almost traitorous.

As if he understood her reluctance, Payton clucked. He pulled her closer, so that they were almost touching, so that she could feel the strength of his body all around her. "Donna deny me this," he said quietly. "I've no use for a Lockhart luckenbooth if ye willna have it," he said, and reached up, casually slipping two fingers into the bodice of her gown.

His fingers skimmed her breast, instantly warming her flesh—Mared bit her lip to keep the little mewl of titillation from escaping her. She looked up at him as he pulled the cloth of her gown from her skin and smoothly pinned the luckenbooth so that it rested just over her heart. His hand lingered there with his gaze for a moment as he admired it, but then he looked into her eyes.

His eyes were smoldering, she thought, as if something were burning beneath the surface of him, and it occurred to her that perhaps he felt what she did—a burning. Flames melting her from the inside out.